CW01500267

Beneath

The

Mask

Beneath

The

Mask

Victoria Mae

ISBN: 9798343650297

Cover design by: James Thomsit
Printed in the United Kingdom

For Muzzy.
Always remember, healing is not linear.
You've got this.

Author Note

This is ultimately a love story. Yet, within these pages, I hold a trigger warning. If you, or anyone you know, has suffered from narcissistic abuse, I hope that this can inspire and help you to feel less alone on your healing journey.

You deserve everything.
You are good enough.
You are worthy.
You are loved.

Prologue

There's nothing quite like the roar of a stadium. The palpable excitement, infectious joy and elevating anticipation swell in my chest as a delicious grin of pride spreads across my face. They're waiting for me.

Stepping out of the wings and onto the stage, I feel their hunger. With a wave of my hand, the crowd pulses as one. It's like a collective heartbeat; I'm the conductor and the control is in my hands. I can mould the room to my vision.

As I sweep the length of the catwalk extension, indecipherable voices cry out. I'm wearing those boots that give me more of a commanding presence than Hannah Waddingham in *Ted Lasso*. And then I'm there, on my mark. The lantern lights dance, and the follow-spot is suddenly still, drowning me in its beam; poised to follow my every move. I let myself pause further, allowing the dry ice to wrap around me like a powerful blanket. Here I stand. Ready.

With a powerful raise of my hand, the band strikes up and the crowd explodes. A smile breaks out that I can't keep off my face. It's as if the whole stadium is aching for me to begin. Taking the microphone, I prepare my breath and—

'Soph,' my assistant, Issac, nudges me in the ribs and out of my daydream. 'Did you hear what I said?' Tearing my eyes away from my boss on the stage, I turn to see him nervously fiddling with his hands.

I mute my head mic, 'What's that?', I yell over the sound of the sold-out Madison Square Garden crowd, roaring my boss' name.

'FREYA! FREYA! FREYA!'

Behind the curtains of the backstage area, everyone is heightened and flustered. The octet of dancers next to us bounce up and down with adrenaline. The one to my left is fiddling with a strap on her dress which doesn't seem to want to stay. I automatically put my clipboard under an armpit, and with a speedy flourish and a twist I tighten it, before tapping her on the shoulder with a "good to go" nod. She thanks me and I hug my clipboard, then face Issac once more.

'You've got a phone call.'

'I do?' I fumble in my back pocket for my mobile.

'No,' Issac puts his hand on mine, 'the phone in greenroom two.'

'In the dog creche?' Freya refuses to tour without her two chihuahuas, Sugar and Spice, so there's a whole team who look after not only them, but each member of staff's pets if need be.

'Sorry, no, not the dog creche; greenroom three.'

My heart sinks as I have a feeling I know exactly who it is, but manage to stay composed, 'Well, perhaps you could take a message? The show's just started, I have to be here.' I turn back to the stage, unmute my mic, and talk into the headset, 'Followspot, steady for the first lift.' My eyes trace the entirety of the elaborately dressed stage with its T-shaped catwalk extension, 'A little more smoke stage left please, and…' I pause, awaiting Freya's signal, 'uplights, go. Dancers, go.'

'It's your mum,' Issac confirms my fear, as the dancers bound their way onto the stage from both sides, dancing, cartwheeling and back-flipping to join Freya at the end of the catwalk.

I turn back firmly. 'I am not answering that. Not today.'

'You've waited a long time for this.'

A mixture of anxiety and frustration swirls around the pit of my stomach. Even though I have an American number now through work, my British mobile is still active, and she hasn't tried to call me once. Why is she choosing now, to call me for the first time since I left? 'Wait,' I look at my watch, 'it's like,' I pause to do the time difference maths, 'midnight there.' I feel my face fall. Something's got to be wrong. Oh God, I'm not ready.

'She says it's urgent,' Issac presses.

I scoff, 'It's both "always" and "never" urgent with Aubrey Carter. She's cried wolf so often I never know the truth. Hey, what are you doing?' He's taken my clipboard and headset off me.

'She said it's about your dad.' He gives me a look and my heart sinks. 'Go. It's our final show. I'm your assistant, I've watched you do this for six months, you'll hopefully be back in a second, but for now, I'm good,' he smiles kindly, tucking the clipboard under his armpit, and putting on my headset.

With one last longing glance at the action, I walk reluctantly further backstage, and towards the greenrooms. My internal monologue runs through a list of the worst-case scenarios. A car accident. A bad diagnosis. His heart. My shaking hand stretches for and wraps around the handle of greenroom three; with a gentle turn and push, the door opens with a slight creek. I walk over to the phone and take in the

3

flashing red light of call waiting. So inoffensive, yet I know once I've picked up the receiver and put it to my ear, my world could come crashing down. Taking a deep breath, I decide to rip the metaphorical plaster off as quickly as humanly possible.

'Hello,' I say curtly.

'Finally! Here she is, ladies and gentlemen!' her exasperated tone blasts through the phone, and I immediately feel five years old. 'The *young lady* formerly known as my daughter! How kind and gracious of you to finally give me the courtesy of answering a call!'

I quietly exhale in an effort to steady my voice and remind myself that this is the first time she's attempted to call me. 'Issac said you're calling because of Dad. It's late there, is everything OK?'

'Well, of course it's late, do you have any idea how long I've been on hold? Honestly, it is very inconsiderate and insensitive of you, Sophia.'

'Sophie. My name is Sophie,' an argument that has persisted my entire life.

'Well, as you know perfectly well, *I* wanted to call you Sophia, so that is what I shall continue to call you. I can't believe your father registered your birth with an "i.e." and not an "i.a.", without my consent,' she tells me for the thousandth time, 'really, the man—'

'Yes, *the man*. What's wrong?'

'It's all happening here, and all you're doing is swanning about on this ridiculous holiday of yours.'

'I am on a *tour* with my *boss* for *work*. I am not on holiday. So, Dad?'

'Do you know that it's been two years since we've spoken?'

I clear my throat, 'Yes.' *I am acutely aware of that.* I shake my head; of course, she evades me, while simultaneously answering a question with a question.

'Well, what do you think I am, a mind reader? Since you haven't contacted *me*, how am I to know where you are and what you're doing?' Guilt floods through me. I could have given her my American number, but that wasn't the point. I had to distance myself. Didn't I? And of course, she could have tried to contact me, on the number she's always known but chose not to.

'I had to go on Google to find out where you are.'

I'm guessing she means she Googled Freya's tour locations. I wonder how the hell she got Madison Square Garden to put her call through to the greenroom.

'Anything could have happened since you left us and didn't bother to stay in touch.'

I swallow any feelings of shame about choosing to put myself first for the first time in my life, and decide to wait patiently for her to finish her rant.

'Do you have any idea what I'm going through? Of course you don't. This is extremely difficult for me to even pick up the phone, yet here I am, once again, being the bigger person.'

I catch the scoff in my throat before she hears it; she has never been the bigger person, yet continues to claim that title whenever she can.

'I don't need to remind you how selfish it is that you haven't cared to answer a single email of mine, either.' My mum hasn't sent me an email in the last two years. 'I could be dead for all you know. And the fact that you—'

'Mum!' I cut her off while rubbing my forehead; a headache arriving earlier than anticipated. 'What's going on?'

'You need to come home.'

'I am home,' I say, trying hard not to acknowledge the stabbing pain of guilt in my chest.

'That's the most ridiculous thing I've ever heard.'

'What is happening with Dad?' I force my voice to steady.

'You need to come home,' she repeats.

'Is he ill?' I prompt, thinking about his heart scare, four years ago.

'I'm not talking about this over the phone, Sophia.'

'Sophie,' I correct. 'Did something happen?'

'If you were here you would know.'

My building frustration escapes in the form of a loud exhale. 'I am at work. Is something happening or not?'

'Oh, well, I'm so sorry to disturb you, Miss High and Mighty! I know your life is so much more important than ours. Look, this conversation is starting to upset me. I am too distraught over your behaviour. Book a flight for tomorrow or you can no longer consider me your mother. Goodbye Sophia.' And with that, the line goes dead.

Sinking into the leather couch behind me, I maintain my grip on the receiver, and with my other hand, I numbly reach for the pretzels in one of the large bowls of snacks in front of me.

Two years.

I've waited two years for the first phone call from her. A tear rolls down my cheek, as I pop three salty, wheaty treats into my mouth, and realise a small part of me believed that she would ring to apologise. Sighing, I push that thought to the back of my mind, and put the greenroom phone down, before pulling out my mobile to scroll to Dad's number. I pause, knowing that if everything *is* OK, it's highly unlikely he'll answer a call at gone midnight, but regardless, I swallow my feelings along with the pretzels and then dial.

My eye draws to the TV screen in front of me, displaying front-of-house. The TV's on mute but I can hear the faint sound wafting into the greenroom from the stage, through the door that's ajar. I watch as Freya commands the stage with ease: dipping, twirling and entertaining her crowd. How confident and at home she looks.

I wonder what that's like.

The phone continues to ring and eventually goes to voicemail. I hang up and shut my eyes, forcing myself to take another breath.

You have to.

I open my eyes and before I'm ready, find his number, and hit dial. Freya is now being hoisted upwards by her dancers, mid-song; the crowd throw their arms in the air and go wild. *It's ringing.*

'Hello! You've reached the voicemail of Christopher Carter,' my big brother's voice sings through the phone, and upon hearing his tone, a wave of fury rises in me; I almost throw my mobile across the room.

'GOD DAMN IT!' I scream at the empty room.

'Phone call go well?' Issac pops his head around the corner of the door I've left ajar.

'I have to go home,' I say to my hands.

'You don't *have* to do anything,' he says, still rooted to his spot in the doorway.

Subconsciously, I bring my hand to my forehead, 'I think there might be something wrong. Or I *fear* that there's something wrong.' I shift in my seat, 'Speaking of, where are we at?'

'First instrumental backup dancers break as she heads into her first costume change.' I glance at the TV screen to confirm that and watch as Freya disappears dramatically through the trap door on the main stage. We've got exactly three minutes and twelve seconds to get back. 'Safe to come in?' Issac checks, gripping the door in fake fear, and laughing at his expression, I wave him in. He makes his way over to the couch. 'We've got the two festive weeks off now. Maybe this is coming at the best time?'

'There is never going to be a *best time*.' I bury my face in both hands and muffle. 'I vowed to myself that I would never spend another Christmas with them, after—' I don't allow myself to finish the sentence, so let out a large sigh instead.

'Well,' I feel Issac sitting down gently next to me. 'I am on the other end of the phone whenever you need me.'

'My home town is like a black hole; there's rarely any reception, especially if it rains or snows. Once you're in, you're trapped there. But thank you.'

He puts an arm around my shoulders, and as I lower my hands from my face, I turn to look at him. 'Alright, well, we can bitch about it all when you come back for the European leg, in the new year.'

'*Um.*' Biting my lip, I try to ignore the dread that has decided to fill my entire being. I shift to face him, 'I guess I have to look at flights after the press conference and before the party?' I ask as more of a question than a statement. 'I'm sure Freya won't notice me leaving,' I scrunch my nose as I get to my feet.

'You're her right-hand woman,' Issac reminds me, standing once more. We walk together to the greenroom door. 'You'll have to stay until she's ready for you to leave.'

I exhale, knowing that's true, and as I move through the door Issac's holding open for me, I force myself to mentally leave my mother in the greenroom.

Chapter 1

What should have only taken about ten minutes, took close to forty-five, as somehow, the whole of New York City caught wind that Freya was driving from Madison Square Garden to The Plaza, to host a post-US tour press conference. Freya's entire team and I line the inside of the black stretch Hummer, each playing musical chairs, taking turns to prepare her for her exit.

When the car comes to a halt, Andy, the larger of her two bodyguards, exits first, followed by Hans, who holds the door open for her. The screams are almost deafening.

'FREYA! This way!'

'We love you, Freya!'

'On your right!'

'You're stunning!'

'MARRY ME!'

Even from inside the vehicle, you can feel the street vibrating. Who wouldn't want to catch a glimpse of one of the world's biggest pop stars? She's been on the music scene for about ten years now. Everything she does is bigger and better than the last, but her latest album was something else. Along with her die-hard fans, new generations have swarmed in and are buzzing about, hopeful tonight, I'm sure, for an announcement before she tells the press; it wouldn't be the first time. Sometimes Freya's impatience gets the better of her. I'm surprised she hasn't leaked the news by now, to be honest.

Exiting the behemoth vehicle with as much grace as I can, I stand back against it, with Issac and the others, and watch as Freya greets her people. The screams are deafening from the wall-to-wall crowd that has formed behind security-controlled barriers. Freya first poses in the middle of the cordoned-off area in front of the hotel, and the crowd goes wild. People are standing with homemade posters and banners, declaring their love for her, or stating all kinds of things from: "It's my birthday! Give me a kiss", to more, let's say, graphic requests. Turning to the left, I watch a fully-grown man faint and take out a row of teenage girls behind him. Freya now moves swiftly along the front row of the crowd, starting on the right, stopping to sign whatever people are holding out for her, or pausing for countless selfies. As she moves expertly around to her left, I watch as people burst out crying, shout out in delight, and honestly, utterly lose their shit, seeing their favourite star in person.

As well as Andy and Hans by her side, we've hired a full team of private police, who are lined up in front of the crowd, ready to pounce. Regardless of security, I glance around at her entourage, each of us would do anything for her; we're like her personal army, ready to attack whenever commanded. We follow Freya's lead and make our way towards the steps to the hotel, but hold back.

Freya then graces the steps of The Plaza. We make sure to continue to give her space; she'll want this photo opportunity the most. Sure enough, when she's mid-way up the central flight of stairs, and with a whoosh of her floor-length, faux fur coat, she turns dramatically and poses. The night almost turns into day with the number of flashes; good thing she's wearing sunglasses. She's in her absolute element. Then with one final wave, Freya turns and walks in. That's our cue to follow.

The Plaza has been home for the past two nights, and I can't wait to get back to my room. Hopefully, this won't take too long.

Opening the doors to the Grand Ballroom, we navigate the next round of camera flashes. Issac, myself, and the rest of the team weave through the world's journalists, guiding Freya safely to the top table. She removes her coat, hands it to me, and somehow sits elegantly down in her oversized black and white, poofy-sleeved number, that looks as though we've borrowed it from the character, Moira Rose, in *Schitt's Creek*. I place a water bottle down in front of her. It's not filled with water.

Freya's sunglasses remain on her face, despite the fact that it's nighttime and we're inside. We all take our seats alongside her on the top table, a microphone in front of each of us, in case we need to step in and block her from, or bat away, any inappropriate questions. Behind us, the wall has Freya's latest album cover, *Fire*, emblazoned upon it.

Freya lifts her hand to wave at the crowd and then leans forward, her Midwest American accent purrs into the table microphone, 'Did you enjoy the show?' A fresh wave of appreciation flows over her, from the press, and a sense of pride washes over me; we've all worked extremely hard in both the lead-up and the entirety of this stretch of the tour. 'Thank you all for coming, I'll get right to the point.'

What she means is that she's ready to go and party, and is regretting not "accidentally" leaking it, or sending out a press release. During one of our initial meetings, she agreed this would have more of an impact; unusual for her to keep her word.

'As you know, my tour continues in Europe in the new year. I thought you might like to know what I'll be up to afterwards.' She pauses dramatically, and you can hear a pin drop. 'I've just signed a contract to write the next *James Bond* theme song, and I have agreed to play a small role; filming will begin in the fall.'

Freya isn't one for being modest; she's contractually not allowed to state that she's the main love interest. The room goes wild with question after question, and Freya continues to coo the attentive crowd. Leaning forward, I can't help but stare at this undeniably intoxicating creature too, not quite sure where my luck came from, to be this close to her. I sort of fell into this position, really. My cousin used to work with someone who'd done Freya's makeup before and heard through the cosmetic grapevine that Freya was looking for a new member of the team. The job description was vague but ultimately, she needed a new personal assistant who was willing to do whatever was required. Several glowing references and a Zoom interview later, I was suddenly on a plane to New York; fantastic timing on my part after everything that had happened that Christmas.

'Freya!' A young man wearing a blazer and Cookie Monster T-shirt combo, waves his hand in the sea of phones, recording devices, and cameras; with his booming voice, he manages to grab her attention, 'So excited to meet you. Big fan. After completing this record-breaking, sell-out, US tour, how will you be spending your time off before the European stretch?'

'Well, first of all, thank you. It's something that *I alone* worked so hard on...'

A wave of annoyance crosses my face at her egotistical disregard of our efforts. Rearranging my expression into what I hope is a pleasant one, I remind myself that there are cameras everywhere, and that she is the star, not me; not that anyone would be taking my photo, but still. I am a nobody. A silent cog in a shiny machine.

'I'm leaving for Bali in the morning for a solo relaxation experience.'

'So, no Sugar and Spice?' Cookie Monster man asks.

'Sadly not. I need to be 100% focused but, don't worry, my chihuahuas will be having their very own retreat, right here. Next question?'

When Freya talks to the press, her favourite line is that deep down, she's just a calm, quiet girl from Wisconsin. As someone who has been her personal assistant for the last two years, I can safely say, without a moment's hesitation, that is total and utter bollocks. I've seen my fair share of evidence that she's chaotic and reactive, which to be honest, is amusing to watch. But when I have to clean up the mess or adapt to her mood swings, that's a tougher pill to swallow; particularly when they begin with the emotionally-driven spontaneity of firing people, and evolve into me, having to wear whatever hat they had on: from personal shopper to stagehand or tour director, hence me running the show tonight. My job role is so incredibly blurred now, that if I left, I'm not sure what I'd put on my CV.

My assistant Issac once said that Freya's an evil, glass book, that you can see right through. I'd agree with that, yet, she has this magical power that mesmerises and dazzles you, without warning, and suddenly you're under her spell, not quite sure how or why. Everyone adores her. And you know what? Frustratingly, for some reason, so do I. I am so drawn to her, fascinated even. I crave her strength, her aura, even her wrath sometimes, and I've no idea why. That's not true. I know exactly why. Because of the way I was brought up. It's almost as though I'm desperate to be berated, or told that I'm not good enough, and I hate the fact that I'm thirsty to prove that I am. Something I've been working on, but don't quite yet believe.

'Yes, it's more than just a cleanse for the body. It's for the mind and soul too, at a silent retreat. I demand so much of myself, but hardly anything of others, so it will be nice to give myself that space to breathe, relax, and—'

Not demanding. Ha! I will my eyebrows to stay where they are. I've been a PA for over a decade, but Freya is unique. Three a.m. phone calls to get her favourite bubble bath or whatever it was that suddenly took her fancy. Jumping out of my sleep in a state of sheer and utter panic seems familiar to me. Do you know that feeling? It's the one where cortisol shoots from the top of your head, down to your toes, then bounces up once more to land squarely in your heart.

'Where in Bali?' the man continues.

'Oh, I couldn't possibly tell you. I'm very much going to be out of the spotlight in *Uluwatu.*'

Of course you are Freya; that's why you're telling the world's press exactly where your resort is. There will be photographers in bushes and undercover journalists at every retreat in Uluwatu until word gets out that she's "hiding" at The Palm. Normally, Freya insists I go with her everywhere, but this time, after reading a self-help book, she's going by herself, and a part of me believes that she's seeking a new-found sense of self. Ever the delusional optimist.

Ah, man. It suddenly occurs to me that I have to kiss goodbye to my two-week break, alone. Freya extended my stay at The Plaza for the holiday season. I don't have my own home here; I still own half a flat in England, which I've been meaning to sort out. I shake my head slightly, willing my inner monologue to shush, and try to focus back on Freya.

'Ever since I watched *Eat, Pray, Love*, I've wanted to go there.' I smile, as it was me who recommended it, then she insisted I watch it with her.

When I first moved, from England, Freya's PA position was in-house and has remained that way. So, for the last two years, I've lived mainly in the guest wings of her East Coast estate, and occasionally at her holiday retreat on the West Coast; wherever her job demanded. But since she's going to be away, and she has major trust issues, she didn't want me alone in her house, hence the extended Plaza stay. I can't believe I have to go back home.

I feel my insides sinking. I was looking forward to a wintery walk in Central Park, a window shop peruse, enjoying the decorations and lights, and a cocktail at the top of the Knickerbocker Hotel with Issac.

Glancing at my watch, I internally urge the conference to hurry up, so we can get to the after-party, and then I can start looking for flights. I hate that I've lost the ability to be present; I'm always trying to plan twelve steps ahead. How many people would kill to be in my position, yet, here I am, wondering just how soon I can run away.

'I'm looking to find a new sense of self. I want to refocus and reflect. I want to relax my mind and body, and my voice of course.'

I want that. I wish she had invited me now; I'd then have a real excuse not to go home. I find I'm shaking my head slightly, as I know that regardless of an invitation from Freya, I'll be getting on a flight to England; my fear won't let me choose myself.

After only about ten more questions, the press conference concludes due to Freya's short attention span, and want to party. We follow Freya out of the Ballroom and up into the 18th and 19th-floor apartment that used to be owned by Tommy Hilfiger, for the party. I can't believe my life sometimes.

Away from the press and the prying eyes of those who would be desperate to see what she's really like, I scan the room of people Freya deemed worthy to join the afterparty. One hundred flawless yet forgettable people are sprawled smugly across the impressive, Central Park view, apartment. Freya stands, barefoot on a glass table, (what could possibly go wrong?), wearing her red silk kimono, open, to reveal her black lacy underwear, hugging both chihuahuas, while also clutching a champagne glass.

'Cheers to you, you fabulous people!' Freya calls to the bursting room, already tipsy thanks to her "water" from earlier. 'I am a star! Let's celebrate me!'

'Wonderfully contradictory as always,' Issac whispers in my ear. 'Now, when are you leaving and when are you going to tell her?' He sips his champagne.

'Well, I've looked and can't get a flight out until hideous o'clock.'

'What does that mean?'

'I think it was leaving at quarter to one in the morning, with a stop in Charles de Gaulle.'

'Whoof; rather you than me.'

'But that's great news really, because I have to help Freya get away first.'

'God, I hadn't even thought of that; good thing you're in charge. Well, come on treacle, sooner rather than later.' He gives me a shove in Freya's direction and I'm suddenly fearful, even though she doesn't technically have to know. *Maybe I won't tell her.* My legs have carried me over to her before I'm prepared.

'Great speech,' is my first line.

'Thanks, darling.' She puts Sugar and Spice down, to roam free, then leans in and gives me a huge kiss on the lips. They're soft and taste like vodka with a hint of champagne. When she pulls away, her eyes linger on my lips and then meet my eyes, 'Do you know, it's been a while since I swam in the lady pond, but there's something about your glasses that makes me—'

'Thank you. Thank you.' I subconsciously fiddle with them and stop her before I'm accidentally talked into a harmless bit of lesbian experimentation with one of the world's biggest stars. 'I need to tell you something.'

'You're right,' she straightens up, 'we shouldn't mix business with pleasure. I am horny though.' She huffs. 'Who do you think would want me?'

That's a trick question. She wants me to say, "Everyone," so I smile, 'Everyone and anyone you want, but, before we get to that, I've just had a phone call from home. I think there may be something wrong with my dad.'

'You *think*? Why only *think*? Why wouldn't you *know*?'

'Because my relationship with my mother is…' I search for the right word, 'complicated. She told me I needed to book a flight home. Tomorrow.'

A wave of something crosses her features, but it's gone as soon as it appears, 'Well, that's fine. Just cancel your extended stay here.' She waves a hand at me, 'But you have to help me pack, drop the girls off, then accompany me to the airport and make sure I'm OK on the jet, first.'

'Of course.' I nod. I hate that I feel I'm asking permission, and waiting for approval as to how to spend my holiday.

'Fine.' She shrugs. I know she hates talking about anyone other than herself for more than a few seconds.

'So, who takes your fancy?'

***

At every opportunity I can during the party, I flee to my room to get organised. My top priority is to throw all of my clothes that need washing into a bag for housekeeping, to do a speedy turnaround for me. I didn't bring all that much with me on the U.S. tour; saying that, I don't have that much more at either of Freya's houses. I travel extremely light.

Freya grabs my arm on a couple of occasions throughout the night, dragging me back, and insisting that I do a drinking game with everyone. Then, she has me filling up everyone's drinks, or refreshing the snacks, even though there's a perfectly good team of catering staff.

Next, I have to update her socials, give her tiny little animals a walk around the block, then arrange for her red silk kimono to be dry-cleaned overnight as she wants to take it with her, and she tells me she may have thrown up on it. Presently, she's wandering around in nothing but her lacy underwear, which doesn't leave much to the imagination. A normal occurrence. I decide to get started on her packing too, then finally, by 4 a.m., when Freya has passed out facedown on the bare stomach of a woman that I've never met, I slip away to my room for the night.

Sitting on my bed—a four-poster—I get the urge to try my brother again, as it's now 9 a.m. in Surrey, but then a rocket of fury shoots through me, so I stop and breathe instead. Trying to gather, I reassure myself: it was important enough for Mum to ring me to demand my presence, after all this time. I'll just have to wait to find out what's happening. It's then that I realise I haven't checked in, so, instead of calling anyone, I use my phone to confirm my seat, and reaffirm all the details. It's amazing how I can organise someone else's life but have no real grasp on mine right now; an occupational hazard of rarely putting myself first, I guess.

Throwing my phone down beside me on the bed, I glance around my room. Everything is wooden, and the ceilings are insanely high.

You don't deserve to stay in a place like this, I hear a voice say inside my head. Frowning, I try to remove the destructive thoughts, with a deep breath, but instead, anxiety begins to fill my entire body, from my toes, up to my heart.

I suddenly doubt that I have everything, including my passport, even though I know I've packed all my freshly washed clothes, and I always keep my passport in the same place.

Before checking, I stand and force myself to try some somatic exercises my therapist gave me. As I jump lightly on the spot, shaking my hands, I try to convince this feeling of inadequacy to leave my body. Committing to a full thirty seconds before giving up, I then carry myself over to the desk where my overused handbag is located. I unzip the side pocket, and sure enough, there's my passport. Regardless of the tour, I've learnt to keep it on my person due to Freya's spontaneity.

Next, my eye falls on my carry-on-sized case by the door, ready to go, apart from my toiletries which are in the bathroom, that I'll gather in the morning. I numbly walk over, double-checking that I'm not insane and did in fact pack all my belongings. Unzipping, I nod, as I see everything all neatly folded. Then after closing it, I pause briefly and reach for the front zip, which I purposely haven't opened in two years.

Pulling slowly, and wondering why I'm deciding to do this now, I sigh, then allow myself to reach into the depths of the open pocket, knowing full well what's wrapped in there. Gently, I take it out, let the scarf it's wrapped in fall to the ground, and allow myself to look at it. It's the only thing, apart from clothes, that I took from our apartment. A small, framed photo that I've hidden from my eyes and my heart, but couldn't bring myself to get rid of. I prepare myself to take it in. Without warning my senses go into overdrive. The smell of onions, sizzling on the BBQ. The taste of ever-flowing cocktails on my tongue. The sound of unadulterated, unbridled fun with your favourite people, celebrating nothing more than the glow of being together. The delicious warm combination of the sun on my skin, and the warmth of his body beneath me. Nick is sitting on the large egg chair in Gabby and Scott's garden, and I'm sitting on his lap. His arms are around my waist, my hands are on his. Gazing at the photo, I breathe in the memory further and can almost smell his comforting woody yet spicy aftershave. I feel a sting at the sparkle in both mine and Nick's eyes. We were so happy back then. I frown, roughly pick up the scarf, and with a half-arsed effort, rewrap the photo, and return it to its hiding place.

Chapter 2

18th December - 19th December

Freya did not want to get up at 7 a.m., the time we had agreed, to get her ready, allowing enough time to catch her flight. She then rudely reminded me, still face down, that it was her plane, and she could dictate when the hell it took off. So, after contacting the flight crew that they would be on standby for the day, I took that opportunity to catch up on emails, have a little nap myself, and double-check that I was ready too. I then dropped the girls off with the canine team—I'm shocked she's not taking them with her to the retreat, but, hey, I don't ask questions, I just make things happen. When 10 p.m. rolls around, I receive a heated phone call from the second pilot of the day, so I decide to shake Freya awake, fireman lift her to the shower, and then dress her myself; the general public would love to see what I see on a daily basis.

We make it to her private jet that's kept at JFK airport, and after securing her in her seat, with a fresh "water bottle", I wave goodbye to my boss, to check in, and wait for my own flight.

It was ridiculously bumpy, particularly on my connecting flight from Charles de Gaulle. I normally don't mind a little turbulence, but that was hideous; according to the pilot, we flew right through the snowstorm that's headed towards the UK. I'm trying to ignore the fact that it feels like the universe is telling me that when I land, I'm in for another bumpy ride.

Arriving at Gatwick I attempt to balance and brace myself, and that has nothing to do with the flight I've just been on. Mum messages to say she'll meet me as she doesn't trust me to rent a car in the snow that's due—despite the fact that I'm in my mid-thirties, and perfectly capable. I'm more surprised than anything at the concept of her driving; something she hasn't done in years. Maybe we'll get the train?

The doors open at the *Arrivals* gate, and I glance around the festively decorated terminal, seeing happy smiley people embracing the person they're there to collect for Christmas. People are holding up handmade signs to one another, accompanied by enthusiastic waves and shouts of joy. It pains me that that's not the welcome I'm about to get. That's never been the welcome. Then, pulling my case and pushing my glasses further up my nose, feeling increasingly like The Grinch, I spot her. She's smaller than I remember; distinctly older, but with her standard strong head of dyed mocha brown hair, and just as much intimidating poise as ever.

Taking a deep breath, I walk closer and spot…my dad. He looks happy and healthy. Not that I'm not grateful that that's the case, but I stop in my tracks, frown, and watch as Mum runs over to me.

'Now, don't be mad,' is her opening line.

Dad looks down sheepishly, clearly playing the role of a pawn in her game of deception, as he's always done. I divert around Mum's open arms, attempting to drape me in an unbearable hug and walk straight over to Dad. 'Are you OK?'

'Yes, fine, darling; how are you?' He's embarrassed.

'Your heart's OK?'

'Yes, of course, why would you think it wasn't?'

I turn to my mother, frowning.

'My gosh, you've aged considerably since I've seen you last.' She leans in, 'You might need to get a little work done on your face, Sophia, particularly your forehead. Do they do that in New York? You're already starting to get some lines.' Standing taller, she grins, smugly, 'Personally, I didn't get any until I was well into my 40's. Good skin, you see. Shame you take after your father's side.' She continues to examine my face, and her expression becomes concerned, with an accompanying head tilt, 'Such a shame that you're wearing your glasses; where are your contacts?'

'You lied.' Mentally exhausted, I ignore her unsurprising, yet expected analysis of my appearance.

'No, I didn't.' Her tone is triumphant and laced with pride. 'I merely *inferred* something might not be right. That's *your* fault for jumping to conclusions.'

'I can't believe this,' I breathe. 'I'm so stupid.' Without much thought, I turn sharply, my subconscious determined to finally walk out of their lives for good, but she grabs my arm. 'Fine. You want to know the real reason?'

'No.' I shake her off and say one of the many things I've practised saying to her in my head, 'You are incapable of telling the truth. You twist everything and it's always somehow my misunderstanding. I can't do this anymore. Have a nice Christmas.' I walk off, half proud, half shocked for allowing myself to be truthful, and look for a sign for *Departures*; I'm determined to fly away, regardless of the cost. She hurries to keep up with me, matching my power-walk speed.

'You abandoned your family for the last two years, for no reason at all.'

I scoff and make it to a desk wrapped in tinsel. 'I need a flight to New York, please.'

'No, she doesn't.' Mum grabs my arm again and tries to pull me away.

'Stop it!' I wiggle out of her grasp.

'I'm not well!' she whines.

'I'm sure a licensed professional would say the very same thing.' I turn to the lady behind the counter once more. 'How's it going with finding me a seat the hell out of here?'

She taps away, then pauses, 'I'm sorry, there are no seats left on any flight to JFK, LaGuardia, Newark, or anywhere nearby, if I'm being honest; Christmas rush.'

'Fine. Europe; anywhere! I'll take your best judgement. Pick me a place, and book me on it.' I slam my passport and purse down on the desk.

'I'm not allowed to do that, I'm afraid. Plus, between you and me, the snowstorm that's currently sweeping Europe is heading our way, so they've started grounding and cancelling flights to numerous destinations within Europe, which might spread to each continent and—'

'You just don't care about your family; you never have.'

'You will not draw me into a debate,' I aim at my mother, then turn back to the lady behind the desk. 'A flight. Anywhere in the world. I don't care. Please. Find anything.' I whoop out my credit card from my purse and slide it towards her.

'I have dementia!' Mum yells desperately at me.

'Oh, I'm so sorry ma'am,' the lady says sympathetically to her. 'My dad had that.'

'She doesn't have dementia,' I say with confidence.

25

'And how would you know? I *could* have dementia,' she reasons.

I look at her squarely, placing a hand on my hip, '*Do* you have dementia?'

She falters for a moment. 'Well, no. But…'

'I'm sorry, there's a message that's just popped up here on my screen. It says—'

'*Ladies and gentlemen,*' the tannoy interrupts, '*until further notice, there will be no flights arriving or departing from London Gatwick, due to unpredictable and unforeseeable weather conditions. Please visit your nearest customer service desk. Thank you in advance for your patience. We anticipate large waiting times in all queues.*'

'Oh, there we are!' My mum is elated. 'Problem solved!' Mum slaps the counter then turns to my dad, 'Richard!' She waves him over.

'Take Sophia's bags, we're going home.'

***

Silently, I'm somehow obediently following my parents to the car park. As my feet carry me forward, it's as if I've pressed mute on the world. I can't hear my parents' conversation or the commotion of thousands of deserted passengers. I tune in, instead, to the snow, which is peacefully falling with increasing urgency.

We climb into my Mum's Land Rover Discovery Sport; I guess Dad's Jaguar XJ is sitting at home. I sit in the middle row, my parents are both in the front, and I glance back at my luggage in the seats behind me—the boot is apparently full. As we exit the Short Stay car park, I wonder why my parents have a seven-seater car in the first place; perhaps they're anticipating a boatload of grandchildren?

Classic FM hums quietly in the background, as we join the motorway; my dad's attempt to create a calming atmosphere. My mum counters this as she begins her monologue as a passenger who would much rather be driving, but in reality, hasn't driven in the last decade, and is in denial that she no longer drives. I shut my eyes and pretend to fall asleep.

'Did you see that? Break, Richard, break!...We nearly crashed; you need to pay more attention...The sat nav is wrong, take this road...Why did you take this road!...Where did that person learn to drive?...Watch that pedestrian, they could dive out at any moment!'

I force myself to try and focus on my breath, but my internal monologue is on fire:

You are so stupid. You haven't learnt anything in the last two years.

'You are driving too fast!'

My dad is the slowest driver known to man.

'Sophia, did you see that? Hello?' I play dead. '*Huh*, I guess she's asleep.' She lowers her tone, but I can still hear her, 'I can't believe she came, can you, Richard? After she just up and left us for no reason. So very selfish, wasn't it, Richard; wasn't it?'

My dad remains silent. I imagine he knows I'm not asleep, but he also knows better than to disagree with my mother, there's just no point. She'll just wear him down until there's no evidence of a backbone.

My parents still live in the house I grew up in, situated in a chocolate box of a town, one village over from Shere, in

Surrey, where parts of the Christmas favourite, *The Holiday* was filmed.

'This snow is getting worse, Richard, you'll need to slow down.'

'We're nearly home, darling.'

I'm not sure if that's aimed at my mother, or me, as a heads-up. My dad has a calm, kind, and soothing voice; I've missed it. I cautiously open one eye and see my parents both have their gazes ahead, so dare to glance at where we are. We're driving along the High Street—a map of my childhood but iced in decorations, and lights. The first detail I notice is the town's red phone box. It used to be the meeting spot on a Friday night, but I see it's been converted into a lending library. Then one after the other, I spot the place where I had singing lessons and learnt to play the piano. The shop where Gabby and I would get sweets during lunchtime. Our primary school. The bus stop where I had my first kiss with Toby Campbell. The corner shop where Gabby and I bought beer for the first time. The park bench where I threw up said beer after realising that I didn't like it. And then I dare to look at *his* family home. Nick's mum still has the same wreath hanging on her door that she's had since we were teenagers. The holly and fake red berries look a little wonky now, but it still has a little glitter and a lot of charm. Plus, it holds a special memory, involving Nick, and the first time he kissed me. I swallow that thought and continue to drink in the town that holds such a big place in my heart.

The whole place is covered in a light coating of snow now, making it look even more delicious than I remember. *I'll stay one night, sleep off this nightmare, and then grab a taxi back to the airport*, I decide. Maybe the flights will be back on by then?

Dad slows, reverses into the driveway, and suddenly we're here.

'Why don't you park next to the Jaguar?', Mum asks.

'I'll reverse into the car port later,' he reassures. I'm sure that's to avoid her criticism and panic that he'll hit the other car.

'Because more snow is due and…oh good, you're awake!' Mum's face has turned to mine, with an expression that implies I've offended her already. My parents exit the car first and for a split second, I wonder if I can dive into the front seat and race back to the airport. Seeing that, obviously, my dad hasn't left the keys in the ignition, I heave a sigh, unbuckle my seatbelt, open the door on the right-hand side, and then head to the backseat for my suitcase.

'No, no,' Dad puts a kind hand on my back, and gently smiles, 'let me get that for you, sweetheart.' I step out of the way as he leans into the car, grabs it, and the case lands on the pebbled driveway with a soft crunch, thanks to the snow. 'I'll put it in your old room,' my dad says kindly, then swiftly moves towards and underneath the outdoor, covered porch, and fumbles slightly with the house keys. Their tabby cat, Truffle, appears from underneath the snow-covered rose bush. She shakes from her head to tail, then sits, waiting patiently to be let back into the house.

'I'm going to stay one night and then head back to the airport in the morning,' I say, to the back of his head, as he unlocks the house and moves inside at speed, almost stepping on Truffle, pretending he hasn't heard me. I try to say this with as much strength as I can muster, which, admittedly, isn't much. My initial fury has worn off and I'm now just feeling immense sadness.

'Look.' Mum has silently slithered around to the right-hand side of the car to join me, her hands on her hips. 'How else was I to get you here at Christmas? I had no choice. You wouldn't have come.'

'I'm not staying for Christmas.'

'Of course you are. How stupid it would be for you to not stay after all this time.'

'You know why I left, Mum,' I say in a small voice, feeling every part of the introverted, don't-want-to-cause-a-fuss, little five-year-old that sometimes rules my head, instead of the thirty-five-year-old woman I am; there's a slight tremble in my hands.

'I have no idea what you're talking about.' Her face is poker-straight, immediately making me feel like I'm talking absolute bollocks. 'You're always so cryptic and mysterious; it's very frustrating. Now, let's go inside, the snow is ruining your hair.'

I'm too tired to get into everything now, so I obediently follow her. I walk towards the porch, wipe my feet on the external mat, while taking in the elaborate wreath on the door, and then move inside.

It smells the same, like coffee and burnt toast; my mum's speciality. I'm filled with familiarity, and I hate that a part of me feels comfort from it.

My parents haven't re-decorated since I was five and Christopher was eight, so there's a strange nostalgia filling me from my head to my toes. Standing next to my mum, in silence, I unbutton and take off my coat, placing it on the already overstuffed rack. Despite it being just the two of them living here, there must be a good twenty coats on there.

My mum is what you would call a closet hoarder: everything looks pristine, but if you open any cupboard, an avalanche of clutter will fall out. As she removes her coat, I look around; it's superficially neat. She only ever tidies when guests are coming. Perhaps I should be honoured that she must, therefore, consider me a guest. Still in silence, she removes her shoes, while I take off my scarf. I think growing up like this is what led me to decide to have such a small number of possessions; like I said, I don't even have a home right now. Well, I do here, I guess. Fuck, I guess I should muster up the courage to talk to Nick while I'm back.

As I place my scarf on the rack, and Mum fiddles with placing her gloves in a drawer she's pretending isn't already full, I take in the overstuffed umbrella stand that sits next to the rack, and think about the life I've chosen. If I don't have clarity around me, I don't have any clarity in my head. Stuff overwhelms me. This house, and everyone in it, overwhelms me.

'I'm going to go to bed, OK. I'm a little jetlagged,' I aim at the back of Mum's head as I take off my boots and go to head upstairs.

She spins and frowns at me, 'Don't be ridiculous, I've been cooking all day. You might want to get changed and put something on your face, you're looking, and, dare I say, smelling, awful.'

'Please, don't hold back how you really feel!' I say weakly as Mum disappears down the hallway and into the kitchen. Sighing, I numbly climb up the staircase to my old room, taking in the winterberry garland that's twizzled around the bannister; that's new. As I walk up the creaky stairs, I contemplate why I've reverted to the wallflower I've always been whenever I'm here, then shuffle defeatedly to my bedroom—the second one on the left, at the front of the house.

When I open the door to my room, my dad's still in it, sitting at my old desk by the window, playing with the handle of my suitcase, clearly waiting for me. 'I'm sorry sweetheart. I didn't want to be a part of this, but,' he shrugs, 'you know your mother. It's her way or the highway. Her opinion is the only one.'

I shake my head and blink away any tears that start to manifest there, 'Anything for a quiet life, *huh*?' I say tightly, my tiredness wanting to consume me.

He smiles sadly, 'That's right.' He takes me in as if for the first time, and his smile turns warm. 'I like your hair. It's longer than I remember.'

I shrug, 'It's been two years.'

He nods resolutely. 'Has it really?' He stands and walks over to me, touching my cheek gently with his hand. 'I've missed you, sweetheart.'

I feel myself soften, even though the hurt and disappointment of his actions still sit firmly in my heart. I let him hug me, but I don't fully commit to giving one back. He feels warm and safe. I wriggle out of his arms, not ready to completely forgive him. Even if he was only the bystander, not the instigator, he still watched me, for years, mentally suffer. And he did absolutely nothing. I sniff, 'So, dinner?'

'Your mum's cooked a roast.' He scrunches his nose slightly and I let a small giggle out. I guess it wasn't burnt *toast* I could smell.

Beneath the Mask

***

So, despite my better judgement, I shower, throw on a small amount of makeup, brush my hair, put on my smart black jeans and my simple yet elegant cream H&M jumper, and make my way back downstairs. Maybe after all this time, things will be different. They'll seize this opportunity to apologise, or, I don't know, take some responsibility, or accept accountability for something. Anything. I'm willing to believe it's a possibility. I have to believe it's a possibility.

When I arrive at the bottom of the stairs, I hear a certain laugh and automatically stop in my tracks. *No. She wouldn't dare invite them, would she?*

Slowly, I creep down the corridor, taking a moment to procrastinate by glancing at the festively decorated front room. It's the same as it's always been: an artificial tree with bland, uniform decorations and timed lights, and tired tinsel hanging from every corner of the ceiling, crossing in the middle. I note that behind the neat line of Christmas cards, Chris' sport trophies from school still take pride of place upon the mantelpiece. I frown at the reminder that any evidence of my achievements—from Head Girl, to straight A's in all my exams, volunteering efforts, or simply starring in every lead musical role my secondary school put on—had to remain in my room.

I sigh then take in Truffle, asleep on the carpet, enjoying the heat from the flames of the roaring fire. Smiling at the cat, I continue my way silently down the corridor, turn the corner, and step into the spacious kitchen.

Sure enough, sitting at the central island is my brother, Chris, and his girlfriend, Aria. My feet have come to a halt as if my subconscious won't let my body move any closer to these toxic people.

'There she is! Hello, sis!' Chris jumps off the bar stool in excitement, and strides, proudly towards me; before I can stop it, he drowns me in a large hug. He squeezes me tightly and then lets go. I'm grateful he hasn't rubbed the top of my head like he always used to. 'How was your flight? Great I bet. But then you always did get all the perks of working for a famous person, didn't you? Lucky bitch.' He jabs me in the arm, hard enough so I feel the need to rub it and watch as he picks up a mug.

I've only ever worked for one famous person.

Chris strides away and helps himself to what I assume is a top-up of mulled wine, that's gently simmering on the stove.

'Sis! How are you? Great to see you.' I hate that Aria calls me sis. Before she started dating Chris a little over three years ago—on and off again, I might add—she was my secondary school bully, and I'm still mildly afraid of her. Aria doesn't leave her seat, which I'm grateful for. 'So much has happened since you left us, you naughty minx. Just to fill you in, we got engaged!'

Aria wiggles a large diamond at me, the size of which I'm surprised Chris could afford. I glance at my mum, whose expression portrays nothing short of giddiness. I try to swallow my pride; apparently, my brother and Aria have different rules to follow. Nick first asked me to marry him when we were eighteen. My parents said we were too young and hadn't been together long enough, which, I guess we were, and I supposed we hadn't. He asked me again when we were twenty-two; after all, we'd been together for five years by that point, and they said we were still too young, and I reluctantly agreed. He asked me a third time when we were twenty-eight (going eleven years strong) and my mum said to stop asking for her blessing and that she would never approve. Knowing that it would break my heart to have a wedding without my family present, Nick and I made the decision to be together, but to never bring up the subject of marriage again. And we didn't.

'*Annnnd,*' Aria snaps me back to the present, in a singsong tone while moving her hand to pat her stomach, 'we're expecting! Due in February.'

Everyone cheers, and suddenly I'm right back where I was two years ago. Numb. Detached. Withdrawn. *What is happening? How am I here?*

'You could congratulate us, sis, bit rude and all that,' Chris whispers to me, then takes his seat once more and begins stroking his wife-to-be's stomach. I shake my head and all I can manage is a tight, bewildered smile.

'So, we're thinking of a very small wedding, like, 200 or so.'

My mum is nodding, 'Absolutely, we'll want all the important people from the village there. They've been desperate for this relationship to succeed from the beginning, of course.'

Yes, an on-again-off-again relationship of three-ish years is a comparative journey, to the sixteen years that Nick and I were together.

'Well, you see, Sophie,' Aria looks at me, oblivious to my inner conflict; from her expression, you'd think she was carrying the weight of the world. 'They've all been on the journey with us. We picked the most darling place to get married—your parents were kind enough to put down the deposit, you see, as your dad had some money freed up from the sale of the G-Wagon, and we just didn't have enough on our credit card—' I look to my dad, who hangs his head. He told me he was putting the money from the sale of the G-Wagon into a deposit for a holiday home. Aria continues, '—and then, it just wasn't...' she pauses, 'the *one*; you know? So,' she continues with dramatic tones, 'this *happened to me* two more times! Again, I felt so bad for your parents—'

Interrupting her, I look at my dad, this time with raised eyebrows, 'You paid for *three* wedding deposits?'

'Four actually, as it turns out, and,' Aria, shrinks in her seat slightly, as if embarrassed—a role that she has never played successfully, 'there's even a wedding dress sitting in a little shop in Newbury—so far away—but,' she touches her hand to her stomach, 'I'm not going to be able to wear it, am I?'

'As I've said,' Mum puts a comforting arm around Aria, 'you can just sell that on eBay and put it towards anything you like!'

Again, I look at my dad, 'So, four *non-refundable* venue deposits, and a, I'm guessing, £1,000 wedding dress?'

'Oh, no! It was, I'm embarrassed to say, nearer to four.'

'Four?'

'Well, five, really, but who's counting?'

I laugh incredulously, 'Yes, who's counting?' My irritation runs through me along with the firm belief that Aria's biggest draw to my family has always been that my dad was on the Forbes 100 List. I look to my dad again, who hangs his head and starts mindlessly stirring the gravy. 'So, let me get this straight—'

'Sophia,' Mum spins around with speed, opens the fridge and hoists something heavy out of it. 'I've done something very special for you: a salmon!' She displays what must be around a 20-pound Chinook proudly: still with its head attached, complete with a glassy eyeball and all, on a plate full of curly parsley.

I exhale, 'I don't eat fish, Mum. I'm a vegetarian,' I say with as much calmness as I can possibly muster.

She cocks her head, 'Are you sure?'

'Yes. Yes, I am. Since I was six years old.'

'No, I think you've got that wrong. Plus, vegetarians eat fish.'

'That's a pescatarian.'

She ignores me, 'Oh, maybe this is just part of your existence now as a fake American. It's because you're watching your weight, isn't it?'

'What?' I hate that I subconsciously put my hands on my stomach and suck it in; a result of her ongoing habit of pointing out if I'd gained a few pounds.

'Because you should be, you're not getting any younger, and it's so hard to lose weight when you hit a certain age. It's all about balancing your hormones. Then you can look as fabulous as me!' She poses.

I clear my throat, 'Right,' is all I can manage.

Her expression drops when she realises I'm not taking the bait to compliment her, 'Well, that's a real shame that I spent a huge amount of money on this for *you* and now you're not even going to eat it.'

My mouth hangs open, and again, I look to Dad. Of course, it's a waste of money for the vegetarian, who doesn't eat fish, to not eat the fish, but perfectly OK to pay for a plethora of unused wedding venues and a never-to-be-worn white dress. Mum noisily throws down the plate of salmon, 'Well, I guess let's all sit and eat then,' she says sulkily as if I've intentionally ruined her day. I feel the need to apologise, then catch myself at how ridiculous that is. 'Come, come!' Mum says and waves everyone over to the table in the dining room.

'Oh, sit next to me, Sophie!' Aria jumps off her seat in the kitchen, skips to the dining room table and with her head over her shoulder says to me, 'You can feel my bump!'

I have absolutely no desire to touch this woman.

Slowly, I walk over to the dining table, and, still standing, watch my brother and Aria take their seats, along with my mum, all happily talking. My dad moves past me to place the gravy boat down on the table, then turns to walk back over to me with a strained but pleasant expression, 'Can I get you a glass of wine, sweetheart?' My dad squeezes my shoulder and I'm momentarily frozen; am I actually going to sit down with these people, as if nothing has happened? I find my head is nodding. Instead of returning to the kitchen for a white wine, or a glass of the mulled variety, either of which would have been my preference, Dad rushes over to open a bottle of red that's sat in the middle of the table; my mum's favourite.

I rarely drink red, but I politely take it anyway and find that I'm being gently pushed to the overstuffed table, filled with steaming-hot, lidded serving dishes. I take a seat despite every bone in my body wanting to run away.

Everyone begins taking off the lids and serving themselves the roast dinner. My plate remains empty, as I watch Mum ladling blackened roast potatoes, 'Well, it's so nice to *finally* have you all here. Even though *some of us* haven't *bothered* to make an effort to be here,' Mum says, and Dad refills her glass in an attempt, perhaps, to shut her up.

'Did I tell you, Sophie?' Chris says from the seat opposite mine, while shovelling onto his plate something orange, that I'm guessing used to represent a carrot, 'Oh, silly me, no, of course not; you haven't been around. After you wouldn't lend me that money, and I lost my job—'

'Were asked to *leave* your job,' I correct, recalling there was a disciplinary and a small court case involved.

'Small details,' he waves me away, 'Since no one has been hiring the last couple of years—'

'You haven't worked in two years?'

'No. Like I say, no one is hiring.' He frowns at me, 'Anyway, we decided to stop paying rent.'

'A wise decision!' Mum says proudly.

I close my eyes and take a deep breath. 'OK.'

'So, Aria and I are currently living here with Mum and Dad; just until we've saved up enough to get our own place.'

'Well, I suppose that's good for you to save what you would have spent on rent or a mortgage, while you're not working, but—'

'Exactly,' he interrupts me, 'and all our food and bills; that's been a relief to not pay for anything.' Chris nods, and I frown at this while he obliviously seeks out his next, unintentionally, mushy veg. 'So, I'm looking for something good enough to support the three of us.' He smiles at Aria, who decided five years ago that work, "wasn't for her."

I down the wine. I don't like it, but I gulp it anyway. My dad comes back over to me, tops up my glass, before I can stop him, walks back around, and takes his place next to Mum.

'And you know what this means, don't you Sophie?' Aria beams at me, as Chris fills her plate for her, 'Since you're here now, we can do *everything* together these next two Christmas weeks!'

There is no way in hell I'm staying here for two weeks.

'It'll be so much fun. We have so much to catch up on. Can you pass the potatoes please, Richard? The baby is just craving carbs, and you know me, I *never* eat them, but here we are!'

'So, no job, four unused wedding venues, a £5,000 wedding dress that won't be worn, a baby, and you're living here?'

'Well, as you well know, Aria no longer engages with her parents after they treated her so badly,' Mum sips her merlot, and I can't help but think of the irony here. 'So of course they were never going to help, but above all, Aria and Christopher had no choice after *you* wouldn't give them any money, Sophie.' Mum holds my gaze intensely.

It's all your fault, I hear her voice say in my head.

I bite my lip. Of course, I feel for Aria, her mum was as toxic as they come, and I'm glad her parents moved to Timbuktu or wherever it was, but my parents? They refused to help *me* with anything financially, or otherwise, when I moved into my flat with Nick, yet expected me to give my money to Chris when he was asked to leave after the disciplinary; Mum was furious when I didn't.

'Would you like some stuffing, darling,' my dad attempts another diversion.

'I'm...' I have no words.

'Oh, did you hear the news?' Mum intervenes. 'Aria is singing a solo at the Christmas Light Switch On!'

'And rightly so with a voice like hers,' Chris coos.

'Wait...' I try to start any kind of a real conversation, but Mum is off again.

'And now that you're back Sophia, I've signed you up to help with the set design of the annual Christmas Eve primary school play. Of course, you know it'll be at the Town Hall as always, but the work will be done at the primary school, then transported over—you can help with that too, and—'

'No.'

Mum shrugs, 'It's all arranged, it will be rude if you don't turn up; you'll make me look bad. You've no idea how challenging it's been for me to keep up appearances after everyone from the village asks how you are, or why you haven't visited. Oh, and speaking of the Christmas Light Switch On, I told them that you're doing something with sound nowadays so you're in charge of that—'

That's not what I do.

'—as the person they've got is not capable of doing a good job.'

I'm pretty sure that person is Nick.

'Of course, the Lantern Parade needs volunteers as always, so, I told the organisers that you said you'd love to help, since you've missed the last two, and—'

'Stop it,' I say quietly, anger starting to brim up inside me.

She continues as if she hasn't heard me, 'Oh,' she yawns, 'I'm so tired from all the cooking I've done today, and, I'm just thinking that since you're not going to eat what I've prepared for you, Sophia, I guess you can cook *your* meals from now on; just don't break anything in my kitchen like you used to. But then again you were always the clumsy, irresponsible one, weren't you; remember poor Smudge?'

I shoot a look at Chris who purposely avoids my gaze. He knows *I* was not responsible for our hamster's death.

41

'Regardless, Sophia, since apparently, I have no idea what you like anymore, you're going to have to fill me in. You've changed your food habits, and—'

Banging the table with my left hand on each word, so the perfectly laid out, three-course cutlery jumps, I find myself yelling, 'I AM A VEGETARIAN!' I realise I'm now standing and visibly shaking. 'No.' My fists are clenched so hard that I fear the wine glass in my right hand might break. 'OK. Let's take a beat,' I say out loud and try to compose myself. 'I'm sorry, but are we honestly going to pretend nothing happened here, that everything's OK, and we're all going ahead with life as normal?'

'Life has gone on as normal, Sophia, you've simply been too busy and important to witness the last two years.'

I feel like I've been slapped.

'Now, you've had too much to drink, lower your voice, and Richard, take her glass away.'

Exasperated, I grip my glass and gesture around wildly in dismay, so a little of the wine escapes and drips onto my mum's crisp white tablecloth.

'Now, look what you've done. I knew you were still clumsy. Go and get a cloth and we can continue our lovely conversation.'

'This is insane. Are none of you going to address *why* I haven't been here for two years?' I scoff, 'I am the only one who's done any inner work, or tried to gain some retrospection!' I say with realisation. 'A part of me berated myself for attempting to live any kind of life away from this…' I gesture around again as if my words will come and find me. '…I don't…I can't…this is just….' I look at my mum with exasperation, 'The money? Really? You're still blaming *me*, despite everything? That's where you're still at?' I turn my focus now to my brother and Aria, 'And you two? The last time I saw you, you had each other arrested and you took out restraining orders! Are we still just pretending that didn't happen either?' I pose this question to the entire room.

'Lower your voice, Sophia, the neighbours will hear you,' Mum threatens with her eyes now avoiding me; something she has always done to show her disapproval of my behaviour.

'I'm…no…it's…ARGH!!' I put the wine glass down. 'I can't do this. I'm…'

'You are so ungrateful,' Mum takes to her feet, 'I've been slaving away for you, now sit back down young lady!'

'I…I need some fresh air.' I storm out of the dining room, through the kitchen, and march into the hall. Stepping swiftly into my boots, I whip my coat and scarf off the stand and hasten to put them on.

'Sweetheart, I know things still aren't perfect, but if you just come back to the table,' my dad pleads.

Frustrated tears form in my eyes, 'Perfect? It's like a crazy time warp! No one is taking responsibility for anything. No one has changed, and no one wants to change!' My dad stands there, helpless. 'I'm sorry, but I can't do this right now, Dad; I can't breathe.' With my shaking hands, I fumble to button my coat, and talk more to myself than to Dad, 'What was I expecting? Self-growth? Some introspection? *Ugh*! I'm the one who's been in therapy for two years, not them. How stupid of me to think that they can look inside themselves and question their actions.'

'You've been in therapy?' Dad looks horrified.

I feel myself deflate completely. *That's all he heard from my soliloquy.* 'I'm sorry but I have to go.' I grab a spare key

43

from the dish on the windowsill where they've always lived and leave the house.

Chapter 3

An icy wind hits my cheeks as soon as I've closed the door behind me, making me inhale sharply and struggle to steady my breath. Looking around, I take in the snowy mountain that used to be Dad's car—I guess he didn't move it to the carport in the end—and stomping past it, I make fresh tracks in the carpet of snow up the garden path, my boots crunching angrily as they go.

I have no idea where I'm going, all I know is that I need to get the hell away from that house. This is why I left two years ago. This is why I had to go and try to create a life of my own; I couldn't breathe in the box that I'd been told to stay in. *For fucks sake!* Have I learnt nothing in therapy?! All these terms that were so new to me two years ago, whirl through my brain like a large tumble dryer on a fast spin, each causing more pain than the last. *Narcissism. Enmeshment. Co-dependency. Gaslighting. Trauma bond. Mother wound.*

I hate that a part of me is so glad to see them and another part wants to scream until my face turns blue. My conflicted feelings churn inside my stomach, and I wonder momentarily if I'm going to be sick. Pushing that thought down, I pick up my speed and turn towards the High Street. This is ridiculous. I could be alone in my room at The Plaza right now, with a glass of sauvignon blanc in one hand, a book in the other, enjoying the view of Central Park, and celebrating my achievements, but where am I? Right back where I was! This is unbearable! How am I expected to get over this? I'm— '*Oof!* Oh, I'm so sorry, I....' With the familiar soft scent of exotic wood harmonising with a warm bitter spicy nutmeg, I look up at the man I've crashed into. *Perfect.*

'Sophie? Wow. I didn't expect to see you back here.'

'Yeah, well, here I am!' I say angrily at the person I used to care so much about. I instantly feel awful for taking it out on him, as I always did.

Nick looks at me in the way he always used to, with kind, patient eyes, and I want him to just scoop me up and envelop me in his arms. I miss his hugs so much. 'You're wearing your glasses.' He smiles sweetly at me. I watch his arm jolt, as if he was going to touch my face and then rethought it.

In response, I insecurely reach up and adjust them, 'Yeah. It was always Mum who hated them and forced me to wear contacts, so now I wear them. The glasses. I wear the glasses, yes.' *Oh my God, have you forgotten how to talk like a human?*

'So, you're back for Christmas?' Furrowing his brow, he looks doubtfully at me, knowing that this is the last place on the planet I would choose to spend my holiday, after everything that happened.

I scoff, 'Well, wouldn't you know it, Aubrey Carter—my own mother—lied to me, tricked me into coming here, and now, I'm back and it's like I never left, and I can't breathe, and that's just freaking fantastic because now you're here, and...' I can feel myself welling up. '...and that's just great. Just...' *I have to get away.* '...yup.' I point at him and start to back away. This is not how I wanted to be acting or looking when seeing him for the first time since we broke up.

'Where are you going?'

I can't breathe. 'I have no idea.' I continue to walk backwards, away from him. 'But I do know that I have to go.

Yup. I'm leaving. Here I go.' I stumble slightly in the snow but remain upright. 'I'm going…' I turn. 'I'm gone.' *Ugh. I hate myself.* Forcing my legs to walk faster away from him, I faintly hear his voice but don't turn around.

'Soph...'

Ugh! I hate this. I hate this. I hate this! I'm power-walking now. I turn several corners and then come to a slow stop, telling myself to catch my breath and look around. I've subconsciously headed towards the part of town that hosts a small number of independent stores, and several bars and eateries. I watch as a bus approaches its stop, from the big, out-of-town shopping centre. Most stores here always close early, plus if you want anything branded, you've got to go further afield. I watch the odd shopper get off the bus, and make their way home, through the snow, carrying their overstuffed bags of Christmas gifts.

I continue my aimless wander, and small flakes start to fall once more. As I go, I look inside each window display; everything has changed since I was last here. Shops that I used to love have been replaced, and each seems to have had a makeover; time truly waits for no man. Twinkle lights and Christmas trees of varying designs glimmer optimistically back at me. Christmas has always been a funny time for me. It's filled with the conflicted feelings of wanting it to be a magically joyful time, yet realising—especially in more recent times—it's just a cause for triggers.

Then suddenly I stop and gaze up at the only familiar sign. Its bold font reading: "*Hermanos*", is accompanied by its yellow tuk-tuk logo, swinging lightly in the wind. Sighing, I pause at the warmly lit restaurant. It's full tonight, and I stare at a couple, sitting at what was *our* favourite table—a great view of the street and equal distance between the chips and guac station, and the cocktail bar. I watch in my mind's eye Nick giving me a small, badly wrapped square box, with a twisted ribbon around it; his lack of patience in packaging always made me smile. I quickly tear into it, remove the bow and wrapping paper, and then inside, upon a layer of rose petals, lies the key to his flat, that became ours; it's still ours. I smile sadly as I watch in my mind, the film of the past. Nick stands, leans in, and kisses me over our table of feta, roasted cauliflower, and sweet potato tacos, accompanied by a passionfruit martini for me and a mojito for him. Blinking, I realise the couple at *our* table, in real life, are now watching me, questionably. Uncomfortably, I shuffle along quickly, and sigh once more, my anger wanting to brim back up, but I don't seem to have the energy.

The people I call my family did this.

Attempting to move out of this headspace, I continue my walk down memory lane and turning the next snow-covered cobbled corner, I hear the loud, unmistakable sound of karaoke. Glancing up I realise I've ended up at The Swan. This is the pub that everyone of my generation gravitated towards as teenagers, and as time moved on, no matter where life took us, or who moved away, whenever we came home, this was the place we would all return to, for a reunion. Ever since I can remember, the pub has hosted karaoke on a Thursday. I'd forgotten what day it is. I can't keep a smile off my face, as I walk towards the front doors.

Stepping inside, it's just as I remember. Slightly too warm, loud enough to not be able to hear your thoughts, and brimming with tipsy people, of all ages, here to avoid family conflicts, over the festive period; or maybe that's just me.

Beneath the Mask

Taking off my coat and scarf, I glance around for a spare seat, or some familiar faces, when suddenly, I'm drawn to the singer. Holding the mic with one hand and sipping her drink that's in her other, is a petite young woman, wearing a deep purple turtleneck jumper, that complements her warm, tawny complexion. She's also wearing what I know to be her favourite pair of dark blue skinny jeans, and over-the-top, knee-high black boots. Her shiny, poker-straight, midnight-black hair shimmers in the low light of the pub, and is slightly shorter than I remember; she must have had a haircut since our last video call.

The introduction starts and then her voice begins the opening lines of KT Tunstall's, 'Suddenly I See.' Swinging my coat and scarf over my arm, I stand, smile, and enjoy her performance. Gabby hasn't changed one bit. I lean on the pillar next to me and take her in, committing to completely rocking the song, and entertaining the whole room. A crowd of gents on the nearest table to her, whoop appreciatively and cheer in between each line. With a mix of Malaysian and English heritage, she is without a doubt, one of the most striking women that I know; it's amusing to see that, upon closer inspection, the guys cheering, are a good ten to fifteen years younger than us. Her beauty is timeless.

Then her eyes move to where I am, as the song is drawing to its close, she spots me, screams and in between lines, starts pointing at me, changing the lyrics to: *'Suddenly I see, it's my best friend So-phie/Suddenly I see, what the hell are you doing here?/Suddenly I see, I've really fucking missed you!/Suddenly I see, standing there is my best friend So-oo-ophie!'* As the song finishes, she throws the mic into the booth behind her and runs over to hug me. 'Holy bugger me

49

sideways and call me crazy!' She throws her arms around me. 'Why are you here?'

'It's nice to see you too,' I say, breaking away and smiling at her.

'No, I just mean, after everything...'

I shrug, 'I'm leaving tomorrow. She tricked me into coming back, and—'

'Tomorrow? You're only here tonight?'

'Well, I haven't got a flight yet, but I'm not staying, so...' I shrug and let my voice trail off.

'Well, we need to get pissed,' she says this as a matter of fact and grabs my hand, leading me to the bar, moving people out of the way as we go. 'Excuse me, sorry, yup, this is my best friend, she's only here one night, that's right, move please, thank you!'

'Is Scott here?' I shout over the crowd. 'I haven't seen him in the flesh since you guys came to visit last year.'

'He was, but had a kitty cat emergency.' He's the branch manager at the local animal shelter. 'My song was up next, so I said I'd stay until that. Now I've got an excuse to stay longer.' She grins at me as we make it to the front of the queue for the bar, 'So what will it be?'

'Dad gave me wine, so maybe I should stick with that,' I offer.

'Tequila it is.' She turns to the young man behind the bar and before I can stop her, she's ordered four.

'I don't think we've had tequila together since...' I try to tap into my memory and she finds it for me.

'Our eighteenth birthday party,' she nods. 'We agreed never to touch the stuff again unless there was a real celebration. You're here; that calls for a celebration!' She turns to pay the barman quicker than I realise that I've forgotten my purse. 'It's on me,' she says firmly.

'I've forgotten my bag,' I make a face.

'Then it's definitely on me.' She laughs at my fallen face.

'I ran out of the house without thinking.'

'Neither here nor there; I would have paid for it anyway. It's not every day that your best friend comes for a surprise visit,' she bats away any of my guilt. We both turn as the next singer begins with, 'Bat Out of Hell.'

'Oh my God, is that—?' I laugh.

'Greg, yup.' Gabby sniggers. 'The guy hasn't sung anything else at karaoke since secondary school.' I glance over and he's headbanging and thrusting with all his might.

'He's got a little more creative with his moves, though,' I notice, as he's now grabbing a poor woman sitting near to him and is spinning her wildly around the dancefloor. 'Wow.' He sends her off, back into her seat, then launches once more, into the second verse, closing his eyes to be more emotive with the song.

'This town hasn't changed, has it?'

Gabby smiles, 'Not a single bit. Right, lick.' We both lick the corner of skin on the back of our hands between the thumb and first finger. 'Salt.' She sprinkles a white line on my newly lickcd space on my hand, then hers; the salt sticks. 'Cheers!' She holds a glass aloft and gestures for me to do also; I oblige, awaiting my next instruction. 'Lick.' We lick the salt. '*Ugh*,' she screws up her face. 'Shot.' We both take the shot, '*Agh*; lemon!' We both take a bite of lemon.

'That was horrible.'

'It was,' she agrees. 'Let's do the other.'

***

Two turned to four, four turned to a possible five, I can't remember, and we're now sharing a bottle of New Zealand sauvignon blanc, and feasting on a dinner of crisps and peanuts. I feel thoroughly marinated, my problems sitting just at the edge of my consciousness, but on the far side of my protective booze layer. It's now that I decide Gabby and I should do a duet. We wobble, arm and arm over to the book of suggestions and select our song.

The music starts up and we go for it. I've always loved Kelly Clarkson.

We hit the chorus of 'Since U Been Gone' and Gabby says over the mic, 'Fuck me, I forgot how high this is!' We laugh and continue, bopping up and down and just before the bridge Gabby says, 'Sophie solo!' I hit the high notes as best as I can in my drunken state, to an appreciative crowd. We then dance our way through the instrumental and finish the final chorus and outro with a nice call and response, singing all the parts we can. The crowd claps and whoops. 'And next, for your immediate pleasure,' Gabby gestures to me, 'the fabulous Sophie Carter, fresh from New York, would love to sing you a solo!'

Everyone cheers. I lean into my friend, 'What? Did I sign up to sing something?'

'Nope. I just miss your voice.' She grins at me with her best puppy-dog eyes, 'Please. You don't have to if you don't want to.'

'What did you pick for me?' I ask, feeling fearless with my booze cape wrapped around me.

'SOPHIE! SOPHIE! SOPHIE!' the (just as equally marinated) pub-goers chant. I can't help but smile.

'Your favourite song when you were twelve,' Gabby encourages.

I burst out laughing, trying to think what the hell that was, then read the title on the screen in front of us; I turn back to her. 'What if I can't remember the words,' I suddenly worry.

'They appear on that screen right there, hon,' she laughs. 'I've missed you singing it. Please.' I waver for a moment. 'And anyway, if it helps, everyone's drunk and not really listening to you anyway,' she scrunches her nose.

'OK, I'll do it.' I take a deep breath, and the introduction to Avril Lavigne's, 'I'm With You,' starts. Gabby sits across from me, leaning on her elbows, and cupping her cheeks in her hands, staring, and smiling at me.

'Go, Sophie!' a voice I don't recognise, shouts.

I begin singing, softly at first. I love this song. I put everything into it. As each section builds, without trying I've connected to my emotions from the last two years. I realise I'm trying to sing out all the frustration, sadness, and anxiety that I've bottled up and tried to pretend wasn't there. The line, '...nothing's going right, and everything's a mess...' starts, and that's when I spot him; Nick's sitting at the bar, drinking a pint. I shut my eyes and don't let this throw me. I continue, completely surrendering to the vulnerability of the song and when I'm done, I allow my eyes to head back over to the bar. Nick's not there. I guess he left after seeing me. Even though he's got a great singing voice, he's always hated karaoke; he'd always say that he's an audio engineer, not a singer. I search the crowd once more with my eyes; did I imagine him? I think I need a pint of water. It's not until Gabby jumps up and throws her arms around me that I realise the room has erupted into thunderous applause.

'Have you been practising that? It's even better than I remember!' Gabby guides me to our table and we sit down. My eyes are still focused on the bar stool Nick was sitting at. 'What are you looking at?'

'I just, *uh*, thought I saw…someone.'

'Who?'

'Nick,' I say, now looking at the karaoke performance space.

'Oh fuck, really? Your Nick?'

'You know he's not *my* Nick anymore, but yes, Nick!' I point and Gabby sees him too, holding the mic.

'He hasn't come in here since you left.'

'Really?' That saddens me. He always used to like having a pint with whatever band was rehearsing in his studio.

'Evening everyone,' Nick says, 'I just wanted to say that I found a set of keys outside,' he holds them up. 'So, if you're missing them. I'll be over there,' he points to the bar.

'GIVE US A SONG!' a drunk voice shouts from somewhere.

'Oh, no, thank you. I don't sing.' He hands the mic back to the owner of the karaoke.

'Yes, you do! And rules are rules, man: you touch the mic, you have to sing!'

'This is ridiculous,' I hear him say.

'Well, if you're shy, how about a duet? Where's Sophie?'

I instinctively grab the menu that's in the middle of our table and hide, unsuccessfully, behind it.

'There she is!' I hear another voice and attempt to shrink further into my menu.

'We're not letting you go without a song,' I hear the karaoke guy say.

'Soph?' I now hear Nick's voice, 'Can you please help me out here?'

'Excellent!' Gabby's voice comes from next to me. 'Love it. Love you. Love him. Love everything about this. Yes!' I feel the menu being grabbed from my hands.

'What are you doing!' I bark at Gabby's excited face.

'Helping!' she smiles, then guides me to my feet and over to where my ex-boyfriend is standing.

'*Ah*, didn't they make such a cute couple! I can't believe you two broke up,' the karaoke guy says over another mic, and I feel my face flush a Rudolf-nose-red. 'Here you go, Soph.' I take the mic he's offering me, and feel myself sobering up with every second. 'And I know just the song that people would like to hear from you, guys.' Glancing at the screen in front of me, the words *"Shallow – from A Star is Born – Lady Gaga and Bradley Cooper"* appear. I gulp. I turn to the karaoke man.

'I don't think this is a good idea.'

'I don't think we have a choice here, Soph.' Nick smiles at me, kindly.

The intro starts, with sweet guitar picking and then suddenly, he's singing. *God, I miss his voice.* Initially, he doesn't look at me. He sings to the door, something he always used to do whenever Gabby and Scott would encourage us to sing together. It's not until the last line of pre-chorus one that he looks at me, '*...and in the bad times, I fear myself.*'

I swallow, suddenly nervous, and then I begin my first line. He continues to look at me. I clear my throat a little before continuing into the second pre-chorus. When I get to the chorus, I let go, shutting my eyes. The crowd cheers with appreciation for my top notes. And then he's harmonising with me, '*In the sha-ha-sha-ha-ha-low...*' I'm suddenly transported back into his red Citroën BX GTI that had a temperamental radio. On our road trips, we'd drive for hours in what I called his "tonker" car, and whenever the radio would give out, we'd sing together, the time just blissfully disappearing. After I've sung the climax of the song and headed into the second chorus, I know I shouldn't, but I look over at him, and can't tear my eyes away. He joins in again, harmonising. *I miss this so much.* We finish the song and we're still gazing, sadly, at each other; so much was left unsaid and yet, I have no words.

'Well, wasn't that something?' the karaoke man cries through another microphone. 'Alright, next up we're going to have Winston with, you guessed it: "Hit Me with Your Rhythm Stick"!'

'Hey, can I talk to you for a sec?' Nick grabs my hand as I nod, and he leads me through the crowd, towards a quieter corner of the pub. 'I'm sorry, I don't think I handled seeing you very well, earlier. I just...' he pauses, '...wasn't expecting to see you here. Ever again. Or...ever, anywhere, again, if I'm honest.'

'You didn't handle it? *I* didn't handle it. As it turns out,' my head flops to one side, 'I'm not very well put together!' My balance wobbles with my head movement, I go to steady myself on a nearby table, and accidentally knock several glasses; they smash on the ground and the entire pub cheers.

'Let's get some water.' He smiles at me, walks to the bar, and orders two; he was never one to point out I'd drunk too much, and would only do what was best for me, without judgement. We stand in awkward silence with the surreal soundtrack of Ian Dury. Shifting awkwardly, I don't know why, but I suddenly feel the need to apologise, for everything. The water arrives and I sip it, gingerly, while looking at him from the corner of my eye. *I can't bring myself to say anything.*

'So, how's New York?'

I nod, 'Good. Good.' He looks at me, somehow looking into my eyes and seeing my soul. 'And, how's your work?'

He shrugs, 'Fine. We've got some of the latest Neumann U87 ai's in the studio, so I guess that's something.'

'You always were a sucker for a great microphone.' I nod and sip again. 'And, how are your parents?'

He smiles, 'The same.'

We stand in silence once more and I take the opportunity to gulp the water. *We've completely forgotten how to be with each other.* I could be standing with a total stranger.

'So, I was wondering, since you're here now, we could, I don't know, sit and...*um*...are you alright?'

I shake my head, then regret it. 'I think I need to go home.' I immediately scoff, '*Home.* A mystical illusion where apparently you always feel loved and welcome! Maybe I'll just sleep here. I remember I had a nice snooze in one of those booths one time,' I say pointing behind him.

'Come on. I'll walk you; you'll feel better in the fresh air.' He downs half his pint of water and then places it with finality on the bar.

Before I can argue, he's putting his arm around my waist, and steering me towards the door; it feels nice. I meet eyes with Gabby who's striding towards us. 'Here you go.' She hands my coat and scarf to Nick, and he helps me put them on. I feel like a child who needs assistance and can't do anything for herself. 'I'll ring you tomorrow and hopefully, we'll grab breakfast before you fly home.' Gabby gives me a hug.

'You're leaving tomorrow?' Nick says, mildly horrified, or maybe that's just how I want him to feel.

'I'll book a flight tonight before I fall asleep,' I wave the thought away. I'm not able to think straight right now.

Gabby gives me another hug, 'I love you.'

'I love you too,' I grin at her, then feel concerned, 'Hey, you ready to go? You could walk with us?'

'Oh, no, I just need to chat to someone; you two go on ahead.' She exaggerates a wink; subtlety has never been her friend. 'Goodnight you two!' she calls as we walk towards the door.

As soon as we're outside, I inhale the night's air, attempting to find a bit more clarity. It's still persistently, but lightly, snowing. 'Well, isn't this something?'

'What?'

'This,' I gesture to us. 'Here you are, rescuing me from myself once more.' I go to smile but all of a sudden just feel the overwhelming urge to cry.

He keeps his eyes on the ground for a moment as we walk, searching for his words, then he finally looks at me, 'I was never rescuing you from yourself. I was always rescuing you from...'

'I know.'

'Anyway, I'm...just...glad you're here. You left a hole in my life, you know?' Nick says vulnerably.

I stop walking for a second and put my head in my hands. 'Yeah, well...' What do I want to say to him? I dare to lower my hands to look at Nick, and figure, what the hell, 'I have no life without you. I'm helping someone else live theirs.' I shrug and let my eyes fill with tears. We continue walking. If I hadn't drunk so much, I definitely wouldn't be saying any of this right now, but I keep going regardless, 'I hate what happened, but I had no control over them, and I wasn't strong enough, and…I'm so sorry.' I exhale, attempting to release some of the heaviness. 'Anyway, we can't take it back, can we? And I guess we'll never know what could have been, because they just…they just…took everything away, and,' I wipe away a tear, 'it's all just a bit too much. I'm sorry.'

Nick shakes his head, 'You don't need to apologise.' I feel there are a million little things that I need to apologise for, but instead, I fold my arms, and we fall into silence.

When we're finally at my parent's house, we stop just before the driveway, and I look up at it with distaste. 'I hate this place.'

Nick follows my gaze, 'Me too.' Then after a moment, he meets my eyes once more, 'How are you getting to the airport tomorrow?'

'*Um*, I don't know; cab maybe?' I shrug.

'Let me take you. Just message me a time, OK?'

'OK.' I smile, and without discussion, we silently walk side by side towards the front door. When we're under the porch cover, he smiles sadly at me and lingers, his eyes drinking me in as if it's the first time he's seen my face. *Is he going to kiss me?* Then just as quickly as I've allowed myself to raise my hopes, he shakes his head ever so slightly, as if silently changing his mind, then he nods. 'Goodnight, Sophie.' He turns and begins to walk back up the path.

'Nick!' I stage whisper, stepping off the porch into the snow. I want to run into his arms, but instead, I catch myself and stay rooted.

He stops and turns. 'Yeah?'

'Do you want…' *No, I can't ask him that.* 'I just, *um*.' I exhale. *Don't go there, Soph; you can't*. Instead of inviting him in, I decide to say what I've wanted to, for a long time, 'I'm sorry I didn't fight for us.'

He shakes his head, 'I'm sorry I didn't fight to keep you.'

Those words strike my heart harder than anything else. Can you ever guess what someone else is thinking? Or do you merely stand there assuming and compiling your own story? The silence remains between us, but as our eyes remain locked, it's as if we can understand each other in a way that no one else ever has. *Good God. What are you afraid of Sophie? Just reach out and be with him!* And yet, in spite of myself, I do nothing.

'Well, sleep well,' Nick finally breaks the silence, and I fear there'll never be another moment.

'Sweet dreams.'

With one final small smile, Nick turns, and walks the remainder of the garden path, then down the street, and out of my life once more. I watch him go, and wonder if this was my closure. A small part of my soul feels like it's healing, but at the same time, feels even more broken than before.

Realising that the snow is becoming increasingly persistent, I make my way back towards the house, then wipe my boots on the mat outside, sheltered on the covered porch. I turn the front door key as quietly as possible and step inside. Removing my boots, coat and scarf, I tiptoe to the bottom of the stairs. I hear the TV—my mum will be asleep in front of it. My dad will be in bed, and I truly hope that Chris and Aria are as far into dreamland as is humanly possible. I creep my way up the stairs, being sure to avoid the right of the third, and the middle of the fifth steps that have always had the loudest creaks. Safe now, on the landing, I weave left towards my bedroom. Turning on the light and closing the door, I exhale once more; *made it.*

Beneath the Mask

Glancing around, I numbly take in my place of solace from my childhood; something that clearly, I was too exhausted to acknowledge earlier. My bedroom has the same floral wallpaper and the bed's in its usual place, but there's a running machine in one corner, a Pilates machine in the other, and countless stacked boxes filled with God-knows-what. I let my bag fall to the floor and look at the desk by the window. I told my parents, when I was younger, that I needed to move it from its original position, facing the wall, to get a little more natural light to do my homework. But in truth, at a contorted push, I could see Nick's house from there. I girlishly make my way over and lean across the desk, moving my face closer to the window. A dark figure in a long black coat moves through the snow. It suddenly stops and turns. It's Nick. I wave and he steps directly under a streetlamp, so I can see him clearer; something he always used to do. He waves back at me with a large nostalgic grin on his face, then he turns back around, and I watch his silhouette disappear into the darkness.

Chapter 4

20th December

Fuck my head hurts.

Eyes still closed, I scrunch my nose and try to figure out where I am.

The bed feels weird.

Oh. I'm at home.

Sighing, I pull the covers up in disgust. *Ugh, what's digging in my back?* Fumbling around, my fingers find my phone. Grabbing it, I force my eyes to open and I press my thumb to the screen to biometrically open it while simultaneously reaching for my glasses on the bedside table with my other hand. Glasses, now on my face, the screen comes into focus.

Fuck.

The page that stares back at me is a timed-out screen on the British Airways website. Guessing I passed out before doing anything useful, in my horizontal position, I refresh it and search for flights.

Delayed. Cancelled. Grounded, are the only words that greet me. 'Fuck!' I say out loud this time and throw my arm back down on the bed, still clutching my phone. It rings in my hand and I bring it up to my face to answer.

'So, I'm guessing you're not going anywhere today?' Gabby's voice, more gruff than usual, asks.

'No, I fell asleep before I could book anything and now it seems nothing is available.'

'Because of the snow,' she says, knowledgeably.

'Really? It didn't seem that bad last night,' I yawn.

'Have you looked outside yet?'

'I haven't sat up yet.'

'Hon, I'm not sure you're going anywhere, anytime soon.'

'It can't be *that* bad. *Ugh.*' I force myself up from bed and wander over to the window. My eyes fly open. 'Oh, Holy Jesus.'

'Exactly. I'm sorry to tell you hon, but I think you're home for Christmas.'

***

'This can't be happening.' I'm saying this out loud to my reflection in the bathroom mirror. Taking my glasses off, I splash some cold water on my face.

'Hello! Who's in there? The baby needs to pee!'

The baby needs to pee? Does she realise that's not correct? I quickly grab my towel, dry my face and with glasses back on, open the door.

'Oh, I forgot you were here!'

Charming

'I guess we've all just got used to you not being around. No offence.'

'*Um hmm.* And good morning to you too, Aria.' I go to leave the bathroom and she stops me by wrapping her bony but strong fingers around my wrist.

'No need for you to leave, I'll just pee quickly and we can have a little chat.' Before I can say anything, she's led me to sit on the side of that bath and is now relieving herself. 'Between you and me, Aubrey did work hard on that meal yesterday. Might be worth a little apology for storming off like that. Oh, morning!' I follow her line of sight and see my dad walking past (a newspaper under his arm) on the landing through the door, she's left ajar. He smiles politely but hurries on and I'm left shaking my head at the continued lack of boundaries in this house. 'Just, you know, put yourself in your mum's shoes for once, is all I'm saying.'

I feel like someone has just punched me in the gut. *She has no idea how much inner work I've been doing over the last couple of years.* Aria grabs the loo paper, does what she has to, stands, flushes, then washes her hands.

'Oh, good you're both up.' Mum now joins the bathroom party. 'We're all due at the school in a couple of hours. Well, not all; your father is going to stay home because his back is playing up, and Christopher has a meeting.'

'A meeting?' I yawn.

'Yes, about a very important potential job opportunity in London.'

I frown as Chris always seems to have some form of excuse not to bend to Mum's every beck and call. Mum reaches over me and grabs her toothbrush, while Aria nabs a hairbrush and starts weaving it through her already picture-perfect hair. I watch, somewhat detached from my brain, as Mum applies toothpaste and continues to talk to us while brushing, 'So, I spoke to Mr Frances last night. You remember your old sixth form teacher, Sophia? He's now headteacher at your old primary school—you'd know that if you'd been here—and he is just thrilled that our family has *reunited* for Christmas. Did you know he's a religious man? He said he's been praying for your soul, Sophia.'

Praying for my soul? I highly doubt those words came out of his mouth. I will myself to lower my shoulders and take the high road. Plus, I'm too hungover to tell her that we are most certainly *not* reunited, but, like I always used to, I remain quiet. My opinion isn't valued in this household. Even if I did speak up, my words would get twisted or thrown back at me, and I'd end up forgetting what my point was in the first place. It's easier to be quiet.

Before I left this environment, I didn't realise that my relationship with my family was filled with a type of emotional manipulation called gaslighting. When my therapist said it's a type of psychological abuse where someone distorts your reality by telling you that things aren't the way they actually are, to the point where you question your own judgement and sanity, I burst out crying. There was finally an explanation or definition really, of what it was that I was feeling. I wasn't going mad; I had a label. I like labels. I like boxes. They help me feel in control.

I look now at them both, chatting away without a care in the world, not torturing themselves over their words or behaviour, or trying to make sense of a situation. This is exactly why I felt crazy when I was here; no one else seems to be suffering, so I must've been the one in the wrong, right?

'Fantastic; exactly what I was thinking, Aria,' Mum's voice brings me back to the present. 'Sophia, we think perhaps you should go a little earlier. Mr Frances might want to speak to you before we get going.'

I clear my throat. I've no intention of going there at all, never mind early. 'No, thank you,' I try to say with strength.

'No, thank you?' Mum repeats back at me with an impatient hand on her hip. 'What will everyone think?'

I really couldn't give two fucks.

Victoria Mae

Resisting the natural urge to concede, I stay quiet, and we just continue to stare at each other. *I'm not backing down.* I hear my therapist's voice in my head:

You do not have to attend every argument you are invited to.

'Not eating my food yesterday, and now, refusing to help the community; you've really changed.' She finally shakes her head and avoids my eye contact. 'I don't recognise my own daughter.' Throwing her toothbrush down, she then strides off in her dramatic fashion and stomps out in a way that was always designed to make me run after her and apologise, regardless of it almost always being her fault. But as uncomfortable and wrong as it feels to stand up for myself, I stay rooted, my fingers gripping onto the side of the bath for support.

Aria exhales loudly, 'Well, I think that was incredibly rude of you Sophie. Why did you bother coming back here if you weren't going to make amends and apologise for your behaviour?' Aria places her hairbrush down gently, then with poise walks towards the hallway, pausing in the door frame for a moment, she looks over her shoulder at me, 'You really are incredibly selfish.' And with that, she's gone.

***

'Well, what a complete and utter bitch.' Gabby twirls her celery stick around her bloody mary, while I recount the bathroom story to her and Scott, in our favourite brunch venue, The Mad Platter. 'She's saying *you're* selfish; how ironic is that?'

'All she cares about is her image. She's just as manipulative as she was in school,' Scott chips in. 'Her and that Whitney What's-Her-Chops who used to bully the shit out of you.'

'Thanks,' I say sarcastically.

'Sorry.' Scott makes a face, 'I'm a little testy; it's the shelter. We don't have to get into it now.' His face contorts in pain, his full attention elsewhere.

'No, I want to hear. Still struggling?' I guess. They've kept me up to date with the decline in funds since I left.

Scott nods and heaves a huge sigh. 'Yeah. I don't want to admit it, but I'm not sure we'll be open much past the new year.' I go to reassure him that something will work out, when he continues, 'Oh, speaking of Whitney and Aria, did I tell you that they tried to come to the shelter with a photographer and journalist, to publicise in the local paper how *they're* helping to support us, just because Whitney's husband runs the paper now, and she fancied a bit of publicity?' I shake my head and his face continues to crumple, 'Aria and Whitney have been in the shelter one other time, which, by the way, was when Whitney brought in a collie pup with mild behavioural issues, saying she found it, but I had a hunch that it was *her dog*! You could tell by the way he reacted to her walking away.' He shakes his head in anger, 'Vile people.' Gabby shakes her head, as I'm guessing she's heard the story before, but Scott looks at me, and my mouth is open in disbelief; how the hell can a human do that? 'Sorry, but what I'm saying is, once a shit person, always a shit person, and once a bully, always a bully,' Scott drinks his large oat cappuccino, then angrily licks his upper lip for the chocolate-covered-foam-momentary-moustache to disappear. 'The fact that Aria is still friends with a person like that, speaks volumes. I always hated the way they treated you. It wasn't OK then and it's not OK now.'

Taking a deep breath, I feel like I'm caught in this limbo between frustration and helplessness. 'It's like Aria has this power over me. And it doesn't matter that I'm now a grown-ass woman, who should be able to stand up for herself, it's like I've just stepped back in time, and become the person I always was around her. Not in a nostalgic way like with you last night,' I smile at Gabby, 'but in the absolute peak of my introverted, co-dependent, shell of a human phase; I hate transforming back into that version of me. It's like I've completely forgotten everything I've been working on for the past two years.'

Gabby shakes her head, 'It's a process, hon. It was never going to be easy seeing them again, no matter how much time had passed. I'm sorry. I wish there was something I could do. You could stay at ours?'

Smiling at my friend I know, regardless of the size of their house, that there'd be no room for me. Scott's an only child, whose parents have now both sadly passed, but Gabby's entire family are back in town for the holiday season; every bedroom, including the converted garage guest house that they normally Airbnb, will be full. Gabby is one of five kids: two brothers and three sisters in total, she's the eldest. Her parents, aunt, uncle and grandma are coming too, having all gone their separate ways, yet they remain as close as ever. Since everyone likes to return "home", and since her and Scott's place is the biggest (their long-term plan is to have a home filled with both human and fur babies) she always offers to host. 'And where would I stay exactly?' I ask kindly.

'In my bed.' Her tone is matter-of-fact.

'I'm sure that'll be nice and cosy.' I laugh and raise an eyebrow at Scott to challenge the situation.

'I'd take the couch for you, you know that,' he says with all seriousness, and Gabby looks lovingly at him. I grin at my friends. We've all known each other since primary school, and he's as much of a best friend to me, as Gabby. I watched the two of them have various relationships—none of which I'd particularly warmed to—so I was secretly happy when either of them broke up with whoever they were with over the years. I always thought they belonged together; they both love animals and activism, but they were such close friends that neither saw each other in that light. It took them reuniting after Gabby had finished veterinary school, moving back to town to work at Paws and Claws, and her volunteering at Scott's animal shelter, for them to realise that they were in love. They've been together for five years now.

'Anyway,' Gabby refocuses, and sips her bloody mary, 'back to you. You were saying...'

'I have no idea.' I shake my head.

'The bathroom debacle,' Scott confirms, then shakes his head. 'Jesus Christ, you put up with a lot. I'm not sure I'd be able to handle it,' he says honestly. He looks at me, not with pity, but with the strong, platonic love of a replacement brother. 'Please know that we love you, and, I'm sorry, but they're all dicks.'

I burst out laughing. 'God, I've missed you guys.'

'You've no idea how much we've missed you.' Gabby reaches over and takes my hand, 'But we know how incredibly shit it is for you to be back in this town, so, I just want to say, even though you know it: please don't go into yourself. It's OK to talk about how you're feeling, hon.'

Clearing my throat, I allow myself to question how I feel; something that I'm still working on, as I have a strong habit of suppressing everything. 'I feel...' I search for the right word, 'disappointed. I allowed a little part of me to feel this small, optimistic glimmer of hope, that something would have changed.' I shrug, 'Like, my lack of presence would have forced them to look at themselves.'

Gabby leans forwards, and squeezes my hand even tighter, 'I hate to say it hon, but if your absence meant nothing to them, then they don't deserve to be in your presence.'

'You didn't message.' Nick is suddenly at my side, and I gaze up with confusion.

'Was I supposed to?' *God, he's handsome.*

'Mate! Come join us!' Scott gently pushes the empty chair with his leg from under the table, to slide it out for him, but for now, Nick smiles and stays put.

'You said you'd message me your flight details and I said I'd give you a lift to the airport. When you didn't message or ring, I figured I'd find you here.' He stands with his hands in his pockets and looks kindly down at me.

'You always were a smart guy,' Gabby grins at Nick before raising her glass to him.

'I'm so sorry.' The sinking feeling of shame shoots from my heart to my feet. 'I don't remember that.' I look at my phone which has no notifications, or reception for that matter, then I gaze sheepishly up at the man I used to love. *Still* love. 'My phone didn't ring.'

Nick shrugs, 'This town's a black hole; reception's always a bit hit and miss, isn't it?' He unwraps his scarf and points to the empty seat next to mine, 'May I?'

'Of course.' I smile and resist the urge to lean my head on his shoulder after he's sat down. It feels formal. I hate it. Nick stretches his hand out to shake Scott's and they chat for a moment. Gosh, it's like we're back to normal, the four of us having a meal together. My heart fills with sadness, then Nick turns to me.

'So, what's your plan, then?' He looks at me with patient eyes.

I exhale. 'I keep checking, but no one's flying out.'

'Well, I guess that's normal, being five days before Christmas.'

'They're now saying it's not only due to snow, but to heavy winds, and lack of pilot visibility,' Scott fills him in.

'I suppose that's *kind of* important,' I say sarcastically, then drink my mimosa.

'Oh, here's something,' Gabby's on her phone, 'It says there's a BA flight to JFK on the 26th.'

'Fantastic.' I smack the table. 'Book me on it!' I practically scream, diving under the table to grab my bag, then sitting back up, I throw my purse down and scare every table around me. 'Sorry,' I say, making a face and willing myself to get a grip. Why do my family make me act like a crazy person? Gabby passes me her phone and I swiftly complete the booking.

'You'll miss my Boxing Day charity night.' I look up from the confirmation page to Nick. He's trying to raise a playful eyebrow, but I just feel desperately guilty for not even remembering that's what he's done for the last ten years: host a themed party for the town, feature talented musicians, and raise money for charity.

'Sorry,' I say weakly, regretting booking my flight with such haste.

'He's chosen the shelter this year,' Scott announces proudly, although his expression says that that still won't be enough to save it.

'That's great,' I try to say with gusto and fail miserably.

71

'Well, more importantly,' Gabby clears her throat, clearly sensing my uncomfortableness, 'you'll be here for my birthday!' She grins.

'That's the first time I think I've ever seen you smile about your birthday,' I say.

'I'm sorry, but it sucks having your birthday two days before Christmas. No one buys you separate presents.'

'I do.'

She smiles at Scott, 'I know you do.'

'And so do we,' I say with false outrage and feel my cheeks redden as I realise I've said "we" without thinking. I give a small smile to Nick.

'Present company excluded, obviously. Sorry, that makes me sound ungrateful. Maybe I should just tell everyone I'm celebrating my birthday in July or something.'

'Now there's a plan,' I say, taking another sip of my mimosa.

'So,' Nick clears his throat, 'as well as the birthday,' he nods at Gabby who once again raises her glass to him, 'that means you'll be here for Christmas,' Nick says, optimistically. Or maybe that's just how I want him to sound.

I nod gravely, 'So it seems. *Oh*, fuck.' I shut my eyes and breathe deeply.

'What is it?' I hear Nick's voice.

Looking at him, I admit, 'Now, I haven't got any excuse not to help with the set design or whatever it is, for the kids' play.' I tilt my head, 'Or the Lantern Parade. Or Light Switch On and,' I sigh again, 'what am I going to do about Christmas Day?'

'Oh, don't worry about that,' Scott waves his hand. 'You're absolutely spending it with us.'

I smile at my friends. 'Thank you.'

'Or…' Nick clears his throat. 'You could spend it with me and my family.'

I scrunch my nose. 'Really? You don't think that would be awkward, bringing your ex to Christmas dinner?'

'Oh, I'm counting on it.' He smiles and I feel my insides start to ache. I love his family. 'But they'd all love to see you, especially my folks; they miss you.'

Smiling sadly, I reply, 'I miss them too. Alright, well, I've got two options then, haven't I? And speaking of sharing a meal, have you eaten?' I ask Nick, gesturing to the menu that's in front of him.

'Have you already ordered?'

'We have. We're having the—'

'Oh, no don't tell me,' Nick playfully interrupts, picks up the menu, scans it, then after a glance and a nod, he pops it back down, 'Apart from the obvious selection in front of me of liquid starters for the girls: mimosa with more bubbles than orange, and bloody mary with extra spice,' he gestures to our glasses, which we both raise, 'oat cappuccino for the lacto intolerant gentleman in front of me,' he gestures to Scott and we all laugh. 'I'm guessing a simple sausage sarnie,' he points at Scott who nods, 'the avocado sourdough with a side of hashbrowns for Soph, and the Mexican pancake stack for Gabs, with a side of bacon.' He folds his arms triumphantly.

'Yes, but you've missed two things,' I say, matching his posture, playfully.

He purses his lips in concentration, '*Hmm*, alright.'

'He won't get it,' Gabby doubts him.

'No, no; have faith,' Scott gives his friend the benefit of the doubt.

'Oh, I've got it.' He points at Gabby and I, 'Açaí bowl to share, which you'll both only pick at because you love the granola and almond butter, but in reality, yoghurt when hungover makes you feel even worse,' that was aimed at me, 'and you,' he looks at Gabby, 'hate the texture of sunflower seeds in yoghurt, and you both knew that subconsciously, so you also ordered a side of fried halloumi, which in reality, is what you wanted in the first place.' He sits back triumphantly and folds his arms once more. Scott applauds him.

'Well, aren't you just a big fat know-it-all?' Gabby jokes while nursing her liquid starter.

'How do you remember that?' I tilt my head and lean on my hand. Two years have passed since we've all sat here together.

He shrugs, 'Every time we came in—after going out the night before—I'd end up eating the açaí bowl, for all the reasons I've just said.'

I burst out laughing. Then heave a big sigh, 'So, what are you up to today?'

'I'm covering for my brother; he signed up to help with the set design of the kids' play at the school, but has to go to work last minute. He said it's nearly finished but there's some painting and costume work left.'

'Which I guess I'm now helping with too?' Neither of us says anything for a time, we just lock eyes. *I wonder if he misses me as much as I miss him.*

He smiles and then is the first to break eye contact. 'What about you, guys? Fancy doing some painting with us?'

'Working,' is Scott's short reply with an accompanying lowered bottom lip.

'Love to,' Gabby bites the end of her celery then talks while chewing, 'but I have back-to-back pooches, a clowder of cats, a rabbit and a ferret,' she swallows.

'What time you starting?'

'11.30,' she yawns while placing her elbows on the table and resting her head in her hands. 'I'm sure I'll perk up in a bit.'

I give a sideways smile to Nick; maybe it'll be fun being just the two of us.

***

After food, Nick and I walk slowly over to the primary school Gabby, Scott and I used to go to, to help with the decorating for the upcoming kid's Christmas play. I attempt to start several sentences but chicken out and swallow each thought before it can make its way out of my mouth. I've forgotten how to be with him.

I've forgotten how to be myself.

We catch eyes a couple of times and smile politely. When we pass the corner shop, I hear my voice saying, 'Are you as uncomfortable as me?' *That's the question you've settled on? No, Hey! Tell me more about work; what's new with your folks? Ugh, I'm ridiculous.*

'Yup.' He nods, and chuckles softly, 'But I'd like to power through to the point of being able to have a conversation with you again if that's OK?'

'Sounds good.' I smile, and it occurs to me that we're walking past the bus stop where I had my first kiss. 'You know I had my first kiss there?' I point to the offending spot.

'Toby Campbell; I remember you telling me.'

'Your memory is ridiculous.'

He doesn't seem to take the compliment, but grins, turns and then points, speaking with all the intensity of a movie voice-over man, 'And back there, you threw up by that bench after drinking beer for the first time!'

I shake my head, 'I have clearly left a vivid impression in your mind.'

He shakes his head, 'I just listened when you talked.'

'You were always a good listener.'

'Still am, if you ever want to talk.' He tilts his head.

'Thanks.' I smile but feel sheepish.

We're nearing the primary school now and I stop just outside the gates with a loud sigh, 'It's so weird to be back here. I swore to myself I'd never step foot in this town again. What am I doing?' I'm not sure if I'm asking him or myself.

He shrugs, 'You're trying to do the right thing.'

I scoff, 'The right thing,' I repeat back at him. 'I don't know what that is anymore. God, I don't think I can go in. Heaven knows half the town will be in there and I dread to think what my mum or Aria, or my stupid brother have been saying to them all.'

'I don't care about that. And neither should you.' He looks at me squarely.

He's not wrong. 'Um,' is all I say out loud, gripping the iron gates and gazing up at the clouds above us, wishing I could just up and fly away.

In my periphery, I see Nick, placing a hand on the gate too. He then laughs, 'I'm looking forward to seeing their faces when we walk into the room together. After everything that's happened, I bet this'll have them gossiping scenarios well into the new year. But like I said, I don't care what they have to say. It's just nice to see you, and...' he puts his left hand gently upon my right, 'I'd like to spend more time with you while you're here. If you want,' he adds quickly. I turn back to face him; he's smiling softly at me.

'I'd like that.' *What are you doing?* 'It's really nice to see you too, Nick.' I feel myself softening even more. *You're not over this guy! You're going to get hurt all over again!*

I nudge my inner commentary roughly in the ribs, as Nick gently removes his hand from mine, then gives the gates a little tap, 'Well, we're late, we better head in.' He opens the gate and heads down the path. Suddenly, he stops in his tracks, 'Screw it, can I be honest?'

I gulp, 'I guess.'

He takes a deep breath, 'I wasn't sure that I'd ever see you again, and now that you're here—' he stops, lifts a hand to my cheek, and I allow myself to snuggle ever so slightly into it. '*Ugh*, why is this so hard?' His hand stays where it is, his thumb stroking my cheek lightly.

'Because it turned out that my family hated you, they wore us both down, they lied, manipulated, gaslit and confused me, then broke us apart?'

'Well, yes, I suppose that's why.' He smiles at me and his eyes land upon my lips, only for a moment. We step an inch closer, then he opens his mouth to speak and—

'If it isn't Moreland High School's favourite couple!' Nick's hand drops as we hear Mr Frances' voice and my cheek suddenly feels naked without his warm touch. Glancing up I see the familiar round face of my favourite teacher.

'Sir!' Nick holds out his hand and Mr Frances shakes it firmly.

'Nicholas, long time no see. And Miss Sophie Carter. It's been even longer! I hope New York is treating you well.'

Victoria Mae

'Hi.' I hold my hand out and he accepts it warmly. 'Really nice to see you again, Sir. New York is treating me well, thank you. I hear you've been praying for my soul,' I say without thinking if that's rude.

He laughs, 'Well, I wouldn't have put it quite like that, but,' he lowers his voice, 'you know your mother and her interpretation of words.'

'Yes. We both do,' Nick protectively answers for me. 'So, what's left?' Nick puts a hand on Mr Frances' back and encourages him to lead the way.

'The stable, focusing on the manger is where I'd like you, Nick. And Sophie, I thought you'd like to spend more time with your mother—'

You thought wrong.

'—she's working on the three kings.'

'Oh, no,' I try to say as casually as possible, 'Thank you, but I thought I'd work with whatever Nick's helping out with.'

'I'm afraid I'm not in charge of that decision, Sophie. All jobs have already been assigned.'

'Great,' I say with a straight face.

I fall a little behind, as we make our way through the playground, around the school, down the Christmas tree-lined path at the back, and, taking a deep breath, I enter the school hall. It smells the same: oven-fresh sausage rolls, and instant coffee, but with the added mix of paint fumes.

'I'll catch up with you in a bit,' Nick says supportively, as I'm frozen to the spot. I manage a nod and then glance around. I spot the same tight clucks of helpers, heads down, gathered together in gossipy groups. I suddenly feel eight years old again. No one's seen me yet, I could just back up and reverse, silently out of the door.

'Nick's here?' I hear someone say, followed by meerkat movements and hushed tones.

Oh, man. I can't do this. I feel my feet shuffling backwards.

'Sophie?'

Dammit. 'Hi there.' I wave at a group of mums whose kids used to bully me along with Aria and Whitney, 'How are you all?' My feet won't let me budge.

'Well, we are shocked to see you here!' The head mum of the group, who I recognise as Whitney's mum, stands up and walks over to me, placing an unwanted arm over my shoulder, guiding me reluctantly in. 'Since you ran off to New York, leaving Nick and your family, we'd love your take on what happened.'

'Excuse me?' I'm shocked at her lack of tack.

'Your mum said you left without any reason or prior warning, and, it's been, what? Two years? Oh, and, particularly after everything that your poor brother has been through getting unfairly dismissed from work, and you haven't been here to support; I'm sure there's just something that we're missing in this puzzle.'

'Well, it's a long story.' I feel sick. I subtly try to shake her off, but it now feels like I have a piranha on my arm; no sudden moments or it might chomp down even harder.

'OK, well, I'll find you later when we have more time. Whitney will be here soon, and we want to hear absolutely everything.'

I have no intention of being here when Whitney the: *I gave away my own dog to try and prove that I'm somehow a good person,* arrives. 'Alright then, if you wouldn't mind,' I gesture to her arm. 'I better get on.'

'Of course, of course! Great to see you.'

79

I hurry off to the corner with no real sense of purpose apart from getting away from her. As sheer bad karma would have it, my eyes narrow, as I realise I'm headed straight out of the flames and into the fire.

Mum looks up from sewing a King's robe. 'Look who finally decided to show!' she says quietly, but loud enough for me to hear. Then she drops the King's robe and holds her arms open for me. This is purely for the show of others and has nothing to do with warmth.

'Hello,' I say tightly, then crouch down and out of sheer habit to save face in front of the town, give her a limp, one-armed hug. It's then I realise this is the first hug we've had in over two years. I bite my lip to stop myself from tearing up. Of course she told everyone that I left for no reason; it had to be my fault. I wish I was brave enough to speak up instead of numbly standing there in disbelief while she tarnishes my character.

When I let go, Mum takes in my expression but won't dare say or do anything to imply anything is wrong with our "perfect" family. She lowers her arms, sits up straight, knowing that she's being watched, and gives her best fake laugh, as if I've just made a joke, 'Oh, Sophia, you are so funny! Why don't you help yourself to sausage rolls over there.'

'Because I'm a vegetarian, Mum,' I say quietly.

'Oh, yes.' This throws her for a second, but then she steadies herself, 'Well, that's not my fault,' she says even quieter, then slaps on a fake smile. 'Would you mind getting some more of this red ribbon for the sash, from over there, please, darling?'

If I didn't have this feeling before, it suddenly hits me in the face with all the subtlety of a cream pie: I need to get away from her before I say or do anything I know I'll regret, so make a split-second decision, 'No, sorry, I'm going to help Nick.'

'Oh, I'll get it for you, Mum.' Aria stands, gives me a look as if I'm in the wrong, then sashays her way over to the box of material.

She called her "Mum"?

'OK then. No need for me to be over here.' I turn, spot Nick, and march towards him. He's already got a paintbrush in his hand and is painting the manger.

'How is Mummy dearest?' he manages to say with a straight face.

I plonk myself down and grab a spare brush, talking in as low a tone as possible, 'I'm going to explode. She is freaking unbelievable. Did you know that she's been telling people that I left without any reason or warning? Like, I just, up, and left! Left you, left them! Abandoned my *poor brother* in his hour of need. Of course it's my fault, and I'm in the wrong.'

He calmly focuses on his paint lines, 'Yup.'

'Yup? How are you so calm?' I gesture to him with the paintbrush.

'Because, I've had two years to process this, and like I said, I don't care what they, or anyone else thinks happened. *We* know what happened; *we* know who is at the root of this; that's all that matters. You don't need to defend yourself to anyone.'

I feel my shoulders lower. This is just one of the reasons why he was so good for me; he was my voice of reason. Apparently, I don't possess one of my own. 'I miss you calmly making good points. You always had a way of making me feel better.'

'*Do* you feel better, now?'

I want to say that, yes, all my frustration has completely vanished without a care in the world, but I can't, 'Of course not!' I say in my low tone, 'She's blaming everything on me! I am, once again, the frigging scapegoat, and I'm just supposed to take it? *Ugh*!' I dunk the paintbrush in the pot at speed, then take it out, splashing myself, Nick, the floor, and the manger.

'Hey! You're ruining all my good work here! Give that to me.' Nick wrestles, playfully, for the brush.

'No, you have to fight me for it.' He attempts to pry the brush out of my hands and I grip on tightly, refusing to let go. I wave it around and accidentally decorate his jumper.

'What the hell? This was a gift from Adam!' he says while laughing. 'Alright, you, give it up!' Nick grins while aiming for my jeans, but I swivel and swirl out of his reach.

'Never!' I giggle. *God, I miss this.* 'Hey!' he's painted my nose. 'Take that!' I give his cheek a swipe of the brush.

'Oh, that's how we're playing, is it? Alright, then.' He puts the end of the brush into his mouth, so both of his hands are free and uses them to pin me down on the floor.

'No, alright, I surrender,' I say in between laughing and him moving his face around to give my face a painted makeover. He then stops, his eyes steady and it's then I realise that I don't care who's watching us; I will him to discard the brush, lean in, and kiss me. I scan every inch of his face, not wanting to miss a single second of this moment. I wonder if he wants to kiss me too.

'*Fid ou yant t'ake uh yalk ahfta is?*'

I laugh, 'What?'

He spits out the brush, but his hands remain where they are, 'Did you want to take a walk after this?'

'Let's take a walk now.'

Chapter 5

After a swift trip to the loos to wash my paint-splattered face, and while no one was looking, Nick and I dove out of the building in amused silence; I feel like we're teenagers again, sneaking out of last period with "Doctor's Appointments". When we've rounded the corner, I breathe a sigh of relief.

'So,' I take him in. 'Where do you want to go?'

'Coffee,' he nods, 'and then anywhere the moment takes us.' A mischievous grin spreads across his handsome face.

'Sounds like a plan.' Without a word, we naturally head towards what was one of *our* favourite spots in town, Frankie's. Frankie is a local guy who, at the age of forty, decided that he hated his corporate job in London, so packed that in, and put his life's savings into this café. He wanted to recreate recipes his Italian grandmother used to make, as well as create his own. I remember the grand opening—I think I was about six—and this place has been a staple of my life ever since.

Pushing the door, a blanket of cosy instrumental Christmas tunes wraps warmly around us. It's as popular as it always was, with every table, occupied with happy customers. Inhaling, I breathe in the scent of freshly baked goods, and bean-to-cup coffee. 'Oh, I've missed this place,' I say as we join the fast-moving queue.

'I bet there are a thousand coffee shops in New York.'

I nod, as we shuffle forwards, 'There are. But there's just something about here that feels like a warm hug.'

'That'll be Frankie,' Nick raises a playful eyebrow as we become next in line.

'Hey,' I say, pointing outside, 'that's Chris, what's he doing here?'

'He does live in this town,' Nick says, nonplussed.

'No, Mum said he's got a meeting in London.' I watch as he shifts, awkwardly from foot to foot, glancing at his watch, and carrying a large, overstuffed backpack.

'Maybe he's about to go there now?'

'Maybe?' I watch him suddenly dart off and out of my sight.

'Are you kidding me? Has my Christmas come early? My darling Sophie! How are you?' Frankie's warmth helps to drop any cares I had about my brother. He rushes from behind the counter, towards us and envelops me in a large hug, smelling like a sugared pastry. 'Now, you tell me, darling girl: does anywhere in New York compete with my croissants?' His face contorted with seriousness.

I make a face, 'There's a place in Brooklyn that comes close, but, absolutely not.'

He frowns, '*Hmm*, Brooklyn, *huh*?' He says this like the place is his arch-nemesis. 'Well,' he dives back behind the counter, 'wait until you try this!' Frankie picks up some tongs, snaps them at me playfully, then selects what looks like a perfectly ordinary, plump croissant. He places it delicately onto a plate, then hands it to me, expectantly.

'You want me to eat this right now?' I say, self-consciously, as the queue is steadily growing behind us.

'Of course.' His eyes steady on me, as if nothing in the world is more important to him.

I take a bite, nervous for a moment that I won't like it, and prepare my mouth to say otherwise and arrange my face into some sort of pleasant expression. But of course, there's no need to pretend; I feel my shoulders subconsciously relax, as I close my eyes blissfully. Not only is the pastry light, and fluffy, with a satisfying flaky finish, but the flavours explode in my mouth like a culinary firework. I swallow, 'Oh, my God, what's in this?'

Grinning ear to ear, he folds his arms triumphantly, 'Homemade fig jam with the last of my honeycomb from the summer. Take that, Brooklyn.'

I shake my head in amazement, 'You certainly haven't lost your edge, Frankie,' I smile at him.

As there wasn't a free seat in the house, we ordered two coffees to go (much to Frankie's protests) and another couple of croissants—none of which Frankie would let us pay for, so we left a generous gratuity in the Santa tip jar, and ran out before he could give it back to us.

Laughing and catching my breath in the brisk afternoon air, I take the lid off my to-go cup and blow on my gingerbread latte. I look over at Nick, watching me with a smile, 'What is it?' I take a sip, then put the lid back on.

'Nothing.' His gaze is warm, and I enjoy the sensation of our elbows touching now and again as we continue our walk. My stomach flutters as the spark is still very much alive, at least for me. The sun suddenly appears from behind a cloud, catching the snow and making it glisten. I gaze around at the Tudor houses with smoke billowing out of the chimneys and realise my mouth has started voicing my thoughts without warning, 'As much as I hate to admit it, I've missed this town. But at the same time, I'm desperate to leave; it's confusing being back here.' My boots scrunch in the snow as we continue our walk, heading towards the local park.

'Go on,' Nick encourages me to flow in a stream of consciousness.

I gesture to our surroundings, 'I love these streets, and the snow makes it even more magical. Seeing Gabby, Scott, and, Frankie, and…you.' I dare to smile at him, and then I feel my heart and face fall, 'But *them*? They are just where I left them: slowly sucking out my soul and making me feel small and insignificant and worst of all, guilty. But they're my family,' I say, as if that excuses their behaviour. 'And, you know…' *Am I brave enough to say this?*

'What is it? You can tell me anything, you know that.'

I take a sip of my coffee, then decide, what the hell, 'You know what hurts the most? *You* were my family, and now you're not. I hate that.'

He sighs, 'I hate that too.' Nick nods, 'But, you had to get away; I get it. And now you work for a superstar.' Nick frowns, 'If I had anywhere to go, I would have gone there.' He stares ahead, lost momentarily in thought.

You could have come with me. I find myself saying in my head. I wish I had the confidence to say that out loud.

'I think what you did was brave,' he interrupts my thoughts.

'I'm not sure *brave* is the right word, leaving to work for Freya; insane, maybe.'

'No, I mean, leaving and walking away from *them*.' He takes a sip of his coffee. 'If I'm being honest with you, I wasn't sure you were capable of that.'

I frown, not sure if that's a compliment or not. 'Thank you?' We turn another corner, and with not a soul around, it's as if we're the only two people on the planet. Just us, and the silence of the snow.

'You know what I mean. They have this invisible power over you when you let them and, honestly, it made me feel proud of you. It takes a lot of strength to stand up to people like that.'

'I didn't stand up to anybody, I ran away. And I don't think it was strength. It was more like, I...' I shake my head, '...I had nothing left to give. I couldn't fight anymore to try to be seen, heard, or understood. I was sick of trying to defend myself, or you,' I gesture lightly at him with my cup, 'for things we hadn't even done.'

'Trying to make people like that understand the truth when they've already created a false storyline, is exhausting.'

I suddenly stop, 'It was exhausting.' I raise an eyebrow, 'It's still exhausting.'

We return to silence as Nick reads me with his eyes.

'I'm sorry,' I find my mouth saying.

He smiles and shakes his head, 'You need to stop apologising.'

'No, I need to keep apologising until this pain goes away,' I bite my lip. Nick takes a step closer to me, and for a moment I think he's going to kiss me. But he reaches his hand forward, takes my cup, and places both mine, his and the bag of croissants on the nearby, snow-covered wall. 'What are you—?

Without warning, Nick scoops me up in his arms and holds me. I melt into his embrace. God I've missed these arms, the warmth of his chest, the sound of his breath. I breathe him in; his woody, spicy scent, familiar and comforting. 'No one and nothing can take away your pain,' he says softly into my hair. 'You have to decide that you're ready to let it go.' I close my eyes and nod. I feel like if I talk, my voice will crack. 'I wasn't ready to let you go,' Nick almost whispers.

'What?' His comment surprises me, but I don't loosen my grip.

'Two years ago. After the Christmas blowout and everything, I knew we had broken up, but you leaving when you did, just felt so sudden.' He continues to hold me tight, and I'm grateful; I'm not ready to let go of him either.

I lightly shrug, 'When my cousin's friend Sarah vouched for me for the Freya position, the interviews happened so quickly; I guess I just dove before I could talk myself out of it. Suddenly I was on a plane, and the next minute I knew, I was looking after a pop star.'

He exhales and before I want him to, he loosens his arms, and they fall to his sides. Nick smiles down at me, and I'm not sure if I feel sad or happy. He then reaches for the croissant bag and our coffee cups; he hands mine back to me. 'So, tell me. What's it like working for an international superstar?'

'Oh,' I take a sip of my coffee, to recover from our swift transition from deep, to small talk. We begin walking once more, 'It's exciting; knackering; ridiculous. I do everything for her, from picking up gluten-free, dairy-free, fun-free pizza, to managing her show, and scheduling her life.'

He nods, 'Sounds intense. But I'm sure you're nailing it.'

'I don't know about that.'

'Still can't take a compliment, *huh*?'

'Absolutely not,' I smile at him.

We then walk in silence for a time, both contemplating what we're doing here, and trying to process how we're feeling, or perhaps that's just me and he's giving me the room to breathe. 'So, are you dating anyone?' I decide to ask as we step through the park gates. Trees iced in thick layers of snow surround us like we're entering a Christmas card.

'I was for a couple of months, but it didn't work out.'

I feel like I've been stabbed in the heart. What was I expecting though? That he'd wait for me? That we'd eventually end up together? How could that even be possible with my family? 'I see. Do I know her?' *Why the hell are you asking that?*

He nods, 'Remember Chelsea, from school?'

'The girl who was obsessed with you since sixth form? No, I can't remember Chelsea,' I can't keep the sarcasm out of my voice.

'Well, I was at the Lantern Parade last year, and she was back in town visiting family and came over to say hi; we went for a mulled wine, then…' I think he stops talking as the pain from my heart has clearly started showing on my face 'Sorry.' He's sheepish. 'I don't know why I even went out with her if I'm honest. I guess I thought, a year had gone by, I hadn't heard from you and…'

'And what?'

He purses his lips then says quietly, 'Why didn't you call me?'

'Why didn't you call me?' I can't help but ask the same question.

'Would you have answered if I did?'

'Yes.' I make a face. *I'm not sure I would have been brave enough to.* He gives me a sceptical look. 'Well,' I clear my throat, 'I didn't think there was any point in calling you; you'd made your point pretty clear that night.'

He licks his lips then opens his mouth to speak, but then closes it again. I wait patiently for him to gather whatever it is he wants to say. 'I was mad at you,' he says eventually.

'I'm sorry. I was mad at everything if I'm honest. I didn't mean to storm out. They make me crazy.'

'They make me crazy too. Oh wow!' I can't help but say out loud as we walk towards the bandstand; it's been completely renovated since I was last here, but more importantly, dressed up for Christmas. Fairy lights are wrapped around the newly painted, racing-green columns, and continue onto the brand-new roof that I'm seeing for the first time.

'I thought you'd like it. They finished it last year.' We walk up the steps, and I take in the lights that continue to wrap around the inside of the wooden beams in the domed roof, creating a warm glow in the twilight.

'This is magical.' I smile, looking around, then take a seat. 'Like something out of a Hallmark film.'

He laughs, 'Oh my God, I'd forgotten how much you like those.' Nick looks around. 'Or, maybe I haven't.' He gestures with his coffee and huffs slightly like he's surprised himself, then takes a seat next to me.

'They have a whole Hallmark channel in America, you know?'

'I thought they were just on Netflix?' He gives me a look somewhere between horrified and amused; the number of cheesy rom-coms he sat through with me is quite impressive. 'So, you like the lights, *huh*?'

I nod while sipping my coffee.

He looks around again, 'Yeah, Christmas kind of gives you the feeling of hope, somehow, doesn't it?'

I look down, 'I haven't had that feeling in a long time; I've forgotten what it's like,' I say honestly.

Nick's hands clasp together and I suddenly wish his hands would reach out and hold mine. He clears his throat and asks softly, 'Are *you* seeing anyone?' His tone indicates the answer will hurt him either way.

I gaze at him and give a half smile. 'No. I'm not seeing anyone. I went on a couple of blind dates a while ago, but I wasn't ready.' *I'm still not ready.* We silently sip our drinks; our truths coming out as slowly as both our guards will allow.

'And here we are.' He looks at me sadly.

'Here we are.' *God, I've missed those eyes.* 'So, what do we do now?' I ask self-consciously.

He takes a deep breath and sighs it out, creating a smoky cloud in the frosty air. 'We can try being friends?'

I can't help but smile again. 'Well, alright then. As a *friend*, what are you doing tonight?'

'I've got a band rehearsal.'

'Since when are you in a band?'

'I'm not, I'm in charge of the studio, remember?' He grins, 'There's a band rehearsal going on tonight.'

I sigh, 'Man, I wanted an excuse not to go back to my parent's house.'

'You want to come with me?'

'Is that allowed?'

'Like I said, I'm in charge of the studio. I can do whatever I want…as my boss is in Cornwall with his family.'

I laugh, 'Alright, it's a date!' I suddenly feel awkward, 'Not a *date* date; you know what I mean.'

His eyes flicker with warmth, 'A non-*date* date it is.'

Chapter 6

I'm not meeting Nick again until eight, so I make the most of avoiding going home. I pick up presents for Gabby and Scott, then return to Frankie's to curl up and read a couple of chapters of a book from the phone box lending library.

Feeling slightly smug I wiggle further into the best seat in the house: one of the two leather armchairs by the fireplace. The crackle of the fire draws me in, and I zone out, listening to some soft folk music playing. 'Here you go, Soph. Sorry about the wait.' Frankie places my hot chocolate, served in a red and white striped mug, on the table.

I turn, 'No problem at all, *oh*,' I take in what he's just placed down.

'That is what you ordered, isn't it? I got the last two orders mixed up,' he makes a face at me.

'Yes, yes, it is. *Um*. Never mind.' I'll just scoop them out, it doesn't matter, I say in my head.

'Is it because there are marshmallows in there?' he tilts his head to one side.

I cough, 'Yes. I'm sorry, I shouldn't have said anything.'

Frankie places a warm hand on my shoulder. 'You didn't say anything to apologise for.' He looks at me kindly, 'I've been serving vegan ones for the last couple of years.'

'You have?'

'Yeah, you inspired me to finally do that; why should vegetarians and vegans have to miss out,' he smiles gently.

'I'm impressed you remembered.'

'What? That you're a vegetarian?' I nod. 'How could I forget that? You made the decision when you were six,

93

didn't you? I remember it was around the time I opened the café.'

I smile at him and tears fill my eyes, the face of the salmon my mum got for me yesterday flashing before my eyes tauntingly.

'You OK, sweetheart? Was it something I said?'

I clear my throat, 'Yes, but not in a bad way. Thank you for remembering.'

'You're my Sophie.' He gives my shoulder a loving squeeze. 'Now, enjoy.' He goes to walk off and I stop him,

'Oh, who's playing right now?' I point to the speaker next to me.

'Not sure who the artist is, it's an independent music channel that people submit to, what's it called?' he frowns to remember, and rubs his face contemplatively, leaving a light dusting of cocoa powder on his chin. 'Oh, yeah, *Alex Rainbird Music*. Nick recommended it to me.'

I smile, 'Of course he did.'

'Can I get you anything else?'

'No, I'm good. Thank you.' Out of the corner of my eye, I see the queue continuing to grow. 'You should think about getting some more help in here, Frankie.'

He opens his mouth, then closes it again, before smiling at me and heading back behind the counter.

That was weird. Well, I guess it took him forever and a day to admit that he needed help at all, and finally, reluctantly, hired two people after years of doing everything himself. I pick up the mug and gently blow to cool it down, sending the five mini marshmallows sailing from one side to the other.

A couple of hours fly by, and after checking my emails— amazingly, there's nothing from Freya yet, so I message her to see if she's OK—I grab a sandwich for dinner from the local bakery, then walk my way over to Nick's studio. Luckily most things in this town are within walking distance, yet I use the short journey time to steady my beating heart over the thought of spending more time with him.

Wiping my snow-covered boots on the welcome mat, I walk in, and it's just as I remember. The studio was built in the 1970s with the idea of imitating Rockfield Studios in Monmouthshire, attempting to entice famous artists to record. However, to my knowledge, nobody famous has ever set foot in this building; it's merely a hub for local bands to rehearse, members of the public to come and record something for fun, and for the local music school, that Nick encouraged me to help out at when they didn't have a vocal coach for about a year. It was a part-time job alongside my work as a PA, and I loved every second of it.

As I walk the length of the corridor, I remember Nick telling me when he first got this job as assistant audio engineer, he had the idea to take inspiration from the halls of Abbey Road Studios in London; apparently, they have black and white photos lining each wall in the corridors, of every artist who has ever recorded there. I love that this collection, however, is a story of the town, rather than anyone famous. From Frankie who wanted to record, 'My Way', for his daughters, to Nick's nephew, Adam, and his friends who wanted to record a pop artist, that I'm afraid to say I've never heard of. I gasp, and stop. There's one of Nick and I. I've never seen this photo. Stepping closer, I scan the black and white shot, to identify when it was; I used to sing in the recording booth all the time, just for fun, when Nick wanted to practise setting levels.

Gazing at the photo, I take in what I'm wearing, and suddenly remember; we were singing 'Shallow', from *A Star is Born*. At the time it was all my vocal students wanted to sing, so I thought I'd try it out with Nick first; I had no idea that someone had taken our picture. We're singing into the same mic, our eyes are locked, and it's obvious to anybody's eyes that we're very much in love in this snapshot of the past.

Feeling suddenly flushed, I take off my coat, tear my eyes away, and head to the control booth. From the sounds of it, the band has already arrived and is casually tuning up. I tap on the small square window of the control booth door while pushing it ajar; Nick swivels in his seat in front of the intimidatingly large mixing desk, to face me, and warmly welcomes me in. The room has a couple of tired couches, a snack cupboard, and a mini fridge. I know the fridge is always stocked with water and beer. In a past life, Nick would get wine for me too, whenever we'd stay late. I push down that feeling and continue familiarising myself with my surroundings. There's a small TV screen showing a live feed side angle of the recording room, and a large window, to look directly into the recording area. Tentatively, I take the seat next to him.

'Long time no see.' He grins at me then clears his throat, gesturing to the band, 'They're called, Rise and Shine. Out of all the bands that rehearse here, I think you'll like them the most; they've got a real Reggae/*Sugar Shack Sessions* kind of vibe.'

'What's a *Sugar Shack Session*?'

He looks at me like I've suddenly sprouted horns. 'Are you kidding?'

'No.' I give a small smile, leaning over to put my coat and bag on one of the couches.

'*Sugar Shack* is principally a music channel, but they've grown into a multi-media company, based in Florida. If you watch any of their videos, they feature all kinds of lesser-known bands doing a set among luscious palms in a garden, sometimes in thunderstorms.' His eyes sparkle as he talks, 'It's really cool, you get to discover all kinds of artists you've never heard of; you have to check it out.'

'I love how passionate you still are about finding new bands. It's like when you introduced me to *Tiny Desk* concerts.'

He throws his arms up in the air, 'They're the best! You know I went to see Lake Street Dive last year?'

'Without me?' I say automatically and then instantly regret it; they were a band we discovered together while watching their *Tiny Desk* concert on YouTube, and we always planned on going to see them.

'Well, next time, let's go together, yeah?'

'Agreed. So,' I swivel my chair away from Nick, to the window, to hide my embarrassment, 'Rise and Shine, *huh*?'

'Yup. They travel from about half an hour away, each week, just to rehearse, but they're recording a demo today, or, starting to, anyway; this is the first of three sessions.'

'Nice.'

'Hey, Nick, we're ready when you are,' a voice says through the speakers, and I take in the band of late-20-something musicians; four guys and one girl.

Nick presses the talkback on the control desk to respond, 'Alright. Guys, this is Sophie, she's going to be assisting me today.'

I give a small wave as they all greet me, completely unphased that someone else has joined the party.

'Let's check the levels,' Nick says, then he lets go of the button so the band can't hear us.

'I'm assisting you?' I laugh.

He waves his hand, 'Sure, why not?' he grins.

The lead guitarist begins a riff. It's somewhere between funk and soul with a voice like Michael Franti. One by one the five-piece take turns, while Nick adjusts and twiddles knobs and buttons in front of him. He glances sideways at me, and I don't realise I've been staring at him. 'What?' he laughs.

I shake my head, 'I'd have no idea where to start. I've always been impressed watching you do this.'

'Well, we want a balanced sound between the musicians. So, Gina, over there,' he points to the left, 'she's got a powerful voice, but softer tone than Jerry—guitar and vocals—so, I'm bringing up the overall volume, and the high mids on her voice, to make it brighter and stand out from his raspy timbre, giving them some separation clarity in the frequency domain. Then keys,' he points to the middle of the recording booth, 'is a tad heavy-handed, so it makes sense to bring him down a bit. We want a rich sound from the bass there,' he points to the right, 'who's a great player but his instrument doesn't do him justice, so I'm bringing up the bottom end whilst at the same time cutting out around 600Hz to reduce some of the unwanted artefacts. And then finally on the drums, we've got a load of different instruments from bongos to a cowbell and zils, so I'm still dialling that in.'

'See,' I wave my hand over the thousands of buttons in front of me, then gesture to him with an open palm, 'impressive,' I say, still smiling.

He turns once more to focus on the band, and after a few more twizzles and slides, he presses the talkback again, 'OK, why don't we try one?'

Jerry, the leader, gives a thumbs up, and Nick presses something again; the boxed sign above the window turns red, and reads, "recording", in white letters, and the little lightbulb in the studio turns red.

The band is excellent. I'd pay good money to see them live and I'll definitely be buying this album when it comes out. I take in each musician, immersed in their own world, all pulsing to the beat in harmony; it's magical to watch. I love the female singer; her breath control is insane, and if I were confident enough to compliment myself, I'd say we have a similar tone.

'Do they have representation?' I find myself saying when they're into their third song; Nick doesn't tear his eyes away from them, his head fully in producer mode.

'Nope, not yet, but that's why they're recording. They've got a massive following already, so I've got a feeling it won't be long until they do.'

'Me neither.' Maybe I could talk to Freya's label? They're always keen to snatch up fresh talent.

The band continues for a good couple of hours, with only a small break, clearly making the most of their time in the studio. But before I know it, the band has gone for the night, and I feel like I've just had the pleasure of attending a secret concert. 'Well, thank you for this,' I say as I put my coat back on. 'It was a welcome distraction.'

'You could come to the rest of the recordings?'

'Really?' I scrunch my nose, afraid of overstaying my welcome.

'Yeah, why not? I'll message you the schedule.'

'Well,' I contemplate in my head: I would love to spend all my time here with Nick instead of in some forced social situation with my family. 'That sounds like something *friends* would do together,' I say slowly while nodding, 'So, yeah, that would be great. Thank you.' I stand awkwardly for a minute, not sure if I want to hug him, or pounce and straddle him in the chair, so I stay rooted, unable to trust myself. 'Well, goodnight then,' I end up saying.

'Goodnight, Soph,' his eyes glistening with joy. Smiling, I somehow remember how to use my legs to leave. 'Oh,' Nick says as I've reached the door. 'Did you see the new addition to the photo wall? What d'you think?'

I turn and grin, 'I love it.' And with a satisfied nod, I turn, walk through the door, and let an audible sigh out, as I exit the building.

***

By the time I'm sneaking into my parent's house, it's gone eleven. Hopeful of the fact that no one will be up, I sneak my way towards the kitchen to grab a glass of water and a snack. I tiptoe past my mum, assuming her usual position, fast asleep in front of the TV that's still casting its light across the otherwise darkened living room; the fire, extinguished, and the timed Christmas tree lights, long gone off. In the kitchen I head to the fridge, suddenly ferociously hungry; my small sandwich of a dinner, clearly not quite enough. Opening the Smeg door, I look in and grab the water filter jug first. The salmon, still untouched, is now wrapped tightly in cellophane, and judgingly staring up at me from the second shelf with its one visible eye. I poke my tongue out at it and shut the fridge door. Then turning, I see my dad tiptoeing in, in his fluffy plaid dressing gown, with matching pyjamas and tired slippers.

'Hi sweetheart,' he whispers. 'Just fancied a little midnight snack. Care to join me?'

'Sure,' I say quietly and smile at him as I sit on one of the stools at the central island. 'Thought you weren't allowed snacks since your heart scare,' I say lightly.

He looks guiltily up, chuckling slightly, 'That's why it's a midnight one.'

Dad walks over to the glass cake dome, lifts the lid, and selects two mince pies before placing them gently down once more.

'How's your back?'

'My back?'

'Mum said you couldn't help today because your back was playing up,' I grin.

'*Ah*, yes, yes, much better, thank you.' We both lock eyes, smiling, knowing that that was a little white lie. 'You know,' he continues to whisper as he walks over to me and takes the adjacent seat, 'I remember when you were little, the first thing you wanted to do at Christmas time was buy a box of mince pies.'

'Well, I had to, Mum insisted on baking them.' I make a face. She's as good of a baker as she is a chef. 'Looks like she may have improved her recipe though,' I say, remarking at the perfectly pleasant pie, complete with a sugared star on top, or maybe it's Chris' work; he always did like baking.

'Nope, store-bought,' Dad whispers, and we have a silent chuckle together.

Of course my mum would display them in a way that looks like she baked them.

'I've been thinking about you all day, sweetheart. Where have you been?' he asks kindly.

I shrug, 'Just out.'

He nods, knowing that I want to avoid as much conflict as possible. Although, from the look on his crestfallen face, I suddenly feel guilty for not sharing anything, 'I spent most of the day with Nick, actually,' I confess, while slowly peeling off the foil case.

'Nick? Wow. How is he?'

'Don't you ever see him in town?'

'I do,' he removes his mince pie foil case, then continues, 'but Mum makes a point of quickly changing direction or leaving whenever we see him, so I haven't spoken to him since...' His voice drifts off and he takes a large bite of his mince pie so he doesn't have to finish his sentence.

'Sounds about right,' I say, and take a bite of mine. We both munch and after I've swallowed, I turn to him, 'He's good, or, at least I think he is. Still as passionate as ever about bands and, *man*, he's talented behind that mixing desk. What have you been up to today?'

'Nice quiet one, as the girls—I mean, your mum and Aria—were at the kids' Christmas play preparation day.' He makes a, *please don't tell them about me lying* face, and I nod. 'I've no idea where your brother is, but I had the house all to myself; read the paper, had a nap, and watched some TV.'

I smile. 'Sounds like your perfect day.'

He nods, 'Sweetheart, I know how hard it must be for you to be back here, but, I have to say, I've missed you, and it's so nice to walk into the kitchen, and see you standing there; it's been too long since I've seen you.' His eyes seem to water a little and I feel my insides fall with shame. 'But I understand why you left,' he adds, placing his hand on top of mine, and giving it a gentle pat. 'I know it wasn't just because of your job.'

I find my eyes are starting to glisten too, and I give a little sniffle. 'Thank you for saying that, Dad. I needed to hear it.'

He gives my hand another pat, then we sit in comfortable silence, finishing our store-bought snacks.

Chapter 7

21st December

Call me ridiculous, immature, or what have you, but I'm determined to avoid all contact with my family unless absolutely necessary. So, I set my alarm for 6 a.m., to sneak out of the house before anyone wakes up, with a small bag of whatever I might need for the day. I'm doing an early morning Boot Camp at the leisure centre with Gabby, and then I'll figure out my day from there.

As I reach the bottom of the stairs I freeze. I can hear rustling in the kitchen. Maybe it's just Truffle? Instantaneously, the tabby cat extinguishes my theory, padding down the stairs, rubbing her head on my legs, and allowing me to give her a small pet before striding confidently towards the kitchen. The rustle of an unidentified human continues. *Crap.* Too late to turn back now, I tiptoe over to my coat, scarf and boots, and placing them on as quietly as possible, I put the key in the lock. I wince at the small click that unbolts the door but without looking back, I hurry out, closing it as quietly as possible. I go to lock it again from the outside, but with an unexpected *whoosh*, the door opens with my hand still on the handle, making me stumble back into the house. When I've steadied myself, I look up and see my big brother.

'What are you doing up?' Chris whispers then steps over the threshold, his speed is so quick I almost fall back the other way, into the snow. In an attempt to compose myself, I step backwards off the porch, creating a more acceptable space between us.

'Just out for some exercise,' I smile innocently and hope for no further follow-up questions. 'And you?'

He's already dressed in smart trousers, heavy Timberland boots, complete with a duffle coat and rucksack. He shifts uncomfortably on the spot, 'Nowhere. I've, *um*, just come back from the gym,' I frown at his perfectly non-sweaty appearance, doubtfully, 'and...I'm just taking the rubbish out.'

I look down at his empty hands but as I don't want an interrogation, I'm not going to give him one. 'Great stuff. Well, see you later, then.' I quickly turn, before he asks anything else, and head towards Gabby and Scott's house.

When I turn the corner, I peek back and watch as Chris hurries down the garden path, and speed walks in the opposite direction from me, head down, with his hands in his pockets. *Hmm, that's weird.* As I continue my journey, I wonder what he's up to, but I'm soon distracted by the town's charm. The streets are—understandably—quiet at this hour, as the sun hasn't even risen yet; I love how peaceful it is with nothing but birdsong to accompany me on my short walk through the snow-covered Tudor village. It really is like walking through a Christmas card.

When I reach Gabby's door, she's already outside, I assume not to wake Scott, her family, or their fur babies: British shorthair, Gunther, the Maine coon, ironically named, Tiny, Dolly the ragdoll, their two sleepy but playful Australian shepherds, Lilo and Stitch, and however many fostered dogs they've decided to take on right now. Lilo and Stitch were long-term fosters that they fell in love with and, unintentionally, became part of the family.

She twiddles her large bottle of water as I approach the gate. 'There she is!' She glides towards me in her bobble hat, 'So, tell me everything; how was your date with Nick?'

'It wasn't a date.'

'Of course.' She puts her hands up.

'It was just two friends hanging out.'

'Who used to be so madly in love with each other, they couldn't hide it.'

'Hey!' We turn right and start ploughing our way up the road, making fresh tracks in the sparkling powdered path, untouched from last night's snow.

'What? All I'm saying is that you've grown excellent at hiding how you feel about him.'

'I have no idea what you mean,' I say, feeling my pace increase with my heartbeat, and I have to force myself to slow down. I don't need to run away from her or deny these feelings; I'm safe here.

'Yes, you do.'

'I know,' I give in. 'Did you know he dated Chelsea?'

'For like a second,' she says matter-of-factly.

'Why didn't you tell me?'

'Because what good would that have done?' She puts her hand up to her face, mimicking a phone, 'Hey hon, you know Nick, that you're still madly in love with but can't be with because your family are crazy? Yeah, well, he's now dating the girl you hated throughout secondary school!' She drops her hand and then puts her arm around me. 'Hon, he was miserable the entire time he was with her, in fact,' she makes an "*aha*" face, and nods, 'he's been miserable the entire time *you've been away*. Anyone with half a brain can tell that he's still not over you. You were together for what, sixteen years? You grew up together,' she tilts her head and gives me a small smile, 'we all did. You don't just stop caring about someone after all that time.'

'I know. It's strange to be around him and not be with him. There's so much history. But at the end of the day, I hurt him,' I shrug. 'And my family hurt him, for years. How could we ever come back from that? But even if we could, I live in New York now. If we got back together, would he move to be with me? Would I move back here? My job is insane, we'd probably never even see each other, although I could probably get him a job with Freya, and—'

'Hon,' Gabby interrupts my crazy talk, 'you're spiralling.'

'Thank you.' I take a deep breath to gather myself together as we turn the corner and continue our trudge through the snow towards the leisure centre; a workout in itself. 'You know, even before we broke up, it was like having this huge elephant in the room. We could never fully just,' I gesture with my hands, not quite sure what I want to say, 'I don't know, relax, be free, and plan our lives together, with the ridiculous stories they made up about him just getting more elaborate over time, eating away at my sense of reality. I hate that I started questioning everything.'

'I know hon.' Gabby squeezes me, before removing her arm from my shoulders, and then links it through mine. She knows the whole story but like a true friend, she smiles to encourage me to get it off my chest.

'I still can't believe they made me think, even for just a second, that I didn't know what was going on in my own life; they actively told me that I was wrong, and they were right.'

'That's called gaslighting,' Gabby nods. 'That would make anyone crazy, hon.'

'*Crazy* is exactly the word.' I bring my hand up to my face, to push my glasses back up my nose, and I realise how cold they are; I'm suddenly annoyed that I've forgotten my gloves.

'But you guys were so good together. Please don't tell me you've just blanked out all the good times because there were so many of them. I was there. I witnessed it.'

I feel myself soften, 'No, I haven't forgotten the good parts. I just wish I'd been a little more mentally present for some of them, instead of beating myself up.' I sigh.

'Beating yourself up for having a good time?'

'Yeah.' I say sheepishly, 'I know it doesn't make sense, but all the fun Nick and I had, the road trips we went on, and all the joy I experienced, the majority of the time, I felt like I didn't deserve any of it; especially when my brother was going through a tough time.'

'Just because someone has put themselves in a situation, doesn't mean you have to join them; it's not your job to solve a problem that somebody else has created for themselves.'

I point at my friend, 'No, actually, this is something I've learnt in therapy: the way I was brought up, is called enmeshment.'

'What's that?' She shakes her head.

'There are no clear boundaries of where you end, and someone else begins. You are supposed to feel and think the same things collectively. If someone has an opinion, you're all meant to share it; if something has happened to someone, you go through it as if it were your problem to solve. You own nothing, not even yourself.'

My friend looks at me, not with sympathy but with so much love in her eyes, it almost makes me cry, 'I wish you'd shared more with me. I might not have been able to make any of it better, but I could have listened.'

I take another deep breath. 'I didn't realise how much I was holding in if I'm honest.'

'Fucking arseholes.' Her comment makes me burst out laughing. 'Do you still feel—what did you call it—enmeshed, after the distance and time?'

I think for a second, 'I don't know. I feel like a part of me has grown, but it's the logical part. I now know what happened to me, and I've got an explanation as to why I have this gut-wrenching shame in the pit of my stomach constantly; I'm still working on the emotional side. I know I haven't forgiven them. I'm not sure it's something that you completely get over, is it?'

'There's a hell of a lot to get over, hon; it's going to take time.'

'I'm so tired of carrying this; I wish it were just as simple as putting it down.'

'Well, maybe it can be, even for just one morning; trust me, you won't be able to think about anything during this Boot Camp.'

***

The exercise class was ridiculously intense, and I did work out some tension, so much so that as I lie here on my mat, sweating profusely, I feel like there might be something seriously wrong with me; I try to catch my breath. The moment the class ended, Gabby had to rush off for work, but I couldn't bring myself to move, so, here I lie, alone, in an empty room, after promising the teacher I'd get up before the next class started. *Maybe I could just have a little nap here?*

Maybe not. Hearing voices echoing through the space, I decide it's time to peel myself off the mat, clean it, and then head to the showers. As I'm psyching myself up, I begin to wonder just what I'm going to do with the rest of my day, when a familiar voice prickles in my ears.

'Oh my God, Sophie? I didn't know someone's face could go that colour?' Her face glares down at me, still from my horizontal position, accompanied by a group of girls I don't know. They're clearly on their way to a class without a hair out of place and faces fully made up.

'Hi, Aria, what class are you headed to?' I sit up and get to my feet, hating the feeling of being looked down upon.

'Oh, we've just been—pre-natal yoga—such a workout, wasn't it, girls?' They all nod. I take in Aria's petite bump, but the others honestly don't look pregnant at all; my stomach has looked more bloated after eating a burger.

'You just missed Whitney!'

Thank God. '*Aw,* what a shame,' I try to say with more *oomph* than I feel. I drag my mat over to the sanitising spray and resist the urge to squirt them all in an attempt to get them to back off.

'She'll be sad she missed you.'

She'll be sad to have missed the opportunity to take the piss out of the colour of my face.

'Well, anyway, I happened to look in the window, and couldn't believe it was you; didn't have you down as a working-out kind of girl.'

I finish drying the mat, hang it up, and turn, straight-faced to her, 'There we are then.' I go to move past her, but she stops me.

'I've got Dad's car, so let's get showered and ready, then we can do a little Christmas shopping together!'

I feel my eyebrows twitch together, 'Oh, I don't know, it's—'

'I won't take no for an answer.'

I don't know whether it's the pressure of being stared at by her friends, or the lack of energy that I've got left, thanks to the class, but before I know it, I hear my defeated voice, 'Sure. I'm meeting someone at one though, so we'll have to be done by then.'

'Oh, absolutely. I'm having my nails done then, anyway.'

It's just a couple of hours. How bad can it be?

***

'Oh, this is fun; just like old times!' Aria beams as we speed away to the nearest out-of-town shopping centre.

'It's only 60 here,' I find myself saying out loud like an old lady, afraid that we'll skid in the snow.

'It's fine; there aren't speed cameras here anyway. Dad never says anything about my driving.'

Of course he doesn't, he's far too polite. 'I can't believe Dad lent you his car,' *or that you call him "Dad", for that matter.*

'Oh, he doesn't mind at all. Every time I bring it back, he cleans it for me.'

Glancing out my window, I know that'll be because she's left crap all over his car and he can't stand it. He hates people eating in his car and even though she'll deny it, she is a serial snacker, regardless of being pregnant. Dad hates confrontation, and will never say anything, giving the impression that he doesn't care, but secretly, I have the distinct impression that it chips away at his soul.

As the town disappears, and we weave around the snow-covered country lanes, I wonder just what the hell I'm going to talk to this prize moron about for the next couple of hours. I breathe deeply but as quietly as I can, so it doesn't come across as a sigh or a huff.

'It's basically mine anyway as Dad lets me take the car whenever I want, and always fills it up for me; isn't that nice?'

'*Umm,*' I say non-committedly, knowing it's nothing to do with her, and everything to do with the fact that he likes a full tank, regardless.

'It's just been so tough financially since Chris lost his job you know, and with the baby coming and everything, we just need to save as much as we can, so, it made sense to sell our car, right?'

'Right.' I try to focus on the stitching on the dashboard to calm myself; so neat and uniform.

'The girls from the gym have been ever so nice. Of course, me and Whitney are still close, but they're my new group of friends. Did you like them?'

I nod this time, not bothering to make an agreeable noise. She seems to always have a change in friendship group, saying there's a lot of bitchiness and backstabbing; she fails to see that she's the common denominator. Aria glances over briefly at me then brings her eyes back to the road. 'Is something wrong? You're awfully quiet, Sophie.'

I swallow, 'Well, I don't quite know what to say to you,' I decide to be honest.

'Why? You've always been able to talk to me; you can tell me anything.'

That's not quite true. I made a concerted effort to let go of any negative feelings when she transitioned from my bully to my brother's girlfriend. Aria made no such effort. Now, so much has happened, and I'm not sure I'm ready to confront her. I start to rub my forehead, 'Aria, let's not get into this now, OK?'

'Into what?' she says innocently. 'I'm being perfectly pleasant here, wouldn't you say?'

'Sure.'

'I invited you on this shopping trip, even though I didn't have to.'

'You did.'

'And I'm the one making the effort to talk, wouldn't you say?'

'Yup.'

Aria exhales loudly, 'You're being impossible. You're giving me nothing to work with here. I guess it would be better if we were just silent.'

'Perhaps it would.'

Aria huffs, then sporadically looks over at me, tries to start a conversation, and then repeats the pattern, for a solid five minutes.

I do not have to attend every argument I am invited to, I repeat to myself, as we continue to sit in uncomfortable silence. We reach the shopping centre, park up, then exit the car and walk in, neither of us now wanting to make small talk. We head first into Lush and then have to leave as the smell is too intense for Aria. Still in silence, we weave in and out of each store, both picking up items and gathering more bags between us.

We enter John Lewis and somewhere around the bedding, Aria loses her cool. 'Why aren't you talking to me?' She flaps. 'I haven't done anything wrong here; *you're* in the wrong. You're the one who upped and left the family. But you clearly have something to say to me, so just get on with it!'

My stare must be incredulous because she visibly retreats. 'You are something else! I'm not doing this in a department store.' I make my way around a three-tier pillow display, and she squares up to me on the other side.

'Are you mad that I'm allowed to drive Dad's car?'

'Don't be ridiculous.' I dodge her and head towards the perfectly made-up beds, wondering briefly if I can dive into one and hide.

'Is it that I found you in the leisure centre then?' She matches my pace as we move past curtains and duvets.

'Why the hell would I be mad about that?'

'It's that he fills the car up for me, isn't it?'

Suddenly anger rockets through me and before I've thought through what I'm going to say, I'm shouting, 'HAVE YOU LOST YOUR MEMORY? YOU BROKE UP NICK AND I!'

Aria's hand flies to her heart, as nearby shoppers have stopped to watch our scene unfold. 'I did no such thing. You're starting to upset me, and the doctor said I'm not supposed to get upset during the pregnancy. I think we should go home; we can discuss this in the car,' she says the end of the sentence exactly like my mother.

'I am *not* getting in a car with you.' I stand with my arms folded, knowing that it will take me twice as long to get the bus, but will be worth it, not to be near her.

She stands a little taller, 'Fine. Suit yourself.'

I watch her stride off, then I collapse onto a nearby armchair; my heart beating faster than it did at the end of the workout this morning. I try to focus on my breath and tears fill my eyes. I thought I'd be able to control my anger when I eventually faced them, but I guess I wasn't ready. I needed more time, instead of being tricked into being back here before I've got my head around everything.

You're not strong enough to do this.

I'm stuck here.

Salty tears trickle their way down my face now, and I don't care that members of staff are huddled together, debating whether or not they should ask me to leave. I feel broken, and I don't know how to fix myself. The droplets become more urgent and I let go of the bags I've been gripping onto, letting them fall haphazardly to the floor. I take off my glasses to wipe my eyes and a blurry figure walks up to me.

'Soph, are you OK?' Nick's voice fills my ears and he bends down and wipes my tears away.

'What are you doing here?' I ask as I put my glasses back on and his beautiful face comes into focus.

'Mum loves a John Lewis Christmas duvet set.' Suddenly, without overthinking, I throw my arms around him and start sobbing. 'Hey. It's OK. I'm here.' Nick kneels, stokes my hair and lets me cry into his shoulder.

'I'm sorry. I'm so sorry.'

'Stop apologising; you didn't do anything.'

He holds me tightly and I feel both comforted and desperately helpless. I miss being in his arms. I miss how he smells. I miss the way he calls my name. I miss our life together. The pain continues to bubble up and I let out two years of pent-up emotion. I grip onto him, wanting to make up for lost time; desperate for his touch since the taste of it yesterday.

'Ma'am. I'm sorry, but you're starting to make shoppers uncomfortable. I'm going to have to ask you to leave.'

'Can you please give us a minute, here?' Nick answers for me.

'Fine. Two minutes,' I hear the voice say.

'Always was one to make a scene, *eh*?' I manage in between sobs as they slowly decrescendo.

Nick gives a small chuckle, which sets me off, and then we're both suddenly in hysterics. I finally let go and we look at each other with understanding.

The shop assistant is back and leans in to whisper, 'I'm afraid, you're now scaring the customers, please find your nearest exit.' His comment only makes me laugh louder, and taking Nick's hand, we stand, gather my bags, and run out of the store.

Chapter 8

An hour later, we're letting ourselves into Nick's family home with the promise that it will be empty, and therefore a safe place to be.

'Oh, God, are you sure it's alright that I'm here?' I ask as he turns the key.

'For the millionth time, nobody will be home. My folks are at the garden centre. He pushes the door gently and as we step over the threshold, it smells exactly as I remember; like a bakery.

'What if your brothers or nephew come for a visit?'

'Highly unlikely; one's at work, and the other—as his washing machine broke the other day—is now doing several loads, at my flat right now, or…our flat,' he says after a small hesitation, then gives me a quiet smile. We need to talk about it, but neither of us is quite ready; we both stay firmly planted in an unspoken agreement. 'And Adam's at school,' he adds to break the tension.

Nick shrugs off his coat, then hangs it up on one of the empty hooks on the floating wooden refurbished plank that reads, "Foster Family" in a friendly, cursive font. 'Anywho, I'm sure we can hide out here for a couple of hours,' he smiles at me, then offers to take my coat.

'Ever the gentleman.' I unbutton and remove my coat, then unwrap my scarf, and hand both to him. 'You know, it's not that I don't like your family; it will be nice to see them after so long, I just,' I shrug, 'don't feel at my most presentable right now.'

Nick hangs up my things before pausing for a beat to regard my face. 'Of all the people I know, you are the only one to successfully pull off a *pretty* crying face.'

'Shut up,' I say with disbelief.

'No, I mean it. It's like you've practised in the mirror or something. No ugly crying faces to be seen. Mine, however…' He contorts his face.

'I've known you for sixteen years—'

'Eighteen; I met you when I moved for sixth form.' Nick's Adam's apple moves up and down, his voice not allowing him to say I've failed to add the two years that have just passed.

'Fine, eighteen,' I smile, wanting desperately to keep everything light, 'and in all that time, I think I've only ever seen you cry twice. Once when I accidentally threw hot coffee over your foot and the nurse at the hospital was peeling away your dead skin with tweezers.'

'*Oof*, that was grim. I've still got the scar, you know.'

'Sorry.' I make a face. 'And the second time was when Bruno died.'

'Oh, Bruno. He was the best.' He glances lovingly over at a picture of the deceased furry family member.

'I miss the sloppy kisses,' I say.

'Are you talking about the beagle, or me?'

I smile, '*Your* kisses were never sloppy.'

'Glad to hear it.' His eyes sparkle and I allow my mind to remember, just for a moment, what it felt like to have his lips touch mine.

'Do you want cake?' he asks, snapping me out of it.

'Does the sun rise in the morning?'

Nick leads the way to the kitchen, heading to the fridge. Unlike my mother, Nick's mum is an excellent cook and an equally impressive baker. Any time I came to visit, she would look at me, guess my mood, and know what cake to whip up. Cookies for celebrations, chocolate cake for sadness, homemade ice cream, just because, cheesecake for anger. Whatever it was, she was right, and it always made me feel better.

'Oh my God, she's made her Christmas chocolate fudge brownies!' I exclaim as I enter the wooden country cottage kitchen, and take in the plate Nick's holding.

'Yup, and I swear they're even better this year. No idea what she's done to them, but I'm sure she's added something.'

'Can I help?' I play with the tired, knitted tea cosy that's sat on the side.

'No, no, I've got this.' He smiles, and placing the tea cosy back down, I subconsciously pull up the chair I always sat on whenever I was here in the past; ever a creature of habit. Leaning my elbows on the table, I wait patiently as Nick warms two brownies up in the microwave. He walks over to the freezer, and gets out salted caramel ice cream, to accompany the sweet treat. I watch in silence as he plonks the frozen tub down in the centre of the table in front of me with a grin, before getting out some plates and spoons, bringing them over to the table, then returning into the kitchen, to wait in front of the microwave. I let my eyes trace from his toned shoulders, down to his strong back, and perfectly squeezable arse; everything feels deliciously familiar. When the microwave pings, he brings the now-heated brownies over and sits opposite me. We grin naughtily at each other then dig in.

'Oh my God, how does she make these?' I groan with pleasure after my first gooey mouthful.

'Told you, right? Something's new.'

I swallow and let my taste buds try to answer the question. 'More vanilla?'

'Nope, I asked her. She said she used the same amount. It's more…I don't…earthy maybe? Whatever it is, she just grinned and told me I would never guess.'

I giggle, 'Maybe it's a "fun" brownie?'

He looks at me with disbelief, 'Can you honestly see my parents putting *weed* in their brownies?'

'Maybe not *weed*, but CBD oil?'

He thinks for a minute. 'Oh my God, I think you might be right. She took a trip to that new Health and Healing store in town.'

We sit laughing for a minute and then I smile once more at him. 'Thank you, Nick.'

'I literally did nothing. Mum made the "fun" brownies.' He chuckles.

'No, I mean, for somehow being in the right place at the right time. Again. You always knew how to rescue me.' I take a large spoonful and enjoy the contrasting warm brownie with the cool ice cream.

'Well,' he plays with his spoon, 'you always seem to have a talent for putting yourself into situations that need rescuing.' He looks up, not quite sure how I'm going to take that.

I nod, 'Yeah; what the hell was I thinking getting in a car with Aria this morning?'

He points his spoon at me, 'Exactly.' He takes a mouthful and I hear keys turning in the door. We both look startled for a minute like we're not supposed to be here, then hear voices.

'Is that Nick's coat?' Nick's dad's voice travels to our ears, then I hear his mum reply,

'But whose coat is that? Is it—?'

'Hi, we're in here,' Nick calls to his parents.

Before I've braced myself, they've rounded the corner.

'Sophie! I thought I recognised that coat! Oh, pumpkin, how are you?' I stand and walk over to her open arms; my heart suddenly feeling fuller.

'Hi, Hattie.'

'Oh, I've missed these hugs!' She squeezes me even tighter.

My stomach falls at the guilt of everything. I love Nick's mum. She's so kind and warm, and, although I've never told her this, she's always reminded me of Mrs Weasley from *Harry Potter*.

'Don't keep her all to yourself,' Nick's dad, Fred, smiles warmly at me as Hattie reluctantly lets me go. He wraps his arms around me and I suddenly want to burst out crying, with the greeting of love that on some level I feel like I don't deserve, but somehow, I keep it together.

'We heard you were back in town; didn't think we'd have the pleasure of finding you in our kitchen!' Fred says cheerily, finally letting me go, he smiles, and takes in my face. 'It's as if no time has passed at all.'

'And already eating my brownies! Should have known!' Hattie plays while walking over to the kettle. 'Who wants tea?'

We all raise our hands.

'A pot it is!'

'How was the garden centre?' Nick asks as we retake our seats; I know he's doing this to try and take some of the attention away from me, and I love him for that.

'Horrendously busy,' Fred says quietly, with a weary raised eyebrow, while walking over to the cupboard to get four cups.

'It was fabulous!' Hattie beams. 'I've finally got the artificial tree I've always wanted.'

'You bought another tree?' Nick laughs at his mum's tradition of adding or replacing a tree with a new one each year; (donating the old ones to the local hospital). Without fail, she'll always declare that this is now the "perfect" one.

'Yes, it's the perfect one! It's nice and small, covered in snow and lights; it can replace the one in the upstairs window.'

'Maybe you can think about replacing that old wreath on the door? It looks so tired now, Mum.'

Hattie pauses, tea cosy aloft with a look of horror on her face, 'Absolutely not, that wreath has too many memories attached to it; I'll sooner trade your father in than I would that wreath.'

'Nice to know where I fall on the scale of importance.' Fred kisses his wife on the cheek, knowing she means no harm.

'Oh, shush, you know what I mean. There's something special about it; it's always brought good luck.'

'Has it now?' Nick asks before taking another mouthful of brownie.

'Yes, of course. The year I bought it, I married your father—'

'It's forty years old?' I say, incredulously.

'Forty-two!' Hattie says proudly while pouring hot water in the now teabag-ready pot. 'Anyway, then when I was having trouble getting pregnant again, after you, I gave the wreath a sparkly makeover, then I found out I was having your brothers,' she nods at Nick.

'The twins certainly bring some sparkle,' Fred says, then looks to Nick, 'As do you, of course, son.'

'Thanks, Dad.' Nick grins, accepting the compliment along with the cup Fred's holding out for him. I take the one that's offered to me too.

'Call me superstitious, but I believe, it continued to bring us luck: with your father's job, the move to this house, and then the first Christmas after we moved here, I lost it; could not find it for the life of me.'

'I remember this,' I find I've said out loud.

'Yes, see, even Sophie knows how special it is; go on dear.'

'We were seventeen. We'd been assigned to work together on a project for Business Studies, remember?' I look to Nick.

'No idea.' He shrugs.

'Oh, come on, of course you do, your memory is better than mine. We came back here to work on it, and your mum was putting up the decorations around us. We took a break and I offered to help look for it. There were a bunch of boxes in the loft, and even though they didn't say "Christmas" on them, I had a feeling to look in there, and I found it with some photo albums. We hung it up together, and—' I start smiling.

'And what?' Nick says, now taking the teapot from his mum, as his parents sit down with us.

'You don't remember?' I give him a pointed look.

He taps into his memory and then starts smiling, 'That was the first time you kissed me.'

'I believe *you* kissed *me*,' I say, embarrassed that we're having this conversation in front of his parents, or that we're having this conversation at all.

'You see? It brought beautiful Sophie into our lives,' Hattie grins. 'So, it is a part of this house and our family.'

I suddenly feel a knot of sadness in the pit of my stomach again and it undoubtedly shows all over my face, as Fred regards me. 'You will always be a part of this family, kiddo.'

'Thank you.' For a beat no one says anything, there's just warm understanding and love floating around the table. 'So, Nick and I were discussing what your possible new ingredient could be,' I say to Hattie, gesturing with my brownie, and keen to move the conversation on.

'You will never guess,' she says confidently.

'We think it came from the Health and Healing store,' Nick offers, with a challenging eyebrow.

Hattie is flummoxed, 'How on earth did you guess that?'

Laughter fills the air as Fred speaks up, 'I knew I felt more relaxed after having one.'

***

I stay at The Fosters' until it's time to go to the studio with Nick. When we arrive, the band hasn't yet, so I allow myself the luxury of asking for a tour of the newly refurbished recording booth. I say booth, it's a spacious room. A large round carpet graces the floor and various foam spiky things have been stuck to the wall for optimum acoustic perfection. The mics are still in place from the band yesterday, so I carefully weave through the snakes of cables that lie like a neat obstacle course on the floor.

'So, this is the famous Neumann U87 ai, *huh*?' I take in the condensing mic, subconsciously picking up a pair of headphones and placing them on my head.

'Make yourself at home,' Nick laughs.

'God, I love the inside of a studio,' I say as Nick watches my gleeful face examining every inch of the mic. 'It's one of my happy places.'

'I would have imagined that you'd been in countless studios in the last couple of years, though, no?'

'The inside of the *control* booth while Freya's doing her thing, absolutely yes. The inside of the *recording* booth, no. Oh, unless you count handing Freya water, that isn't water from the door?'

'No, I wouldn't count that. Well, let's make up for lost time then, shall we?'

I laugh, 'What do you mean?'

'As you said, you haven't been in a booth for years, you're all set,' he gestures to me in front of the mic with headphones already on, 'let's make the most of it.' He cheekily grins then practically runs out of the recording space, and into the control booth.

Nick plonks himself down and swivels in his seat, then presses the talkback, 'Alright, shall we try one?' he asks playfully as if I were a recording artist.

'No,' I say with a slight hesitation in my voice.

'Well, I heard definite hesitation there,' he plays, 'What would you like to sing?'

'I am *not* singing! I haven't sung in years.'

'So, that wasn't you who sang karaoke a couple nights ago with me?'

'Oh, I forgot about that,' I admit out loud. 'Hey, drunken karaoke doesn't count.' I wag a meaningful finger at him.

'Alright then, may I please be the person to remind you that you used to be a vocal *coach.*'

'Well...sure,' I stutter. 'But not really. It was only for a short while; many moons ago; in between finding my feet as a PA, as you needed someone to fill in. I was never really that good, according to my mum—'

'I'm sorry, didn't you win an award?'

'I may have been voted favourite teacher at the music school the year I was there, yes.' I feel myself standing a little taller with pride and then immediately squash myself, 'But it doesn't count as a real award.'

'And wasn't it you that used to have this amazing power to inspire the kids out of their comfort zone, so much so that the quietest child in the music school, ended up doing a solo, and won a competition?'

'OK, sure, that's true, but *I* wasn't singing there, was I?'

'Always ready with a come-back,' he shakes his head, but I can tell he's not ready to give up. I'm secretly enjoying this banter and urge him to continue.

I shrug, 'I'm sorry, I guess I'm just not cut out for it anymore,' my tone is playful as I stroke the mic stand in front of me.

'Well, that's a shame,' he starts playing with his phone as if he's scrolling to find something, 'I guess we'll just have to move on then if there's nothing I can do to convince you.' He attaches a cable to his phone, presses something and the little recording lightbulb comes on; then he taps his phone and out of the headphones blasts the intro to 'Don't Rain on My Parade', from the musical, *Funny Girl.*'

'That's not going to work,' I stand with my arms folded but I'm smiling.

'You're right, too big too soon.' The music stops, 'How about a little of…this!' Miranda Lambert's, 'Mama's Broken Heart' comes out of the speakers now.

'Appropriate, but no.'

The music stops abruptly, '*Mmm,* maybe a little too on the nose, *huh*? Alright, next up in our intro game,' he scrolls, smirks, and 'Ex's and Oh's' by Elle King starts playing.

I burst out laughing, 'And *that's* not on the nose?'

'Fine, fine. *Ooh*, how about this?' The speakers are now graced with Smash Mouth's, 'All Star.'

'I'm sorry, you're not even close, I'm not even a little bit tempted at all, not one bit, just…*Somebody once told me…*' I can't help myself, I lean in, grab the mic stand, and start singing the opening lines. Nick, grinning from ear to ear, takes to his feet once more and dances around as I sing. I'm just about to hit the chorus when the music stops. 'Hey!'

'Oh, I'm sorry, I thought we should stop because you're not enjoying yourself,' he says with all seriousness, then Olivia Rodrigo's, 'Good 4 U' starts.

'That's how you want to play?'

'Yup, he grins, 'begin that tune!'

This time he lets me get to the chorus, but when I'm starting verse two, he stops the music again.

Next up is Billie Eilish, 'Bad Guy.'

'Are you trying to tell me something here?'

'Absolutely not,' he says innocently as I start singing and as soon as I've begun, he's pressed pause again. 'Alright next up, back to a little country!' The unmistakable guitar riff of 'Jolene' by Dolly Parton fills the booth and this time he only lets me sing two 'Jolene's' before hitting pause. I burst out laughing. And he's onto the next. Michael Franti's 'Sound of Sunshine' comes on.

'Oh, this is a tune!' I start bobbing up and down. 'It's a little low for me, but I'm up for the challenge!' He allows me a verse, a chorus, the refrain, and part of the second verse before hitting stop once more.

'Yeah, we should definitely stop this; you're not having a good time.' He tilts his head, playfully.

'I guess we should,' I say, hoping he's not finished yet. After a small beat, he plays the intro to 'Paper Rings.'

'Oh, I love Taylor Swift!'

'I know you do; I remember.' He grins as I start but this time, he doesn't even let me get halfway through verse one.'

'Oh, come on!'

'Fine.' He presses to resume the song. Our eyes both seem to sparkle when I get to the chorus, yet there's no time to be embarrassed by the lyrics, as he presses pause once more. 'Alright, I think I've got it.'

'You haven't got it,' I tease.

'Oh, I'm confident.'

'Bring it on, Foster!'

I square up to the mic, as he plays Pink's 'Trustfall'.

'Oh, you mean business.' I allow the music to go past the entry for vocals.

'What do you think?' He regards me with kindness, the music playing lightly in the background, a soundtrack to our conversation. I nod and he pauses, then restarts the song.

'*Picture a place where it all doesn't hurt…*' I begin the song softly and this time I know he's going to give me the room to sing the whole song. He sits slowly down in his chair and doesn't take his eyes off me the whole time. Occasionally I have to shut my eyes as the intensity of his gaze is overwhelming. Then I allow myself to let go. There's something about singing where you can lose who you are.

You connect with the lyrics, become the beat, and before you know it, you're gone; there is no you, no song, everything is fluid. After the breakdown, I allow myself to look at him, and I maintain eye contact until the last bar. When I'm done, I just stand there, gazing at the man I'm still so in love with. Then the door to the control booth bursts open. The band has arrived and clearly witnessed at least some of that. I see them silently applauding until Nick presses the talkback for me to hear them in the sound booth; their whoops of appreciation make me blush.

'How do you feel?' Nick beams at me.

I exhale, 'Free.' I smile and then take a small bow for my unexpected audience.

Chapter 9

The band continues to shower me with applause as I step back into the control room.

'You have some serious pipes!' Jerry, the lead, says as he gives me a pat on the back.

'Thank you, thank you,' I say, absolutely mortified that it wasn't just Nick who witnessed that, but secretly on some level, feeling proud of myself.

The band files out of the control room, and into the recording booth to set up, and I sink into the seat next to Nick, burying my head in my hands. 'I can't believe people saw that!'

'And?'

I sit up, 'And? People *heard* me.'

'People used to hear you all the time. I don't get it.' His brow ever-so-slightly creases.

'I'm just…not very good. That's all.'

He gives me an enquiring look, 'You are full of absolute bollocks, you know that?'

I shrug, 'No, it's true. The musicals at school don't count, and then for a year, I was the vocal coach, not the vocalist. I felt safer behind others, or when I was encouraging others, rather.'

'And why do you think that is?'

'I've no idea.'

He looks at me squarely. 'Yes, you do.'

Nick knows I know exactly why. 'Fine. Maybe it has something to do with my confidence being verbally beaten down for years; that might do it.' I give a sad smile and hear how desperately depressing that is, now that I've finally said it out loud for the first time. *Why have I never admitted that to him or myself?*

He shakes his head at me, 'You have no idea what you're capable of. If only you could see yourself as I see you.'

'And how do you see me?' I can't help but ask.

'Alright, Nick, we're ready when you are.' Interrupted, we both look through the glass and see the band staring back at us. Nick presses a few buttons, setting to work without hesitation, then hits record, and gives a thumbs up. For a moment I'm mesmerised by the band once more, that I forget I'd asked a question; their music is transportive and joyful; I feel my shoulders instantaneously relax.

Nick positions his chair towards mine, but I can't bring myself to look at him, 'You are more talented than anyone I know, and I've seen a lot of gifted people grace this booth.'

Blushing, I turn towards him with my eyes down, noticing his hands are twitching to reach out to mine, but he doesn't quite let them. Daring to look into his eyes, I feel myself almost ache for him. *Does he feel that too?*

'You have this ability to lift others and support them to see their light. I just wish you'd do it for yourself.'

I shrug, 'It's hard to find the light in your own darkness.'

Nick considers this, 'Then I guess it's about looking for the glimmers until they become your light.'

I give him a small smile, wishing it was that easy. 'It feels impossible to instantly change the worst parts of yourself.'

'Who says you have to do it instantaneously? Or all at once, for that matter?'

'Me,' I say firmly. 'Like, if I haven't changed or perfected everything straight away, there's no point in trying.''

131

'Well, that's just your mother talking.' I nod, silently, feeling mildly deflated. 'Sorry,' he says in a small voice. 'You've always had a habit of setting impossibly high expectations for yourself.'

I scratch my neck, starting to feel uncomfortable. 'It's fine. And true,' I admit.

He smiles at me. 'You're a lot stronger than you think you are, Soph.'

'No, I'm not,' I say in a small voice.

'Like I said, if only you could see yourself, as I do.'

***

A few hours of small smiles and sideways glances later, I thank Nick and the band, and head over to Gabby's vet practice, to wait for her to finish her shift. I could have hung out with Nick for the whole day, but there's a part of me that's trying to protect my heart, no matter how much I yearn to be in his company; I can't grow too attached again. He's not mine anymore, and we're not an "us".

As I trudge sadly through the snow, I try to shift my mind to happier thoughts and find myself humming the band's latest tune; it's unbelievably catchy. I can absolutely see them filling stadiums like Freya does. I take out my phone to set a reminder to contact Freya's label when I'm back at work, then return it to my bag.

Pushing the door into the vet practice, the bell above the door announces my arrival, but you can barely hear it over the chorus of animals, waiting to be seen. I glance past a Dalmatian with his head hung, a husky that's howling, and a German shepherd next to him all riled up, then a Jack Russell joins the song, as I turn to the young receptionist, who can't be older than seventeen. She's sitting at the desk and greets me warmly, 'Welcome to Paws and Claws! How can I help you today?' She smiles widely, looking like the "after braces picture" that hangs in the local dentist.

'Oh, I'm good, thank you. I'm just here to meet Gabby.' Although, looking around, I count seven dogs in total, and something that I'm assuming is a cat, in a travel box, so it doesn't look like she'll be done anytime soon. 'Actually, maybe I'll just message her. Thanks.' I smile and go to leave.

'Do you have an appointment?' she persists, 'Is it a consultation for a pet you've not brought with you?' She twiddles a pen in her hand and tries to work me out.

'No, no pet. I'm her best friend. I was thinking I'd just hang out here until she's done, but—'

'Oh, you must be Sophie!' The young receptionist excitedly exclaims as she stands up and walks around the desk, extending her hand. 'You work for Freya, right?'

'That's right.' I accept the hand offered, giving a tight, but I hope friendly enough smile. This rarely happens but when it does, I know she's going to say one of two things to me: She's a singer, and has always wanted to be in the industry, and could I introduce her to Freya; or, Freya's latest album "spoke" to her on so many levels, and could I introduce her to Freya.

'Freya is such an inspiration to me.' *Hmm, option two.* She clasps her chest with her left hand, her right still gripping onto mine. 'I'm a singer-songwriter too!'

'*Umm.*' *Oh, option one.*

'I've had a small following for about three years now. I've done several covers of Freya's, my most popular being, 'Fire', and *she liked* it! I just couldn't believe that *Freya* saw

133

it and liked it. So inspiring that she reaches out and encourages her fans like that, isn't it?'

Raising my eyebrows slightly, I haven't got the heart to tell her that that was most definitely *me*, not Freya; she wouldn't even know the username, never mind the passwords for any of her accounts. 'Well, she just loves her fans,' I commit to saying out loud.

'*So* exciting to meet you. I bet you've got a million stories.' She leans forward slightly, hoping I'll share one of them. But I just smile kindly, not saying a word, so she continues to speak, 'I bet you could do a podcast or something! Or I could interview you on my channel!'

'Wouldn't that be something,' I barely trust myself to voice my thoughts, never mind exposing the inner secrets of my boss.

She finally releases my hand, and walks towards the door closest to us, from the five that surround the room, 'Think about it. I'll just tell the boss you're here.' She reaches out for the handle and just when I think our exchange is over, she turns, and practically shouts over the barking, 'I don't suppose you could connect me with Freya could you?'

I shake my head, 'Afraid not, but I'll pass on everything you've said.'

That seems to satisfy her, 'Oh, thank you. I'm Madison. No last name; I'm like Adele and Beyoncé.'

Strong stance.

'I'll give you my handles. Take a seat, I'll be right back.' Madison knocks on "Room 1", and heads in.

Selecting a seat, and wishing that I had an ounce of her confidence, I lean forward and reach for a magazine to flick through. The dog next to me catches my eye. It's a solemn French bulldog, with a blue doughnut like an aeroplane travel pillow, around its neck. I smile at the owner and wonder what that's about.

Settling my eyes on the magazine, Freya's face stares back up at me; I subconsciously give a small sigh as memories come flooding back of every detail of that photoshoot: from me peeling her out of bed, into the car, and in front of the camera, to thanking and bribing the team at *Hey There!* with tickets to Freya's show, in exchange for not printing how dramatically intoxicated she was. Shaking my head, I place it back down on the table in front of me and push it away. I could definitely tell some stories which people would love to hear, but deep down, I know that my soul wouldn't let me; everyone deserves the trust and respect of others, and Freya is no exception. I take out my phone again and scan my emails. Still nothing from Freya. I pause over a new message, then quickly type one to say I hope she's enjoying the retreat and to message me if she needs anything. It feels weird that she hasn't got in touch.

A moment later, Madison, the receptionist returns, walking enthusiastically back towards me, 'Gabs said to go on in. Can I get you a coffee or anything?'

'No, I'm good, thank you,' I say, standing and hiding my phone just in case.

'Tea? Water? Really, it would be my pleasure to get you anything at all.'

'Thank you, I'm good,' I confirm, as I walk away from her and into "Room 1". I make sure to firmly shut the door when I'm on the other side. 'Wow,' I whisper.

'I know she's a bit intense, isn't she?' Gabby's dressed in her usual scrubs and tending to a golden retriever paw. 'Does it make you feel about 100 when you realise you're practically twice someone's age?'

'Scary, isn't it?' I walk further into the room, '*Aw*, what's this guy in for?' I walk over to the table he's lying on.

'He has a large thorn stuck in his paw.' Gabby's wearing a pair of glasses that magnify, so when she looks up at me, she's reminiscent of Edna from *The Incredibles*. 'Alright, we are done.' She straightens up with a pair of tweezers in her hand, grinning.' I take in the dog, who's completely still.

'Is he OK?' I ask with concern.

'He's under. That's the only way I could get this out; he's a bit of a drama queen. You can pet him if you want; he'll come back around shortly.' She starts to clean up, 'Sorry, I happened to mention Freya to my receptionist.'

'It's fine.' I bat her away, knowing she wouldn't have done it on purpose.

'I was dealing with Mrs Chowdry's tabby, Pepper; she's always a handful.'

'Mrs Chowdry or Pepper?' I laugh.

She raises an eyebrow, 'Both. Anyway, sorry, it just slipped out.'

'It's all good,' I say, petting the long blonde fur, remembering just how much I'd love to have a dog. 'Hey, can I ask you a question?'

'Of course.'

'Do you think I don't believe in myself?'

'What makes you ask that?' my best friend questions while taking off her nitrile gloves and placing them in the bin.

'Just something Nick said.'

She grins, 'Oh, I am loving how much time you're spending together.'

'You're avoiding answering my question.'

'Well,' Gabby is now washing her hands in a small sink, 'I guess I need a bit more context.'

'No, you don't.'

She turns off the taps and starts drying her hands on paper towels, 'Fine. When you're rallying behind someone else, you're astounding to watch. But when it comes to being your own cheerleader? You've never fully believed in yourself.' Her comment lands hard, like the finality of the bin that's just slammed shut.

'Well, that's a pretty harsh realisation.' I return to focus on the furball in front of me, as my best friend comes and stands close.

'You've spent so much of your time in the position of a…what did you call it once? The opposite of a narcissist?'

'Co-dependent?'

'Exactly. What do you expect? Like you were saying earlier, you neglect your own needs and feel bad if you have any.'

'Man, that's heavy.'

'You've always been like a chameleon.' Gabby now starts petting the golden retriever too.

'What do you mean?'

'Well, you can look at someone else and see exactly what they need or want from you, and you bend, and mould yourself into whatever person *they* need you to be. No wonder you don't believe in yourself; you've no idea who you truly are. You're just whoever someone else expects or demands you to be.'

I shrug, 'I'm a people-pleaser.'

She considers me for a moment, 'No, I don't think you're a people-pleaser; it's more than that. You know what it's like to feel insignificant, and you never want anyone else to feel that way; you want everybody to feel seen and heard.'

I exhale. 'Why have we never spoken about this until now?'

Gabby smiles, 'Maybe it comes with maturity? When you put down the booze, cigarettes, or whatever, the truth has nothing to hide behind. Plus, how many self-help books have we bought between us in the last ten years or so?'

I think for a minute, 'I gave most of them away when I moved, but I've got at least five in New York.'

'Right, so I reckon all together there's about twenty-five or so. Now more than ever it's common practice to dive into the psyche, and to be open and honest, right? I think it's a good thing.'

Gabby reaches out for my hand and gives it a squeeze.

'Well, right now, I'd like to just put everything down for a beat. It's kind of overwhelming.'

'Well, you can forget all about it tonight at the Lantern Parade.'

'Oh, I'm not sure I'll go.'

'Are you kidding? You used to love the Parade! The whole town will be there.'

'Exactly.'

She gives me a look, 'My whole family are coming; they'll protect you from evil!'

'Couldn't I just hide at your house?'

'You could,' she nods. 'But you know the bigger part of you—the little girl in there—wants to go. You love the Lanterns. You and your cousin, Liv, used to go nuts each year, wherever she came to visit. Didn't you lead it one year?' She taps into her memory.

I burst out laughing, 'I did. However, it was Liv's idea; I never would have done that. My cousin's way more confident than me.'

'*Ooh*, how's her handsome Australian man?'

'He's American; he just sounds Australian because he grew up between England and America. They're good. They were venturing around Fiji last time I spoke to her.' My cousin, Liv is a globe-trotting travel journalist, and her husband, Dom, is a professional photographer. They used to work for two different magazines, but are now both at National Geographic full-time, which continues to pay for their adventures. She always tells me that work doesn't seem like work to her; something I've always envied.

'How the other half live, *huh*? So, you're coming, right?'

I take a deep breath, 'Fine. At least it'll be crowded and I can avoid my family.'

'I think it's hilarious—I mean absolutely necessary—but hilarious, that you're avoiding them while staying in their house.'

'I've got to. There's just no point in bringing anything up, not yet anyway. Maybe I'll revisit it after I've done the European stretch of Freya's tour.'

Gabby sighs, 'Well, shit. For a second there, I'd told myself that you'd moved back.' She looks at me and folds down her bottom lip. 'I have to watch you leave again. But I know you have to,' she adds, not wanting to add to my guilt.

I nod, wishing that things could be different.

Chapter 10

Gabby's right. The Lantern Parade was my favourite event in the town as a kid. Something akin to *Gilmore Girls* Town Square charm. Everyone in the village creates a lantern, and, you guessed it, parades around, finally ending in the town square, to the accompaniment of local music acts.

Smiling, I can't help but feel protected walking with Gabby's entire family to the town centre starting point. I know waiting for us at the end of the parade will be numerous stalls from local restaurants, selling everything from spiced fries to warming chilli, and buttered popcorn.

I gaze at these people talking excitedly around me. I've always felt like they were part of my extended family. Scott is beaming at Gabby's side, and next to them are her parents, aunt, uncle, grandma, and siblings. I suddenly feel blessed to know each and every one of them.

As we make it to the starting point—my old primary school—there are several food trucks lined up by the gates, selling hot beverages and Christmassy snacks. Taking a deep breath, I enjoy the aroma of spices from mulled wine to fresh mince pies.

'*Ooh*, let's grab a mince pie before we start!' I can't help but exclaim, spotting a dessert truck.

'You go ahead hon, I'm still full from dinner,' Gabby says, swinging Scott's hand slightly; they're like a pair of joyful teenagers, so in love, and clearly enjoying the night as much as me.

'Yeah, I'm good, thanks, Soph. Meet you by the tree?' Scott points to the large oak to our left, and with a nod of agreement, I make my way over to join the queue for the dessert truck, waving at my old sixth form teacher, Mr Frances, as I go, who I spot standing with his family.

Taking my place in the queue, I wait and enjoy my surroundings. The snow has stopped falling but it blankets every surface around, icing rooftops, windowsills, cars, and each path in every direction. The road has been cleared for the parade and the safety of the town, so mounds of snow line the route. I watch as a group of teenagers make snowmen and throw snowballs at each other. There's an air of excitement and I allow myself to feel it too. *I deserve to feel excited about something.*

'Should have known I'd find you waiting for a mince pie.'

'Auntie Soph!' I'm suddenly being hugged from the waist down.

I turn to see Nick all wrapped up and looking cuter than ever, standing next to (what I'm guessing is) his nephew, Adam, now with his arms around my hips and head on my stomach.

'You know me, can't resist,' I aim at Nick, smiling, then a thought occurs to me, 'Aren't you in charge of sound tonight?'

He shakes his head, 'Got one of the guys from the studio to cover; I couldn't miss this.'

'Well, I'm glad.' I beam at Nick while hugging Adam back, marvelling at how much taller he is. 'How are you?' I beam down at the little man I always considered to be *my* nephew too, who must be…what? Seven now? I quickly work out in my head.

Adam pulls away, holds Nick's hand, and looks sheepishly up at me, 'Can I still call you Auntie Soph?'

I smile, and bend down slightly, 'I'd be very upset if you didn't.' That's clearly the right answer, as Adam grins. 'And you're missing a tooth!' I straighten up and take in his missing front-middle-left incisor. 'When did that happen?'

'Last night,' he says proudly. 'It's my last baby one!'

'He was annoyed as he's the last in his class to lose them all,' Nick says quietly to me.

'I see. And did the tooth fairy come?'

Adam gives me an exasperated look, 'Come *on*, Auntie Soph; the tooth fairy doesn't exist.'

'Since when?' I'm horrified.

'Since always,' he says with the air of a fully grown adult, and I hate that I've missed two years of his life.

'Just like the Easter bunny and San—'

Both Nick and I hurry to shush him, with the entire town's young folk here; I'd hate to play the role of Grinch, taking away the magic of Christmas. We shuffle forwards in the queue now.

'What? *Everyone* knows!' Adam says with a voice that's laced with injustice.

'Not every kid knows. Who told you that?' Nick asks.

'Ruben.'

'Well, I'll be telling your dad about that.' We move forward again.

'Who's Ruben?'

'A new kid,' Nick answers first.

'He's my *best* friend.'

'I thought Benny was your best friend,' I say with a little sadness.

'He's my *second* best friend, or maybe my third best friend,' he says, considering this as we make it to the front.

'So, what'll it be?' I ask Nick and Adam, taking in the impressive list of mince pies with a twist.

'A snowman biscuit,' Adam says without hesitation.

'Great, and what about you, Nick?' I smile.

'I'll take a reindeer brownie, please.'

'You didn't have enough brownies earlier?' I grin at him.

'What can I say? I'm a sucker for a good brownie.'

'Me too,' I admit.

'Alright, I'll have—' I go to get out my wallet and Nick stops me.

'Oh, no, it's absolutely on me.'

'You sure? You know I'm going all in.'

'Of course,' Nick grins, knowing that when I'm faced with too many choices, I overbuy. 'And then I can try whatever you can't eat.'

'Oh, you will, will you?' Suddenly we're seventeen again.

'Guys, you're holding up the queue!' Adam says in a loud, embarrassed voice.

'OK, Alright then! *Um*, let's see,' I waver momentarily, 'I'll go for the mixed bag selection of mince pies, please; a salted caramel and rum, a billionaire, the luxury amaretto and almond, a chocolate and hazelnut, *ooh*, pecan and maple syrup, and….an original.'

'Are you going to eat *all* of them, Auntie Soph?' Adam asks in surprise as we're each given our treats by the laughing lady in the dessert van, while Nick pays.

I go to open my mouth but Nick answers for me, as we're walking away, 'Nope, she will take a bite out of each one, decide which she likes the most, eat them in that order. Then have maybe, two, three, at the most, then she'll offer them to me. Or you,' he adds.

'*Ugh*. I hate mince pies.'

'I thought that too when I was your age, but it turns out it was just my mum's baking.'

We all laugh as we head over to the oak tree. 'So, what lantern have you made this year?'

'I've gone for a pirate ship.'

'I was talking to Adam, but thanks for sharing,' I grin at Nick while opening the bag, and picking the billionaire's mince pie first.

'I've made a rocket.'

'Well, that's neat.'

'I want to be an astronaut when I grow up.'

'Not a zookeeper anymore?' I ask as that's what he's said since he was about three.

'I like animals,' again, he answers like an adult, 'but we were watching this thing on YouTube, and it's so cool.'

'He's super into space at the minute. Started with planets and then we were watching NASA's live stream of the International Space Station,' Nick confides in me while taking off one of the pretzel antlers from his reindeer brownie, then he throws it in his mouth.

'Did you know astronaut means "star sailor?"' Adam challenges me.

'Oh, I see, so that's why you've done a ship and you've done a rocket!'

'Total coincidence,' Nick says, 'but I like it!'

'What lantern did you make, Auntie Soph?'

'Oh, I wasn't planning on coming, so I didn't make one.'

Adam looks crestfallen and I suddenly feel awful.

'What are you talking about, you joker,' Nick elbows me in the ribs, 'Yours is right over there!'

'What are *you* talking about?' I whisper to Nick.

'What are you whispering about?' Adam says irritatedly.

'My mum's holding yours for you; remember?' Nick nods at me.

'Oh, yeah! Of course.' I smile at Adam and then make a face at Nick when our nephew isn't looking. We walk over to the oak tree, and standing next to Gabby's family is all of Nick's; his parents, twin brothers, and their wives. Everyone stands chatting animatedly and I try to swallow my nerves; I'm not part of this family anymore. Suddenly I feel a gloved hand squeeze mine. I turn to Nick, who smiles gently.

'You'll be fine,' he says softly then frowns, 'Your hands are freezing.' He lets go.

'I forgot my gloves this morning,' I shrug.

'Here,' he uses his chin and his chest to get his right glove off, as Adam is still holding onto his left, 'take one of mine.'

'I can't take one of your gloves,' I laugh as we near his family.

'You're right,' he turns to Adam, 'Hey bud, can I have my hand for a sec?'

'Only for a sec,' he says, as Nick takes off his other one, and hands it to me. Then retakes Adam's hand once more. 'There you go,' he grins.

'Nick, you're going to freeze.'

'You need to warm up. When you have, I'll take them back,' he reasons.

'Fine. Thank you.' I put them on and instantly get a little feeling back in my fingertips.

'So, what do you think of your lantern?' Nick nods to the one his mum is holding.

'You made me a star?' I say with surprise.

'I did. When you couldn't get a flight home until Boxing Day, I thought you'd love to carry something in the parade, so…'

I'm speechless and can feel my eyes sparkling at him. 'You really are the best, aren't you?'

Chapter 11

Surrounded by all of these amazing people, I can't help but have a full heart. Each family member around me gives me a squeeze, and welcomes me, without question or hesitation, back into their lives. On too many occasions to count, one of them has helped to lift me, make me laugh, or support me in some way. For a moment I forget just why I left this town.

'Sophie!' Nick's mum, Hattie, greets me warmly with a one-armed hug; her other arm, strongly holding onto my lantern and making sure it doesn't swing and smack me in the head.

'Nice to see you too, Mum,' Nick teases, as she lets go of me and envelops him in a strong hug.

'Oh, shush you, I see you all the time.' She pats him on the back then turns back to me, 'Here's your lantern, pumpkin.' I accept it while thanking her, then take it in. The main part of the lantern is made up of willow sticks for the frame (that I know will be from Nick's parent's garden) taped together with masking tape, wrapped in fairy lights, with white, crafting, tissue paper over the top, to make up the star. At the highest point, there's a little loop of lacing wire, with a hook through it, that's attached to the bamboo hook holder. I hold onto it firmly, lift the lantern high and let it swing freely. Whenever I made one of these in the past, it never looked like this; I've only ever made a huge mess.

'Nice lantern,' Gabby says, as she and Scott come closer to examine it.

'There's something different though?' Scott smirks.

'Well, I just took my time with this one,' I lie.

'Says the girl famous for her more of a patchwork quilt style of lantern,' Nick challenges.

'Well, I'm a changed woman. I remembered this time to apply the PVA first, to stretch nicely over the frame, and glue to the edges of the willow,' I say with false pride.

'*Ah huh*, so that's the first step, is it?' Nick teases me.

'It's, *um…*' I look at the star, and I'm exactly where I've always been. Clueless. 'Yes?'

'Don't you loosely lay the paper over the frame, cut to size, remove, and *then* add the glue?' Gabby asks.

'Yes, yes, that's what I meant.'

'I miss your pickled creations,' Scott says. 'This is a little too perfect.'

We all look at Nick and he shrugs, 'Well, thank you.' He blushes in the glow of the streetlight. 'Do you like it?' Nick carefully considers my face.

'Well, as we were saying, it's not quite as good as some of mine in the past,' I grin, 'but, you know, it'll do,' I joke.

'Oh, yes, I'm sure the lady who was notorious for setting hers on fire, would have done a much better job.'

'I never could quite figure out why that kept happening,' I make a face.

'You'd always forget to leave a little chimney at the top of the lantern,' Scott contributes.

'Or would never make the access door big enough to safely light the candle, so it would always go up in flames,' Gabby adds, clearly remembering all too well.

'Alright,' I make a face, 'everyone's an expert. Thank God they decided to switch to fairy lights, *huh*?' I say.

'I think you may have been a contributing factor in that decision,' Scott winks at me.

Laughing, I look around. The town has gone all out this year; or maybe it's just been too long since I've taken part, to remember properly. Everybody would come along to the Town Hall, weeks before, and design and build their lanterns together. You can, of course, do it at home, but where's the community in that?

I smile once more at my lantern, then at Nick, 'But with all seriousness, thank you. You really are a bit of a master at this.'

'I do think it's one of my best,' he says without any ego attached to it.

'Oh, it's up there, for sure, but I think my favourite was the giant microphone you made for me.'

His brow lifts for a minute, as he taps into his memory, 'Yeah, that took weeks. Worth it though!'

'I remember my mum being furious at you for deviating from the theme; whatever it was that year.'

'I'm rather proud of inspiring others to forget about a theme and just make whatever they fancied.'

Looking around, I notice lots of people have gone for animals. There's a bumble bee, a jellyfish, a hedgehog. Then next to that, deviating from any kind of theme, there's a giant red heart, a Santa face, a big moon, and lastly, a selection of more traditional, lantern-shaped lanterns.

Thanks, apparently, to my clumsy nature, each one of these will be fitted with their own battery-powered fairy lights. We're all told not to turn them on until we're given the signal to the countdown; it's my favourite moment. I wait with anticipation in the crowd, and I take this opportunity to slide off Nick's gloves and sample each of my remaining mince pies. My favourite is the pecan and maple syrup, which I continue to annihilate in one sitting.

'You are a champion,' Nick laughs while watching me.

After swallowing (it takes me a beat before I can) I retort, 'Well, I was going to offer you one but now you're just going to have to miss out. What a shame,' I tease.

'I didn't want one anyway,' he plays, then gives me a sad puppy dog face with his bottom lip lowered.

'Alright, how about the...' I debate with myself as all of them are equally as delicious. '...amaretto and almond?'

'Sounds great. Thank you.' He takes it gleefully, and then there's a bellowing voice from one of the volunteers of the event; she was never someone who needed a microphone.

'Ladies and gentlemen, boys and girls! Are we ready for our Lantern Parade?!'

While putting the gloves back on, I cheer with everyone else and giggle at how young I suddenly feel; 35 going on 15.

'I'm pleased to tell you, we're ready for our countdown! Please have your switch at hand to turn your lanterns on AFTER we've reached the number ONE!'

Momentarily, there's a smattering of lanterns that flick on and then off quickly; a mix of people either jumping the gun or wanting a test run to make sure that theirs still works.

'OK, on my count. FIVE...'

The crowd joins in with gusto, 'FOUR, THREE, TWO, ONE!'

'HAPPY NEW YEAR!' Nick shouts from next to me, something that he's always done just to make me laugh. As predicted, I burst out laughing, while all around us, the lanterns flicker on; it looks like a fairytale wonderland. The air is filled with "*oohs*" and "*ahhs*" and sprinkled with chatter and applause.

'Alright!' The volunteer shouts. 'Enjoy everybody! Let's go!'

The sound of a drum, calls everyone's attention. I take the opportunity to pop my paper bag of mince pies into my handbag. A short fanfare blasts from the town band, up the front, and we begin our procession through the snow-covered streets. Soon after, the crowd starts singing Christmas carols.

'I've missed this,' I say to Nick, who hasn't left my side and is singing a heartfelt rendition of 'Little Drummer Boy'.

'I know,' he says simply, then smiles sweetly at me. For a moment I wonder what life would be like if I just left my job, and moved back here. Would Nick take me back? If so, I could move back into our flat, maybe we could go against my mum's wishes and finally get married, or start a family. Maybe I'm strong enough now to believe that it doesn't matter what my family does—I can't change them, I can only change myself.

'What are you thinking?' he asks with a head tilt, and it's not until that moment that I realise that Nick's still looking at me.

'Sorry, I'm...' I stop myself from completing the sentence truthfully, '...just...grateful to be here with everyone, you know?'

We approach the town square—the end of the parade—the band stops, and we are graced with the melodic greeting of a choir. As we wrap ourselves around the front of the small stage, I enjoy an unexpectedly snazzy version of 'Carol of the Bells'. The parade continues to gather, and I marvel at each lantern as it passes me, especially the wonky, not-so-good ones.

I spot a giraffe, a penguin, a manor house if you can believe that, and a giant book that reads: "'Twas the night before Christmas..." A Scrooge follows closely behind with a large, crooked nose, and then I can't help but let my jaw fall. At the back of the parade, bringing up the rear is a ten-foot bee-keeper lantern, courtesy of a man on stilts. I guess he stayed hidden until the start of the parade. Although how that was possible, I'm not quite sure.

He weaves around the large crowd that's gathered, to appreciative applause with the accompaniment of the choir. I enjoy people parting like the Red Sea to let him through. He's got a large lantern net that he's swotting around, close to people's heads. Kids laugh and scream with joy, then he heads towards the choir leader. The beekeeper bops her on the head, much to the amusement of the crowd, but you can see the choristers getting a little stressed as he then blocks her conducting completely from their view, and tries to take over, waving his arms around with gusto to lead them. Finally, he continues past her and stops in front of Nick and I. When he gets close, I can see it's Frankie from the bakery.

'Hello, you two!' he shouts from up high at us.

'Since when are you able to walk on stilts?' I shout back.

'Took a circus class with my grandson; great fun!' We laugh and wave as he continues his journey to stand at the back of the crowd and listen to the rest of the choir set. There's an eclectic and rousing mix of Christmas tunes with a couple of pop classics thrown in.

About fifteen minutes later, the mayor carves her way through the choir and takes her place centre stage, her Civic Regalia catching the stage lights.

'Thank you. Let's give a big final applause to the Rock Choir!' Everyone cheers as they clear the stage, and leave the mayor to stand alone. 'We have lots of excellent acts lined up for you this evening, but first, hello and welcome everyone! What a display of talent this evening!' She gestures to the crowd. 'I think you can all agree that you have outdone yourselves this year! Please give *yourselves* a big round of applause!'

Nick smiles at me as if I've created the star I'm carrying, 'Really, bravo. I must say that yours is particularly excellent.'

'It is.' I grin, then see his face fall as he glances back to the stage.

'What? What is it?' I follow his line of sight and see my mother standing on stage, just behind the mayor. 'What's she doing up there?' The applause simmers down and the mayor continues,

'Ladies and gentlemen, to introduce the next act, could you please put your hands together once more, for the Town Secretary, Aubrey Carter, who tells me she has something special planned for you.'

'What on earth could my mum have planned?' My stomach sinks as I remember the last time she did this; an act had dropped out at the last minute, of the town talent show, that she was in charge of, and I ended up singing an unplanned, acapella solo, on stage at the Town Hall, having to be creative on the spot, as I hadn't intended to sing anything at all. I was only ten, but still, it's one of my worst recurring nightmares, even to this day. I hate not being prepared.

'Good evening, everybody.' My mum has put on her best public speaking voice, which is purposely posh, and reminds me of Mrs Bucket from the show, *Keeping Up Appearances*.

Victoria Mae

'I am delighted to see you all here this evening, and I am so pleased so many of you have gone with *my* theme.'

'What was her theme?' I whisper to Nick.

He looks at me and rolls his eyes, 'There was no theme.'

'Is she trying to get credit for something?' I guess.

'Who bloody knows.'

'As you know, this parade has been a tradition in this town for many a decade, and it gives us the chance to showcase some of the town's talent! As per your programmes,' she waves hers around, 'we have the timings and list of each act performing tonight. All the surrounding schools will be with you momentarily, but I couldn't help but add one more, last-minute, unannounced act!'

'Oh God,' I find I've said this out loud and my mind immediately starts to reel through possible songs for me to sing. Then I catch myself and remember that I'm a fully grown-ass adult, and I don't have to do everything that my mum demands of me. Still, my stomach continues to do somersaults.

'This is someone you haven't heard sing in a *long time.*'

'This can't be happening again,' I turn to Nick, whose worried expression shows he still remembers my childhood nightmare too.

'She has a voice like no other!'

'OK, maybe she's not talking about me,' I reason to Nick, who's silently in shock and we return to stare at the stage.

Mum has a look of pride on her face, 'But this is a person who I love very dearly.'

'Definitely not me, then.'

'It's not every day that you can showcase someone in your own family.'

154

Nick and I look at each other once more. 'You don't have to do anything,' he tries to reassure me, and I think I'm about to have a panic attack.

'Ladies and gentlemen, boys and girls, please give a warm welcome to the stage, my daughter—'

'Fuck,' I say, Nick mirroring my look of horror.

'ARIA!'

I feel my stomach drop with relief, but then rage immediately races through me.

'What the actual fuck?' Suddenly, Gabby is on my other side, with Scott closely behind.

'Way to ruin a perfectly good evening,' Scott says in my ear.

I frown at the stage. Angry tears start to well in my eyes. I didn't want to get up there, but why the hell was it so easy for Mum to say those things about Aria, and never me, especially after all this time? Hasn't she spent any time at all reflecting on things?

'I thought for a horrifying moment she was going to get you up there again,' Gabby makes a face at us both. 'I still remember that. You nailed it though. Best rendition of "Dream a little Dream of Me", I've ever heard.'

I shrug, 'It's my dad's favourite song,' I wipe away a tear that's escaped, 'so it was the first thing I thought of,' I reply numbly, not quite here in the present moment. I return my gaze to the stage, staring at this over-the-top-probably-for-my-benefit-only scene of Mum and Aria hugging. Mum now leaves the stage with a wave to the crowd as if she's been declared president.

'Good evening, everyone,' Aria's voice beams through the mic, so comfortable being in the spotlight. 'As you all know, The Carters have been so good to me since I joined their family.'

I want to yell that's because she's taken advantage of them, yet immediately after, I feel my anger being replaced with feelings of worthlessness; she's the daughter Mum always wanted, not me, so maybe it's all for the best.

'Anyway, with all that being said, my first song, I would like to dedicate to Richard.' Her expression adopts a serious expression, and she shifts her feet slightly on the spot to ground herself and to get into a performing mode, as the opening bars of, 'Dream a Little Dream of Me' start.

I stare at the stage in bewilderment then move my eyes to Nick, Gabby, and Scott, who all take the opportunity to guide me away from the stage, in silence. We weave our way through the crowd, and although some are watching as Aria sings the first verse, not everyone is paying attention; I can't help but think that that's something I love about this town. As much as there's an evening of performers and they wouldn't want to be without that, most people are more interested in enjoying each other's company, and sampling the food and drink all around, so, they're not all staying still, rooted to the spot, or being quiet for that matter, listening to the acts. When Aria breaks into the chorus, our little group of four arrives at the back. Nick leads us around a corner and when I finally face them, we all lose it.

'Not a patch on you!' Scott starts with.

'What a complete and utter bitch!' That was Gabby.

'Is she trying to replace me?' I gesture wildly and nearly knock my star off its hook.

'In her mind, I think that's already happened, hon, I'm sorry to tell you,' Gabby was always the one to tell me as it is.

'There's no point in trying to find logic in this situation, Soph,' Nick places his free hand on me and his pirate ship lantern sways gently in the wind, as if it's bobbing up and down on an imaginary sea. 'They're clearly trying to make a point after what happened this morning in John Lewis.'

'I just can't…' my eyes fill with tears, 'I just don't…get it.' I sigh so deeply, and will my tears to bugger off. 'What is so incredibly wrong with me?' I desperately ask them all, and they take turns to answer. I ping-pong my head between them; Gabby starts:

'You grew up and they didn't like it.'

'It's like they're punishing you for having your own life,' Scott says.

Nick scratches his head in frustration, 'There is nothing wrong with you.'

Gabby takes over, 'You don't need to compete with Aria. They made you compete with Chris your entire childhood, and it only ever made you feel like shit.'

Then Scott takes my hand, 'You are here for the next five days, there's nothing you can do about that, but you can make the most of being here.'

'We'll help you avoid them,' Gabby agrees.

'Move into mine tomorrow,' Nick stops, I think, surprising himself, but then continues, 'or, no, actually, why don't we do that tonight before they get home.'

I open my mouth but Gabby talks first, 'You do not need to give them an explanation,' she says with force.

I guiltily think about my dad, a part of me so desperate to spend more time with him, and really, he hasn't done anything wrong. I then stop those intrusive thoughts; he might not have caused the trauma, but he was a bystander who didn't stop it.

Then Scott gives me a stern look, 'They are toxic people and it will be our mission for the rest of the time that you're here, to keep you away from them, as best we can.'

'I reckon we can do that; they are predictable.' Gabby nods, clearly making an action plan in her head already. 'They do the same things, go to the same places.'

I smile sheepishly at them all, feeling that I don't deserve this level of love or protection. '*Ugh*, it's exhausting being in my head.' I give my temples a small massage and hope my intrusive thoughts will bugger off. 'Thank you,' I manage to wobble. I sniff, then try to gather myself, and look at Nick, 'When shall we go? I don't want you to miss Adam.'

Nick waves my comment away, 'It's fine. We'll go now—no need to stay for Aria's set is there? Then there's three schools before Adam's, so, if we hurry, I'm sure we'll be back in time for that.'

'Thank God all the surrounding schools take part, *huh*?' Gabby agrees.

'Just in case it takes longer, we'll stay so I can film it, if you're not back,' Scott offers.

'Thank you, that would be great. I wouldn't hear the end of it from Adam, I'm sure. But we'll make it.' Nick smiles at me and I feel so protected; it hurts that we're not still together.

'Can you take both of these?' Nick opens his left palm to me and for a moment my free hand goes to take it, but I catch myself in time and pass him my lantern.

'Of course.' Gabby takes the pirate ship and Scott takes my star, to join both of their Lego-like, cat lanterns.

'Alright,' Nick looks at me, 'let's go.'

Chapter 12

Sneaking around the outskirts of the crowd, we manage to slip away unseen and unquestioned and head to my parent's house. When we arrive, I unlock and open the door; Nick stops in his tracks.

'What's wrong?'

'It's…I don't know, I guess I always just promised myself that I'd never set foot in here again,' he looks around as though the house is going to yell at him, or something.

I exhale, 'I know. Me too.'

We both take a moment then Nick snaps-to. 'Alright,' he steps over the threshold to join me inside, shuts the door, and immediately we both take off our coats and boots and tiptoe up the stairs.

'Why are we sneaking?' I whisper.

He searches for an answer, 'I don't know,' he whispers back, then we both laugh loudly and continue our way up, taking pleasure in stepping on the squeaky steps as we go, suddenly filled with the excitement of skulking around together.

I rush to my bedroom and gather my things; thankfully there's not much to gather as I made a conscious effort to not unpack completely—physically or mentally. Nick leans on the doorframe and looks around, 'Gee. It's as if you were never here, right?'

'It is always as if I've never been here. I never fitted in this family,' I say while throwing my toiletries in my carry-on with purpose.

Victoria Mae

'Damn good thing, I say.' Nick walks in. 'Alright, how can I help?'

'You know, I think…' I pick up my pj's, '…that's it.' I give the duvet a swift stroke to flatten it out.

'Do you have anything in another room?'

I shake my head, 'Nope, but it's always good to check, isn't it, just in case I've overlooked something.'

We check the bathroom and study, then head back downstairs. Nick scans the living room, while I take the kitchen and dining room. Feeling satisfied, with a mild side helping of anxiety, I nod at the empty kitchen, as if to say goodbye for the final time.

'Soph?' Nick calls from the living room.

'Yeah? Did you find something of mine?'

Nick walks in slowly, carrying something, 'I think so.' I look down at the seemingly harmless hardcover notebook, then, walking closer, I realise it's my diary.

'Oh, great thanks.' I take it and then stop. 'Wait, where did you find this?'

'On the sofa,' he says simply.

Momentarily confused, I shake my head as if I've gone mad. 'I don't remember writing in it down here.' Then anger swooshes through me, 'Where on the sofa did you find this?'

'On your mum's side.' He presses his lips together before continuing, 'It was face down, and open to yesterday's page.'

Shutting my eyes, I exhale, then open them once more and look at Nick, 'Of course she would go through my luggage and read my diary. I forgot she used to do that.'

'As if you needed any more reasons as to why you're leaving,' he says, clearly thinking that my mother couldn't get any worse, 'Invading your privacy like that, isn't OK,'

Nick says in disbelief, 'but then again, I'd expect nothing less, if I'm honest; she never respected your privacy before, why start now?'

'No boundaries,' I shrug, annoyed that my tone is almost excusatory. 'Alright.' I will my shoulders to lower from their place just below my ears. 'There's no guarantee that she hasn't taken out anything else, but,' I nod my head, 'it's time. I'm never coming back here; she can keep whatever else she might have felt the need to take out of my suitcase.'

We walk towards the door, and I take this moment to look at the family portrait that's above the mantelpiece in the living room. This is the only picture displayed in the house of me; I know there are more, but they're tucked away in a box somewhere. I look at us all, Mum sitting, Chris and I on either side behind each of her shoulders, and my dad, in the middle, behind her back. We're all smiling as if we're the happiest family alive. I always had to smile and pretend that everything was OK. I couldn't question the little flickers of doubt that tried to hint something didn't feel right, yet questions sat in the pit of my stomach for decades. I've always known that if I ever voiced this, I would be told that I was too sensitive, or, not to take things so seriously. I learnt as a kid that my feelings don't count and my opinion doesn't matter. I don't want to live that way any longer. I deserve more, don't I?

We leave my parents' house in silence without looking back, and walk to Nick's apartment, ten minutes from there. When we arrive in the mews courtyard, behind a row of shops where we used to get a cheeky Friday night bottle of wine, I pause, and stare up at the flat I used to call home; a wash of sadness flows over me and my former life. It's a renovated Tudor barn, and ours is the one on the upper floor.

To the right of the lower level flat, there are covered, exterior stairs to get to ours. Without question, Nick takes my case from me, and we climb the stairs in silence. Then it's my turn to stop outside the open door.

'I know it's a bit weird, Soph,' Nick says from inside as I remain, hesitant, at the top of the stairs, 'but it's either here or your parent's house, right?'

'Indeed,' I say, feeling suddenly desperately lost. Stepping closer, I look at every inch of the doorframe and then I can't keep the sadness out of my voice, 'You painted the front door,' I say numbly as my hand reaches out to stroke its now duck-egg blue, that used to be yellow.

'Yeah, I needed…wanted a change after you left,' Nick stutters. 'The colour seemed too happy for how I was feeling if I'm honest. I'm sorry,' he hangs his head slightly.

'No, I get it,' I say numbly, stepping inside and taking a deep breath. *I'm home*, I hear my inner voice say with an attempt to comfort me, but this feeling is immediately preceded by grief, as I know that's simply not true; it's not my home anymore and hasn't been for two years.

I walk in further, hugging my arms as I look around. The layout of furniture has been kept much the same. I smile at our impressive entertainment unit; the heart of the space that created the soundtrack to our lives. Several speakers sit next to amps, mixing desks, a record player, a CD player, and some bells and whistles that I loved, but couldn't ever hope to understand. Around that in a perfect arch, hosts our collection of CDs and vinyl. The sofa teasingly invites me in to the memory of us sitting for hours, right there, listening, laughing and living. I note the throws and cushions have all changed. Our TV hangs on the wall above the log burner, and the floating shelf between them remains, but all our pictures and knick-knacks have gone. The small dining table for two, or a close four, just off the petite kitchen, sits harmlessly in the corner, and memories of all the dinner parties we hosted with Gabby and Scott rush instantly into my mind. Looking closer, the place settings have been changed from bamboo to a dark grey, and a Yankee candle no longer sits in the middle; it's been replaced with an iPad stand. Our lives have been erased from time, leaving no trace of anything we built together.

'Are you OK?' Nick asks, softly.

'I loved our life,' I quietly admit with hot tears now prickling my eyes.

'So did I.' His expression falls further, and he takes me in, with an overwhelming deep sadness that I recognise. Before I know it, he's scooped me into a hug, both of us mourning the life we used to have. I realise I'm shaking with my sobs, and although he was never one to cry, I can hear his breath shortening. Neither of us move for a time, we just soak each other in. I hold onto him like it's the last time I'll see him, or afraid that if I let go, he'll disappear.

Eventually, my sobbing abates, but he continues to embrace me, as he always did. When I've stopped crying completely, he loosens his hold and looks at me, bringing his hands up to my cheeks, and softly wiping away my tears. 'I think we both needed that,' he smiles. I catch my breath and he tilts his head, 'Or, we need help.'

'I'm already in therapy,' I admit.

'*Um*, to talk about the people who should be in therapy!'

I smile at him. He was always my best friend first and foremost; perhaps that's why it felt impossible to leave him. You forfeit a piece of your soul, don't you, when you lose a love like that?

163

'Man, I really didn't think they could get any more ridiculous, and now this. Yelling at you in a department store, embarrassing you at a public event, reading your diary?'

Shaking my head, and giving a small chuckle, I wipe away more tears that are gracing my cheeks. 'I'm not sure if they're from crying or laughing,' I admit out loud.

'Perhaps if you can somehow view this trip with humour, it'll make it a hell of a lot easier. Plus, you've got me, Scott and Gabs, and everybody.'

I look at him and feel a wash of gratitude. There's no need to express this, he knows, but I say it anyway, 'Thank you, Nick.'

'I've got you.' He smiles sweetly and I know that although we can never be together, he will always hold a place in my heart, and I in his. 'Alright,' Nick claps his hands together. 'We'll put your stuff in the spare room when we're back; it's ready for guests, just like we always had it.' I don't allow myself to fully feel how strange that is, and I watch as he weaves a hand through his hair; I resist the urge to touch it too. 'You ready to go, or do you need a minute?'

I rub my cheeks once more and take a deep breath. 'I'm good, but maybe I'll just quickly splash some water on my face.'

'Of course, take your time.' Nick automatically puts his arm out to show me the way and then clearly feels ridiculous. 'Sorry, of course you know where it is.'

I smile sadly, then head towards the main bathroom. I loved how we decorated it when I moved in, even though it was mainly used by guests; our room had our en suite. As I put my hand on the handle, I tell myself, that however different it looks in there, it doesn't matter, and that I'll be

OK. The phrase, "This too shall pass", comes into my head—a phrase that I've always tried to remind myself of, to keep calm. Coincidentally, it's also what Gabby had tattooed onto her left butt cheek when she was drunk on her twenty-first birthday; we both thought it was hilarious with its double meaning in that particular spot.

Taking a deep breath, I push the door and step inside. I smile as I look around; it's exactly the same. The fluffy cream bath mat and relaxing neutral shades greet me. Walking over to the sink, I put my glasses on top of my head, run the cold tap, then splash a little water over my face. 'This too shall pass,' I whisper to myself as I dab my face with a towel. Replacing my glasses I look at my reflection in the mirror above the sink and say once more, 'This too shall pass.'

But I don't want it to pass, I hear my inner voice reply.

'I know,' I say in response.

Subconsciously I reach out and open the mirror that's hiding a small bathroom cabinet behind it. I smile as there's an unopened tub of my moisturiser sitting there, but as it's the one for guests, I feel I can't open it. Instead, I reach into my handbag and take out the Barton Reynolds Revitalising Spray that my cousin sent me, and give my face a spritz.

Closing the mirror door, I look at my reflection once more. I suddenly hear Mel Robbins in my head. I loved her book, *The High 5 Habit*, which I read a couple of years ago. I must have left it at Gabby's when I moved to America, but from what I remember, she tells you to put your hand on the mirror and give yourself a high-five, while saying, "I see you, I believe in you, and I am here with you; you've got this." Admittedly, I haven't done this since I read the book, giving in to my resistance, thinking how ridiculous, and that

I don't deserve a high-five. Yet, I decide now is as good a time as any to look deep into my own eyes, and try to feel the words instead of just saying them. When I'm done, I nod at my reflection and exit, heading back into the living room.

Nick's standing there holding something, 'Here. So I can have mine back.' He chuckles and offers me a pair of gloves, that when I accept them, notice they're mine.

'I guess I left these here, *huh*?'

He nods, 'Actually, there were a few things you left here; we can go through them later if you like.'

'Let's do that.' We smile sadly at each other, any small hopeful wisp of a reconciliation evaporates, and we head out the door.

Chapter 13

During the walk back to the parade, we stay in understanding silence. As we approach the main square, we hear the sound of children singing; I make a face at Nick, 'Have we missed it?'

He's as cool as a cucumber, 'Nope. That's "Frosty the Snowman". That's not on their setlist,' he says knowledgeably.

I grin at him.

'He wanted to practise with me,' he explains.

Ignoring the voice in my head that's saying what a good uncle he is, and therefore what a great dad he'd make, we weave our way around the edge of the crowd, hunting for our lanterns, to locate Gabby and Scott's position.

'*Ooh*, there,' I point to our left. Scott, Gabby and her family are still next to Nick's. We walk over and I feel a mixture of relief from seeing them and panic for what I've just done.

Scott spots us first and bops the lanterns up and down to join him in a happy dance. 'They're next. Adam's just lining up backstage.'

'Did anyone notice we were gone?'

Gabby nods, 'Yup, both mine and Nick's families, but I said you had something to take care of and you'd be right back. No one asked any follow-up questions.'

Taking back our lanterns, I think just how strange that is for no one to give me the third degree. As a kid, and even as an adult, I couldn't go anywhere or do anything without my actions or intentions being questioned. I thought that was normal.

The school kids on stage come to their final melodious line, and after a bow, are applauded, and exit backstage. They're immediately replaced with Adam's school. This is clearly now a military operation, and far from the circus I'm used to. All the kids are in neat rows, some smiling, some looking completely petrified. Adam's on the front row, stage left, so, luckily, directly in front of us. He smiles and waves at us all; not an ounce of fear on his face. We wave back and the group starts to sing, 'A Marshmallow World'.

'He's so confident up there,' I say, swaying with the beat.

'Yeah, something happened about a year ago; I think it was his growth spurt that helped.'

'I remember he stood there and cried during his first performance at the Lantern Parade, and didn't sing a single line.'

'I know, bless him.'

'Well, *there* you are! We have been looking everywhere for you,' a voice with fake sincerity that makes the hairs on the back of my neck stand up, says from behind me. I turn and Aria is squaring up to me, with Chris and my parents slightly behind.

I have nothing to say to this woman.

'We thought we'd find you here; you'd never miss the Lanterns. What did you think of my set?' Aria asks, her eyes challenging me to not compliment her.

'Oh, it was just wonderful, wasn't it!' my mum says while looking at me.

I have nothing to say to this woman either.

I gaze at Aria, confused by her wanting to seek me out in the crowd after yelling at me in John Lewis. 'Why were you looking for me?' I can't believe the words have come out of my mouth.

'Why wouldn't I, sis? You're so silly!'

'Our fight earlier?' I offer.

She furrows her brows, 'We didn't fight earlier.'

I shake my head, feeling, once again, like I'm going mad. 'In John Lewis?' I prompt. Maybe it's baby-brain?

She waves her hand, 'None of that matters,' in one sentence she dismisses my feelings, once again, as irrelevant. 'I see you're with Nick,' Aria states judgmentally. 'Why?'

'Always a pleasure to see you, Aria,' Nick responds dryly.

'No need to be rude to my fiancé, Nick,' my brother decides to defend Aria's honour.

'I think you'll find he has *every* reason to be rude to her,' Scott snarls at Chris.

I place a hand on Scott's chest as he leans slightly forward as if to challenge my brother, 'Alright, let's just leave it; we can get into this later.'

'Now, don't make a scene, Sophia,' my mum threatens, ignoring the fact that I'm attempting to defuse the situation; she places blame directly on me. 'I know you've been avoiding me all day, and now we're all together; this could still be a very nice family outing, don't ruin it.'

'*Phah*,' I scoff, 'How am *I* ruining anything?'

'Like I said, you're completely avoiding me and I don't know why.'

'You don't know why?' I say in disbelief.

The choir finishes their first song and the audience claps.

'You're getting out of hand, Sophia; we'll talk about this at home.'

'No, we won't,' I say, stronger than I feel.

'Well, we're not doing this in public,' Mum says through gritted teeth, giving her best fake smile to a few people who have started to watch. The next song begins its introduction.

'No, I mean, I'm not going back to your house.'

'Fine, I'll keep all of your stuff, shall I?' Mum's tone is sarcastic.

'My stuff isn't at your house.'

'Of course it is. You think it just disappeared?'

'I've decided to stay somewhere else.'

'Well! Can you believe the audacity? My daughter; too good to stay with her parents!'

With all the courage I can muster, I decide to confront her, 'Just placing aside for a moment all the crap from two years ago, you went through my things and read my diary!'

She looks like someone has slapped her. 'I did no such thing.'

'It was on the couch in your spot,' Nick chips in.

'Well, clearly you must have left it there. How dare you suggest I would do such a thing, Sophia.'

'Her name is Sophie!' Nick practically yells.

'This is not OK Mum.'

'Well, I had the plumber in today; perhaps it was him.'

'Why would the plumber go through my things, Mum?'

'I don't know, you'll have to ask him.'

'I think that's enough,' Gabby speaks up for the first time. 'This isn't going to go anywhere helpful.'

'Excuse me, Gabriella, no one asked for your opinion,' Aria snarls.

'And people beg for yours?' Gabby gives Aria a death stare and I suddenly feel the situation spinning wildly out of control.

'Is there a problem here?' Nick's mum is suddenly at my side too.

'Oh, no, of course not, Hattie,' my mum flusters. 'How...how are you? Well, I trust?'

Hattie nods politely, 'Just fine, thank you.' The two mums have a staring competition for a moment, neither ready to have a full-on fight in public that's been brewing for years because of my and Nick's situation. For a moment we all stop with the background soundtrack of Adam's school singing, 'Santa Claus Is Comin' to Town', filling the air. I look at my dad, his expression reads extreme discomfort. He's so helplessly bashful compared to these strong women. I exhale and I wish for the millionth time that he'd just stand up to Mum and Aria, and take my side for once; something I know that he could never do.

Another applause breaks out and I look up to see Adam frowning at us all from the stage; I suddenly feel super guilty. 'Look, let's just enjoy the rest of Adam's set, shall we?'

The choir breaks into 'Grandma Got Run Over by a Reindeer' and I can't help but burst out laughing at the timing. 'Who put that on the set list?' I look at Nick.

'Brilliant, isn't it?'

'Look, Mum, why don't we go? We'll have this conversation another time.'

'Good idea, Aria.' Mum stands tall, despite her small frame, and links arms with my soon-to-be sister-in-law. 'See you all soon.' My family leave, and I hear Hattie say,

'Not too soon, I hope.'

***

Despite the gnawing uncomfortableness in the pit of my stomach telling me this is far from over and the worst is yet to come, I enjoy the rest of the evening without bumping into my family again; maybe they all went home in protest. Gabby and Scott try to reassure me that my family don't deserve another second of my attention, so, I try to shift my focus onto the musical acts instead.

The rest of the night's entertainment is excellent. After all the schools have performed, Madison from Paws and Claws takes to the stage, starting with, an admittedly rousing version of Freya's 'Fire', which is followed by an acoustic duo, then to finish the evening, Rise and Shine take to the stage for the finale. After seeing them in the studio, it's quite something to see them live, working a crowd. They're by far my favourite act of the evening, and I'm impressed to admit that due to the repetition of recording, I know most of the words now to a couple of their songs; I gleefully hum the rest.

Nick and I return to what used to be our shared home, with at least two mulled wines in us, alongside the remainder of my mince pies, allowing any remaining awkwardness to dissipate. We enter the flat once more, and instead of the familiar feelings of dread and disappointment, I feel blissfully at ease.

'Why don't you take the main bedroom? I'll just change the sheets.' Nick goes to walk off and I stop him.

'Don't be silly, I'm more than happy to take the spare room. No point in creating extra laundry for you.'

'You sure? Our bed was always comfier than the spare.' He makes a face as he realises what he's said. *Our* bed.

'I'm sure. It's not for long, is it?'

'No. No, it's not.' I can't read his expression. I think it's disappointment.

'Well, it's all set up for you. Do you want me to take your case in for you?'

Ever the gentleman. 'No, I'm good. Thank you.'

'OK, then. I'll see you in the morning.' Nick glides over and kisses me on the cheek. His lips are soft and I wish they'd linger for longer, but he just straightens up, and smiles, so I take that as my cue to end the evening.

When we didn't have any guests, the spare bedroom was somewhere that we created as my zen space. Alongside my aunt, Nick encouraged me to get into meditation to calm my nervous system, and in the past, this was always where I headed when I needed to re-centre.

Stepping into the spare room and glancing around, my heart lifts. Nick bought everything that's in here, surprising me one day when I came home from work. It didn't feel right to take anything when I left, but seeing it all after so long, I realise how much I've missed it. There's a Buddha head that you plug into the wall and pop little wax melt cubes in to allow the incense of sandalwood, rose, or lavender to flow around the room. I smile at the pictures gracing the walls. Nick selected my favourites from my cousin's husband's portfolio: a picture of light refracting through trees on their trip to Sequoia National Park; a line of gold Thai figures from the Grand Palace in Bangkok from the trip that they went on where they fell for each other; a night image of Bruges where everything has a warm glow of orange about it; a triangle view of Venice from inside the Bridge of Sighs; and finally, the shot that he won *National*

Geographic Photographer of the Year Award with; a close up of an emperor penguin chick from their trip to Antarctica.

To some, they might not match or make sense, but to me, they help free my mind and calm me down. I smile at the two pillows emblazoned with elephants, and sit gently down on the bed, gazing at it all. Is it strange he's kept it this way? I'm not sure. I glance up at the sound of a knock on the door. 'Come in,' I call.

'Thought you might like some water.' Nick offers me a glass and standing once more, I take it and thank him. We then stand there in understanding silence until he shrugs. 'I couldn't bring myself to redecorate this room,' he says simply. I smile and he knows he doesn't need to say anything else. 'OK,' he smiles at me, 'sleep well.' He turns and heads to the door.

'Hey, Nick?'

He stops and turns, 'Yeah?'

'Thank you.'

'For?'

'Just take it as a blanket thank you. One size fits all.'

He smiles at me, 'Sweet dreams, Soph.'

Chapter 14

22nd December

I sleep surprisingly well, feeling safe and warm under the protection of the 15 tog, winter duvet. Taking my time, I snuggle a little further under the covers. *What if I just stay here forever?* I breathe in the fabric softener and move my hand over the luxurious cotton sheets. I watch the morning light dance on the ceiling from my horizontal position. The curtains we bought for both bedrooms are thin, and designed to let light in. We also decided to pair this with a pulldown blackout blind, that sits behind the light curtain, the idea being that you have the option of waking up naturally with the sun, or not. Last night apparently, I chose to let the light in. Maybe my spiritual self can do the same.

Thanks to these curtains, I smile at the memory of Nick and I excitedly jumping out of bed, awake before the alarm, and going on our morning routine hike out of town before work each day. Wherever we ended up, we'd spend hours imagining our aspirational lives: me as an international global singing star, obviously, and him as a world-class sound engineer. We made a mental list of all the event venues across the world that we'd love to work and perform in. We talked about surrounding ourselves with music, fun, and friendship. Living a life that we dictate and design, with no boundaries, limitations, or drama. Seemed idyllic. Could we have ever allowed ourselves to create that if we'd stayed together? I'm not sure, but in those times, it felt exciting to pretend.

Nowadays, I allow my life to be dictated by Freya; no time for me, a morning routine, or a dream. Even if I let myself wonder what a dream life would look like now, I'd have no idea where to start. I frown and push that aside, not wanting to think about work right now, or my lack of sense of self.

As I shift slightly in the bed, I suddenly feel squeamish. Never being one for being able to sit with my thoughts for a long period, I reach for my glasses on the nightstand, and then for my phone, for some immediate distraction.

First, I check out the weather. Bleak with a side of frost now, and some further snow promised later. Then I check social media. A mixture of updates from people I don't talk to anymore and other accounts of Influencers which I follow that make me feel bad about my own life decisions. I frown at my phone, hating that I compare myself to strangers, and I wonder, not for the first time, if I should just delete all these accounts. I then log into Freya's socials for a quick bit of maintenance, and finally, I head to my work email.

Freya is someone who, if she wants you to answer, will not only email but also text, call, use messenger, DMs, or carrier pigeon. Since she hasn't done any of those, I know she hasn't tried to get hold of me. It gives me an unsteady feeling—what fire do I have to put out? When is the next shit going to hit the fan? Something's not quite right with the world. I contemplate ringing her, and Google what time it is in Bali. It's seven hours ahead there, so two in the afternoon, I work out. With my finger hovering over the dial button to call Freya, I pause; maybe she's taking the silent part of the retreat seriously. I'm sure if she wanted or needed me, she'd get in touch.

A tap on the door interrupts my internal questioning, 'Come in.' Leaning on my elbows, I push myself up to a seated position and readjust the covers to fall over my knees, which I'm now defensively hugging.

'Thought you might like a coffee.' Nick walks in with two mugs. I let go of my phone that I'm gripping and reach out as he hands me a steaming mug. He then sits on what was always his side of the bed. 'How'd you sleep?'

'Well. Thank you for this.' I take a sip and it's perfect, almost as if he waited for it to cool to the perfect sipping temperature before coming in. 'How about you?'

'Honestly? It felt weird knowing you were in here.'

'Oh. I'm sorry. Look, I'm sure I can stay on Gabby and Scott's couch or something, I—'

'No,' he interrupts my insecurity of feeling like I've outstayed my welcome, 'I mean,' he shrugs, 'it's us, and our apartment. It felt wrong to have you in *here*.'

I laugh, 'Well, I'm not sure how to take that.'

'Take it as a compliment.'

'OK, I will.' We sip our morning coffee (like we always used to after getting back from our hikes), then a thought comes into my head. 'Is our bedroom the same?' He gives me a sideways glance, 'I'm sorry, I don't know why I asked. Forget I said anything.'

'Do you want to come and have a look?' he tempts.

'No.' He looks at me with a questioning eyebrow, 'Yes,' I say honestly, this time.

'The box of your stuff that I was talking about last night is in there too, so we could go through that.'

'Oh, good,' I say sarcastically while reluctantly removing myself from under the covers but not committing to getting up yet. 'I've been waiting to have that cliché, "here's your stuff in a box" moment, with you.'

'I don't know what to say to that.' Nick gets off the bed.

'I'll just nip to the loo first,' *and check my reflection real quick*, I say in my head. He walks towards the door, then stops and turns, 'Nothing about our relationship was ever cliché. It was always more than that; I thought, anyway.'

'It was.' I smile, 'I'll just be a sec.' Nick leaves me to it, and I slowly climb out of the warm bed, grab my washbag, and make my way to the main bathroom.

Stepping inside and shutting the door, I put my coffee and washbag on the windowsill, and do the necessary. As I'm washing my hands, I check out my reflection. Not bad morning hair, I nod at myself. I give my teeth a quick brush, pop on some deodorant, and give myself a quick spritz of perfume, then, picking up my mug, I shuffle along down the corridor, sipping my coffee as I go.

When I walk through the open door of what used to be our bedroom, it's both comforting and sad. I loved our room. A calm oasis from the craziness of my outside world. Again, he's changed a few things, like the pillow and duvet covers, and the photos (that were of us) have been replaced with generic things you'd find in TK Maxx or somewhere; perfectly beautiful, but no personal touch.

Automatically, I walk over and sit on my side of the bed. He stops for a minute to take me in, and then recovers quickly, walking towards the closet. He returns a moment later, placing an innocent cardboard box on the bed between us, then fluffs the pillow, and sits on his side.

'OK, I'll just dive in.' I place my coffee on the bedside table, happy to see the coasters are still the same, then after a deep breath, I turn back to the box, and look in. At first, nothing seems too bad. A scarf that I was convinced I'd lost. Another pair of my gloves. Some miscellaneous socks whose partners I took to New York with me, which are long gone after I was sure Freya's washing machine had eaten them. My copy of Mel Robbins' *The High 5 Habit*. Then it gets a little harder.

Always one for wanting to print photos out, instead of keeping them on my phone, I spot my photo albums from the last fifteen years or so. I don't need to open them. I know what's in there. Our lives. Or, our past lives. Not overwhelmingly heavy or many, as I'd always print out one highlight from every month or two, as a reminder of our good times. Next to that are the knick-knacks that used to grace our floating shelf under the TV and above the log burner, my favourites being the framed, pressed rose that Nick gave me when he asked me out in sixth form; a miniature bottle of wine that reads "Malibu Rocky Oaks Estate", from my cousin's wedding; the curvy sign saying, "Home" that we picked out the day Nick gave me a key; and finally, a photo frame.

This frame is special because it has two sides. The left says, "How it started" which has a picture of us when we were seventeen, arms shyly around each other, and on the right it says, "How it's going." On this side, we'd always update the picture each year or so with our latest road trip or favourite moment. The final photo we put in it was of us standing on top of a mountain from the last trip we took together, to the Lake District.

I exhale, 'Wow.'

'I know.' Nick sips his coffee then places it down on the side. 'This feels very final, doesn't it?'

I nod, not sure how I want to respond. For me, at least, I've felt like it's been final for a while, but this is a new level of…I don't know what…grief, maybe?

'Should I not have shown you this? I could just put it back in the cupboard?'

'No,' I say softly, 'I'm glad to have them.' I reach in and carefully pick up the frame with two pictures, and gaze at it more closely. 'Gosh, we were so young,' I say, looking at us both from our school days.

'And now we're so old.'

I laugh, 'We're not old. We're…a little more seasoned, but definitely not old.'

'Yeah, *seasoned* is the right word; I'm starting to get grey hair all over the place.'

'All over the place?' I laugh and raise an eyebrow.

'I meant on my head.'

'*Ah.*' I grin and look over, enjoying his sprinkle of salt and pepper. I shrug, 'I like it.'

'You say that because you're not going grey; just you wait!'

'Nothing wrong with grey hair. I always liked that about you.'

'What? The grey hair's a new thing!'

I smile, 'Oh, right, my mistake.' In the last couple of years that we were together, a few of his strands had started to lighten, but I never said that I'd noticed. I have always loved the idea of knowing someone your whole life and growing old together.

'Well, I didn't have any before all the crap happened with your family. Clearly, they brought out the best in me.'

'Sorry about that,' I say, looking at him with remorse.

'It was never you,' Nick takes this moment to delicately brush a strand of my hair aside.

'Wasn't it? God, I wish I was stronger then. Or, no, I wish I was stronger now. I couldn't even stand up properly to my mum last night, never mind two years ago.'

He shakes his head, 'When you're right there in front of someone, saying what you want to can seem impossible. Plus, I guess it depends on how far along on the healing journey you are.'

'*Um.*' I look back at the picture, feeling completely lost and overwhelmingly lonely. 'I've no idea where I am on my healing journey. I thought I had moved on a bit, maybe, but...' I stop myself, as I realise I'm not talking about my family. My voice trembles, barely audible in its whisper, 'I never wanted to lose you, Nick,' I bite my lip, not daring to look up.

'Soph?' Nick says softly.

'Yeah?' I tentatively turn back to him, still holding the photo.

He doesn't say anything, he's just drinking me in. I feel my stomach flip. His eyes look longingly into mine. He edges slowly forward, so subtly that I think I might have imagined it. All the same, I edge towards him ever so and wait.

And wait.

Just as I think he's going to back away, he leans in.

His lips tenderly grace mine and I sink effortlessly into his embrace. Like no time has passed we instantaneously find our rhythm as the pad of his thumb gently traces my jaw. With a slight clang, I realise I've dropped the photo frame back into the box as I fall further into him. The kiss starts to intensify and without overthinking, I break away, place the box on the floor, and return to straddle him, just our plaid pyjama bottoms and T-shirts separating us. The warmth of his chest heaves unevenly as he cups my face and the kiss becomes more passionate. With no concept of time and space, his strong hands hold onto my hips as he slides us down the bed, to lower our bodies, his head, resting on the pillow. Teasingly, he trails his fingers under my T-shirt and draws me closer; I feel him longing for me.

He combs his hands through my hair while kissing my neck in that secret spot that only he could ever find. My whole body tingles, alive at the electricity of him. Forgetting who, and where I am, I allow myself to let go and whisper his name. Hungrily, he nibbles kisses from my neck to my shoulder, and with his hot breath upon my skin, his voice confesses, 'I want you, Sophie.'

'Then take me,' I find myself saying, pulsating with anticipation.

Effortlessly, he rolls me, our fingers sieve into each other and then with one effortless sweep, he pins my arms above my head and kisses me deeply. Nick then gently pulls away enough to look into my eyes, his expression soft, vulnerable, 'You've no idea how much I want you, but is this a good idea?'

'I think it's an excellent idea. The best idea we've had,' I say smiling while trying to ignore the nagging feeling of doubt that's surfaced to ruin the moment. *Sleeping with Nick won't make losing him again any easier.* I feel my smile fade, 'Maybe you're right. Let's stop this, before anything happens, yeah?' I go to move my arms but his remain where they are.

'Alright.' He nods, then, clearly changing his mind, leans down and kisses me again, this time, almost achingly slowly.

Nick releases one of his hands and keeps me pinned with the other, he draws an invisible line from my wrist to my side, to the top of my thigh, and back up again. A pleasant shiver journeys my entire body.

'So,' I say in between kisses, 'what are we doing right now?' He breaks away.

'Enjoying the moment,' he rolls and lifts me, to lay on top of him once more.

I groan with pleasure then laugh, as he kisses my delicious sweet spot, again. 'Isn't this exactly what we're supposed to be avoiding here?' I push away and slide my legs up, but can't help myself. I've had a taste of him and it's not enough. My body doesn't want me to stop. Our tongues entwine and then with our lips still together, he sits up, as I adjust to wrap my legs around his back. He interlocks his fingers at the base of my spine.

Nick pulls away to gaze into my eyes, his face beaming at me, 'Yes, absolutely, let's stop this. It's going to get us nowhere.'

Desire, overruling logic, we rip and tear at our unwelcome pyjamas, discarding them onto the floor. My body melts into his as our bare flesh reunites. His thumbs lovingly massage my lower back, but my hands are desperate to rediscover every inch of his toned body. I can't wait any longer. He pulls me somehow closer, whispering, 'God, I've missed you.'

And suddenly, it's happening.

***

Lying, panting, very glad that I went to the bathroom before entering this room, I attempt to catch my breath. Nick and I stare at the ceiling, holding hands.

'Well,' I clear my throat, 'that…was…*um…*'

'Two years in the making,' Nick breathlessly finishes my sentence, and we start laughing. We both roll onto our sides to face each other. Nick leans on his elbow, 'You've no idea how badly I've wanted to do that since the second I saw you were home.'

'I think you've just shown me how badly,' I grin, then lean in to kiss him once more. I break away, deciding to be honest, 'Me too,' I say, close to his lips, then lean back on my side to take in his beautiful face.

'So, what now?' Nick strokes my cheek.

'Now? Now we lie here and enjoy this, and not think about what's next. The outside world doesn't exist.'

'I like that.' He wiggles closer and kisses me, and that's where we stay until night falls.

Chapter 15

The band is recording again tonight, and I take my place, once more, in the co-pilot seat of the control booth. I'm not paying attention to the band this evening; I'm staring at the man I just had sex with three times. Sitting with my right leg tucked beneath me, my left leg dangles so my toes just about touch the ground. My right elbow is placed on the armrest, and I'm leaning my head on my hand, still marinating in post-coital deliciousness. I like that it's a secret right now just between us; no one knows it happened, and to add to that, I don't know what's going to happen next. It feels exhilarating, instead of scary. No, it's better than that, it feels like home; *he* feels like home.

'Do you have any idea how hard it is to concentrate right now?' Nick says looking forward, rather than at me, and adjusting a few levels while smiling.

Grinning and spinning the chair side to side slightly, I feel playful, 'Yes.'

Nick presses the talkback button as the band comes to a finish on their latest song, 'Light in My Fire', another tune that will stay pleasantly in my head all night. 'Alright guys that was great. Let's maybe just take it from the bridge one more time?'

'Let's do it,' Jerry, the band leader, calls; they clearly don't want to waste a second of their time here. He nods at Nick.

'Alright, we'll do a drop-in from bar 50.'

Jerry nods. Nick presses record again. 'And five…, six…, five, six, seven, eight.' The band do another take, which to

185

me, sounds just as good as the first one, but Nick's nodding, grooving with the music.

'That's better,' he says under his breath, to himself rather than me. I love watching him work. He can hear things that I've never been able to; I've no idea if something needs less "bottom end" or whatever it is he comes out with. He's a genius at what he does. Nick then turns to me, my gaze remaining on him. 'You are a problem.'

'I'm a problem?' I say with amusement, knowing he doesn't mean anything bad by it.

'Yes. I'm supposed to be concentrating on my work here, and all I want to do is take you right here in the booth.'

I laugh, 'With an audience?' I gesture to the band. 'That's new.'

He presses his lips together in thought, 'Yeah, it needs a fade-to-black feature on the window, doesn't it?'

'I'm sure they've got that in the budget somewhere; you should ask them.'

He tilts his head then rolls his chair over to me, so his face is inches from mine. 'God I've missed flirting with you.'

'Are you going to kiss me in front of the band?' I'm not sure if I'm panicked or not.

'Yes, I am. That's not a problem, is it?' he asks kindly.

I pause, 'No.'

His lips are soft and tender and before I want him to, he's pulled away in time for the end of the song.

'Nice work,' Nick says into the booth to the band.

'I was going to say the same to you,' Jerry, the band leader replies, and I giggle. 'We'll take five, then get back to it, Nick.'

'Great stuff,' Nick says over the talkback, presses a few buttons, then wheels his chair back over to me. He parts his legs, bringing them either side of mine, then draws my seat closer to his, leans in and kisses me. I can hear my internal monologue wanting to over-analyse this, but I don't let it; I drop into the moment and stay there. When we finally break away Nick smiles at me. 'God, I've missed doing that.' His eyes sparkle into mine and my heart flutters under his gaze. 'Do you want a drink?' He gets up and heads over to the small fridge in the corner.

'Sure, what do you have?'

'Beer; sauvignon blanc.'

'Since when do you stock wine in the fridge?' I play, knowing he must have gone especially out of his way.

He grabs the bottle along with two mugs that are sitting just to the right, 'Well,' he moves over to the couch, and I stand to join him, 'if I'm being honest, I picked it up the other day, just in case you might stay late,' he grins.

'How very presumptuous of you,' I sit down gently next to him with a playful smile. Entwined with the day we've just enjoyed, the tasty memories of our past late-night couch adventures flash naughtily across my mind.

Nick pours the wine and we sit in silence, sipping in a memory of two. I suddenly feel like I've been magically transported into the past, back before my world imploded.

'Can I be honest with you?' Nick snaps me out of my memory lane headspace.

'Always,' I say, meaning it, but slightly afraid of what he's going to come out with.

'I love your idea of "the outside world doesn't exist right now". And I want to stay in this bubble with you, and to just—' he reaches to brush a lone strand away, 'enjoy you

187

and us, and whatever is happening right now. What do you think?'

'I think it may come back to bite us on the arse,' taking in the depth of longing in his eyes, I realise I couldn't care less if it's a bad idea or not, 'But I think I feel the same way,' I answer honestly. 'I don't want to overthink or over-analyse. I've done so much of that over the last two years; it's exhausting.' I take a sip of wine and then continue, 'Sorry, we don't have to get into that.'

'No, I want to.'

'OK.' I clear my throat. 'Well, I mean, in therapy, it's important to go over things to get to the root cause, but I've learnt that I tend to want to punish myself by ruminating or sitting in a negative thought. I remember the worst of everything, and I end up ruining a perfectly good moment.' Nick's eyes remain steady on me, the seriousness of what I've said sinking in, explaining so much of our past in a single sentence. 'Like right now, over-explaining, and, stumbling over my words, ruining the moment.'

'Don't be daft.' He takes my hand, 'I'm glad you're in therapy.'

'Me too.' Nick encouraged me for years to talk to someone impartial; I just felt so much shame for even thinking about talking to someone about it all, that I stopped myself from seeking the support I knew, deep down, I needed.

'Is it helping?'

I nod, 'Yeah, it is. It's undoubtedly the best decision I've ever made, but it's also kind of sad.'

'Go on.' Nick squeezes my hand.

'Well, it's reassuring, as I now know I wasn't going mad, and I realise it's quite a common thing to have a narcissistic parent and a co-dependent child, style of relationship; plus, it gives it a label, you know?'

'You do love a label.'

'I do.' I smile at him smiling at me. 'But,' my face drops, 'even though I've done all this work on myself: trying to explore who I *really* am, not who I was told to be, and allowing myself to consider what my values and beliefs are instead of just obediently and mindlessly living according to my mum's rules, being back here, all that inner work feels pointless; I feel like I'm right back where I started.'

'Because you've done all this work but they're right where you left them?'

'Exactly.' I exhale.

'Well, I'd say the fact that you are attempting to take control of your own life and thoughts and feelings, is the point. They're where you left them because that's where they choose to be. You're never going to convince them that they've done something to hurt you.'

I shake my head, 'It's been so hard to dig everything up.'

'I can imagine.'

'Plus, I wasn't ready to come back, but I did anyway.'

'Because you're a good person,' Nick reasons, and I take the opportunity to sip the wine.

'This is good.'

'It is.' He looks at his glass and swirls it around, 'It's from the new wine shop on the corner. They do tastings; we should go while you're here.'

I smile, 'I'd love that. But I meant, *this* is good; talking to you. I've missed it.'

He puts his glass down and takes the opportunity to stroke my cheek.

Victoria Mae

'You are so special, Sophie. I've always hated just how much they made you believe that you're not.'

We look longingly at each other; I wonder if he's still in love with me. He leans in and kisses me with purpose; God I want him. Apparently three times this morning wasn't enough. Nick gently pulls away and then smiles at me, 'Alright, so, we agree. We're not letting the outside in and we're not going to go crazy from the inside out.'

I laugh at this, 'It may be too late for me.'

'Nonsense.' He takes hold of his glass once more and holds it out to me, 'Here's to us and to enjoying a perfectly good moment.'

'A perfectly good moment,' I repeat, and our glasses clink; we sip while keeping eye contact.

'Hey Nick?' Jerry, the leader has just entered the control room, 'And, Sophie, wasn't it?'

'Yup, hi. Thanks for letting me gate-crash this; I'm loving it, by the way, you've no idea.' I beam at Jerry.

'Well, I'm glad you feel that way. We were just wondering if you'd be up for something. Gina was just about to lay down some harmonies for the next one, but we wondered: would you be up for it?'

'Up for what?' I ask, clearly a little slow.

'Singing the harmony,' he says simply. 'She...we,' he corrects himself, 'loved your vocals when we heard you sing the other day. Gina thinks your voice will blend seamlessly with hers, adding a layer of richness that's been missing, and I agree. We'd love it if you're up for it.'

I sit in shock, 'Me? You...you want *my* voice on your record?'

'Yeah,' he says, amusingly looking at me, waiting for my response.

I laugh, 'Well…I…I don't know…I'm not really a singer.'

'Not really a singer?' Jerry says with an air of disbelief, 'Then what the hell was that in the booth the other day?'

'That was *um*…'

'Oh, you're a closeted singer?' His eyes widen with excitement. 'Awesome. Fancy coming out of the closet with us?'

I laugh, 'I'm not *in* the closet, per se, I used to sing all the time. But I just…I'm, just a…'

I have no idea what I am. All I know is that I do not feel good enough.

I gulp my wine, suddenly very glad that I have the glass in my hand.

'Why don't you try it?' Nick's reassuring voice calms me a little. 'Might be fun? Plus, I believe in you.'

I turn to him. *He's the only one who has ever believed in me.*

Taking another sip of wine, I try not to overthink, and go with my gut, 'OK.' I put the glass down. 'What are we singing?'

***

'It's been ages since I was in a booth,' I say nervously, trying to excuse myself to the band just in case I completely cock it up.

'Apart from yesterday,' Nick's voice chimes in through the speakers from the control desk.

'Oh, yes. Apart from yesterday.' I feel small and completely out of my depth.

'Soph?' Nick's calming voice sounds in my headphone ears. His beautiful face beams at me through the glass. 'I'm only talking to you; the others can't hear.'

I've always loved that feature about a studio, the control booth being able to talk to individual musicians if they wanted. I give him a small smile.

'Just take a deep breath; you've got this.'

'Alright, let's go for it.'

The band is kind, funny and supportive throughout the whole thing. We go over the harmony parts several times and I shock myself as to how quickly I pick them up; clearly forgetting that I have any kind of training, and find it's both easy and fun.

'OK, shall we try one?' Nick says from the booth and I nod nervously.

The driving beat of the track plays in my ears; I anxiously fiddle with my headphones but I naturally start to get into the groove. I swallow a few times and feel the need to clear my throat as my entry is drawing nearer. The track is now a few bars before, I think about my breath, prepare, and then I'm singing. Urging myself to relax into it a bit more, I give it my all. They were right, my voice does blend nicely with Gina's. We connect, looking at each other while singing. When I come to my last line, I can't help but smile. The music stops, and the band applaud with appreciation and compliments. I'm embarrassed and try to push down the feeling that I don't deserve that kind of praise.

'Fun, right?' Nick says from the control room. I nod and breathe to push away my mum's voice analysing my performance in my head.

We do a couple more takes, then when we're done, I get smothered in a group hug from the band.

'You know, we're singing at the Light Switch On tomorrow; fancy popping on stage for this one?' Gina says to me as the band begins to pack up.

'*Um*, I don't know.' Alarm bells start to ring in my head. It's one thing to sing in a booth where you can do as many retakes as you want, but singing *live*? That's a whole different kettle of fish. 'That sounds like a lot of pressure,' I admit in a small voice.

Gina pops an arm around me, like we've been friends forever, 'Well, think about it babe. We'd love it if you're up for it, no pressure if you're not. I can use my loop pedal; that was my plan anyway. But just so you know, your voice kicks some serious arse. People need to hear it, in my opinion.'

'I'll think about it.' I smile, not sure if I mean that, but wanting to.

When the band has gone and just Nick and I remain, I head back into the control booth, and sit on the couch, exhaling loudly. 'I can't believe I just did that.' I hug the pillow that's next to me. 'Do you have any idea how long it's been since I sang in front of people?' Nick's standing, leaning on the mixing desk, silently taking me in. 'I mean, my vocals are going to be on an album. *My* vocals. That's insane.' I reach for my wine glass which I left on the table and take a large gulp. 'This is insane.'

'I'm proud of you.'

'You know what? Me too.'

Nick walks over, takes a seat next to me, and leans in to kiss me. He then leans back, and takes my free hand, 'I don't think I've ever heard you say that before.'

'Say what?'

'That you're proud of yourself.'

I think for a moment, 'Really?'

'Not once in the entire time that I've known you.'

'*Huh.*' I exhale again, 'Well, maybe the therapy is helping more than I realise.'

'You know, no one's here now.' Nick raises a suggestive eyebrow.

'And what could you possibly be implying?' In anticipation, I place my wine glass back down on the table and give him an innocent head tilt.

We just look at each other for a moment, and then dive in, hungrily, hands everywhere and I realise I don't care if anyone did walk in right now. I kiss him like there's a time limit. 'God, I've missed kissing you,' I say between breaths.

'I've missed everything with you.'

He wraps himself around me. I surrender. And three times becomes four.

Chapter 16

23rd December

'And then what happened?' Gabby twists her body slightly, the new waterproof I bought for her birthday (today) narrowly avoids the wave of snow slush being fired through the air from her Australian shepherds, as we walk through the park.

'Then,' I find I can't keep the smile off my face, 'we walked back to our flat—his flat,' I correct myself, reconsider, then revert while making a face, 'our flat, and we talked until we fell asleep.'

'In your old bed?' She throws a stick for Lilo, her white fur with patches of grey and tan is darker than normal, soaking wet from the snow.

Stitch is now at my feet and tries to weave in between my legs, but I remain upright. His fur—mainly black with a white belly, and sporadic tan colouring—is not quite as wet as Lilo's. He prefers to stay close instead of jumping into the snow mountains around us like Lilo. 'Yes, we were in our old bed,' I say, smiling but Gabby's face doesn't match mine. 'What? What is it?'

'Please don't get me wrong, I know I said I was loving how much time you're spending together, and I am. You guys mean everything to me, and I was distraught when you broke up. I guess I'm just afraid for you, that's all.'

I stop walking for a moment, 'I'm safe with Nick,' I say so strongly it almost echoes through the trees. 'What Aria said to everyone about him two years ago, was complete and utter bollocks.'

'No, I know that hon,' she rubs my shoulder and we continue on our walk. 'Anyone who knows you guys knows that. Why the hell your ridiculous family didn't ask me or anyone close to you guys what your relationship was really like, is beyond me.'

'They're not interested in anyone else's opinion, and even if they were, they wouldn't have believed you anyway.'

We walk for a few moments in silence then she says, 'I'm just afraid of you getting your heart broken all over again. Like, what's your plan here?' Gabby looks at me with deep concern, as the dogs bound along next to us. 'How has the situation changed? What makes this different? Are you moving back? Is he moving to New York?'

'You sound like me.' I smile then shake my head, 'I don't know.'

'You don't know,' she says, her eyebrows furrowing.

'Nope,' I swallow and wonder what the hell I'm doing, 'and we've agreed we're not going to talk about it just yet. We're going to enjoy being in the moment.'

Gabby stares at me, sideways, as we make our way back towards the fairy-lit bandstand, where we started our loop of the park. 'You are?'

'I am.'

'Just, enjoy the moment and not overthink it?'

'That's right.'

'My best friend, Sophie Carter, the person who used to take 45 minutes to pick a cereal, is not going to overthink this?'

'That was one time.'

'What about the time that you couldn't decide where to go on holiday, so you didn't go anywhere?'

'Yeah, that was stupid.'

'Or any time in the past, when you've been paralysed by your own indecision after being offered a choice in a restaurant, or a bar, or—'

'OK, point taken. I over-think. I can make choices to organise someone else's life, but decisions are hard if they're for me.'

'I know, hon.' She whistles for the dogs to come back from running around the bandstand, and puts them back on their leads. 'I don't mean to be mean. I just love you and want to protect you.' She exhales. 'Alright, well, if you do want to talk things through, I'm here.'

'Thank you, you know I will; just, not now. We're in this blissful bubble.' I plunge my hands into my pockets and raise my shoulders, as we make our way towards the park gates.

'I just don't want you to get hurt when the bubble bursts, hon.'

'I don't want to get hurt either, but I also don't want to stop whatever this is between Nick and I. I haven't had him for two years; I'm making up for it.'

Gabby gives me a sympathetic look, 'Leaving Nick was the hardest thing I've ever seen you do.'

I take a beat as her steady gaze remains on me, 'I'm not over him, Gabs; I never have been.'

Gabby nods, 'I know, hon.'

We walk in that comfortable silence that only best friends can, as we exit the park, and head back into town, towards her house.

'So, how did you leave things this morning with him?'

'He said he had an errand out of town to run, and, honestly, I'm glad, as I thought we could use some air. So, I said I'd meet him at the Light Switch On, later.'

Gabby nods, taking that in, then a sneaky smile spreads across her face, 'Four times. Man, and I thought my one-time, bit of birthday sex before Scott went to work, was impressive.'

I giggle, 'I didn't plan on it, but sometimes you just have to go with the flow.'

'And with that flow you went! I thought you had a bit of a glow about you,' Gabby laughs. '*Ah*, man, well, I hope you know what you're doing.'

'I definitely don't. But I'm determined to be present with all of this.' We round a corner, and I grab Gabby and pull her back to hide.

'What are you doing?' she laughs.

'Look.' I whisper, pointing around the corner.

'At what?' she asks with amusement.

'Chris. He's getting on a bus!'

She looks at me with concern, 'Are you OK?'

'I think I'm paranoid. Something's going on with him.'

'He's getting on a bus, hon; what's suspicious about that?' she asks patiently while humouring me.

'Well,' I try to think of why I care so much. 'I don't know, but something feels off. It's a sibling thing, I guess. I know he's up to something.'

'Last minute Christmas shopping!' she says with a dark voice. 'The bastard.'

I laugh, as we watch him get on the bus and travel in the direction of the out-of-town shopping centre. 'Fine. It's all in my head. Maybe I want him to be up to something suspicious.' I link my arm through hers and we continue our walk. 'So, what do you have planned for the rest of your special day?'

'I've got to swing by the vets.'

'On your birthday?'

She shrugs, 'They're short-staffed, Scott has to work anyway, and it'll be nice to get away from my family for a bit. I love them, but family can be a lot.'

I laugh, 'You don't have to tell me.'

***

After a birthday lunch (on me) in The Mad Platter, Gabby heads off to work and I take the opportunity to stroll around the town. Having an aimless wander is therapeutic. In the last two years, I'm not sure my feet have touched the ground; Freya was like a whirlwind I was happy to get swept up in. It was a very welcome distraction. I throw my scarf in another loop around my neck and snuggle my gloveless hands into my pockets.

Perhaps it's time to decide to step out of the self-inflicted emotional tornado and into the sun. This year's nearly over. What do I want out of the next twelve months? If I allowed myself to think for a moment about this next year, where would I even begin?

Nick, a small voice says instantaneously. *I'd begin with Nick.*

My face spreads into a smile, not a subtle, small one, but a *show-all-of-my-teeth-at-the-same-time*, one.

And of course, it's at that exact moment, I see my parents. Across the street, Mum points at something in a window of the local haberdashery, and my dad patiently nods. They suddenly turn, so I do the same, ready for a speedy escape, but it's too late.

'Sophia!' Mum's voice bounces off every building and even if I wanted to deny that I'd heard her, it would be impossible.

Reluctantly I spin my body towards them, 'Hello.' I wave, and I watch, as they carefully cross the road.

'There you are. We're going for coffee,' Mum's cold eyes bore into me.

'Well, I won't keep you; enjoy.'

She disregards my comment and holds onto my arm, not linking hers through mine, more steering me in the direction she wants me. 'Come come.'

Dad and I stand in the queue at The Coffee Pot, Mum's favourite; I much prefer Frankie's. The Coffee Pot is unwelcoming and pretentious; black and white interior with no colour or sign of festive cheer apart from a token silver garland. It's not joyful or warm, which, I tell myself, is the perfect setting for coffee with my mother.

Mum is doing her usual rounds of finding the *right* table. The one I know she wants to sit at already has people on it. She's standing uncomfortably close to them, and I'm sure, will soon make them move. I look to my dad. 'So, how's it going?'

'Fine, fine. And you?'

Why can't he ever be honest? There must have been some tension in the house after I moved my stuff out of it. I exhale, failing to see the point in trying to have an open conversation with someone who doesn't want one, 'Fine.' I nod and look at the menu. 'What are you going for?'

'I'd like a gingerbread latte from Frankie's,' he says in a small voice. The honesty makes me laugh so loud, that my mum turns to scowl at me.

'Me too,' I say at the same volume, 'But since there isn't even a winter spiced blend, I guess just a standard latte, *huh*?'

'Good plan.' He nods.

We place our order and while waiting I turn to see Mum's progress. Sure enough, she's now sitting at the *right* table, its previous occupants having moved, disgruntledly, two tables over.

The frosty barrister places the drinks down and I carry the tray over to the table.

'Yes,' is Mum's opening remark, as if I'd ask her a question, 'Aria went to the doctors, and all is looking well for baby Carter.'

'That's good.' I say, meaning it, but wonder what exactly I'd like to say to this woman. May as well make the most of this. Maybe I could be brave enough to address something small; her reading my diary. I clear my throat, and go for it before I'm ready, 'Can we talk about the other night?'

'Which night?' Mum says, 'The one you stormed out after I'd been on my feet cooking all day?'

'No, the night of the Lanterns.'

'Yes, wasn't Aria wonderful.'

'I meant, you reading my diary, Mum. Can we have a calm conversation about that, please?'

She looks shocked, gazes around and slaps on a fake smile, 'I did no such thing.'

'You used to read my diary all the time when I was a kid.'

'I did not. I have no idea where you get such crazy ideas from; that Nicholas probably, he's always been a bad influence.'

I exhale. *Of course, we can't have a rational conversation.*

'Anyway, as I was saying, she's been so sick, poor thing. It's wonderful she was able to stand up and give such a rousing performance at the Lanterns; no one would have known what she's been through. She's just fantastic.'

'Right.' I swallow, and from nowhere, decide to continue being brave, 'So, maybe we could talk about why I left when—'

'She's so very strong, Aria. I'm proud of her. I honestly don't know what I'd do without her; there would be a huge hole in my life if she wasn't around all the time. Well, her and Christopher of course. It's important to have the people you love around you every day.' She sips her drink and I wonder if she's any idea how insulting that is. Perhaps that's the point? *OK, not the time to talk about something so deep.* I'll go for light instead,

'So, what are your plans for Christmas day?' I decide to move the conversation along in any other direction apart from the Aria and Chris fan club.

'Usual family affair. Aria's traditional breakfast.'

Since when did she have a tradition?

'Christopher is working so hard on finding the perfect job. I know the right thing will come along soon. He was so good at everything at school, any company would be lucky to have him.'

I always did better than Chris at school, but for some reason, his achievements were always viewed as greater than mine—still are, it would seem.

'Good thing he hasn't got a job just yet, it would be so horrible not to have him around on Christmas day, it wouldn't be the same without him.'

I clear my throat, noting that my lack of presence the last two years obviously meant nothing.

'The holiday season really is trying for a pregnant lady.'

I frown at the whiplash change of conversation.

'All the shopping, and the planning. She should just sit back, relax and let her loved ones take care of everything for her…'

After a solid twenty minutes of her talking *at* me, I make several attempts to steer the conversation then give up. She is determined to return my attention to Chris and Aria. I attempt to talk about my life, and my job, then again try to address anything real, including why I left two years ago, but she continues to spin me around in circles, never quite ending up where I began, dizzying my thoughts, making me forget what I'd said in the first place. Occasionally, I glance over at my dad; I'm not entirely convinced he's listening to a single word she's saying. He nods from time to time, but his eyes are glazed over, like my heart.

When we part, Mum says how nice it was to catch up after all this time of me being absent from their lives, having learnt absolutely nothing about me, and affirming in my mind, just how much Aria and Chris mean to her. I walk absent-mindedly to Frankie's with a desperate need to feel the warmth of his welcome and a sense of belonging.

***

When night falls, I peel myself out of my favourite, fire-side seat, and meet Gabby once more, my spirit feeling a tiny bit

203

brighter. We walk along to the main square, with Lilo and Stitch, following the sound of music. 'So, why is the Light Switch On only happening two days before Christmas?'

'Something to do with trying to save money, I think.'

'So they allowed the fairy lights on the bandstand, but not the tree or the main street?'

'The lights on the bandstand are solar powered; that's what they call a compromise.'

'*Huh.*' The icy wind hits my face as we turn a corner and a shiver runs down my spine. 'God, it's freezing,' I say, pulling my scarf up in an attempt to cover as much of my face as possible, then I blow on my hands and rub them together.

'Well, you're not wearing your gloves, again.' Gabby nods to my red-tinged cold hands.

'I left them at home—at Nick's I mean.'

Gabby shakes her head, 'God, please be careful with your heart, hon. I just hope you're not playing with fire.'

'Oh, I'm definitely playing with fire, but right now, it feels worth it.'

'Speaking of your flame,' Gabby nods towards the sound desk gazebo that's set up next to the stage, adjacent to the 20-foot Nordmann Fir, and a sizable, soon-to-be-lit, reindeer. Nick's in there, headphones on in concentration, getting ready to play the next track. He glances up and spots us; I give a shy wave. His face lights up when our eyes meet.

'Oh my God, he is still so in love with you.'

'Do you think?' I say, feeling my cheeks flush.

'Oh, I think you're both in trouble, hon.' Gabby smiles and waves, saying all of this through her teeth.

'Good evening, everybody, and welcome to this year's Light Switch On…' Nick greets the crowd. 'In just a few minutes, the mayor is going to turn on the reindeer!' Nick's face falls as he realises what he's just said over a microphone to the entire town. 'I mean, turn on the *lights* of the reindeer, the tree and, yeah, anyway...' A smile creeps across my face as he continues to make the audience laugh. I always loved watching him rally a crowd; he could easily be a stand-up comedian if he wanted to be. 'Next up we'll have a little Christmas favourite. Feel free to sing along,' Nick says through the mic and 'I'm Dreaming of a White Christmas' by Bing Crosby comes on. Nick places the mic down, takes off the headphones and comes over to us. My heart soars at the sight of him. I'm scared of the can of worms I've opened, but seeing his face, I know deep down that I'd do it all again. 'Hey there!' Nick stops in front of us. 'I've got something for you.' Reaching into his pocket, he fishes out my gloves.

'Thank you. What would I do without you?' I take the gloves, bashfully, regretting saying that out loud, as I am, technically, in reality, *without him*. I put them on and it's not until that moment it occurs to me: my family might be here.

'So, busy day, Gabs?' Nick asks, I reckon trying to sense out if I've told her or not.

'Not too bad; that Staffy was in again.'

'What did she eat this time?' he chuckles.

'A peach pit. I swear, I'm going to install her with a zip soon.'

'At least it wasn't glass this time,' I remark, remembering her telling us about this dog eating her way through a glass jar of peanut butter; the owners fed her bread for a few days to bloat her out, and miraculously, a few days later, she pooped out the shard of glass with no injuries.

'I think she's a cat deep down; she's had at least six lives so far; bless her.'

'Alright, well, I'll get back to the booth. Come over if you fancy.' The last part was aimed at me.

'Thanks, I might do that.' We lock eyes and he knows that I don't want to draw too much attention to myself or to the fact that we're…whatever we are. I resist the urge to kiss him good luck, and he turns back to the mixing desk gazebo.

'Like I said, you are both in big trouble.' Gabby bends down to pet the dogs and I watch Nick go.

The crowd starts to grow and excitedly gathers in front of the stage. Nick's the bread of the entertainment sandwich tonight, playing before and after the band. I still haven't decided if I'm going to go up and sing a bit of harmony yet. The band is super relaxed about it and told me to go with my gut when I arrive, so, I'm going to let my gut decide at the last moment.

I gaze around nervously, biting a nail, feeling the anxiety of potentially performing, mixed with the dread of waiting to spot my family, and for the shit to hit the fan once more.

'I don't spot them either,' Gabby says from my side, knowing exactly where my head is.

'They'll be lurking in some dark corner ready to pounce on me.'

Gabby laughs, 'Good to know you're not over-dramatising the situation.'

I raise an eyebrow, 'Habits are hard to break.'

More people are arriving and my anxiety is starting to worsen. 'I don't think I'll get up and sing,' I say to Gabby.

She shrugs, 'There's no pressure hon. Would be nice to see you up there, though,' she smiles encouragingly at me.

As we move around and say hi to a few people, I keep glancing over at Nick, each time I do, he's looking over at me too. We smile at each other and then look away quickly; there's no way either of us wants the town gossiping over this. When one person knows, everyone knows.

Nick's now playing, 'Warm This Winter' by Gabriella Cilmi. I smile as he knows that's one of my favourites. I'm pretty sure that he's created a playlist just for me, as each song has a memory or story behind it that he's played so far. I feel like he's talking to me through the music.

Out of the corner of my eye, I see the band arriving, I try to swallow my fear, and get out of my own way, 'You know what, I think I'm going to do it,' I say to Gabby, ever the person to swing wildly from one decision to another.

'Good for you! Let's head over there before you change your mind.' Gabby puts an arm around me. As we walk over, I see the guys, who, honestly, look a little nervous themselves.

'Hi, everyone, this is my best friend, Gabby.' They all shake hands but there's an air of loss. 'Everything OK?'

Jerry looks at me, 'Gina's sick. Throwing up everywhere. She said she ate some questionable sushi earlier, so I don't know what we're going to do. We can make a few of them work where she's the lead, we've done that before, but…' his voice drifts off as he looks at me.

'But what?' I ask.

'I've seen you singing along as we've been recording; how well do you know the songs, would you say?'

I let out a hoot of laughter, 'Oh, no. I can't sing a full set, are you kidding me?'

'I know, it's a lot to ask, considering you were just going to pop your vocals on one track tonight, but, look,' Jerry hands me the set list, 'it's all the songs you've heard us record, plus a couple of Christmas ones.' Glancing down the list I know that as terrifying as this is, I could pull this off. I return my eyes to his eager gaze; he looks confidently at me, 'I just have a feeling.'

'All set guys?' Nick joins us backstage.

'Gina's sick, we were asking if Sophie would be up for singing the whole set,' Jerry the lead, catches Nick up.

Nick looks at me, sensing how overwhelmed I am right now.

Jerry continues, 'We've got stands for our iPads, we'll stick that to yours,' he takes the set list piece of paper from me, 'And all the charts are on my iPad here, you can use that; it'll be right in front of you the whole time.' My head is starting to spin. 'If you can sing Gina's line for each song, apart from the track you recorded, just stick with your harmony, I'll do Gina's part. No point in confusing things. I wouldn't ask if I didn't think you could pull it off.' He looks at me seriously, 'Do you think you can do it?'

Chapter 17

My heart is now in my mouth as everyone is staring, awaiting my answer. I swallow and say the first thing on my mind, 'There's a big crowd; the whole town is here.'

'That's a good thing,' Jerry says, casually. 'The bigger the audience, the less pressure.' I look at him doubtfully, so he continues to try to convince me, 'I find if you're just singing to one person or a smaller group, it's much more intense; they pay closer attention. Luckily on a gig like this, most people have had a few mulled wines or spiced ciders; they're not really listening to us.'

'It's just like karaoke,' Gabby chips in.

'There's no pressure though if you don't want to, Soph,' Nick looks at me. I feel safe under his gaze. I trust him and somehow, he has always managed to calm my nerves. 'But if you're up for it, you know you've got this.'

I subconsciously rub my forehead. I did feel amazing after recording the track, plus, once upon a time, on some level (the one before my mum's criticism wore me down), I did love performing at school. I exhale nervously, 'OK.'

'Alright!' The band high-five, 'Can't tell you how much we appreciate this, Sophie. *Ooh*, what's your last name?' Jerry questions.

'Carter.'

'Well, Sophie Carter, you have made my night.' He smiles and I nod, somewhat numb to what I've just agreed to do. 'Take my iPad, have a look through the charts. Any questions, I'm here.' The band resumes setting up, and I try to settle my nerves while reading the charts and reminding myself of the songs I've heard on repeat, over the past three days. I go over a few bits with Jerry, right up until the moment I'm about to go on. The rest of the band walks up the stairs at the back of the stage, and I grip onto the railing.

'What the hell have I agreed to?' I say, looking alarmingly at Nick.

His expression calms me, even before he's said anything, 'Having a great time, and showing off your talent.'

Still backstage, away from prying eyes, Nick kisses me swiftly on the cheek, 'And if it helps, I believe in you.'

And that does it. I nod and turn, the feeling of his faith in me carrying my legs up the stairs, and onto the stage, to join the band. I place the iPad I'm hugging on the stand, and say a couple of "one-twos" to test the mic, all the while trying not to look at the faces in the audience, and glancing just above their heads; my eyes focus on the scissors sign of the hairdressers, Nick's mum used to own.

'Alright, we've got one more song from me,' I hear Nick's voice, talking to the audience, 'then we'll be switching on those lights and welcoming the up-and-coming band, Rise and Shine!' Nick presses play on Mariah Carey's, 'All I Want for Christmas.'

'You alright?' Jerry asks, and I nod, ignoring the fact that I feel like I'm going to throw up. I try to allow myself to believe that I can do this, then without warning, I spot them, wearing shocked expressions, and staring right at me. My body freezes, judgement reads all over my mum's face and Aria looks like someone has just slapped her. My brother is frowning and whispering something to Aria with his hand over his mouth, right into her ear, like a five-year-old bully. My dad gives me a weak smile and a thumbs up. Suddenly, I find my body turning, and my feet walking backstage. 'Hey, where're you going?' Jerry calls after me, but I don't stop.

Climbing back down the stairs, my breathing has gotten heavier. Nick catches my eye, then removes his headphones and rushes towards me.

'They're here...I can't...it's too much...it's...I...no...' I gasp for air, clearly on the brink of a panic attack.

He puts his hands gently on my arms, and strokes them slightly, 'You're OK. You're safe. Breathe. Can you repeat that for me?' he says calmly. 'You're OK.'

'I'm...OK'

'You're safe.'

'I'm safe.'

'Breathe.'

I try to take a deep breath and find I can't catch my breath at all.

We repeat this several times until I feel my heart rate lowering. Nick's eyes stay steady on me. 'You don't have to do this, but remember that you are more than good enough, and worthy.'

I feel my eyes prickle with tears as I repeat his sentiment, somewhat unconvincingly, 'I am good enough. I am worthy.'

'Yes, you are. And not that it matters, but Aria had a whole set the other day and her voice isn't a patch on yours. You can do this.'

Losing myself, I grab his face and kiss him on the lips. When we break apart, I exhale, and look at his slightly shocked expression, 'Whoops.'

He laughs, 'We're backstage, I doubt anyone saw that.' His expression reads that he doesn't care either way if it remains a secret or not. 'You've got this, Soph.' He takes my hand and gives it a squeeze.

'Thank you,' I squeeze back then let go. Mariah is approaching her famous high note in the song's outro, and I take this opportunity to walk back on the stage, this time, with some newfound confidence. Screw them. Plus, if I can watch Freya do this every night to tens of thousands of people, I can absolutely sing to a couple hundred.

Jerry looks relieved as I take my spot next to him, 'Sorry about that. I'm ready now,' I say with slightly wobbly confidence.

As Mariah (and the crowd) are finishing her song, the mayor walks up on stage to join us, 'Nice to see you, Sophie! Didn't know you were in a band?'

'Well, I'm not, really, I'm just covering.'

She smiles at me, 'Well, I can't wait to hear you; it's been far too long since we heard that fabulous voice of yours.'

'Thank you.' I step aside so she can use my mic, as the song fades out.

'Good evening one and all!' The mayor has a warm, approachable nature, despite having worked alongside my mother for years. She's been the mayor for as long as I can remember. No one has ever wanted to go up against her, and she's never wanted to step down. She must be in her late 70s now. 'Who's ready for a countdown?'

The crowd cheers and Jerry leans into me, 'The set list is here,' he points to a sheet of paper, sellotaped to my stand. 'I believe in you.' I smile and glance down to the set list and reassure myself I know the order; we're starting with the one I sang harmony on, so at least that will ease me in.

'Alright, in, THREE, TWO, ONE!'

I glance over to Nick, who, I see from the corner of my eye, mouthing, 'Happy New Year!' at me, making me smile. It's stupid, I know, but sometimes the stupid things in life force you out of your head and into the moment.

The lights above our heads, on the tree, and in the reindeer, flicker on and the crowd cheers. I turn back to Jerry, and smiling, he counts the band in. The intro starts and the mayor segues, 'Please give a warm welcome to Rise and Shine!' Everyone claps, and I tell myself that the crowd is there to support, not analyse me. Every other person has a phone up, clearly ready to record. I try to swallow my fear of being immortalised in video form. I spot my high school bully, Whitney, alongside some of the busy-body mums; I will myself to look away. I don't allow myself to look over to the spot where my family is standing, instead, I look to Gabby. She's now standing next to Scott, who I guess has just arrived. They both cheer me on.

As I near my entry, I promise myself that I'm going to enjoy this. When I begin, I'm nervous but somehow don't sound it. The guys are encouraging and by the end of the second chorus, I'm really into it. I don't care that my family, among others, are out there, probably judging me; something takes over my body, and it's like I was always supposed to be up here.

When we get to the end of the song, the audience erupts into applause. I grin as Jerry talks effortlessly, and charismatically plays with them; I've always been so envious of people being able to talk to a crowd. I don't think I could ever be that person; I reckon I'd get in a pickle, saying everything backwards or mixed up somehow, and get laughed at. Plus, the persistent voice in my head tells me that nothing I have to say is important enough to hear.

Jerry looks at me, snapping me back into the present, and I force myself to stay rooted to the stage and out of my head.

As we make our way through the set, I've no idea how, but I feel more and more at home. Each of the four original songs I enjoy performing, with, admittedly, a little improv on my part in places, but the band seem more than satisfied.

I breathe a sigh of relief when we arrive at the Christmas songs. First up is, 'What Are You Doing New Year's Eve', followed by 'Baby it's Cold Outside'. I remember teaching both of these songs in my brief side job as a vocal coach, so, I feel like the pressure is off a bit.

'Ladies and gentlemen, I'd like to share something with you,' Jerry says as I sip from a bottle of water I've just been handed by the bassist. 'To my right is Miss Sophie Carter.' To my surprise, the crowd cheers the loudest it has so far, making me giggle with embarrassment and I give a little wave. 'Tonight, she was just going to add some harmonies to one song, but after telling her our usual female vocalist had fallen ill, she stepped up. So, just before we get into our penultimate song, can you please show your appreciation, once more, for Sophie!'

I can't help but smile and I glance over at the sound desk gazebo; Nick's beaming at me and enthusiastically cheering more than anyone. I push away the voice that says I don't deserve this and breathe in the moment. I look out at the faces in front of me and this time focus on the positive people: friends I used to go to school with, some old teachers, shop owners, and neighbours I've known since I was little. They're cheering. For me. I shake my head slightly and allow the clapping to die down before saying, 'Thank you', shyly, through the mic.

'Alright, so, next up, we've got a Christmassy duet for you—'

'Actually, that's not quite right,' I realise I've said this over the mic, and Jerry, the lead, looks at me with amusement.

'It's not? Pray tell, Soph.' He leans casually on the mic stand.

'Well…' I clear my throat, 'the daughter of Frank Loesser, who wrote the song, said he used to get annoyed when people sang it at Christmas time, as it was written about a relationship where the guy is so keen, he wants to know if they're in a long-term relationship, so poses the question, "What are you doing New Years' Eve?" during Spring time.'

'*Huh*,' Jerry takes me in, impressed, and continues to talk through the mic, 'fascinating. Well, all the same,' he picks up a ukulele from its stand to the left of him, 'it's the next one in our set list, so, hopefully, Mr Loesser won't mind.'

I laugh loudly through the mic, along with the crowd, then press my lips together, not quite believing that I said that so casually in front of a crowd. I make eye contact with the band and nod to say I'm ready. Jerry starts strumming the uke, creating a Hawaiian vibe. I'm just about to start singing when I hear Scott's voice over a microphone.

'Sorry, sorry, everyone.' The band stops and looks around to see where this disembodied voice has come from. 'I hate to interrupt, but there's just something that I'd like to say.' I turn and Scott is making his way to the front of the stage, with a wireless hand-held mic in hand.' I step to the side to make room for him, glancing over to Nick, whose playful eyes sparkle at me. Scott is now at the front of the stage, looking out. 'Evening, everyone. For those who don't know me, my name's Scott.' There are several murmurings in the audience and my stomach goes into an excited knot; I know what he's about to do. 'And,' he clears his throat, 'for the past five years, I've been going out with that lovely lady right there,' he points, 'Gabby.' The audience hushes. 'For those who don't know her either, it's her birthday today.' Cue a smattering of applause and cheers before returning to silence. I take in Gabby's face, somewhere between horrified and excited. 'She always says to me that nothing special can ever happen on her birthday, as it's so close to Christmas, so, I wanted this year to be a little more…memorable.' He grins. 'Would you mind letting her through to the front please?' The crowd parts instantaneously, and she and the dogs start to walk to the front. I see one of her brothers come out of nowhere, and grab the leads, so she takes a solo walk to the front. 'Gabby. We've been together for five years, but I've been in love with you since I was five years old.' I stand back further, letting him have the stage, as he gets down on one knee, producing a ring from his back pocket; the audience gasps, 'We might not have everything figured out, but I know that wherever I'm going, I want you there with me.' I glance over to Nick, who's watching me, not Scott. 'Gabby,' I smile at Nick then bring my eyes back to Scott, 'would you please do me the honour of becoming my wife?' Gabby's eyes are filled with tears, and she nods before shouting,

'YES! YES!! Of course I'll marry you.' Scott leans down, places the ring on her finger, then leaves the mic on the stage, before hopping down to kiss her. The audience erupts into applause, as, misty-eyed, I watch two of my best friends embrace; my heart brimming with joy.

'Ladies and gentlemen,' Jerry takes the lead, 'Please give it up for the newly engaged couple!' he then leans into me and says off mic, 'You able to keep going?' I clear my throat and nod. 'Alright, we'd like to dedicate this next song to Gabby and—' Jerry looks at me.

'Scott,' I say off mic.

'Gabby and Scott, this one's for you.' Jerry replays the intro, and this time there are no interruptions. The fun duet reminds me of a version Nick showed me, that Zooey Deschanel and Joseph Gordon-Levitt did. As I'm singing, I smile down at Gabby and Scott, arms around each other, but occasionally allow myself to look back over to Nick, who's looking at me like I'm the only person on the planet. When Jerry and I reach the last line in harmony, applause breaks out once more, and I realise I don't want this to end. I'm loving every single second.

Our final song flies by with the audience joining in with gusto. Both Jerry and I take our mics off the stands and move around the stage as if we'd rehearsed a choreographed routine. At the last line, he grabs me, we twirl, and he dips me. Straightening up, Jerry gives me a huge hug, 'You freaking rock, Sophie,' he says in my ear.

Returning our mics to the stand, the rest of the band come to the front to stand next to us, making a line. We all hold hands and bow together to thunderous applause.

'Give it up, for Rise and Shine!' Nick's voice sounds through the speakers, 'And let's hear it once again, for Gabby and Scott; congratulations guys!' then he plays Elton John's 'Step into Christmas'.

Heading backstage the band is delirious. 'We nailed that!' the drummer says, patting me on the back.

'That was insane,' the bassist gives me a hug,

'Can't thank you enough, Sophie,' the keyboard player exclaims.

'It was fun! I can't believe how well that went if I'm honest,' I admit as I watch Nick, once more, leaving his mixing desk to walk over.

When he reaches my side, he scoops me up in his arms, 'Man, it's good to see you up there; you were incredible.'

'That can't be our last performance with you, Sophie,' Jerry says as Nick reluctantly lets me go.

'Well,' I shrug. That would be awesome, but I don't allow myself to say that out loud.

He points at me, 'That was not our last performance,' Jerry says as a statement.

I smile, 'OK, then. Alright, I'm going to find Gabby and Scott and congratulate them,' I say but then my heart sinks.

'Well, that was unexpected,' I hear her voice before I see her face and feel my whole body deflate.

'Backstage is for performers,' Nick says, not able to hide the spite in his voice.

'I am a performer,' Aria says arrogantly to Nick then turns to me. 'So, what was that about? You felt the need to upstage me?'

'What?'

'I performed yesterday, so you felt you had to? It's a bit sad really. And that stunt with them getting engaged to distract from you? Pathetic.'

'Hi, we haven't been introduced,' Jerry holds out his hand to Aria. She looks him up and down and then a welcoming smile spreads across her face.

'Aria; I'm Sophie's sister-in-law.'

'...to be,' I correct her.

She shrugs, 'Much of a muchness. You know, if you're ever looking for a *real* singer to dep, I'm available for events and touring.'

'Are you? You're pregnant,' I remind her.

Again, she shrugs, 'Yeah, so? Your parents can always babysit. Anyway, just saying, as I thought you might want more…options.' She looks me up and down and I suddenly feel embarrassed.

You didn't do a good job.

'I think that's enough, Aria,' Nick says protectively.

'Why don't you mind your own business, Nicholas? Anyway, I'm just back here to invite you for drinks at ours.'

'At *my parent's* you mean?'

'Yes, ours,' she says arrogantly.

I feel a jolt of guilt, but I'm not sure that's the right thing to do. 'Thanks, but I don't think that's a good idea, do you?'

'Well, if I'm being honest, no, but Mum requested.'

We stare at each other, each knowing full well that it's never a *request*, it's an expectation.

'Plus, Dad wants to spend more time with you.'

And there it is, the guilt bomb; statements that are always closely followed, to make me feel ashamed for doing anything else, other than spending time with them. I feel myself wavering.

You should. You're not planning on spending Christmas with them. How selfish you are, Sophie.

'Well, we're all going to go for a drink now in The Swan; maybe you could join us?' Jerry's friendly offer hangs in the air, oblivious to any family tension.

'Sure. We could do that,' Aria says, aiming to match his tone but I can sense something bitter in her voice.

219

I exhale, as Jerry looks at me, misreading my expression, 'Unless you'd rather be with your family?'

I don't know how to respond to that politely. 'I'd really like to go for drinks with you all,' I commit to saying out loud.

'Then it's settled then,' Aria glows. 'I'll rally up the family and we'll see you there.' We watch her sashay off.

'I've got to finish the set, but I'll come as soon as I can. Maybe an hour?' Nick looks at me with worry and I try to reassure him I'll be alright.

'We'll be in public; nothing dramatic will happen.'

'I'm sure Gabs and Scott will be up for a congratulatory drink too.'

'They're both working early tomorrow, but they'll probably come for one. Don't worry, I'll be fine.'

Nick looks doubtfully at me, 'I'll get there as soon as I can,' he repeats, then shakes each of the band members' hands, 'Great set, guys. See you later.' And with that, he darts off before the track finishes.

'I'm sorry, did I misread the situation there?' Jerry asks, and I shake my head.

'Don't worry about it. It's a long story.'

'Families, *eh*?'

I shake my head. 'You've no idea.'

***

Gabby and Scott are beaming and it warms my heart. After a debrief of what just happened—of course, Nick was in on it—I marvel at her blue topaz princess cut ring. Then two soft drinks later (and since my family are actually behaving themselves, sitting in a corner, not interacting with anyone) my best friend and her new fiancé decide to head home.

'Remember, you can leave any time you want to,' Gabby reminds me of my own free will, as she gives me a hug.

'We're in public, my mum won't say anything when people are watching.'

'All the same,' Scott puts his arms around me and gives me a squeeze, 'leave if you need to.'

'I will. Now, go get some sleep,' I raise an eyebrow at Gabby, knowing she won't be going straight to sleep. 'Congratulations again guys.'

'Remember that you are strong, brave, and brilliant,' are Scott's parting words as I pet the dogs goodbye, and then go back to join the band.

I can't believe that my family hasn't come over yet. I pick up my glass of wine and take a sip.

'You're getting low,' Jerry nods at my glass, 'let me get you another.'

'Oh, no, don't worry. I'll get the next ones.'

'Absolutely not,' the pianist goes to stop me, but I'm too quick and grab my purse from under the pile of coats.

'Same again?' I point to all of them, and they give me a mix of "thanks", thumbs up and "cheers". I head over to the bar to place the order.

'A large sauvignon blanc, two bottles of Heineken, a BrewDog IPA, and a Guinness, please.' The barman goes to start my order and a skinny hand stops him with a clearing of her throat while simultaneously wrapping her fingers commandingly around his wrist.

'We'll also have a Coors with lime, a large merlot, a single brandy, and a cranberry juice please,' Aria loosens her grip and the barman raises his eyebrows but doesn't say anything. He obediently gets to work as fast as he can, beginning with the Guinness and IPA to let them settle.

Taking a deep breath, the whole family comes over to join me. 'Hello,' I say as pleasantly as I can, and look at them all, awaiting their analysis of my performance, or to somehow make me feel small or need to apologise for something I haven't done.

'Oh, so nice of you to acknowledge our presence!' Mum says, looking me up and down, like I'm the one in the wrong, as always.

'You could have come over to me,' I say, stronger than I feel.

'You could have invited us over.'

Excellent point, Mum. I wonder why I'm reluctant.

The barman continues to place the drinks down in front of us, avoiding eye contact with each of us.

'I'll get these darling,' my dad says, getting out his wallet.

'No, it's fine, I'm buying for the band too. It's no problem.' I smile weakly at him.

'Well, how kind of you, Sophia,' Mum says with sarcasm. 'Please don't go out of your way with an act of generosity on our account; we know money is an issue for you when it comes to helping out your family.'

I open my mouth to say something but my dad speaks up and changes the subject. 'It was lovely to see you on stage, sweetheart. How did that come about?'

'Yes, we're all dying to know,' Aria's the one with sarcasm this time.

I'm reluctant to tell them that I've been spending time at Nick's studio, always one to share too much and have it come back to bite me on the arse. I hear my therapist in my head reminding me that I have a right to create boundaries and that I don't have to share everything. 'Right time, right place, I guess,' I commit to saying out loud, as the bartender hands me my wine, not a moment too soon. I gulp a little and wait for the next interrogation.

'Instagram says the band is from a few towns over, how did *you* meet them? Have they been in New York, or something?' My brother tries this time to find out how I could possibly have this kind of connection.

'I've come to know their music only quite recently,' that's kind of true, 'and the normal female lead was sick, so I was asked to cover.'

'Oh, that makes sense,' Mum says, 'it did sound like you weren't too familiar with the material.'

I shut my eyes for a moment and try to focus on my breath; it's caught in my chest.

'I thought you sounded lovely.'

'Thanks, Dad.' I give a small smile at his attempt to stand up for me.

'What did you think, Mum?' Aria asks, glowing with anticipation of the pre-empted assassination of my talents.

'*Hmm.*' Mum makes a face, 'Oh, my opinion doesn't matter.'

I glare at her, knowing that she's going to give it anyway. 'Go on,' I can't help but say, instantly knowing I'll regret it.

'Well, if I'm being completely honest,' Mum puts her voice to a whispering level, 'the lights were catching your glasses, which was very distracting; I told you, you should always wear contacts. Speaking of lights, they completely washed you out—when did you stop wearing makeup? Plus, you were a little sharp in places, Sophia. It showed that you've been in the wings of the stage rather than on it, and truth be told, I was a little embarrassed for you.'

'Wow. OK, then.' I put my Visa on the card reader to pay, then stand a little taller, and pop my wine on the tray of drinks, to take over to the boys. 'Well, thank you.'

'Thank me? For what?' Mum asks with shock and wavering pride.

'Thank you for showing me exactly why I have chosen to distance myself from you; you've shown me exactly who I don't want to be.' I pick up the tray, shocked that I've said that out loud, and go to walk off. 'Enjoy your drinks.'

'Let me help you with that, Soph,' Jerry is now at my side and takes the tray from me before spotting the rest of the Carters. 'Oh, you must be the family!' He pops the tray back down and extends a hand to them. 'I'm Jerry, leader of Rise and Shine.'

Mum's the first to accept his hand. 'I'm Aubrey; Sophia's Mum.' She puts her left hand to her heart and fake tears fill her eyes, as if the thought of me being her daughter, and that I've achieved something, is too much for her to handle.

'Sophia? I thought it was Sophie.'

'It is,' I say quietly to him and he gives me a confused look but doesn't question further.

When Jerry hasn't reacted to her emotional display, she introduces everyone, her tears suddenly vanishing, 'This is my husband, Richard, my son, Christopher, and daughter, Aria.'

I feel my skin prickle at the warmth in her voice as she says, "...daughter, Aria", and try to focus on my breath.

'Pleasure to meet you all. You must be super proud of Sophie here, *huh*?' Jerry says, casually leaning on the bar.

'Oh, yes, of course we are. We were just telling Sophie so.'

I scoff and try to pass it off as a cough before sipping my wine again and placing it back on the tray.

'Our socials are blowing up,' Jerry looks excitedly at me, 'Light in My Fire' has had 50,000 views already.'

'Excuse me, what? 50? As in 5-0?'

Jerry grins, 'Yeah crazy, isn't it?' He turns back to my family, 'So, does music run in the family then?' Jerry leans in.

'Well, I hate talking about it…'

That's rubbish, she loves talking about it.

'…but when I was younger, performing was my life. I was a lounge singer you see, and a backing vocalist, performing regularly in the West End and on Broadway; I even danced with The Radio City Rockettes for years. But then I decided to sacrifice my dreams, to have a family.'

'Amazing. No wonder Sophie's a natural on stage.' My mum's face screws up, she won't like him now, as he's complimented me, and taken the attention away from her. 'Would you like to join us?' Jerry offers considerately.

'Thank you, but, no. Don't want to disturb your afterparty. I think we'll just drink up here, and then better get going. Aria's pregnant, you see, so she needs her rest.' Mum places a loving hand on her and it somehow feels like a rejection towards me; we couldn't possibly stay and celebrate something that I've achieved.

Jerry holds my wine out for me to take, then grabs the tray again, 'Alright, well, great to meet you all. I'm so glad Sophie came to the studio. Thanks for these; see you over there in a bit.' He smiles at me kindly, then walks off, not realising what he's just done.

'So, that's where you've been hiding, at *his* studio,' Aria says with distaste.

Victoria Mae

'Good evening, Carters. How are we?' Nick's voice is behind me, then suddenly he's at my side.

'Well, here he is, Saint Nicholas, to save the day!' Chris says, looking Nick up and down and clearly wanting to do nothing more than punch him in the face.

'Wasn't Sophie spectacular up there today?' Nick says strongly, completely ignoring my brother or any tension.

My dad smiles kindly, clearly his voice has been lost once more.

'Of course,' is Mum's response. '*We* asked to have a drink with *her*, didn't we? We are always so proud of her achievements.'

'Heard you say you're off now. Shame you can't stay for a toast to Sophie, then,' Nick tests my mum's level of support. You can tell she's wavering. She's stubborn, so she won't back down, or be proved to be wrong. She looks over to the bar, takes the glass of merlot, and raises it. 'To Sophia—'

'Sophie,' Nick interrupts and corrects her.

'That's what I said.' She looks at me as if it's so hard to find something positive rather than critical to say, 'Congratulations.' Her face is straight as she takes a sip, and with no warmth in her eyes, or love in her voice, there's just a cold iciness that runs down the length of my spine. And with that look, the little voice in my head takes over, all pride in what I've just done instantly washes out of me.

You do not deserve to be celebrated.
You've hurt them, not the other way around.
You don't deserve to have these feelings.
You've shone too brightly.
You really are selfish.
It's all your fault, Sophie.

226

Beneath the Mask

You should never have gone on that stage.
You don't deserve to be seen.
You should never have come back here.
You don't belong anywhere.

Chapter 18

After a few sips my family left, leaving the drinks I'd just bought them, mostly undrunk.

I tried to be fully present and celebrate with Nick and the band, but I'd travelled too far down the negative thought train. I'd let myself feel everything. The negative and untrue thoughts curse through my veins disguised as truths. Their words of criticism display as facts in my mind. But the strongest, was my mum's stare, burning right through me somehow, creating suffocating yet unexplainable shame.

Whenever that would happen as a kid, I learnt to push it down, smile, and pretend that everything was OK. I learnt that unless feelings are positive, or reflect well on the family, they are not to be shared. Now I've been in therapy, everything is just below the surface; I've dug around, found the things I've been hiding or denying, and sometimes it's so overwhelmingly painful, I wish I could just bury them all again to feel "normal." Funny how we learn to live with toxicity running through our veins and define it as normal, and when it's not there, anything that's truly safe, feels wrong or, sadly, "unsafe." And regardless of all the work I've done on myself—the inner work—it's excruciating sometimes, and liberating the next. In this moment, none of it matters. My coping mechanisms feel unreachably far away, and I've surrendered to the powerlessness of it all. I've got to the point of wanting to shrink, curl up, and retreat from the world.

Even as Nick and I walk back to the flat, I can't find the words. I share what Mum said, but nothing more. Nick gives me the mental space for us to walk in silence.

We arrive back, I take off my shoes, but then walk over and sit numbly on the couch, still wearing my coat.

'You're going to get a little hot wearing that,' Nick says kindly while lighting the log burner. He offers a hand to me to take my jacket.

'Yeah.' I wriggle out of it, pass it to him, and then find I'm staring at the flames dancing in the fire.

He walks back to the coat stand, hangs it next to his, then pauses in the doorframe, 'Do you want to be left alone?' I shake my head. 'Do you want me to sit with you?' he checks, and I nod. Nick comes over and sits next to me. I shift, bring my legs up onto the couch, lower down, and place my head on his lap. As I snuggle in, Nick starts stroking my hair. I like it. I shut my eyes, caught, once again between contentment and feeling like I don't deserve to be. 'How are they still like that?' he asks.

A hollow laugh escapes my lips, 'Like you said, they don't think they need to change. I hate them, but I also love them. It's like a never-ending mind-fuck.'

Nick makes a sad agreeable noise, then we return to a comfortable, understanding silence. I try to match my breath with his. I try not to overthink. But I'm triggered, and my negative habits are too strong; my mind starts reeling.

Regardless of all the crap that we went through with my family, the lies they told, and the drama they caused, the unnecessary divide they created, this is the main reason Nick and I broke up; we couldn't have a life together because I was so all-consumed with my family. Not that either of us ever admitted that, but whenever I did something for myself or us, it was deemed "selfish", and I believed it. Whenever I had a difference of opinion, I'd be "betraying the family", and I believed it. Whenever I didn't drop everything for them, just because they demanded it, I was "too busy and important", and I believed it. I became a shell of a person, with nothing to give myself or the relationship. My focus was constantly on them; how they would react, what they might say, obsessing over what they did say, and what that implied, how I was supposed to clean up their messes and lift them up to make them feel happy, seen and heard. I believed I didn't matter because that was what was implied. Even in my childhood, if I was successful, I was told to be quiet because it might upset Chris; I guess I just carried that into adulthood.

Throughout our entire relationship, I was living in a state of constant hypervigilance, mixed with survival mode. In some ways, I still am. Nick tried to support me, and tried to stand up to them when he could. But of course, they didn't like that, and so he was written as the villain of the piece. He was fucking up the status quo. He tried to show me how unhealthy my relationship was with them, and I couldn't believe it, it was too hard to accept that as truth. He tried to help me find my voice and place in this world, but I fought so hard against it, believing that I wasn't good enough, worthy or deserving of success, or even love. Love has to be earned, doesn't it? Love is conditional, right?

I had no idea what I truly had with Nick, or how lucky I was to have it. I think I took our love and life for granted because I didn't understand that what we had was *unconditional* love. He saw me for all that I was and loved me for all that I wasn't.

'I'm sorry for all I put you through when we were together.'

He lets out a little laugh, 'What are you talking about?'

I stay in my horizontal position, staring at the fire. 'The way I allowed my past to dictate our present and suffocate our future.'

He exhales, 'You really want to talk about this now?'

'I don't know,' I say honestly.

Nick exhales once more, 'Alright, well, first, you don't need to apologise. Second, it wasn't always, but, yeah, I suppose that's true. It got to the point where your family became the only thing we talked about; there was no room for us. We'd try to make sense of the latest thing that they'd done to you, or I'd lose you for days while you struggled with the fear of what might happen. We couldn't plan holidays or occasions until we knew what they were doing. We'd tiptoe around them like a bomb that was about to go off just to avoid an explosion. It was tough, and then…how they were in the end, just became too much, you know?'

'I know.' I sigh loudly, watching a mesmerising flame flicker.

'You were trapped in a world you felt you couldn't get out of. I guess you're still kind of there.'

'It's hard to rewire your whole brain.'

'I bet.'

We fall silent again then I roll over onto my back to look up at him, 'I'm sorry.'

He shakes his head, 'I told you, you don't need to apologise, I get it.' He continues to stroke my hair.

'No, I do. I'm sorry for not being present in our lives. I just…it just felt impossible to let go of them and live my own life. Even tonight, I let them barricade my mind and belittle me to my face.' I can feel tears wanting to form in my eyes.

'Tonight,' Nick looks at me with fierce conviction, 'what you did was freaking awesome. You'd known those songs for what, three days? And you went up there, like the pro that you are, and performed the set like you'd been doing it for years.'

'It wasn't that impressive.'

'You never allow yourself the grace to give yourself a compliment.'

I shrug, 'The small voice in my head's saying, "Well, that's because I don't deserve it; it could have been better", followed by, "Exactly, it wasn't perfect, was it?"'

'All that voice is, is the worst version of your mum and Aria. I know it seems impossible, but you don't have to tune into it.' He sighs, 'Please give yourself credit for what happened tonight.'

'I'm trying.'

'I think you need to get out of your head.'

'No kidding.' I wipe a tear away that's escaped.

'Maybe tomorrow we can do something to get your mind off everything.'

'Like what? It's Christmas Eve; everything worth booking is probably already booked up by now,' I say sulkily.

'I don't know.' He thinks for a minute, and a smile spreads across his face, 'I've got a few ideas.'

Chapter 19

24th December

Nick and I slept next to each other, but not *with* each other last night; somehow, that felt closer. Without question, he held me tight and gently kissed my shoulder, before I fell asleep wrapped in his arms. Maybe we're done with the other kind of intimacy and perhaps four times was enough?

I look over at him as he's driving me to a secret location in his Mercedes E Class, and a naughty smile spreads across my face; four times is definitely not enough.

We wind along the country lanes and I wonder where he's taking me. I've made guesses but he won't give any hints as to what he's got on his mind. After about 45 minutes, we pull up at an industrial estate. If I weren't with a man I completely trust, I'd think I was about to be bumped off.

'Here we are!' Nick says excitedly, as if we've pulled up at Disneyland or something. He puts the car in park, then pushes the button to turn the engine off.

'And where is *here*, exactly?' I smile, looking around at numerous closed, metal-shutter-fronted units around us.

'You'll have to just wait and see, won't you?' His enthusiasm rubbing off on me, we quickly undo our seatbelts and get out of the car. The settled snow scrunches under my boots, as I walk to the front of the car. I can see a plough has pushed the weeks' worth of snow to one side, creating a little mountain. Nick joins me and takes my hand before leading me slowly forward.

233

'Now, I know you don't want to admit it, but there's most likely some anger still in you.'

'You think I'm angry at you?' I say, horrified.

Nick smiles, and looks at me pointedly, 'No.'

'At my family you mean?'

He nods, 'At your family, the situation, the past, the present; I thought you might like to let some of that go.'

'And how exactly?' I look around at the inoffensive buildings presented to me, and he guides me towards one.

'In here.'

I smile as I read the door's sign, and we step in.

'Welcome to The Rage Room!' A smiley guy who looks like he's never had an angry day in his life welcomes us. 'Is this your first time?'

'Yes.'

'No.'

Nick and I answer at the same time.

'You've been before?' I look amusingly at Nick.

'Oh yeah, maybe three times in the last two years?'

'Great,' the smiley guy waves us over.

'The reservation's under Foster.'

Smiler looks down at the screen in front of him, and makes a few clicks, 'The package for two, perfect,' he taps away at his computer then pushes two clipboards towards us, 'If you could just fill this out: health and safety, etc.' As I take a look down at the sheet of paper, intimidating words shout back at me with titles such as: "Waiver of Claims", "Assumption of Risks", "Liability Release", and "Indemnity Agreement." We both sign our lives away, then hand the clipboards back. 'Alright, for legal reasons, please now verbally confirm that you understand this is an activity of emotional catharsis and not the only solution to mental health conditions.'

'Yes,' we both answer with a small smirk.

'You understand that as a company, we recommend after your visit, other forms of healthy release, such as anger management, seeing a therapist and or meditating.'

'Yes,' we answer together once more. I'm one step ahead there.

'Great, and finally, just to reiterate Paragraph Twelve, Section C, you understand that The Rage Room holds no legal obligation for any injuries you might endure during your time with us.'

I look to Nick who reassures me, 'We'll be fine. No one's getting hurt today.'

'Yes,' we both reply together, for the final time.

'Alrighty, thank you. Will you be using any music today?'

'Music?'

'Yes; yes, we will.' Nick takes out his phone, slides it to aeroplane mode, taps a playlist, and hands it over to the guy.

'Super.' I notice Smiler plugging it into a mixing desk on the channel that says, "Room 2". 'These are for you.' He hands us both a sizeable bag that's surprisingly heavy. 'Please put everything that's inside the bag on, then place any valuables, or items of clothing you don't want to wear underneath, back into them, and leave in the changing rooms; the lockers are free. How are you for footwear?' He comes around from behind the desk and looks down at our boots. 'Perfect. Now if you follow me, we'll get you all sorted.' We follow him through a door that reveals a long, thin corridor with several doors to each side. 'Ladies are here on the left, gents on the right. Meet you back in five?'

I nod and excitedly walk through to the ladies' changing room. Placing the bag down, I start unloading, a helmet with a welding shield, goggles, gloves, a chest protector, and a thick, dark blue boiler suit. I place my handbag, coat, scarf and hoodie in the bag and then into one of the lockers around the room, lock it, and pop the key in my trouser pocket. Next, I put on the boiler suit, afraid for a moment that it will be too small, but it fits perfectly. Then I put on the chest protector, pulling the Velcro straps to a comfortable size, and place on the goggles—which, I'm happy to say, are designed to sit nicely over glasses, then the helmet with face covering, thinking that that's a little extra, but guess you can't be too careful when smashing things. And lastly, the gloves. I catch myself in the mirror and smile; I've no idea what I'm about to get myself into, but I have a feeling it's going to be rather enjoyable.

Pulling the door to return to the corridor, Smiler and Nick are waiting for me. Nick grins, 'Looking good, Soph.'

'You too.' I nod at his matching attire while cat-walking over to them.

'Great stuff.' Smiler gestures forwards, 'Let's get to it!' We follow him down the corridor, passing several numbered doors, descending from "12".

'Are any of the rooms being used now?' I ask.

'Oh, yeah, all of them, actually.'

'Really? But you can't hear anything,' I remark, feeling slightly uneasy.

'Yeah, all the rooms are soundproofed,' Smiler says proudly. 'You can scream whatever you like at the top of your lungs and no one would ever know.'

'What if you hurt yourself?'

'The sessions are timed, so not only would we come and get you after 30 minutes, but we have cameras to keep an eye on everyone. OK, here we are.' We stop outside the door labelled, "Two". 'Like I said, you've got 30 minutes in here. Feel free to use any of the tools on the side; everything in there is fair game. Any questions?'

I shake my head, 'I don't think so.'

'Fantastic, well,' he grabs the handle and pushes the door open, 'have fun!'

I walk in first and Nick follows. I hear the door shut behind us and feel my heart begin to drum faster with anticipation. The room is a concrete box. The walls, ceilings and floors are spray-painted with graffiti, and I spot cans of varying colours over in one corner, I guess for you to add to the "art", if you want. There are several sections of the open room. Turning towards the corner to the right of the cans, there's a selection of glassware, vases, china cups and plates. The next has a TV from the 80s or so, with VHS tapes, and the final corner has an old printer on top of a wooden table, then a big tyre. Next to that is a crowbar, a large hammer, a mallet, and a baseball bat.

'What do you think?' Nick asks, tentatively, walking over to pick up the baseball bat, and beginning to swing it around playfully, but not hitting anything.

'I think it's hilarious. And dangerous. And exciting.'

'Exactly the reaction I was going for,' Nick's shoulders relax, clearly pleased that I'm up for this. 'Alright, pick your weapon of choice.' He places the bat back down to include it for my choosing, and waves to them all. I think for a moment and for no particular reason I find myself drawn to the crowbar, so I go for that first. 'Good choice. Now, what will be your first victim?' He walks around the room making small gestures, like a TV game show model, making me laugh out loud.

'Maybe I'll start small?' I walk over to a stack of china cups, pick one up and drop it on the floor, jumping slightly at the sound of it hitting the concrete and shattering. I instantly feel bad.

Nick laughs at me, 'You want to apologise for that, don't you?'

I laugh at myself, 'Yup.'

'Remember, he said, everything in here is fair game. That means you can break everything, you don't have to apologise, you don't have to pay for a replacement, and most importantly, you don't have to clean up! Think of all those times you wanted to throw something in frustration!' he cheers.

I still hesitate, doubting my ability to lose self-control, 'I'm not sure I can do this,' I admit.

'OK,' Nick walks supportively to my side, 'Follow my lead.' We walk over to the weapons of choice, he picks the bat back up, takes a lunge, a swing, and I scream as he takes out a stack of plates. His smile is infectious. 'Go for it; it's therapeutic.'

I pause, then look at a bunch of china that looks like something my mum would never let me use, saying it was "too fancy" and that "I'd break it". Without warning, I swing with gusto; the china breaks apart dramatically, but seemingly in satisfying slow motion. As it hits the floor in a million pieces, Nick's playlist starts, and I laugh at his first choice, 'Break Stuff' by Limp Bizkit.

'Subtle,' I grin at him.

'I had a feeling you'd feel too polite to get going; I thought a little encouragement would do us both good.'

'Something tells me, you don't need any encouragement,' I laugh, raising an eyebrow.

'What gives you that idea?' He gives me an innocent look, then turns and smacks the printer. 'Get in here! It feels great!' Nick waves me over and I go to town. It's mildly frightening how much rage is in my body. I can feel the adrenaline pumping through my veins. Each part of the printer breaks away, piece by piece with each hit, until there's nothing to resemble the piece of office ware.

The crowbar is starting to get a little heavy, so Nick and I swap, then he picks up the mallet. As Nick's phone works its way through the playlist, and we make our way around the room, I commend him on his musical choices: 'In The End', by Linkin Park; 'Fighter', by Christina Aguilera; Saygrace and G-Eazy's haunting version of, 'You Don't Own Me'; the powerful 'Who You Are', by Jessie J, that has a line in it that has always struck me: "*It's OK not to be OK.*" Then I guess we're onto the lighter side of the playlist as the jovial no *effs* given, 'So What', by Pink plays. And then suddenly we're into my pop-punk faze. Thanks to my big brother's influence, I loved Emo bands from the age of about 11, and Nick has taken the time to select some of my favourites, Sum 41's 'Fat Lip, and 'Check Yes, Juliet', by We The Kings, which was always a nod to us, as even back then, at the age of seventeen, it was clear Mum didn't approve of our relationship.

'God I love this song,' I say as Jimmy Eat World's, 'The Middle' comes on.

'I always liked the lyrics,' Nick pauses from taking out the rest of the china, singing the beginning at me. I laugh, step away from the VHS tapes and join in. We turn our weapons into guitars and pretend to be part of the band.

When we hit the chorus and on the second beat, instrumental stab, Nick kicks the air. I continue to dance around, singing at the top of my lungs, knowing no one apart from Nick can hear me. I then walk over to the TV and hit to the beat. Nick puts his "guitar" down and takes a can of spray paint in each hand. He shakes them like maracas, then pops the lids off with his thumbs and as the song continues to its end, he sprays everything while continuing to sing. He then practically skips around me, drawing a heart on the floor, around where I'm standing. I look down to smile at the heart, then back up to him, he drops the cans, as we both take off our helmets with the face shields. He wraps his arms around me, draws me in, and kisses me softly. It's different this time, more tender, which in itself is kind of hilarious, based on our current setting.

'Alright, did we have—oh, I'm sorry to interrupt.' We break apart, but Nick continues to keep his arms around me. Smiler is standing in the doorway, looking amused at our display. 'Never quite seen this reaction from the activity.'

I look back at Nick; God, I'm so in love with this man. What the hell am I going to do?

***

'So, what did you think?' Nick asks as we weave our way through the country lanes, back towards town, munching on the homemade wraps he made for us both to snack on.

'I think you know exactly how to make me feel better.'

'Well, that was just stop number one.' Nick drums the steering wheel with excitement and a bit of lettuce falls out of his wrap. He picks it off his leg and eats it.

I grin, 'What else have you planned?'

He looks at me with all seriousness, 'Oh, that would be telling!'

'You really are a child; you know that?'

'We are all in the habit of taking life too seriously. We're bombarded with crap and bad news on a daily basis; we don't even have to look for it, it's right in our faces. I've come to believe that we've got to tune in to our inner child: what do they want? What would make them happy?'

'And our next stop has something to do with that, does it?'

'Definitely. Shall we grab a quick something from Frankie's before we go though?'

'If it's on the way, sure.'

'It is.' He smiles at me but won't give anything away.

***

'Would you mind running in?' Nick asks as we pull up just outside the door. 'I just need to make a phone call about our next stop.'

'Full of surprises.'

He grins like he did when we were teenagers, 'I am.' Nick puts his hand in his pocket, pulls out his wallet and opens it. 'Here,' Nick hands me his card.

'I'm perfectly capable of buying coffee.'

'I know, but today's on me.'

Reluctantly, I take it, 'Fine.' And after leaning over to kiss him briefly on the lips, I exit the car.

Frankie's is full of people, as always, and I patiently join the queue.

'Hello, there!' Frankie waves at me, as I near the front. 'No Nick today?'

'He's in the car.'

'So not stopping.' He shakes his head. 'Fine, I'm not offended.' Frankie winks at me. 'I'll be right with you.'

'No rush.'

He swiftly serves the person in front of me, then turns his full attention to me. 'Now, don't tell me, two gingerbread lattes?'

'Yes, please.'

'Did you want to try our Jamaican blend? Just arrived this morning.'

'Sounds great.'

He gets to work, 'Did you know that the best quality coffee is grown at altitudes between 460 and 900 metres above sea level?'

'I did not know that.' I grin at him while watching him take pride in what he loves. I glance up at the door and spot Chris walking in.

My heart jumps into my boots, and I resist the urge to run over to my favourite seat in the place and hide behind it; the risk of burning my arse on the roaring fire far outweighs the risk of having a conversation with my brother. Yet, rooted to the spot, we lock eyes for a moment. I pick up one of Frankie's menus to hide my face, hoping I was wrong, and he hasn't seen me.

'You're hiding behind a menu; that's mature.'

I clear my throat and lower the small piece of laminated paper, putting on my best attempt at nonchalance, 'Oh, Chris! Hi! Didn't see you there.'

'Oh, bugger off.'

'There you are, Soph. On the house,' Frankie says warmly.

'No, I'm paying for this one!'

'Nonsense.' Frankie folds his arms in finality. 'Have a lovely Christmas if I don't see you.'

I take both coffees from the counter, 'Thank you, you too. We'll see you later.' I drop a tip in the Santa jar, then turn and expect to see Chris in the same place, but he's hovering awkwardly behind a post across the room.

'What are you doing?' I ask, walking over to him.

He clears his throat, then stands straighter, 'Nothing.'

I suddenly feel like we're kids in a staring match, determined not to be the first to blink.

He exhales and breaks eye contact. He looks broken.

'You alright?' I find my voice asking.

'You care how I am?'

'I've always cared how you are.'

'You have a funny way of showing it.'

'So do you.'

He stares at me again, frustration building in his eyes, I can almost hear his six-year-old self yell, "Yeah, and so do you!" but instead, he says, 'Do you have a second to sit?'

'Sure,' I say with uncertainty, 'Just a sec though, Nick's outside. He's taking me somewhere.' I take in his face, 'I'm not being a dick, it's a surprise; I honestly don't know where I'm going.'

He huffs, 'You and me both.'

We take the two chairs nearest us that are vacant and sit down. He drums his fingers nervously on the table, while I give my coffee a tentative sip.

'So,' he shifts in his seat, 'How are you?'

'*Um*. Well, I'm spending the day with Nick, he took me to…'

'That's what you are *doing*; I asked *how you are*.'

I pause, 'Well…you'll have to forgive me if I'm not quite sure how to answer that.'

He nods. 'So, you and Nick are back together; how's that?'

I shift slightly as we're not technically back together, then a deep, tormented frown covers my face, 'Why on earth would you care about that, when the last time I was here, you took one of the lead roles in ripping us apart?'

He nods once more, taking his time before answering. 'I'm sorry about that.'

'You are?' I say with surprise.

'I am. I had to take Aria's side but I've always liked Nick, I thought you knew that,' he says matter-of-factly.

'No,' I shake my head and can feel anger brimming up inside me, 'No, I have never known that.'

'Well, I'm sorry. I always found him intimidating, so I felt I had to act strong in front of him.'

I stare at Chris, at a complete loss for words.

'Also, I never wanted you to leave; you're my little sister.'

'I'm sorry, since when did that matter to you either?'

'Always.' He nods for a third time.

'What? No. You've always hated me, and made my life difficult, ever since we were little. You even made me cover for you when you killed our goddamn hamster.'

'Yeah, I'm sorry about Smudge. But,' his face transforms from regret to playfulness, 'isn't making their sibling's life difficult, what brothers are supposed to do?' he grins and I struggle to believe he's sorry about anything.

'Did you come here to find me?' I ask. He knows how much I love this place.

'No, I'm here to meet…someone,' he lets his voice drift off.

'A woman? You're not cheating on Aria, are you? Because I quite honestly think that she'll have no qualms in chopping both your balls off in public.'

He laughs, 'No, I'm not cheating on her.' He strokes his night shadow, and upon closer inspection, I see he looks a little gaunt. 'I'm here to have a meeting.'

'A meeting?'

'Yes. I can have meetings, I'm 38 now.'

'I'm not saying you can't have a meeting.' I let silence fall once more then can't help myself, 'Who are you having a meeting with?'

He bites his lip as if weighing up telling me something or not, 'If you must know…it's with Frankie.'

'Frankie? Why are you having a meeting with Frankie?'

'Because I need another job, OK?'

'*Another* job? You've already got a job?'

He exhales, 'I'm a food delivery man from 6.30 am -12 pm; then I have a class at the adult centre, before I wait tables from 4 pm -10 pm, in Maria's, the new Italian, two towns over.'

'What's your class in?' I ask with genuine interest.

'Aren't you going to make fun of me for being a delivery man or a waiter?'

'No. Delivery drivers can earn good money, right?'

'It's not bad per hour, but I signed a zero-hour contract, so it's not a full-time position, and they keep shafting me.'

'OK, well, at least tips are probably good at Maria's, right?'

He nods, 'They are, but it's not enough.'

'So, you're going to work here?'

'I need to pretend that I work here full time.'

'Why do you need to pretend?'

He looks up at the sky, 'Because...I haven't told Mum, Dad, or Aria, that I have a job at all, never mind two.'

'OK?' I question and lean forward for him to continue.

'They're not ones that I'm supposed to have.'

I shake my head, 'What do you mean?'

He tilts his head at me, 'Oh, come on, is this your first day? They'd all be embarrassed. Whereas, if I tell them I'm an assistant manager here, that will be more acceptable.'

I shake my head again, 'Fucks sake.'

'Fucks sake, indeed.'

I lean further forward, 'Look, I'm not sure that my opinion means anything to you, but I'm proud of you for going out there and finding work—good, honest work—to support your family.'

He scratches his head, 'You think?'

'I do.' I lean back. 'So, what's your course in?'

A smile spreads across his whole face, 'pastry chef.'

My expression matches his, 'Well, well, well, you're finally doing it.'

His expression becomes confused, 'This is new; what do you mean?'

'I mean, you were the one who had the Easy Bake Oven, and the person who tried to convince Mum to make different desserts with you every Sunday.' I shrug, 'Not that she'd let anyone ever take over the kitchen, but still. You've always wanted to be a chef.'

His eyes dart from side to side as if finally piecing together his very first puzzle, 'I have, haven't I? You were always the smart one.'

'No, I was the bookworm because I felt I had to be.'

'Well, I felt I had to be the sporty one. What sort of a bloke is like, "Oh, I'd rather be in a kitchen than on a football field"?'

'Anyone, of any sex, can be anything they want to be. Don't get me wrong, I love a box and a label to lower my anxiety, but when it comes to careers, why should we conform to stereotypes?'

He shrugs, 'Society. No...Mum.'

Tears fill my eyes, as mutual understanding flows between us. I nod, 'Mum.'

'You ready, Chris?' Frankie comes to our side. 'Oh, sorry, I've interrupted.'

'No, it's fine, we're done, anyway,' Chris says, getting to his feet. 'Shall we?'

Frankie leads the way for Chris, who goes to follow him without a goodbye, but then he turns, 'And just so you know, Soph, your opinion means just as much to me as Mum's.'

'Then why all this crap for years?' I say in a small voice.

Chris thinks for a moment then shrugs, 'Fear, I guess.' And with that, he walks off.

Chapter 20

About half an hour later, I've brought Nick up on my conversation with Chris; he's just as confused as I am. On the ride, we demolish not only the chocolate orange muffins from Frankie's I bought on my way out (without him catching me paying for something) but also a punnet of grapes that Nick had in the car for us. We hitch a left, and I think I know where he's taking me, but I don't want to ruin his surprise or get my hopes up, in case I'm wrong.

A mental health podcast Nick and I were listening to one time said, if we lower our expectations, we are never disappointed. Therefore, we can then be grateful for whatever does come to pass. At the time, I thought that was kind of depressing, but in reality, it's helped me be more mindful and grateful.

A smile spreads across my face as we pull in and park outside Scott's animal shelter. 'You've brought me to play with dogs?'

'I have. Scott said they had a few volunteers drop out at the last minute.'

I take in this man; he's always had the ability to understand what I need more than I do. Perhaps that was another thing I took for granted when we were together.

'You look sad. Do you not want to go in?'

'No, it's not that, I just…I don't think I ever really thanked you for all the little things, like this, that you used to do for me.'

He shrugs, 'Of course you did.'

I shake my head, 'No, not really. You had this—you still have this—' I correct myself, 'ability to anticipate my needs. I could never understand why someone would do nice things for me.'

His eyes are suddenly glassy, 'Your upbringing has a lot to answer for. I hate that you believe it's not right or normal for anyone to want to do anything good for you, just for you, just because.'

I bite my lip, 'Yeah, it's got to be even, and if my brother doesn't have what I do, I'm wrong and selfish.'

'Fuck me,' he breathes with frustration. Nick unbuckles his seatbelt and shifts in his seat to face me and takes my hands in his. 'You deserve everything good in this world, always, and without question. It broke my heart that I couldn't protect you from them or the version of them in your head that ruins your day, or week or—'

'Life,' I finish his sentence.

'What I want, more than anything for you, is to practise believing that you are worthy of a wonderful life, regardless of anyone else.'

For a time, we just look at each other. Neither of us knowing exactly what to say, yet, hearing each other perfectly. We're going to have to have a conversation about where we are at some point. We're not officially back together. I leave in two days. I don't want to leave in two days. He doesn't want me to leave in two days. He leans in to kiss me. When we break apart, we smile sadly at each other, my conflict reflected in his expression.

'Alright, feel like putting a pin in all the crap and unanswered questions, and just going in?'

I nod, 'Let's go.'

Two years ago, there was a team of about twenty who worked here full time, a handful of part-timers, and the rest were volunteers. They've had to reduce the staff in an attempt to stay afloat; I've no idea what number they're down to now, but Scott said there's more volunteers than staff.

In the past, whenever life felt a little too much, Nick and I would drop by. We'd help out in whatever way was needed. Cleaning out a pen or cage, taking one of the residents for a walk, helping at the front desk, taking calls, hanging out in the Meet and Greet/Training and Enrichment room, or spending time in the outside space, to play with whatever animal needed a little extra love. No matter what I did around here in the past, I always came away feeling like I was doing something good; not only for the animals, and the community, but for my soul. It made my problems fade away and put everything into perspective.

Truth be told, Nick and I always wanted a dog together, but I wouldn't let myself make that commitment; my mum always told me I wasn't responsible enough to look after myself, never mind another living thing, and I believed her. In reality, the root of that story is Smudge's untimely death. Chris wanted to see if the hamster could fly. From an upstairs window. I just dutifully covered for him, and my parents still don't know the truth.

It's ironic really that my mum has made me believe that I wouldn't be good at taking care of anything when in reality, I grew up too fast and took on a caregiver role from a very young age. Feeling solely responsible for their happiness is exhausting.

Along with my inner demons, we walk through the entrance of the animal shelter, and there's the familiar mix of senses: smells—some pleasant, some not so; the distant sounds of howling and meowing; and sights, some of which, I've found, are always hard to swallow at first.

As we step further in, there's a rotund man, who looks like a biker, holding a cardboard box, the contents of which, I can't see, but there's clearly a bird in it, that's chirping loudly in pain. He—the man, not the bird—talks to the receptionist; saying he found it at the bottom of his garden, it must have fallen out of a nest, and appears to have a broken wing. The receptionist kindly tells him that he should have called first and not dealt with the bird himself, but guides him through a door, to bring the bird in.

I turn my head, and watch with amusement as a few ladies are laughing, holding onto a lead; a blue nose pit bull looks excitedly back at them, then pants at the front door, pulling them along the corridor with ease. The tired-eyed man with them is wearing the company T-shirt and wishes them a Merry Christmas, so I'm assuming the pit bull has just been adopted.

To the right of us, is the section of the building where they house the cats. There's a window so you can look in while standing in the reception area. Each of the cats is in their own section, and I watch as a few hide in corners, not used to people, or perhaps still getting used to the soundtrack of tens of animals in one building. There's a shaggy-looking black, white and grey Japanese bobtail sitting up on the window ledge, and seemingly staring right at me through the glass; no fear from him. His right eye is closed, with visible damage to it. There are a couple of deep scratches from his nose up to his right ear, some dry blood matted in his fur, and a few sutures in place.

I walk a little closer to the glass and the cat doesn't budge; it's like he's daring me to get closer. We stare at each other through the glass. It's then that I spot Scott, through the window, just a little further beyond this cat's enclosure. I wave and he holds his hand up to say he'll just be a minute. He scribbles something on a clipboard, hangs it up, and talks to another worker. I watch as he moves along the parallel corridor to where we're standing, disappears, then the door to our right opens.

'Hi, guys! Glad you could make it.' Scott hugs Nick first, as he's closer, and then me. Scott takes in my expression, then nods to the glass. 'That's Tiggy. He was the kitty cat emergency the night you arrived. He's looking much better now.'

'What happened to him?' I return my gaze and Tiggy hasn't taken his good eye off me.

'He was found strapped to a lamppost. Unusual for a cat, it's normally dogs we find that way. No idea how he got there, or what his story is, but he's slowly learning to trust us and his wounds are healing every day, so, all in all, we're happy with his progress.'

'This is the problem with me coming here, I want to take them all home and look after them.'

'Back to New York or...?' Scott challenges and raises an eyebrow, clearly having talked to Gabby, knowing something has sparked again between Nick and I; his look encouraging me to want to move home.

'*Hmm*,' is all I say out loud. 'So, what can we do today?'

'*Ah*,' Scott shifts and waves us both to follow him down the corridor, 'We've got countless volunteers covering every department today, so Nick thought you'd like something a little special.'

'I thought you had some volunteers drop out,' I smile.

They exchange gleeful expressions like they always used to when they were up to something.

'May have been a white lie,' Nick confesses when we reach the Meet and Greet/Training and Enrichment room.

Scott gestures towards the door, 'Nick knows what to do. I'll be back in a minute.'

I watch Scott stride further down the corridor, towards where they house the dogs, and turn to Nick who's holding the door open for me. 'That was rather mysterious.' I step into the room and see an octagon-shaped, soft pen set up that you can step into; my stomach does a little flip. 'Are there puppies?' I ask gleefully.

Nick shrugs, 'No idea.' He steps into the room and closes the door behind him. 'But let's get in here, just in case.' He lifts one leg, then the other over the side of the pen, and sits down cross-legged, surrounded by several soft toys, a water bowl and puppy pads. I follow him in and sit to his right.

'There are puppies,' I say to myself with confident certainty, staring eagerly at the door. A few moments later, I hear yapping; I look at Nick excitedly and he grins back at me. The door opens with Scott leading, and two colleagues behind him; the three of them, are each holding two golden Labrador puppies. I throw my hands over my mouth with excitement and Scott walks over, placing his two in the pen with us. They immediately start lolloping about, over me, Nick, and the toys around us. One of them runs with gusto around the space, and steps in the water, splashing us both. I try to pet them, but they're too fast and into everything around us. 'Right now, we've named them after colours,' Scott says and I note the different coloured collars whizzing past me: one has a yellowy-orange one, and the other has a red. 'They're both girls, Amber and Ruby,' he points to the two he's placed in the pen, then the next colleague puts the puppies she's carrying into the pen too, as Scott introduces them, 'then we've got Emerald and Sapphire, also girls.' They join the others, the one with the green collar chews on Nick's trouser leg, while the blue-coloured one bites Amber's ear. 'And finally, our last girl is Pearl, and the only boy of the litter, we've named Onyx or, O for short.' The last of the colleagues passes the penultimate puppy wearing a white collar, to Nick. The newest golden furball immediately wiggles out of Nick's arms and heads for the toys, and then he hands the final one to me. As the colleagues leave the room, I notice the puppy I'm holding has a black collar, so I'm guessing he's O. 'Onyx.' I tap into my memory, 'The ability to overcome challenges.'

'What's that?' Nick asks.

'Onyx is a stone that my aunt gave me when I was younger. It gives you strength and perseverance to overcome challenges.' I smile at O. He's the only one not darting about and just wants to be held. He looks up at me with his huge black eyes, then snuggles his little head into my chest. I feel his tiny heart beating and my body melts. 'Oh my God.' I pet O's head; it's so soft and fluffy. 'This is it for me.' I shut my eyes and know that I sound like Kaley Cuoco playing 'Pup Quiz' on *The Tonight Show* with Jimmy Fallon.

Scott climbs into the pen with us and takes a seat, 'They came in three weeks ago. They were found in a warehouse. No sign of the mother. We're guessing they're about two months old.'

'Oh, that's so sad that the mother wasn't there,' I say, giving O an extra little hug; he likes it, I think, as his tail gives a small wag, but he stays firmly in my arms. 'Why's this one so timid?'

Scott pets O on the head, 'The others leave him out, they don't seem to want to play with him as much. I'm guessing he's the runt of the litter.'

'But he's perfect,' I say, taking him in. 'Why wouldn't anyone want to play with him?'

'He's a little smaller than the others, so the girls dominate him.'

'Always a problem,' Nick says, and we all laugh.

'Plus, he's not as interested in food or drinking on his own; we've had to use syringes. He's slowly putting weight on though, so, things are on the up,' Scott says, guiding Pearl away from chewing the net of the pen.

I look at Nick who's holding a toy up for Sapphire, and Ruby jumps up instead and pulls it away.

'I love this. Thank you both so much.'

Scott smiles, petting each of the pups, 'No worries, view it as an early Christmas present.

'What's going to happen to them if you have to close?' I say with worry.

Scott's weary expression reads all over his face. 'Honestly, I don't know. Gabby and I have talked about taking as many as possible; I can't think about it right now.' He clears his throat and shakes any tears that are trying to form away. 'Alright,' Scott stands and climbs out, 'stay as long as you want and message me when you're ready to go; we'll come and take the puppies.' Scott leaves us to it, shutting the door behind him.

'I might stay all night,' I admit.

'I'll break it to Adam that you're not coming to his play then, shall I?' Nick grins.

'Fine. Maybe not all night.'

'Adam will be happy to see you in the audience tonight. He told me he loved looking out and seeing you there at the Light Switch On when he was performing; he said it gave him a boost, knowing you were watching, and wanted to show you how much he'd learnt about being on a stage.'

I shake my head, 'I can't believe how grown up he is now, and so confident too.'

'I know what you mean, it's like a spark's been awoken in him. He's constantly on a stage.'

I witness the love in Nick's eyes, and I have a pang of sadness that because of my family, I've missed so much. 'I wish I could have seen him.'

'You did the other night.'

'No, I mean, I wish I could have been here for it all, watching him grow and develop; I feel like we've just jumped forward in time.'

'Well, we have.'

I exhale, 'I know.' I focus on O's soft head. 'I hate that even if I had been here, I know I would have been distracted and missed some of it anyway. I've always had a talent for being physically present but not completely there, mentally.'

'You're here now. Let's make the most of it, *eh*?'

'I'd say we are.' I grin naughtily at him, then laugh as all the girls are now clambering on top of him. 'You always were a ladies' man.'

'Nah. I've only ever loved one girl.' He looks over at me and despite all the puppies, bouncing around us, and the one I'm still holding close, Nick leans in, stopping just before my lips, then whispers, 'I *still* only love one girl.'

I can feel myself wanting to well up, not entirely sure if they're happy or sad tears, perhaps a mix of both, so I close them. I feel Nick's soft lips upon mine. How can I leave this man again when everything in my being is telling me to stay? We break apart.

'Wait until we get home, I've got one more surprise for you.' He wiggles his eyebrows playfully.

Chapter 21

Arriving back at the flat, I feel both lighter and fuller; less anger, more love. As I remove my coat, scarf and boots, I wonder what else Nick has planned. If I'm honest, I don't have a whole lot of energy left and would quite like to sit and do nothing; I haven't got the heart to tell him that though.

'Alright, and now...' Nick whips off his coat and it theatrically lands on the rack, '...the *pièce de résistance! Un momento, por favor.*' He grins then runs down the corridor, and into our bedroom. I take a seat on the couch in amusement. God I love this couch, it's perfect. I swear, nothing in either of Freya's properties that I've stayed in for the last two years, has the same firmness or comfort level. What is it about this couch? The little voice in my head answers:

It was your home and you didn't want to leave. You felt safe here.

I take one of the pillows and give it a hug, feeling a little sorry for myself. A second later Nick pauses in the hallway doorframe, holding something behind his back, grinning. 'So, knowing you as I do, I'd say, you've had a great time.'

He pauses to raise an eyebrow, so I reassure him, 'I have.'

'But you're now a little emotionally tired?'

'Yup,' I nod with amusement.

'Or perhaps even overstimulated, and don't want to do anything, correct?' He points at me.

I smile, 'Correct.'

'I thought that would be the case, and so…' He whips from behind his back a square light blue box with a white ribbon around it. The colours remind me of a Tiffany box, but as it's larger than that, and since Nick and I aren't technically back together, and I realise how ridiculous that thought is, I slowly let that thought go. Nick's excited voice brings me back. 'In this box is something that I have kept since Liv and Dom were last here.'

'Right,' I crease my eyebrows in interest, trying to remember which time with my cousin and her husband he's talking about; he begins to walk over.

'It's something I enjoyed doing as a teenager—one of the many reasons your mum dislikes me.' I immediately know exactly what he's talking about. Nick reaches the couch, sits next to me, and offers the box, 'Merry Christmas.'

I take the lid off and sure enough there's a small *joint* sitting in there. I laugh. 'Are you kidding? I've never done that before.'

'I know. I thought, what better time than Christmas Eve?'

'Before your nephew's Christmas show?'

'To be honest there's no better time than before a children's Christmas show.'

I laugh loudly at this then look down at the innocently rolled, special cigarette. 'How strong is it?'

'No idea. Dom left it here for me about three years ago after their inspired trip to Amsterdam.'

'Is it still in date then?'

'It might have lost a bit of its potency, but should be fine.' He's looking at me with more affection than ever. 'Just to state the obvious, there's zero pressure if you don't want to. I'll just wait until Liv and Dom are back to have it again.'

Victoria Mae

As I contemplate this, I think of my cousin, Liv. She's the one who always encouraged me to take time to do something for myself without overthinking and to jump out of my comfort zone. Ever since we were kids, she was the sister I wish I had, encouraging me to do new things and explore what I love. I never felt like I could, or that I deserved to, but, hey, I loved her for trying to convince me that I was worth it. 'OK,' I say out loud.

'You sure? I haven't forced you?'

'Nope. I'm excited and nervous and would like to,' I say honestly.

He walks over to where the lighter for candles has always lived and brings it back over to the couch.

'Won't the smoke alarm go off?'

'Just turned it off.'

'What will the neighbours say?'

'That's the best impression you've ever done of your mum.'

I make a face at him. 'Fine.'

'Alright! A little music first?' Nick stands to put something on, walking over to our entertainment unit. After swift consideration, I note he's picked up Jamie Cullum's *Twenty Something* special edition album, on CD.

'You're not going for the vinyl?' I question, knowing he prefers the sound.

'Nah, I'd have to get up and turn the record over, then put the next one on and flip that over too.' He grins at me then hits play. 'Sounds far too strenuous.'

As soon as the first five notes of 'What a Difference a Day Makes' grace the speakers, I feel my shoulders relax. 'God, I love this album.' Nick's Dad would play this constantly in their house when we were younger.

'I know you do.' He smiles, 'You always used to say that the first five notes are like sinking into a warm bath.'

'That is exactly what it's like. Why don't I listen to this more?'

'Because you don't let yourself have fun.'

'*Hmm*,' is all I reply and after a beat, 'What a sad thought.'

'Well, no more sad thoughts for now.' Nick lights the fire next, and I enjoy the flames, then he pops to the kitchen and returns with two glasses of water and one of our old tapas dishes.

'What're they for?'

'Always good to stay hydrated.'

'How very sensible of you.'

'And the tapas dish, we'll improv as an ashtray.'

I laugh, 'Always with the quick thinking.'

Nick then sits by my side, looking gleeful, 'You ready?' I nod, feeling like I'm breaking every rule and am about to be told off. I nervously crack my knuckles and will myself to relax. Nick takes it out of the box, pops it in his mouth and lights it. A familiar scent from our sixth-form years wafts through the apartment and he breathes in, holds it for a few moments and then breathes out. 'Oh, yeah,' I see his shoulders visibly relax, and he takes another puff. 'Smooth.' He then offers it to me. I ignore the feeling that I shouldn't, and think of how much of a goodie-two-shoes I've always been. I always follow the rules, I never take risks, and I've always done what I'm told. With my teenage self (who was always afraid to join in) willing me on, I take the cigarette, it feels weird in my hand; I've no idea how to hold it, and if I were in public I'd worry people were judging me, and feel like I were wearing a sign around my neck, stating loudly, "FIRST TIMER!"

Bringing it to my lips, I take a small breath in and immediately blow it out. 'Good start,' Nick smiles. 'Now try breathing in and then when the smoke is in your mouth, breathe in again, hold it, and then let it out.' I do as instructed and this time feel a difference from inhaling it. I immediately cough. And hand it back to him. 'You're a complete natural.'

I laugh loudly and play-hit him on his right arm. We continue to pass it between us, I've no idea how long, talking about anything and everything, until we're about three-quarters of the way through it, Nick suddenly stops. 'You OK?' I look at him, mildly worried.

'Yeah, yeah. I think I need a minute.' He hands it back to me and I continue to take a few more drags.

Then, out of the blue, I feel something, 'Woah.'

'Has it hit you?'

I look towards the fire, 'Yeah, I think so.' I realise I'm staring at the flames. It feels good to stare. Then it's as if a pleasant wave has washed through my body, starting at the top of my head, flowing down my shoulders, through my arms, and then my entire body. 'Wow. No wonder people do this.' I find I've said out loud. I can feel a part of me wanting to judge what I'm doing or trying to hear the inner negative dialogue that's normally constantly running, but it's as if it's been put on mute. No, more than that; like it's not there. I start giggling.

'You alright?'

'Yeah. Are you?'

'I haven't done this in a long time. I think I'm trying to keep my shit together.'

I laugh again, 'What's happening for you?'

'There's just…nothing.'

'Yeah, but at the same time, *everything*, right?'

He laughs this time. 'I have no idea what they've done to these in the last—' he pauses to work it out, 'seventeen or so years, but, wow. I guess they're stronger?'

I'm not sure if I answer out loud, but it doesn't seem to matter. We stare together at the fire. After a while, Nick asks what the time is. I've no concept of time and it feels amazing. He lazily looks at his watch, 'It's only been fifteen minutes, it feels like three hours.'

I smile, not sure I even need to answer him. Did he ask a question? 'Did you ask a question?'

'I don't know.' We both start laughing.

'It's like I can't hear my thoughts; there are no thoughts. This has never happened to me. There's…silence. But not in a bad way, in a "*Heyyyyy*", kind of way, you know?'

'I do know.' Nick now stares ahead and we go back into silence. It's so peaceful.

'It's like you're not in your head, but you're in your body, right?'

'Oh, you are so stoned.'

I turn my head slowly to look at him and he grins goofily back at me. I enjoy his face. Suddenly, I find my hands don't want to clasp together; that feels too restrictive. My left arm flops off my lap and onto the couch. We both look at my flimsy limb then lock eyes, and laugh again.

'You know, Freya does this and then she goes on stage or does interviews. And mixes it with alcohol. How is that possible? I'm not sure I can walk right now.'

'I'm not sure I can talk right now,' Nick says. 'Is my tongue bigger?' He sticks it out at me. 'It feels like it doesn't fit in my mouth anymore.'

'No,' I laugh and notice my body has slipped slightly so the back of my head is leaning further down the couch. Nick's posture matches mine. I want to put my feet up. I try to lift my heavy limbs in slow motion but decide they're just fine where they are.

'I guess it's like alcohol,' Nick answers my question about Freya in a funny time delay, 'people build up a tolerance and it…' Nick fades off without finishing his sentence. It doesn't matter. I feel like I'm floating on a cloud. It's nice. There's no judgement here. I want to have a sip of water so I go to move my arm, but it's like it's asleep. I start laughing.

'You OK? Did I finish my sentence?'

'I don't know.' The water's far away. I sit up slowly, feeling a little like jelly. I lean down to the glass rather than bringing it up to me, it makes more sense that way. I take two hands to lift it a millimetre off the coffee table and sip a small amount before putting it carefully back down. I laugh again as I lay back, 'It's so heavy.' Nick laughs and we return to staring. 'My hands are so small.' I find, once more, that I've said that out loud without planning to. 'I can feel my blood pumping in my veins.'

'I hear music.'

'There is music.' I try to gesture to the CD player, but my arm won't let me, and it makes me laugh.

'No, not Jamie, like, I can hear the heating and the fire, and the kitchen.'

'The kitchen?' I laugh.

'Yeah, it's like a cacophony of rhythms. I can totally get how composers like Sibelius heard symphonies in their heads.' He turns to me, 'I hear music.'

'That's nice.' I tune in further to what's happening with me. 'I feel like my face is relaxing. Like my muscles want a break.'

He giggles, 'That's high.'

'And dry.' I burst out laughing, thinking this is the funniest thing I've ever said.

'What?' He laughs harder, and this time I make a bigger effort to move my arm.

'Jamie. He's singing "High and Dry."' We both laugh and sometime later the song finishes, and there's silence. Somehow, we've listened to the entire album. 'I hear a bird singing.'

'See, a symphony,' Nick says before turning to me once more. 'I think we should go for a walk.'

'I have no idea if I can.' We both laugh again, 'Alright,' I try sitting up first and he joins me; it feels like I'm moving through water. We eventually steady ourselves to our feet and giggle, arms swaying at our sides. 'It's like being drunk but not.'

'It's more relaxed than that,' Nick says, bending down to grab both our waters and laughs, concentrating not to spill any. 'This is heavy.'

We finish the water, place the glasses back down as quickly and carefully as we can, then somehow make our way to the kitchen.

'Do you want a snack?'

'I'm not sure I'm able to eat anything right now; I feel like I might not be able to chew.'

Nick opens the fridge then laughs, 'No matter. There's nothing in there. You always did the food prep.'

'So you haven't eaten in two years?'

'Exactly.'

I love how funny everything seems. 'Alright, maybe fresh air would be good. I'll just go pee.' I stroll slowly down the corridor and when I arrive at the bathroom, close the door. I catch myself in the mirror and smile. I look more relaxed than I have done in years. I haven't seen my reflection without a frown on it, in the longest time. I feel groovy.

When I'm done, I wash my hands, and as I'm enjoying the feel of the soap, I hear Mel Robbins saying in my head, "I see you, I believe in you, and I am here with you, you've got this."

'I do got this,' I find myself saying to my reflection. I give myself a high five, then laugh as I make my way back to greet Nick. He's trying to put on his coat but he's moving in slow motion.

Somehow, we make it out of the door, and down the external stairs, arm in arm, giggling. The fresh air hits my face and makes me laugh even more. 'I'm not sure we can go to Adam's play,' Nick says with what should be a worried tone, but he's glazed over and chilled.

'A few laps and I'm sure we'll feel normal,' I say, not minding either way. 'Everything is so beautiful.' I look at the glistening snow, sparkling like diamonds, decorating every inch of our surroundings. 'Life is beautiful.' I'm not connected to my inner demons, it's as if there's something there waving them away. I turn to Nick who's silent. 'Are you OK? You're the one who used to do this.'

'When I was seventeen and eighteen. Then I realised that I might fail some subjects, so…stopped.'

'I remember. I was there.'

'You were there.'

'And now you're here.'

'We're here.'

'This stuff is hilarious. Thank you.'

Amazingly there aren't many people about as we do several laps around the town. I honestly don't care if there are. It's so pretty out and life feels fluid.

Nick and I don't talk for a time, both in our own worlds and that's OK. It's nice to be in my head without the constant negative internal commentary.

'I should have peed,' Nick says as we take, perhaps, our fifth or sixth lap.

'Well, you're a man, you can have a wild wee.'

'In our town? No, let's go back to the house.'

'So proper.' I get the giggles again as we waft back to the house. I stay in the hallway and stare at the coat rack, Nick heads to the bathroom, still fully clothed in his coat and boots. I don't know how long he's gone, but when he returns, I'm still in the hallway. We look at each other, then laugh again.

'What the hell is in this stuff?' Nick says to me.

'I don't know, you should ask Dom where he got it.'

'I should.' He looks like I've just had the best idea ever.

We both take off our coats and boots then fall onto the couch. Nick gets out his phone, 'Oh my God, this is heavy too.' We laugh and I nod at his iPad on the dining room table. 'Too far.' Nick ponders for a moment, 'Alright, we're smart people, we can figure this out.' He takes his time and then sits up, places his phone to balance on the candle that's on the coffee table and it miraculously stays in position. We both cheer with low-level *oomph*.

Nick taps away, then sits back as a WhatsApp video call starts. I wiggle in slow motion to sit up and see the phone, our reflection staring back at us; we both laugh as we see how blurry-eyed we are, until the picture transforms to move us to a small little rectangle, and Dom's face fills the screen.

'Nick, mate, how are you? Oh, and Soph, is that you?' Dom's eyes widen.

'Yup. Hello,' I manage to say.

'Liv!' Dom calls, behind him. 'Soph and Nick are on the phone,' Looking at the screen, I note they're in their apartment, in Newport Beach, California. I always enjoy looking at all the mementos and pictures from around the world that decorate the background whenever I talk to Liv over a video call. Their home is like a tapestry of everything that fills them with joy. It's inspiring and I wish so deeply that I could be that person too, or, normally I do. At this moment, I feel fabulous.

It's surprising that they're home; they're normally flying off to some glamorous destination, either for work or just because they can.

'Sophie *and* Nick?' I hear Liv's voice in the background. 'She messaged me a story about being there accidentally, but...' her voice stops as her wild curly-headed messy bun enters the screen. 'Hey! You told me you were home but I didn't know you were *home*.'

'Oh, what time is it there?' Nick asks, the only one of us to realise that California's in a different time zone.

'Around ten in the morning,' Dom answers casually, smiling his aqua-blue eyes at us.

'Nice to see you both. What are you doing together? Are you together?' Liv looks excited at me.

I look at Nick and neither of us can quite figure out what we are, so we just laugh.

'We are…currently, next to each other,' I say slowly.

Dom leans in for inspection, 'Are you guys high?'

Nick leans in too, whispering, 'We finally smoked that *joint* you gave me.'

Both of them laugh, then Liv sips from an espresso cup and puts it back down.

'So how is it?' Dom enjoys us for a moment, Liv leans on his shoulder and smiles. I miss her.

I manage a nod and a thumbs up. Nick leans forward, 'I've never felt so floppy.'

'Now, Nick, that's not what a girl wants to hear,' Liv says without a beat.

'Why aren't you somewhere sunny?' I ask.

'We are. We're at home,' Dom says, smiling, the sun is pouring into the room they're sitting in.

'No, I mean, aren't you working?'

'We got the holidays off, so we're spending it together, at home, just the two of us.' Liv looks at Dom and I'm so envious of their love and freedom.

'Why don't you feel guilty?' I ask this with genuine interest rather than hurt.

'For what?' Dom laughs.

'For being…no that's the wrong word…for *doing* what you want?'

Liv takes me in, 'How's your mum?' she answers with a question.

'The same,' I say this and I don't seem to feel any pain. This really is magic stuff. 'How are your parents?' I love my aunt and uncle. My aunt is a super quirky hippy. I've no idea how she's my mum's sister; they're like chalk and cheese.

'They were just here, actually, but they're back home in Spain now.'

'And away from my crazy family; smart. How come you got the fun mum?'

Liv shrugs, 'Just lucky, I guess. Are you hanging in there?' she asks kindly.

'We are currently hanging, yes,' Nick and I start laughing; I'm not able to be serious right now. 'What are your plans for Christmas Day?' Nick asks, from my side and I realise his hand is on my thigh. I like it there.

'We're going to have a lie-in, go for a surf, have some cocktails and tapas, then head to the boat and see if we can find some dolphins. Sarah and Hugo are back from New York and over to ours for Boxing Day, then we'll see my folks around New Year before we fly out to Mexico.'

'Well, that sounds nice.' I tilt my head to one side; how wonderful to live a life that you've designed without an ounce of guilt, shame or doubt. Must be amazing.

'What are you doing in Mexico?' Nick loves hearing about their travels; he's always said it's like travelling vicariously through them when they tell us about their adventures.

'Mayan temples, tropical beaches, checking out the wildlife, food sampling…' Liv smiles.

'Sounds terrible,' I say lightly.

'Can we swap lives, please?' Nick speaks in slow motion.

'And tear you away from that studio?' Dom asks, knowing just how passionate Nick is about music.

'Yeah, I could handle a camera, I've been practising.' Liv and Dom laugh kindly at this which sets me off; everything feels light and easy.

'We miss you guys,' Liv says, picking up her espresso again, and handing another to Dom.

'We'll come and visit you.'

'We will?' Nick looks at me.

'We will,' I nod. 'It sounds totally doable, and fun.'

'Well, alright, we'll arrange that!' Liv says with excitement. 'Hey, Soph, remember that you can handle this; you are stronger than you think, and with that guy next to you,' she points at Nick through the screen, 'anything is possible, OK?'

'OK.' I smile at my cousin, so wise and put together. I put my hand on top of Nick's. It's warm and comforting.

'And, hey,' Nick says before we hang up, 'thank you for the *joint*, man.'

'Yeah, thank you, I've loved every second of it,' I say, still enjoying its magical powers.

'You're very welcome,' Dom laughs.

'Have a great Christmas, guys; we love you,' Liv waves at the camera.

'We love you too,' both Nick and I say at the same time.

'We'll see you soon,' Dom waves, then presses the screen and it goes blank.

'I'd like to be as happy as them one day.'

'Why one day?' Nick asks, 'One day could be today.'

'Today is one day,' I reason. I feel my body flop down a bit more and we enjoy returning to a comfortable silence.

'Didn't we have to do something this evening?' Nick says.

'Maybe? I'm not sure I'm capable of anything right now. How does Freya perform on this while being drunk? Did I ask that already?'

'Perform,' Nick says sleepily at me.

'You want me to perform? Or am I supposed to perform tonight?'

Nick laughs and gives me a goofy grin.

''Cause I like performing but it's just a matter of being able to right now.'

'No,' he composes himself, 'Adam. The show.'

'Oh, that.' We smile at each other, our heads lolling against the back of the couch.

Nick blinks slowly at me, 'I think you're very beautiful.'

'I think you're beautiful too.'

He smiles wide, 'I'll take it.'

'How long do we have?'

'Forever,' Nick closes his eyes for a moment.

'I mean until the show.'

'Oh, you really could get absolutely nothing done on this.' Nick still has his eyes closed. 'I think it starts at 7:30.' We laugh again, 'Well, at least if we see your family, we'll be relaxed about it.'

Chapter 22

Somehow, after a nap and eating a take-out poke bowl in slow-motion, Nick and I make it to the Town Hall for the annual, Christmas Eve, primary school play that Adam's starring in. 'I'm feeling better, but do I look high?' I whisper to Nick as we walk, arm in arm, through the main gates, and up the stairs to the entrance.

Nick looks at me, and I must say he looks much more normal, which gives me some hope that I do too. 'No, you look fine.'

'Just fine?' I tease.

'Alluring, then.'

'I'll take it.' We grin at each other like we're teenagers once more.

We shuffle through the grand entrance with the rest of the excited crowd, passing two four-foot nutcrackers on either side of the main auditorium door, and find two seats at the back. I think we've gotten away without being seen or noticed by too many people we know, with more than a smile and a wave.

I exhale and feel my body relax into the seat. Gazing around it's quite funny to be back in a room you used to frequent all the time, but haven't been to in ages. Growing up, not only would I often come here because it's where my mum works, but all the local schools would use the Town Hall for their bigger events, due to its large stage and backstage facilities.

I feel like I'm seeing it with new eyes after all this time. When I was a kid, I felt that the half-circle barrel vault ceiling was impossibly high, now as an adult, it's so much smaller than I remember. I gaze around at each side of the room, the ornate details I can only now fully appreciate as an adult.

The pillars that mark each side of the room have garlands twisted up and around themselves, several wreaths glimmer along the walls, a forest of fully decorated trees line the edges of the stage, and even though the front-of-house lights are still on, I smile at the thousands of fairy lights, shimmering, above our heads.

'Do you remember the Jazz Band playing here in year 13?' Nick whispers, breaking me away from my appreciation of the decor.

'I remember us skulking off to stand back there and kissing through the whole thing.'

'Exactly.' He raises his eyebrows playfully at me.

Smiling, I tilt my head to one side, 'Tempting, but I think sitting down is probably the best way to go right now.'

'Spoilsport; I'm not offended,' he jokes and wiggles down into his seat.

We watch as several parents and grandparents barge their way as near to the front as they can go. The first six rows or so are already full; I wonder what time they arrived to claim them. Competitive parents always make me laugh. I notice a brunette coming in, wearing a floor-length white coat with a furry hood. It's open at the front, revealing her ruby sequined dress, accompanied by tights and thigh-high boots; she walks around like she owns the place. '*Ugh*, Whitney.'

Nick follows my line of sight, and blows a quiet raspberry, 'Did you know she's currently pregnant with baby number three?'

'Aria told me,' I say yawning.

Nick makes a disapproving noise, 'According to my brother, her eldest is a bit of a bully.'

'Imagine that,' I say with sarcasm, my teenage self feels bad for anyone who that family crosses. I hope Nick and I aren't talking loudly, but admittedly, a large part of me doesn't care. Whatever the reason, Whitney scans the crowd and eventually spots us. She pauses, grinning wickedly then struts over.

'Sophie Carter. And you're with Nick! How are you both?'

'Just fine, thanks,' I say, and after a beat add, 'You?' not caring particularly for her answer, but glad that my voice doesn't give that thought away.

'Oh, you know how it is, two kids and one on the way is a lot to handle. So, are you two back together?'

'Not exactly,' I find my voice saying, not wanting to elaborate and say it's complicated and we haven't yet worked out what we are.

'Are you married then, Sophie?'

'No.' I reckon she knows damn well I'm not married.

'With someone else, at least, then?'

'No.'

'Oh, kids?'

'No.' I'm impressed that I sound and feel so calm.

'*Huh.*' She regards me, 'Such a shame. What have you been doing with yourself then?'

A small voice in my head says I do not have to defend or explain myself to her but before I can put an actual answer together, Nick speaks for me, 'She works for Freya.'

'Freya who?' she asks dismissively, like we're wasting her time, and she checks her perfectly shiny Ruby Fizz-shaded Shellac nails.

'One of the biggest pop stars in the world,' Nick says matter-of-factly and without hesitation.

Whitney's face contorts into confusion, pain, disbelief, and then finally seems to settle on surprise. 'Wow, no wonder you've not achieved the most important and fulfilling jobs then; you've been partying with a pop star.'

I have no idea how to respond to that.

'Well, great to see you both,' Whitney says with false sincerity. We watch as she strides off, waving at other mums as she goes.

'Wow. Good to know that none of my achievements count for anything.'

'She's a moron,' Nick's voice is calm. 'If ever there was someone to pay absolutely no attention to, it's her. And your family,' he adds as an after-thought. 'Oh, look, there's my family.' Nick points to the left-hand side of the room, and there they all are, sitting, laughing, talking, enjoying each other, no drama. God, that would be nice. I allow a huge sigh to come out of my mouth, and I close my eyes to recentre.

I don't consider myself religious, I'm definitely more spiritual, but for some reason, the opening of the Serenity Prayer comes into my head:

> *"Please grant me the serenity to accept the*
> *things I cannot change,*
> *the courage to change the things I can,*
> *and the wisdom to know the difference."*

I say this several times in my head and as if on cue, I hear my mum's voice.

'We need to have a conversation, Sophia.'

Blinking my eyes open, I gaze up and see Mum, standing on her own; highly unusual for her to arrive without the entourage that is the rest of my family. I wonder for a moment where my dad, Aria and Chris are, but my focus draws back to Mum. She's dressed smartly in a crisp, white, perfectly ironed trouser suit, all business, no sign of a nurturing mother—there never was.

'Hello,' I say and look at her, really look at her, for the first time since I arrived back in this town. She has this hardened exterior, from her clothing choices to her perfectly coiffed hair and flawless makeup; nothing is ever out of place, and I've never been able to break through this facade and find the real woman beneath the mask. Maybe I never will. But there has to be more under it all. Why is she this way?

'What are you staring at? Do I have something on my outfit?' She looks insecurely but impatiently down at herself.

'Maybe you were never treated the way you needed to be treated,' I say these words out loud before I realise, or have thought what I mean by them.

'What on earth are you babbling on about? Are you drunk?'

'No. I'm not drunk,' I say calmly and then without warning, I take to my feet. 'How did Grandma treat you as a child.' This is something that my therapist has questioned but I honestly don't know the answer. My grandma died when I was young so I don't remember her, and my mum would never allow me to pose any such question. Mum grew up on a farm and told me my grandma was a great person who she wanted to make proud; that's all I know.

She shudders slightly, but I catch it. 'Why on earth are you asking me that? I said we needed a conversation but that's certainly not the one we'll be having, and absolutely not here with the whole town watching,' she says the last part of the sentence in a low tone, through gritted teeth, and then looks around to see if anyone is looking; she takes a moment to smile and wave at a few people.

'You create such a hardened exterior; I just now wonder, why?'

'Stop it, Sophia.'

'Maybe you're so critical of me, because your mum was critical of you, and hers was to her, and so on, and somehow you think that's the best way?'

'It is the best way. Look at all you've experienced; if it weren't for me, that wouldn't have happened.'

I look at her and suddenly—and I've no idea why—I see a small, frightened little girl, who just wants, and needs, to be loved. I think I want to hug her.

'Something is wrong with you. Stop staring at me.' Her foot does a little stamp, like a toddler tantrum but not quite as dramatic as we're surrounded by everyone in the town. I step forward and without overthinking, I hug her. She doesn't reciprocate at first, and then she brings one arm up and pats me lightly. 'You are embarrassing me,' she whispers.

'I want to hug you.'

'Well, stop it.'

'No,' I say, hoping that she'll finally soften, and melt into my arms.

'Sophia,' she warns, but I grip on even tighter; I feel my eyes starting to well up. 'You are making a scene.'

'I am just a daughter hugging her mother. That's not a scene; it's a sign of affection.'

She wriggles now, 'Come on, I think you've made your point, although, honestly I'm not sure what it is.'

Exhaling, I reluctantly let go and look her in the eyes. 'Nobody cares that I'm hugging you.'

'What will they think that means?' she asks while unruffling her suit.

'Why do you care so much about what other people think?' I feel desperation rising inside me. 'I just wanted a hug from my mother; I shouldn't have to give a reason why or have to analyse what people will think about it.'

She goes to open her mouth and then closes it again, 'I have a job to do.' And with that, she strides off. I sit back down and Nick doesn't say anything at first. He simply takes my limp hand in his and holds it tightly. The lights dim even further and I numbly watch as my mum takes to the stage. I'm pretty sure it's not her job to introduce everything that happens in the Town Hall, but she has always taken it upon herself to do so. As a spotlight hits her, she puts on her show smile and starts talking, it's not until then that I allow the tears in my eyes to spill over onto my cheeks.

'I just wanted a hug,' I say softly to Nick.

He takes a deep breath, and says so softly, that I can just about hear him, 'My dear, beautiful, Sophie, I think you wanted so much more than that.'

'I know,' I whisper, looking up at the stage and watching as she greets Adam's class, with a warmth that I've never felt from her. 'What is so wrong with me that she can't give me that?'

'Nothing. Absolutely nothing.'

'She's never going to be able to give me that, is she?'

He shrugs, 'Never's a long time.'

Exhaling, I gaze forward as the kids file on stage; I spot Adam, looking confident. I feel my heart glow and I do my best to stay in the room, forget, or perhaps accept what has just happened, and try to move on and enjoy the moment. As the show starts, there is so much joy in the room, I desperately want to feel it fully, wrap myself up in a blanket of Christmas love, but it's like I have a barrier just determinedly wanting to swoop in, and crush my soul. I can feel myself wanting to go numb, to detach. I momentarily tune in to my negative inner voice:

You don't deserve a warm glow of love.

I shake my head and take three deep breaths.

Yes, I do. I find a new voice, a quiet one, softly waving at me from the corner of my mind. I've been physically absent from Adam's life for the last two years; I don't want to be mentally absent for this.

I wipe my tears with my free hand and feel Nick's thumb comfortingly rubbing the top of my other. I tune in to the soft touch of his fingers entwined with mine, slowly bringing me back to the present moment; it feels like love.

I deserve to feel love.

I try to tune in to the appreciation of this gesture, feel the gratitude of it, and will myself to come fully out of my head, and back into the room. I squeeze his hand and breathe out the negative thoughts as best I can.

I am in control of what I think, how I feel, and what I do.

And with that thought, I snuggle into my seat, lean on Nick's shoulder, and laugh at a joke Adam's just executed brilliantly.

I'm allowed to enjoy my life.

Chapter 23

25th December

Christmas morning, I wake in Nick's arms. I breathe in a hint of fabric softener, harmonising with his spicy, woody aftershave; a cosy feeling filling every cell. From the pleasant rhythm of his warm breath on the back of my neck, Nick's still fast asleep. I lie, motionless, when I'm hit with the same conflicting emotions that have been drumming around my head since I arrived: grateful that this is where I am, and saddened that my family are where they are.

Even so, today feels different. The weight feels lighter somehow.

Perhaps I'm ready to change?

A small glimmer of light sparks in my stomach at the possibility. I almost nod, as I think it's time that I fully welcome the idea, that it's possible to be happy in spite of the fact that they may never unconditionally love or accept me.

The question therefore stands: do I want them in my life? What would that look like? A new version of a relationship with them would have to be what I contemplate; I'm not interested in the old one.

I synchronise my breath with Nick's and an unexpected wave of hope flows through me, or, no, I think it's strength.

I think I know what I want.

Nick and I weren't strong enough to stay together before, but maybe we could be this time. Maybe *I* could be stronger.

As I lie on my left side, the little to Nick's big spoon, I enjoy the warmth of his body behind me; his toned chest rising and falling close to my back. His stretched-out left arm lays just below my pillow and above my left shoulder, so his left hand is extended and can lovingly hold mine. I shift ever so slightly, not to disturb him, but to gaze at his fingers entwined with my own. I've always felt safe in his arms, he's always made everything better. I'm tired of running away from my feelings or pretending they're not there. But what about my flight to New York tomorrow? Should I give up my job?

Nick must be dreaming, he gives a small happy huff, like he's laughing, then with the rustle of the duvet, he takes his right arm out of the covers, and scoops me in closer, for a cuddle. A warm glow of a feeling tells me I'm home, and unusually, it's not immediately followed by the cold rushing sensation of shame.

I close my eyes again, appreciating this shift.

I snuggle further into Nick's embrace and slowly he starts to stir. Still holding my left hand, he draws that in so both his arms are now cuddling me, then tenderly kisses the back of my neck. 'I love you, Sophie.' His voice is sleepy.

I gently transition out of his embrace, roll over, and kiss him softly on the lips. 'I love you too,' I say when we break apart.

We both adjust slightly, to lie on our sides, facing each other; he brushes a strand of my hair away. Neither of us says anything for a time, lost in our thoughts of each other. Then he adjusts his pillow, 'You've no idea how good it feels to wake up and see you each morning. I don't want that to go away; I don't want *you* to go away,' he corrects himself, vulnerably.

I reach for my glasses on the bedside table, then putting them on, his features come into focus, 'I don't want to go anywhere,' I smile.

'Then stay.'

I make a face, 'I've got a flight booked for tomorrow.'

'Well, delay it. Or, better yet, cancel it completely. Then we can celebrate you moving home at my charity Boxing Day party.'

'I always did love your parties,' I consider, now hugging my pillow.

'That's because they're the best,' he says without a hint of arrogance.

'I can't believe I haven't asked you about it, yet, I'm sorry.'

'You've been a little preoccupied, I understand.' He puts his bottom lip out to pout which makes me grin.

'What theme did you decide on?'

'Masquerade ball.'

'Nice. Doesn't particularly work with my glasses though.' I find my hand subconsciously reaches up to adjust them.

'You weren't here when I was organising it.' His voice is soft.

'Good point.' I smile sadly.

'Rise and Shine are playing.'

'Now, you're just trying to make me feel bad.'

'No, I'm trying to help you acknowledge what's good.'

I exhale and continue to stare at his beautiful face. 'What's good.' I contemplate these words, and a sigh escapes my lips as I reach my hand up to stroke his cheek. 'Why didn't I stay before?'

He exhales, 'Because your family twisted you into a knot so tight that you had to unravel on your own terms.'

'Why didn't you ask me to stay?'

His expression is pained, 'Because I was in a knot of my own. Plus,' he pauses and looks deeper into my eyes, 'I was afraid.'

'What were you afraid of?'

'You losing yourself if you stayed.'

'What?' I don't know what answer I was expecting, but it wasn't that.

'You have no idea how hard it is to have to watch you crumble and become a shell of a person after each comment, dig, lie, or whatever the hell comes out of their mouths.'

I shrug, 'But I lost everything anyway.'

'*Ugh*, why does it have to be so complicated?'

'Because we make it that way. Humans, I mean. To paraphrase the late, great, Dr Wayne Dyer: Life is really simple, but we insist on making it complicated.' We continue to look sadly at each other, not knowing what to say or do next. But it's Nick who breaks the silence,

'Oh, Merry Christmas.'

I smile, 'Merry Christmas, Nick.' Both sadness and joy wash over me; I'm here with him now, but at the same time, we've missed two years, and if I don't change something, it will be our last.

'I got you a little something,' we both sit up, then he reaches over to his bedside table and hands me a small, badly wrapped present.

I laugh, 'I love that your wrapping abilities haven't changed.'

He waves me away, 'You were always the one who wrapped our gifts; I'm way too impatient for all that crap.' His expression falls into vulnerability. 'I hope you like it.'

'What is it?' I turn the gift over in my hands to try and give myself an idea of what's inside.

'You'll have to open it.'

Carefully unwrapping the present, I put the paper to one side. A small purple box with an unintentionally twisty white ribbon is revealed to me. Pulling the satin loose, I let it fall. Butterflies start to flutter in my stomach as I take off the lid and remove some white tissue paper. Inside, lying on a bed of rose petals, is a key; the key to this flat. *My* key that I left here, in floods of tears as I shut the door on our relationship all those years ago. I look up at him with glossy eyes.

'Two years ago, I wasn't strong enough, or clear enough in my head, but what I now know for sure, is that I can't lose you again, Soph.'

'I…I…don't know what to say.'

'I know it's silly. It's just a gesture.' He tries to dismiss what he's given me, but I'm not sure he'll ever know just how much it means to me. 'The key was always yours; like the one to my heart.' He laughs, brushing his messy bed hair away from his forehead, 'Sorry, that was cheesy.'

I shrug, 'I liked it.'

'I was afraid that the last couple of days were just about closure or unfinished business for you. But I never got over you, Sophie, and I don't want to have to.'

I smile, not quite able to find my voice.

'I'm sorry if that's all a bit overwhelming, and don't feel like you have to answer me right now, but please think about what I've said.'

I'm nodding.

'And I know you have a life in New York and a job and everything—an amazing job by the way, I'm so proud of you—I'm not sure how we'll make it work, but what I came to realise over the last two years is that…' Still holding the box, he places his hands on top of mine. 'My life doesn't work without you in it. I have no idea what the future will bring or how we're going to navigate your crazy family, but you have to know that I haven't been excited about anything since you left my life. There's no substance or meaning; my life feels empty without you in it. You're…you're my person, Sophie.'

I realise I'm smiling and crying at the same time. 'You're *my* person.' I lean over and kiss him, knowing in my heart that somehow, I'll find a way to make it work this time. I just need to figure out how. When we break apart, I lean my forehead on his, 'Now, the present I got you seems ridiculous in comparison.'

He shakes his head softly, 'I don't need a present. You're my present.' He kisses the tip of my nose.

A small chuckle comes out of my mouth, 'Well, nonetheless,' placing the key on the bedside table, I pull the drawer, and reach in for his gift. 'Please don't laugh.'

He unwraps it with the enthusiasm of a five-year-old, always so keen to get into a neatly hidden package. When the paper has been discarded his mouth drops open. 'What the?' He brings the picture frame up and looks closer.

'Gabby. She snapped it when you kissed me backstage at the Light Switch On. Do you like it?'

'I love it.' He places a soft kiss on my lips—adding further evidence of why I should stay—then gently stands the frame on the bedside table. 'Oh, no, wait.' Nick throws the covers off and practically runs over to the box of my stuff that I left here two years ago, that's still lying on the floor. He brings back to the bed the frame with two pictures:

"How it started/How it's going", then places it down, grabs the picture frame I gave him, and pauses, 'Do you mind?'

I shake my head and smile, 'I think it's perfect.' I watch with glee as he transports the picture from the solo frame to the dual one.

Nick takes in his handy work and nods with approval. 'We can think about another picture to go in this frame.' He scratches his chin, 'Maybe one of your news clippings?' he says quietly.

'One of my what?'

He looks sheepishly at me, 'News clippings.' He gets up once more and this time opens the cupboard. I watch with curiosity as he brings over another badly wrapped gift. 'This is your real present; I hope it doesn't come across as creepy.'

I laugh, 'Creepy? What the heck is it?' I take it from him with interest and unwrap to reveal what looks like a scrapbook. I open the cover and gasp, turning page after page.

'Freya gets photographed a lot.' He shrugs.

'And so do I, apparently.' I laugh again, then look up at him.

'It started as an accident, collecting all these clippings. A few weeks after you left, there was an article about Freya recording, and there you were, in the background, looking powerful and unshakable. I missed seeing your face. Then you kept popping up in the background of paparazzi photos, and it filled me with pride. I thought you probably wouldn't save any of these, so, I started a collection for you to look back on. My plan was to find out where you lived and send it to you, but since you're here now, I took the opportunity to put them all in a scrapbook for you; that was the errand I was running on Gabby's birthday.'

I'm speechless.

'You never acknowledge any of your achievements; I wanted you to be proud of yourself and everything you've accomplished.'

A wave of love washes through me and I lean over and kiss him gently. 'I think this is the sweetest thing anyone's ever done for me.'

'So, not creepy?'

'If you were some random person, maybe. But since you're the love of my life, I'd say, not.'

Nick heaves a sigh of relief, 'Alright, what are you thinking about today? You know that my family would love to have you there, as would Gabby's. But we'll do whatever you want.'

I nod, 'I want to spend Christmas with you and your family, then pop over to see Gabby and Scott,' I say with confidence. 'But,' I exhale, 'I feel, despite everything, that I need to see them. My soul needs to see my mum, even for a moment.'

He nods.

'There's a part of me that feels I can't be here and not spend at least some of Christmas Day with them.'

'I know,' he says this with understanding and kindness. 'Have you thought this through?'

'No. And yes.' I admit. 'I know that they haven't changed and they're not likely to, which, I don't have to tell you just what an incredibly shite thing that is, but I'm here, and maybe part of the reason *why* I'm here, is to somehow rewrite what happened two years ago. Plus, if I'm going to stay in this town, I need to know what it's going to be like. With them, I mean. I know what it would be like with us, or at least, I hope I do.' He answers me with a kiss, then takes my hand in his. 'And, I think I felt something shift in me yesterday.'

'Sorry about that,' he jokes, making me laugh.

'No,' I playfully bat him, 'not that, I meant at the show. Smoking that stuff my ego seemed to sit down, and I felt something that I've never felt for my mum.'

'And what was that?'

'I think it was empathy. There's still so much hurt, but it was like I suddenly had compassion as to why she is the way she is, without really knowing why. I can't explain it.'

Nick considers my words first, nods, and then gives me a look of concern, 'Do you want me to come with you?'

'Do you want to come with me?'

'No. But I would, for you.'

I smile, and exhale again, 'I think I need to do this on my own at first.'

'Are you thinking you'll eat there?'

'I doubt I'll make it that far. Maybe I'll just go for cocktail hour—'

'The highlight of your family's Christmases.'

I smile, 'It's always helped give the impression that my mum can cook.'

'The only thing she can cook is the nutritional value out of veg.'

I laugh loudly at this. 'Harsh but true. Anyway, I'll aim to stay put until she serves the appetisers. If I only make it through cocktail hour, then at least I'll know I tried.'

'Message me throughout so I know you're alright?'

I nod, 'I will. And then whatever happens, I'll come round to your parents; it wouldn't be the first time they've seen me cry, would it?'

'Well, hopefully it won't come to that.'
'We'll see.'

Chapter 24

Against, perhaps my better judgement, or the little voice in my head trying to battle with my gut, I walk to my family home. Being the person I am, even though these people may have hurt me in the past, I never turn up to a special occasion empty-handed. The tote bag I'm carrying hosts their gifts.

I got my mum her favourite bottle of merlot, and a Yankee Candle—the only presents she's ever approved of me getting her in the past. I got my dad a year's subscription to his favourite newspaper, as I know he always intends to do that but forgets, then a new pair of slippers as I noticed his were wearing slightly. For my brother, if it weren't for the conversation we had yesterday, I was considering framing the job and house section from the newspaper, but I swallowed my ego and resentment and got him a nice stripy scarf from Hobbs and a voucher for the Mexican restaurant, *Hermanos*; I wrote in his card that I only just realised it translates to "siblings". And last but not least, Aria. What gift is appropriate for the woman who used to be the girl who bullied me? Again, I decided to put every thought and feeling I currently have, to one side, and I bought her a mum-to-be pack: a bath thermometer, bath salts, snuggly socks, tummy rub butter (a fancy name for stretch mark stuff), and chocolate, because, who doesn't like chocolate? My current relationship with the parents-to-be might be in question right now, but I'd genuinely love to get to know my future niece or nephew. Maybe I can be their lighthouse in the sea of dark and unchartered waters.

Victoria Mae

As I walk up the slightly less snowy path to the house, I gather myself as best I can and try to swallow my negative feelings. Maybe it all boils down to this moment. Maybe this is the time that it all turns around? Maybe I could move back to my town and live with the man I love without second guessing if it's a good idea or not. Maybe I could try again to be the bigger person with my family, or perhaps we could finally just accept each other. Maybe. I give a brief, steadying inhale and exhale, and before I'm ready, I knock on the door.

Regardless of having a key to the house in my pocket, this feels…I don't know, more proper, or as if I'm standing on ceremony, somehow. I'll drop the key back where it belongs when I leave. I hear some footsteps and then see his shadow in the frosted glass, beyond the wreath.

'Merry Christmas, Dad,' I greet him cheerfully as the door swings open to reveal my father's surprised face.

'Oh, darling.' He envelops me in a hug. 'It's so nice to see you.' I soften as I hear him sniffling. He pats me on the back and then straightens up revealing glossy eyes underneath his reading glasses. 'You came home for Christmas; I can't believe it.'

'Well, we'll see how it goes,' I say, trying to soften the blow or lower his expectations, I guess.

'Yes, yes. Well, come in, sweetheart.'

Wiping my boots on the mat before taking them off, I then step out of them, and swiftly place each one gently to one side, next to the already million and one shoes piled precariously on the footwear stand. I then put the tote on the floor as I remove my scarf and coat. When I'm picking the tote bag back up, I realise my dad is staring at me. 'What is it?' I can't help but ask.

292

He shakes his head, 'You are so much stronger than I give you credit for.'

'The bag isn't that heavy, Dad,' I say, straightening up and giving a small grin.

'Not the physical weight, darling,' he gestures to the bag and then gives a sad smile, 'the emotional weight you've been carrying; I didn't know.' His brow creases, 'I guess I still don't know the full extent, do I?'

I'm shocked to hear my dad saying anything like this, particularly in the family home. 'Thank you.' He places a warm hand on my shoulder, which gives me hope that something will be different this time. 'You've no idea what that means to me.'

His expression then becomes more pained, 'I've been doing a lot of thinking since you arrived back home. And I…I could have reached out, couldn't I? I could have…' he pauses to search for his words, '…got on a plane or at least picked up the phone, in the last two years.' His expression changes, as I watch him battle thoughts in his head, before saying in a small voice, 'But then I'd have to go and find a safe spot to make the phone call.'

'What do you mean by that?' I crease my eyebrows.

'Not, *safe*, I just mean, a *private* spot—like I'd have to leave the house to make a phone call to you, and then your mother or Aria would ask where I'm going or what I'm doing; I've never been a very good liar, so, I figured it wasn't worth the trouble.'

You weren't worth the trouble, the destructive voice in my head announces.

Dad reads my expression, '*You are* worth the trouble, my darling. I'm sorry. Like I said, you are so much stronger than I am.' He leans in and lowers his voice to a whisper.

'You've stood up to both Mum and Aria since you've been here.'

'Not really.' I automatically refuse to accept this as a compliment.

'You've got to give me pointers on how to do that.'

I smile. 'I have no idea. I don't know what I've said.'

'Well, anyway,' Dad continues in his normal voice. 'Since we're here, together, alone in the hallway, I want to say, I'm sorry. And that I was a coward. I'm still a coward. I was too wrapped up in my own struggle, I couldn't see yours. I'm a quiet man and I don't often say what I'm thinking or feeling.'

'Well, there's no room, time or place in this household.'

'I know, but...and I know it's no excuse, but I have to live with them, so, it's easier to agree than to start a confrontation.'

I exhale slightly, and decide to share something that my therapist told me, 'The thing about that, Dad, is that when you don't share it, you end up having to carry everything, and you start a war in your head.'

He nods, knowingly. 'Regardless, you're here.' He pulls me in for another hug. 'I wish I had your strength and resilience, Sophie.'

'Well, we'll see how long for, but a part of me wanted to be here. A part of me never wanted to have to leave; you know that, right?'

He nods, 'You had to go; you were pushed to your limit.' We stand, still in our hug, in silent solidarity for a moment; I finally feel understood. I nervously clear my throat and loosen my grip to look at him.

'So, shall we go in?'

'Are you ready?'

'No.'

And with that, we put our arms around each other, and walk through to the living room.

The only influence my dad has had on the Christmas vibes of the house over the years is the music. He loves Bing Crosby, Dean Martin, and all the crooners. As we walk into the living room, Sammy Davis Jr's playful tones fill the air with, 'Sweet Gingerbread Man'. Mum is in her usual spot on the right-hand side of the couch, with Aria next to her, and Chris in the last seat left on the couch. They all have their backs to me and Dad, facing the roaring fire, and for a moment I wonder if I've made a mistake, and whether there's time to turn back. I think Dad senses this and gives me a little encouraging squeeze. 'There's a delivery,' Dad says and my stomach sinks into my feet, in anticipation.

'Oh, it's probably for me; so many people from the village have been giving me baby gifts,' Aria says cheerily before turning around. When her head turns and her eyes meet mine, her expression drops, 'You? What the hell are you doing here?'

'Merry Christmas to you too.' As I reply, my mum and brother's heads whip around faster than a pair of curious meerkats. Neither of them says anything, so I begin a nervous mumble, 'I thought it would be—' I want to say "nice", but that's definitely not that word, 'the right thing to do, to spend Christmas, or at least part of it, together. I thought maybe we could park everything temporarily and, so, Merry Christmas, everyone.' When no one responds, I take that as my queue to keep going in my babble, 'So, how's your morning been? Opened presents yet?' I put my hand into the tote bag, and one by one, hand out my gifts to them, 'I got everyone a little something.'

Mum, Dad and Chris look at their gifts, in shock, but Aria takes the package like I've given her something disgusting. She passes it to my brother to dispose of, then gets to her feet. 'You have some nerve, Sophie.'

'Excuse me?'

She makes a slow, threatening and purposeful, "this is my territory" walk around the couch to face me. 'You have *deeply* hurt *everyone* in this room,' she says spitefully. '*Your* actions and what *you* did to *us*, since the moment you arrived back in *our* town, are disgraceful.'

I sputter, 'Are…are you kidding me? *My actions*? And what exactly have I done or said?'

'You know exactly what you've done and said,' Aria spits venomously at me. 'Mum, in particular, was deeply affected by what you did and how you acted.'

I think for a moment; is she talking about me hugging Mum yesterday? Surely not.

'Let me get you a drink, Sophie.' Dad loosens his protective arm from my shoulders, and walks sheepishly, but swiftly to the kitchen, 'Wine? Cocktail?' he calls while still on the move, away from any confrontation.

'Anything is fine, Dad, thank you,' I say softly as I stand, rooted to my spot, feeling stronger than I've felt so far on this trip, and pretty sure that I haven't done anything wrong. Then ignoring my sister-in-law-to-be, I turn to my brother,

'Have I deeply hurt you?'

'Well…ha…I *um*…'

Then I turn to my mum. 'Have I deeply hurt you?'

Mum shifts in her seat and clears her throat. 'I hardly think that this is the time for you to start a fight, Sophia. It's Christmas.'

I'll take that as a no. I raise an eyebrow at Aria, silently challenging her to carry on. My therapist always says that *no response is a response.* Aria folds her arms, clearly, two can play this game.

'Here we are! A gingerbread martini!' My dad comes back into the room with a cocktail glass in each hand; I'm tempted to take both and throw them one after the other in Aria's face, but resist the urge. I watch him give one to Mum, and then thank him, as I accept the one offered to me. I take a sip, there's a good dose of caramel vodka mixed with the Irish cream liquor. I turn to my dad, 'I like that you added cinnamon this year.'

'That's not new to us. He's added it for the last two years; you'd know that if you'd been around.'

The back of my neck prickles but I refuse to rise to her bait. This is the moment I can put everything I've learnt about protecting myself and standing up for myself into place. I stride with as much confidence as I can away from her toxicity, and take a seat in the corner, by the neatly decorated Christmas tree, the spot I always used to frequent. My parents' tabby cat, Truffle, saunters in and seems to notice me. She rubs her head and body on my legs, purring. Then with a soft *pat-pat* of encouragement to welcome her up, she leaps and lands on my thighs, circles twice, then curls up contently on my lap. I stroke her with my free hand and sip my cocktail with the other. This seems to infuriate Aria even more.

'I need the loo,' she walks off and out of the room and I am glad for Truffle's soft fur, it's comforting. My dad takes to the vacant armchair opposite me, and our family of four sit in silence until my mum breaks it.

'I haven't got you a gift.'

'I don't need a gift,' I say, finding I mean it.

'I didn't think you would come so I didn't see any point in buying you a gift.'

'I told you, I don't need one.'

'I was going to but then I just assumed—'

'It's OK.'

She sits and stares at me, not quite sure if I'm playing a "long game" or not. 'Well, you should take this back, whatever it is.'

'Don't be silly; open it.'

She does so carefully, unfolding the paper in what I used to consider an infuriatingly slow fashion; I'm proud to say that I think I've just reached acceptance—on something small—but I'll take it. She then puts the paper neatly to one side, to store with the rest of the wrapping that I know she'll reuse. 'My favourite merlot.' She raises an eyebrow, places it down on the side table, then unwraps the next, 'And a Yankee Candle,' she declares to the room, then faces me, 'Aria got me a set of four of these.'

I catch my breath and stop myself from saying anything defensive, 'Well, you've now got one more; perhaps that one can go in the downstairs loo or something?'

'*Hmm*,' she says, then gives it a sniff, 'That's not too offensive.'

That's as close to a "thank you" as I think I'll get. 'Good.'

'Oh, I know!' Mum stands and walks out of the living room; I hear her head up the stairs. While she's gone both the men of my family open their gifts and thank me with, what I think is embarrassment, that I've gone to the effort of buying them something they either need, want, or like, and clearly, they haven't got me anything in return.

I hear Mum's footsteps back down the stairs then she speeds into the room and darts across the carpet, handing me a Pandora bag. I look up at her in surprise. Returning to her seat, her expression reveals triumph.

'You did get me a present,' I say with a small smile.

'Well, I was in Pandora getting the essentials, and you know, I bought *so* much in there, obviously several bits for Aria to add to her collection, and the ladies in the Town Hall, etc, and I spent so much money, that they gave me something for free, so, that's yours.'

I exhale lightly; *did she really need to tell me that story?* I open the package to reveal a plain silver bracelet: no character, no charm; she has no idea who I am, or what I like, but, as she said, it was free, and not intended for me anyway. 'Thank you,' I decide to say out loud, then, placing my glass down on the snowman coaster on the side table next to me, I put the bracelet on.

'You're welcome.' She sits back with pride.

The four of us continue to sit there in silence, with my dad and brother looking increasingly awkward, and my mum, too proud to strike up a conversation first. I sit, quite contentedly, while continuing to stroke Truffle. Sammy has now finished his song and Frank Sinatra takes over with, 'Have Yourself a Merry Little Christmas.' Apart from the Crooners' Christmas soundtrack, the only other sound is the crackling fire. I wish so badly for this to feel warm and cosy, but a sad thought occurs to me: these people haven't been interested in the woman I've become. This might be my birth home, and these people are my birth family, but I can't ever truly relax with them and just be myself. I don't feel at "home" with them.

'CHRISTOPHER!!!' Aria's voice shrieks from the other side of the house. He jumps to attention and quickly strides off. Now alone with my parents, I thought I might have more to say. What would I like to discuss? In the last two years, what have I been dying to share with them?

'It's lovely to have you here, Sophie.' My dad breaks the silence and I smile at his effort. He turns to my mum, 'Isn't it, Aubrey?'

'Well, it certainly is a surprise that I—'

'We have to go to the hospital!' Chris runs into the room and starts gathering up his phone and wallet.

'What?'

'Why?'

'What's happened?'

My parents and I all answer at the same time.

'Aria said she's getting pains. I think it's the baby. I think there's something wrong.'

I gently lift Truffle off my lap, placing her on the seat, 'Come on, then,' I say. I might not like the woman, but I certainly don't want anything to happen to her or the child.

'I've had several of these,' my dad says in panic, gesturing to his now empty glass, 'I can't drive.'

'We've all had several of those,' Chris says, 'We can't ask Aria to drive!'

'I've only had one,' I place my martini glass down, 'I could drive?'

'Don't be stupid, Sophia, you'll kill us all,' Mum staggers to her feet, 'We'll get a taxi.'

'On Christmas day?' I say with disbelief. 'Mum, this is an emergency. You know we can't get a taxi, or an ambulance for that matter, here on a *normal* day in a decent amount of time.'

'Come on, people! My fiancé is very scared and in a lot of pain!'

I exhale, get out my phone and start dialling, 'Get her in Mum's car. I've got this.'

Chapter 25

'So, how is everyone doing?' Nick asks a car full of Carters, and a screeching Aria, as he carefully weaves through the snowy country lanes towards the hospital. Everyone in Mum's seven-seater car continues to talk at the same time. Aria is screaming in pain and shouting expletives at anyone and everyone; Chris is sobbing loudly in between blaming himself; Mum is telling Nick he's going to kill us all and to watch the pedestrian that's nowhere near the car; Dad has had his eyes shut since we set off (he hates all the shouting) but he's also mumbling inaudibly.

As I glance over to Nick, he's amazingly calm— something that I never fully manage to pull off in front of my family. In spite of everything, here he is, once again, saving the day. 'Thank you.' I shift in the passenger seat to face Nick and place my right hand on his left thigh.

He smiles softly but keeps his eyes on the road. 'Don't mention it,' he says quietly enough for me to hear but no one else, not that they could, as Classic FM's 'Ride of the Valkyries' can't even be heard over the Carter chorus.

As we take a left turn into the hospital, I note the car park is packed. Without hesitation, Nick drives up to the drop-off zone, and the moment the car is stationary, my family exits the car faster than I thought possible. As they head for the entrance, Nick leans over and kisses me on the cheek. 'Go; I'll find a parking spot and come find you.'

I shake my head, 'Even after everything, you came when I called.'

He shrugs, 'You needed me. I'm always here for you no matter what they've—'

'SOPHIA!' Both Nick and I jump as Mum knocks aggressively on the passenger window and I press the button for it to wind down. 'We do not have time for you to fool around with this…' she searches for a word, '…hooligan.'

'He's the reason we're here so quickly,' I gesture to Nick then at the hospital.

She huffs and stands tall, 'We absolutely could have got a taxi; we don't need him in our lives.'

'Oh my God, would you just say "thank you" or something resembling human decency for once?'

'You are wasting time, Sophia. Get out of the car. The family needs to come together.'

'Nick *is* family.' She looks as though she's been slapped. 'We're going to find a parking space and then *we* will come and find you.'

She stands even straighter, with one raised eyebrow, waiting for me to change my mind or apologise, and when I don't, she stamps her foot. 'Fine.' Then we watch in silence as she stomps off towards the entrance, like a grumpy toddler with purpose. As the A&E doors slide open, my dad and Chris are just visible, either side of Aria, propping her up, as she bends over-double in visible pain, at the registration desk.

'I hope she's OK.'

'Me too. I mean, I honestly couldn't think less of the girl, but still.' Nick takes a deep breath. 'Alright, let's find somewhere to park.'

After we've circled the car park several times, a space becomes available, and then we head towards the A&E entrance. When we walk hand in hand through the entrance, we spot my dad sitting by himself in the waiting area; clearly my mum insisted on going in with Aria and Chris. We walk past someone who's managed to tangle themselves in multicoloured tree lights, someone with their hand wrapped in a very bloody makeshift plaster, I try not to look too hard at that. A child is crying with an ice pack on her head, people are clutching their stomachs, arms, and feet, and a drunk man is yelling at the lady at the front desk. It's complete and utter carnage, and I suddenly feel very sorry for the doctors and nurses who have to deal with all of this, rather than relaxing at home, spending the holidays with the people they love.

Reaching my dad, he stands to greet us and then extends his hand to Nick. Nick squeezes my hand, lovingly, and then loosens and lets go, to accept my dad's handshake. 'Thank you, Nicholas. We really appreciate you helping us out here.'

'Don't mention it.' Nick smiles at my dad, and we all take a seat.

'You always were a gentleman, even when you were just a teenager.'

'Really?' Nick says in disbelief.

'Oh, yes. I always admired the way you looked after my Sophie.' He stops himself, and nods, saying in a quieter voice, 'I still admire the way you look after my Sophie.'

Nick looks at me, 'Well, you do anything for the people you love.'

I smile as Nick takes my hand once more, then I glance back over to my dad. 'So, is she being seen now? That's quick.'

'Priority. Your mother insisted on going in.'

'Of course she did.'

'*Um.*' Dad is continuing to look at Nick and I, seemingly trying to find his words. 'What Aria said about you that Christmas, wasn't true, was it?' Both Nick and I shake our heads, and remorse covers every inch of my dad's face. 'I should have known, or at least asked, instead of letting them act in the way they did. You've been in our lives longer than she has.' Dad shakes his head, 'I'm sorry for the part I played, Nick.'

'You didn't do anything, sir.'

'No, I did.' Dad sighs, 'I was the enabler; I allowed you to be spoken to and treated in a way you never deserved, and for that, I'm sorry.'

Nick exhales, his eyebrows raised slightly in surprise; I know he never expected an apology from anyone in my family, 'Thank you for saying that, Richard.'

Dad shakes his head, 'You're a member of this family, Nick; call me, Dad.'

'Alright then, Dad.'

Smiling at this warming exchange, I momentarily allow myself to forget we're sitting in a wild A&E waiting room.

'Why would she lie about that?' Dad is looking at the floor; I'm pretty sure his question isn't directed at either of us and I don't think he's expecting an answer, but I give him one anyway.

'Because she wanted to take me down and distract everyone from her own bad decisions. Like taking out a restraining order on Chris, or having him arrested to win an argument.'

'I can't begin to fathom why her mind works in the way it does,' Dad shakes his head.

'I think because of her toxic family, she's desperate for attention or outside validation, and when she doesn't get that, she acts out,' Nick chips in, and then we all fall into contemplative silence.

We stay in the waiting area for several hours with no news and nothing to distract us apart from increasingly ridiculous injuries, before a puffy-eyed Chris reappears to talk to us. 'She's in labour.'

'What? But she said she's due in February; that's what? 30 weeks?'

'32. They said she's just on the border of "very preterm" and "moderate preterm". They've been doing all kinds of tests and were hoping that she'd give birth naturally, but it's looking like it'll be an emergency c-section.'

Dad places a hand on Nick's shoulder. 'What can we do?'

Chris shakes his head, looking as white as a ghost, 'I've no idea. I don't know what to do. The baby's not due for another two months. I'm not prepared, I can't do this. We haven't even packed a bag yet, never mind brought it with us. I was supposed to buy a car seat and I haven't gotten around to it yet. We haven't got the room set up, but then if something happens, maybe we won't need the room…' His eyes fill with tears. 'And, what if something happens to Aria? I can't handle this.'

'Everything is going to be just fine,' I find myself saying out loud. 'Aria is strong and I'm pretty sure your baby is going to be too. Now, they need *you* to stay focused, OK.'

'I'm sure she's in the best hands,' Nick says. 'We can gather together everything you need. I'll swing by my brothers and get Adam's old car seat that I know they haven't sold, we'll get a bag together; what do you need?'

'*Um*,' Chris scratches his head, 'I've no idea. It's all in the birth planner in our room.'

'Fine,' I cut Chris off, 'We'll find that, get everything, and be back before you know it.'

'And I'll stay right here. You can do this, Son.'

'Do you have your phone on? We can call when we're back?'

'I think so.' He reaches for his back pocket and looks, 'My battery's low.'

'Then we'll grab a charger too,' Nick says.

'And we'll let the front desk know when we're back, and they can send it through if we can't get hold of you, alright?' I place a hand on his arm.

Chris nods, then makes his way numbly back through the double doors to the other side of the hospital.

'You OK on your own, Dad?'

He nods with a look of concern. 'Fine, fine. See you in a bit, darling.' Dad gives me a kiss on the cheek, then Nick and I head for the door.

'Never one for a quiet, calm life, is she?'

I laugh, 'Nope, Aria's always got to create some sort of drama. Oh, God, I hope everything's going to be alright.'

***

Weaving our way back through the snowy country lanes, Nick and I are silent. He's concentrating on driving, and my mind is in PA mode; making my own list of everything I think they might want or need, regardless of their planner. We swing by Nick's brother's house first, and with the baby seat secured in the back (thanks to his brother because neither of us had a clue) we head over to my parent's house. When we pull up, I race in, and head to Chris' room.

I almost go to knock then realise how ridiculous that is. Pushing the door open, I step in and don't recognise the room at all; Aria has completely redecorated. Of course she has; the last time I was in here, I think Chris and I were teenagers.

'Alright, where do we begin?'

'The planner,' Nick says, weaving a hand through his hair, 'Chris said everything they'll need is in there.'

So, we start looking around the room. Aria is someone who loves a good list, and over the years that I've known her, she has continued to buy fancy notebooks to organise anything and everything, each needing their own one, of course: food shopping (small white notebook with bananas on the front); clothes shopping (pink with varying-coloured high heels); chore list (blue with a dustpan, broom and washing machine on the front).

'How many notebooks does one woman need?' Nick laughs as he picks up a purple one with "films to watch" on the front. 'We're going to be here all day.'

I finish looking on their desk, enjoying for a moment my favourite notebook I've come across so far: a green one that's emblazoned with "Things that Chris needs to get done", and make my way over to the bedside table. I fan through, "Books to read", "Music to listen to", "Christmas gifts", and "Birthday gifts", then finally spot the planner. 'Got it.' I sit on their bed and open the book, trying to get directly to the list to save time and not get distracted by wondering if she wants a water birth or something. 'Alright, here we go.' Standing, I place the open book on the bed, scanning the top line. 'Use the gym bag on top of the cupboard.' Looking up, there's surprisingly only one there, so I go to reach it, and don't come close, even on tiptoes.

'Here, I got it.' Nick reaches up effortlessly and then places it on the bed.

'Thanks. OK.' I make my way down the list and start opening and closing drawers, feeling like I'm invading their privacy.

I work my way around the room, throwing things onto the bed for the, hopefully, soon-to-be family of three. Aria's dressing gown is next, then Chris' "thick beige jumper in case he has to stay overnight and gets cold", then the list of baby clothes they've already bought that they'd like to take the newborn home in. Each item I place down, Nick refolds neatly, and then puts them, one by one, in the bag. As he's finishing up, I then head to the bathroom to get some toiletries. When I'm back, Nick is sitting reading the book.

'I'm not sure we have time for reading right now,' I say, placing the toiletries in the gym bag. '*Ooh*, Chris' charger.' I walk to his side of the bed, take out the charger from the wall, wrap it up and pop it in the bag too.

Nick watches me, but he's got an unsure look on his face, 'Take a look.' He hands me the Birthing Planner. 'Look at the last item.'

I do as instructed and gaze down the list of what we've prepared for the hospital. I read the last line out loud, 'Ring Sophie…and maybe Nick.' I lift my eyes to Nick's.

'I'm impressed you got a mention, never mind me.'

'It's written in Chris' handwriting, not Aria's,' I note the penmanship has changed from a swirly print to a messy scrawl, then close the book with a firm snap. '*Hmm*. Not quite sure how to process that right now.' I pack the book. 'We'll bring this too.'

It's then that my phone beeps. I take it out of my back pocket, in case it's Chris, then pause as I read who it's from.

'What? What is it? Is it the baby?' Nick's voice is full of concern.

'No.' I exhale, 'It's BA. I can check in for my flight now.' I freeze, Nick and I look longingly at each other, then I put my phone back in my pocket again. 'Can't process that right now either.'

Nick sighs. 'Let's just see what happens today.'

I nod, and with that comment, Nick grabs the bag and we race back to the hospital.

***

'I can't understand what's taking so long.' I want to add, *surely that's a bad sign*, but I can't bring myself to say that out loud. We're sat on the world's most uncomfortable seats drinking terrible coffee and feasting on a make-shift Christmas meal of delights from the nearest vending machine; apparently, it didn't occur to Nick or I to pick up anything edible on our way back.

'Are you sure you can't find out if there's any update?' My dad asks the nurse behind reception for the thousandth time.

She smiles kindly, 'I'm sure they'll be doing everything they can, sir.'

I stare up at the clock on the wall; it's now coming up to 5 p.m. and it was around 11 a.m. when Aria was taken in.

'There's something wrong, isn't there?' I whisper to Nick.

'There's no way to tell. But yeah, I think Chris or your mum would have come out and said something by now. Or at least replied to your messages.'

Dad returns to us, choosing to pace up and down instead of sitting. 'This is ridiculous,' he says under his breath before pacing towards a window.

'I know now might not be the time, but did you want to talk about your flight or anything I said this morning, as a distraction?' Nick looks at me hopefully.

I smile at him. 'I'm not going anywhere.'

'What about Freya?'

'I haven't got that far,' I say honestly. 'But I'm not leaving you; I can't lose you again.' I take him in and we kiss gently.

'She's here!' Chris' voice rings over the hustle and bustle of the waiting room. We all stand and rush over. He's burst out of the nearest double doors, dressed in green scrubs. 'There were some complications, and she's on a breathing machine now to help. Aria's not in great shape either, but they're taking care of her and she's hopefully going to be fine now. But she's here. I'm a dad. I have a daughter. Born at 4.27 p.m., weighing 4 pounds 7 ounces.'

'Four pounds? Oh my God,' I say this without thinking if it's inappropriate or not.

'Yeah, she's tiny, I can fit her in my palm, but the doctors said she's doing really well.'

We each hug and congratulate him, both Nick and I leaving all the emotional baggage at the door. 'Does she have a name yet?' I ask.

'Holly,' he smiles.

'Very festive. Holly Carter,' I smile; I have a niece. I'm an aunt.

'Holly *Sophia* Carter.'

I'm taken aback. It's not my name, but near enough. Mum finally got her: "i.a." instead of "i.e.".

Victoria Mae

'When can we see Holly?' Dad says with pride.
'Now, if you're ready?'

***

We walk with Chris through to the maternity ward. Up one corridor, down the next, three floors up and around several corners, then there's a chorus of babies crying, so I know we're in the right place. But we take a little turn away from the sound of crying and through to another section of the hospital. It's quiet, sombre even. Nick and I are hand in hand, and Dad is walking with his palm on Chris' back. We turn one final corner and there's a large window. A small incubator is visible, and a tiny baby lies within it.

We walk through the door to the right, one by one, and then slowly over to the incubator. Holly is tiny, pink, with fluffy, almost chick-like, sandy blonde hair, just like Chris'. Her eyes are shut, tubes are coming out of her nose, and there's a cannula attached to her left, doll-sized hand. There's a monitor with wavy lines that I have no idea what they mean and various bits of liquid that seem to be pumping into her from bags hanging on metal stands. My eyes fill with tears.

'Hi, Holly,' I say to the small infant. 'I'm your Auntie Sophie and this,' I smile at Nick, 'is your—'

'Uncle Nick,' Chris finishes my sentence. My brother and I lock eyes and there's both an unspoken apology and understanding within his gaze. My eyes continue to well up with increasing intensity.

'Hi, there, Holly,' Nick says looking in, his eyes also showing signs of glossiness. 'It's nice to meet you.'

'This is a family moment; what is *that man* doing here?'

312

'Mum,' I exhale and turn around to face her. 'Stop it.'

She strides in and up to Nick, 'Get out.'

'Excuse me?'

'You heard what I said. I don't know how you can show your face in front of our family.'

'Mum.'

'Aubrey.'

My dad and I answer at the same time.

'Mum,' it's Chris' turn. 'Now is not the time. Nick is welcome here.'

'He most certainly is not. After everything he's done to break up this family.'

I look over to Nick, his eyes are closed and he's exhaling. 'He has done nothing to break up this family,' I say with increasing frustration. 'Your first-ever grandchild has just been born; why don't you focus on that, and we can talk about this another time.'

'How are we doing? *Ooh*, more family,' a cheery voice adds to the party. We all turn and see the door swinging closed from a nurse who's just walked in. She's wearing a bright blue, paper Christmas party hat, with elastic around her double chin.

'This is my dad, my sister and her partner,' Chris introduces us and I clock Mum's frown, but she amazingly stays silent.

The nurse nods at us, then checks a few of the bells and whistles around Holly's incubator, before turning to us once more, taking in all our expressions. 'I've walked in on a family dispute, *huh*? Nothing like a Christmas drama to bring that out of us all.' She looks in on Holly and smiles. 'She's a fighter, this one.' The nurse's eyes come up to meet mine, 'I'm guessing strong, stubborn, and determined, are qualities that run in this family?'

I smile at her, 'You've no idea.'

'Alright, well, nice to meet you all, but I'm afraid I'm going to have to ask you to leave in a few minutes. Apart from you, Dad.' She squeezes my brother's arm. 'We've got a bit more monitoring to do, but Chris insisted on you all meeting her first.'

'Well, I have to stay around too. Aria would want me here,' Mum says strongly.

The nurse considers her words carefully before replying, 'That may be so, Grandma, but—'

'Oh, no, I'm Auntie Aubrey; *Grandma* makes me sound too old.'

The nurse doesn't know what to do with that comment, 'Alright then. Immediate family only from now.'

'I am immediate family.'

'In this case, it means fathers only. Are you the father?' The nurse challenges Mum, and I can't help but let a snigger escape.

'Well, no.'

'Great then. Happy Christmas everyone; what a beautiful gift, *huh*?' the nurse nods to Holly then opens her palm to gesture for us all to leave. 'Chris will stay with Aria overnight. We're not sure right now about the timeline of everyone coming home, but you'll be pleased to hear that despite the appearance, she's doing well. And Aria is too, she's in recovery.'

'That is good news,' I say, 'Thank you.'

She smiles warmly at me, clearly "thank yous" aren't expressed enough here, 'You are very welcome.'

We all make our way out of the door, except for my mum, who's looking back at Holly with her arms folded.

'Come on *Auntie Aubrey*,' the nurse says kindly.

'It's just that…'

'Yes?'

'They can't do this without me.'

'I'm almost positive they can. Now come on, out of that room please.' The nurse waves her arm from the doorway, and with a clearly visible internal struggle, Mum reluctantly joins us in the corridor. 'I'm sure I'll see you all again. Go and enjoy the rest of your Christmas.'

'Thank you,' Chris says to Nick, giving him a firm handshake, then he turns to me, Dad and Mum, hugging each of us quickly. And with that, the nurse puts a palm forward to guide us towards the exit, while she and Chris go the other way, towards where I assume Aria is.

'They can't do this on their own,' Mum says quietly to Chris' back, watching them walk away.

'Come on, darling.' Dad pops an arm around Mum, 'Let's go back home and lift a glass to our grandchild.'

A smile spreads across her face, as she turns to my dad. 'You're right.'

'Well, first time for everything.' Dad turns to me and Nick, 'May we get a lift home with you, Nick?'

'Of course.' He smiles at my parents and for some reason, my mum is silent, and remains that way, all the way back.

***

When Nick has parked in Mum's usual spot, we all exit the car. My dad speaks first, as Nick hands him the keys, 'Thank you, for everything. We couldn't have done this without you.'

'We would have found a way,' my mum says under her breath, then shuts the door with gusto.

'We are really grateful.' Dad's eye twitches.

'Yeah, for that awful driving.'

'Aubrey. Stop it.' Dad locks the car.

Nick and I are just as stunned as Mum's face; my dad has never stood up to her before.

'I beg your pardon?' Dad goes to open his mouth but Mum continues, 'Don't you ever raise your voice to me; people will stare.'

Dad's voice is soft, 'By now, everyone is watching a Christmas classic, or enjoying their families with a glass of something in their hands. No one is curtain twitching. Nick did us a huge favour today. He deserves a thank you.'

My mum wavers but doesn't commit to a smile or a thank you. 'Let's go inside, Richard, it's getting cold.' She goes to turn towards the house, then spins back, 'Are you coming Sophia?'

'I'm going to spend the rest of Christmas with Nick's family. But thank you for the invitation. I'll see you the day after tomorrow.'

'Why not tomorrow?'

'It's Nick's charity ball. But I'll come over on the 27th, OK? Merry Christmas, Mum.' I walk over and give her a hug that she doesn't return. Then, trying not to take it personally, I turn to Dad, 'Merry Christmas, Dad,' and I give him a squeeze.

'Merry Christmas, sweetheart.'

I grin and begin to feel warmth in my heart, as Dad kisses me on the top of my head, pats my arms, then walks over to

Mum, guiding her towards the house. When they reach the step, Mum opens the door and goes in without so much as a backwards glance, but my dad turns and gives us both an enthusiastic wave, before stepping in and closing the door.

Nick steps to my side and puts an arm around me, 'Well that was eventful. How will we ever top that next Christmas?'

'Next Christmas?' I lean in and kiss his cheek. 'Oh, I don't know.' I allow myself to dream for a moment. 'How about we go to an all-inclusive in the Bahamas, and hire one of those neat luxurious huts on sticks, surrounded by turquoise water?'

'I mean,' Nick's eyes glaze over at the blissful idea, 'that doesn't sound too shabby,' he concludes. 'Of course, we'll need to make sure the dog is taken care of.'

'We have a dog?' I grin as he plays along with this fantasy life.

He looks excitedly at me, 'I was thinking, what do you say to us adopting O, the golden Lab from the shelter? You seemed to have a connection with him. Plus, we always talked about getting a dog.' His hopeful eyes look up into mine.

'I'd love that.' He squeezes me, and as we walk up the road, arms around each other, I smile contentedly to myself. The town is quiet, magical even. The fairy-lit houses glow warmly in the twilight, and I begin to let myself imagine just how close to happiness I'll allow myself to get. 'We'll check with Scott if it's too soon to adopt, but maybe we could go on the 27th or 28th? That way you've got the party out of the way?' I suggest.

'Sounds good; I'd forgotten all about the event.' He makes a face.

'Always great to hear that the host is on top of his own party.'

He nudges me playfully, 'Good thing I'm already on top of it all.'

'You sure? No last-minute bits? Nothing you need your *girlfriend* to do?'

He smiles at my use of words while thinking, 'As your *boyfriend*, let me treat you to a dress?'

'Oh, you don't have to do that,' I bat him away.

'I know.' He grins at me, then his expression turns vulnerable, 'Sorry I'm getting a little ahead of myself talking about a dog. You sure you're not going to get your flight tomorrow?'

I allow myself to breathe, 'Well, I'll have to go back at some point; all my stuff is there, plus, I've got to figure out Freya. Maybe I'll see if I can move it. *Ooh*, maybe you could come with me for New Year's Eve, and we adopt O in January?'

'I would love to see New York around Christmas time.' He thinks for a moment, 'Yes, let's do it. We'll rearrange your flight and get one for me when we get to my parents.'

'Sounds like a plan.'

Chapter 26

26th December

Christmas at the Fosters was as delicious as I had always remembered. Warm, inviting, no stress, no drama, too much food, and plenty of drink. Adam insisted on making "Buddy the Elf" chocolate bark with me (a sickly but enjoyable mix of chocolate, ramen noodles, M&M's, and sprinkles, that you put in the oven, and let cool) then we ate it while watching *Elf.* I loved every second of being there, and today, it seems like my life is falling into place.

As I couldn't have predicted getting back together with Nick or being around for his party, when I left New York, I, annoyingly, haven't brought anything appropriate to wear to such an occasion. Maybe my little black dress but it doesn't feel special enough. He told me I could dress up in a bin bag and still be the most irresistible person there. So, with a bin bag as my solid Plan B, I head to the Boxing Day sales in the out-of-town shopping centre, with Gabby and Scott. Scott kindly drove and is now leaving us to have a girls' day, while he hunts for bargains.

I normally hate crowded stores with crazy people, but I feel light, happy and grateful right now. This evening feels special, and I want to make it as such.

'I'm not entirely sure what I'm expecting to find here for a masquerade ball,' I say, combing my hand through a rack of sparkly dresses that would please a disco ball. 'What are you wearing?'

'Oh, I'm wearing that outfit from Halloween several years back, when I was Juliet and Scott was Romeo?'

'The corset number? Nice. Don't happen to have another one of those lying around, do you?'

'Just the one, I'm afraid.'

Starting to lose hope, we leave the eighth store we've tried. 'Let's just head back, Gabs; I'll make do with my little black cocktail dress.'

'No, come on, there must be something here somewhere.' Gabby links her arm through mine. 'Let's grab a coffee and a pastry, refuel, then try the other side of the mall.'

'You have more faith than me.' We turn a corner and spot a wedding dress shop. '*Ooh*! Let's take a break from shopping for a masquerade dress and you try on some wedding dresses,' I beam at my best friend.

'Do you have any idea how much I over-ate yesterday? This is not the time to get into a white, unflattering gown.'

'Nonsense.' Without letting her convince me otherwise, I grab Gabby's hand and pull her into the store. 'You could eat a hippo and still look slim.' As the bell chimes to announce our arrival, I'm surprised to find there are a good twelve brides-to-be in here.

'Do you have an appointment?' a blonde waif of a girl asks us with a wary or hung-over face, I'm not sure which.

'Well, no,' I say, 'We thought we'd just come in and have a look around.'

'Appointment only, I'm afraid.' She doesn't look very remorseful about it.

'Oh, well, not meant to be!' Gabby attempts a swift exit and nearly bumps into a white-haired woman, carrying several gowns over her shoulder.

'Afternoon. Walk-in?'

'Yes, we are,' I quickly answer before Gabby makes excuses.

'It's your lucky day, our next appointment has just been cancelled.' She smiles and gestures around the room, with her free hand, 'Please feel free to look around. Janet will be happy to assist you.' We return our gazes to Janet-the-waif, who slaps on a fake smile.

'Let's start again. Welcome.' Janet stands from her seated position behind the counter, and walks around, 'So, which one of you is getting married?'

'Both of us,' Gabby says, and I give her a strange look, which she grins away.

'You're marrying each other?' Janet-the-waif sizes us up. 'Only one of you is wearing a ring,' she says slowly with suspicion after her eyes return from Gabby's left hand.

'Sophie's one is being resized,' is Gabby's immediate response, without a beat of hesitation, and with mild irritation in her tone for the fake ring scenario, as if she'd planned on saying it all along.

Janet-the-waif makes a face while rubbing her forehead. 'Cool. And you're happy choosing the dresses together? You don't want it to be a surprise on the day?'

'No,' Gabby says with confidence. 'I'm not a big fan of surprises.'

Janet nods while I try to keep a smirk off my face. 'Any idea what you're looking for?'

'None. We are open to suggestions.' She links her arm, lovingly through mine, and tilts her head towards me. 'I'll probably go for a traditional white of some kind, but Sophie was thinking of wearing a colourful one.'

The assistant nods, 'Different, I like it. If you want to have a look through those racks over there,' she points to our right-hand side, further into the heart of the shop, 'and I'll be back in a moment.'

As soon as Janet is out of earshot, we make our way over, and I burst out laughing. 'What on earth did you say that for?'

Gabby shrugs, 'Bit of fun, right?' She grins as she links her arm through mine and adopts an innocent expression. 'If I have to try on dresses, you may as well see what they have in here.'

'*Hmm*. Good point, I guess,' I say with doubt, 'Although I haven't got money for a wedding dress.'

'Me neither, really, but hey,' she points to a sign, 'everything in the store is 70% off!' she says with glee. 'Maybe we'll both get a great deal.' We walk over to the nearest rack, unlink our arms, and begin the search. All the dresses look the same to me, I'm not sure how much help I'm going to be. I stand back trying to see if one jumps out at me and when it doesn't, I get my phone out and Google, "types of wedding dresses". I attempt to match dresses to the picture descriptions that I've found on my phone. Gabby continues to fan her way through several gowns with increasing excitement, before taking one off the rack for closer inspection. 'What do you think of this one?' She places it in front of her body and grins.

According to my picture search, it's a straight, strapless-column dress. 'Looks nice. Hard to tell on the hanger though, right?'

'Yeah, I've no idea. I'm not a dress person, you know?' She hangs onto it, regardless. '*Ooh*, maybe they have wedding *suits*?'

I smile at my friend, 'I'm sure they do. I had no idea how many styles of wedding dresses there are; look.' I show her my phone and she raises her eyebrows. 'Hey, why don't you grab one of each style to see which you like?'

She jabs a finger at me, 'And this is why you're my Maid of Honour; I would never have thought of that.' Gabby hangs the first dress over her arm.

'OK. Here we are,' Janet-the-waif comes over with two champagne glasses.

'Now we're talking!' Gabby says, taking one with her free hand, and I accept the other flute. 'Here's to our wedding, pumpkin!' and with that, she clinks my glass, then turns to Janet. 'So, we were thinking that I'd try one of every style, including a suit if you have one?'

'No, problem. And for you? Same thing but with some colour varieties?'

'Sure, sounds good, thank you.' I sip my free champagne and feel slightly guilty about lying to this stranger.

'And did you want to try on dresses at the same time, or go one at a time?'

'Same time,' we say in unison.

'Great. We'll set you up over here.' Janet fans her palm back towards the entrance, takes the dress that's draped over Gabby's arm, and guides us to the corner nearest the front window. A tad exposing if you ask me, but I guess, who's going to be looking? There's one large dressing room for us, masked by a luxuriously thick, weighted red curtain, then to the left of that, a round podium to stand on, surrounded by mirrors to check out every angle. 'Alright,' the assistant places Gabby's first dress choice in the changing room, 'I'll select a sample for you both, and be right back. Feel free to choose more of your own too.'

Janet scurries off, Gabby heads into the changing room, pulling the curtain behind her, and I take a seat on one of the plush seats in front of the podium, happily sipping my champagne. 'We should do this more often!' I call, enjoying the bubbles.

'What? Try on dresses and drink champagne?' she calls from behind the curtain.

'Well, yeah.' I laugh, then gaze around the rest of the shop. There's light instrumental jazz piano playing which doesn't quite seem to match with the chaos of a dozen excitable brides and their eclectic entourages. Upon reflection, I'm glad we're the furthest away from the dissimulation of brides. When Gabby comes out, I can't help but smile. 'Now, I know you're not a dress person, but you've got to admit, you look fab.' Gabby walks over to the podium and takes in her reflection.

'Jesus.' Gabby stares at herself in disbelief. She spins slightly as if a different angle will tell another story, but her face nods in approval. 'Not bad though.'

'Not bad,' I smile. 'But I think it's a little plain for you, honestly.'

'Yeah, I think I want a little sparkle.' She shimmies her shoulders.

'Oh, not a bad start at all!' Janet-the-waif is back with a travelling rack of dresses, like something out of a hotel, transporting your luggage. Half the rack is full of white, the other, varying colours, that I'm surprised are all wedding dresses.

'Do many people get married in colourful dresses?'

Janet nods, 'Oh, yeah, you'd be surprised. Of course, varying shades of white are the most popular, close behind that is white with a coloured ribbon or some kind of splash of decoration, but more and more people are breaking away from tradition. Why don't you start with this one.' She pulls out a dark, leafy green number and fans it slightly for the full effect. 'This is a lace, scalloped-edge, mermaid style. Don't worry about the size, I'll come back to pin you in.'

Pin me in; sounds terrifying. 'Thank you,' I say, as I take the dress from her and size it up; it's not my style, but I'm game to try anything. Stepping into the changing room and pulling the curtain behind me, I undress, then carefully put on the gown. There's no mirror in the actual changing room, I realise, so I can just look down and guess what it looks like. Pulling the curtain back and stepping out, Gabby takes me in and bursts out laughing,

'Oh, no! You can't wear that.'

'Why? What's wrong with it?' I step, barefoot onto the podium and take in my reflection. 'Oh.' I gaze at myself and spot something akin to a small child trying on her mum's clothing. It's not flattering, and the seaweed green is washing me out.

'No offence, hon, but you look, dare I say it, kind of dead in that dress.'

'Just a few months shy of Halloween,' I shrug, then swoosh the dress around like I'm five years old.

Janet comes forward with some pins and makes adjustments. You can now see my figure, but even so, she shakes her head, 'Nope; I thought that might help but, no. Not the one. How about...' she turns to the rack and takes a ruby, sparkly number, '...this one!'

'That looks a bit much,' I say with wide eyes.

'Well, possibly, but it's red—the colour of love—and I think with the sweetheart neckline, here,' Janet gestures with flair, 'it might just work for you.'

'Yes, yes, go on sweetie; I'd love to see you in that.' Gabby sips her bubbles then turns to the rack to select one for herself. 'I'll try a sweetheart too, then we'll match.'

A small smile twitches at the corners of my mouth. I wait for her to put her glass down on the side table, step in front of me, and then when we're both inside the changing room for two, I close the curtain.

'You are hilarious.' I begin to unzip my dead-mermaid number, while Gabby does the same to hers.

'I think this is the highlight of my Christmas. I've missed doing this with you.'

'We have never done this before.'

'No, I mean, shopping, hanging out just because. I'm going to miss you when you go back to New York.'

'Well,' I step out carefully of my first eliminated number, and hang it back up, 'that was definitely one that looked better on the hanger,' I say.

'Well, what?' Gabby says, now only gracing her underwear too.

'Well, I think I might be...possibly...considering a location change.'

Gabby folds her arms at me, 'Really? Where to?'

'My old flat.' As soon as the words are out of my mouth, Gabby screams and starts jumping up and down, hugging me.

'Everything OK in there? Are the dresses alright?' Janet pushes the curtain open, so we're now exposed to the whole shop, embracing and wearing nothing but our underwear. 'Oh, please no canoodling in the changing room or we're going to have to ask you to leave.' Janet frowns at us both, which makes us burst out laughing.

'We weren't canoodling! Sophie's moving back home!'

'Oh, so, it's been a long-distance relationship? That's lovely.' Janet takes hold of the curtains once more. 'I'm sorry, I'll give you both a minute.' When the curtains are closed again, we laugh even harder.

'So,' Gabby finally lets me go. 'We've been shopping for a good four hours, and you're only telling me this now?'

'I was waiting for the right time. Saying it out loud feels scary. But right.'

'And what about your family?'

'I don't know. I think that I've come to the conclusion that no matter what I do, it won't be supported, and no matter what I say, it will be turned against me. So, I may as well do things that bring me joy. Nick, you, and Scott bring me joy. Plus, the only thing I can control is how to *respond* to their behaviour; they're never truly going to change. I know I want to be with Nick, and I know he wants to be with me.' I reach for the ruby dress and start unbuttoning. 'Christ, I think you'll have to help me into this one. Gabby carefully takes the delicate straps off the hanger from her sweetheart cream number—it's silky with more of a poof at the bottom than the last one.

'This is very exciting.' She steps into her next dress and it fits her like a glove. 'So, did something happen this morning with Nick?'

'Christmas day. He gave me the key to our apartment in a box.'

'Just like he did the first time in *Hermanos*? Gee whizz, that guy's romantic; I need him to have a word with Scott. I got new walking boots.'

'Didn't you ask for new walking boots?'

327

'Yes, but sometimes you want a little something extra too.' She gives me a defeated face, 'Oh, God, is this what our marriage is going to look like?'

'What? You ask him for something and he gives it to you?'

'No, I mean, will the pizazz go away?'

'Pizazz?' I laugh and she goes to bat me but misses. 'He loves you unconditionally, and I bet you anything that if you said to him that you want to be spontaneously surprised with things, he would do it. He'd do anything for you. You need to tell men what you want, sometimes; they're not mind readers.'

She nods her head, 'So wise.'

I finally step into my ruby number then turn around for Gabby to do me up. 'I have no idea how this is going to work; I mean, I've got to deal with Freya first.'

'Oh God, I'd forgotten about her.'

'Me too, to be honest. I still haven't heard from her; I'm starting to get a little concerned; she's never gone this long without speaking to me.' Gabby gives me a pat to indicate she's buttoned me up, and I turn and make a face. 'Oh, well, deal with that later, *eh*? So, what do you think of this one?'

Gabby nods, 'I like it. Very regal.'

I laugh, 'I never thought I'd be described as *regal*.'

'Your dress is regal,' Gabby pokes her tongue out. 'What about mine?'

I take a step back and truly feel my heart melt. 'I don't think I've seen you look more beautiful.'

She comes in for another hug, 'You know, I'm here for you, regardless of where you are in the world: here, there, anywhere. I'm your girl; you know that, right?'

I smile, 'I do.'

She loosens her hug and takes her hands in mine, 'I do, too.'

'In sickness and in health.'

''Til death do us part.' Gabby makes a face, 'I've always found that line a little depressing, haven't you?'

'Absolutely. Mental note taken for you to skip that in your vows.'

'Good idea.' She shakes her head at me and starts welling up. 'I'm so grateful to have you in my life.'

I find tears are now in my eyes too. '*Oof*, me too, hon. You're the sister I wish I had.'

'How are we doing in there?' Janet calls from outside, giving us the grace to not swing the curtain wildly open this time.

'Yes, all good, thank you,' I manage to croak. Gabby takes my hand and we walk out together. 'Oh,' the assistant claps her hands together. 'You know, I have to say, not often do you get to see the absolute pure love between a couple; it's inspiring.'

Gabby and I smile at each other, knowing that there will always be a connection between us, wherever we are in the world, or whatever we're doing; nothing will ever keep us apart.

Chapter 27

An hour and a half, and three glasses of champagne later, Gabby hasn't decided on a wedding dress, but is now sitting, barefoot, in a wedding suit, enjoying the "Sophie show". I've been parading in and out of the changing room, with increasingly drunken confidence, with each brightly coloured dress that has gone from the bizarre to the ridiculous; I can't believe people get married in these. My favourite so far is the one I'm currently wearing: a rainbow number that looks like it belonged to a Barbie doll toilet roll cover. Gabby's grandma used to have a couple of the decorative things. You know the ones? The legs of the doll would go through the middle of the toilet roll, and the dress would puff out the sides, covering the loo paper completely; most sophisticated.

'Smile!' Gabby takes a picture of my latest outfit to add to her collection; I feel like I'm doing the montage from *27 Dresses*. Janet-the-waif is sitting quietly in the corner by the front door, sulking with her elbows on the desk, and her cheeks in her hands. Having given up helping us, I believe she's decided she can't throw us out because we're not quite drunk or rude enough to warrant so, but is holding onto the minute hope that she still might receive a Boxing Day commission. Poor girl, I can't see that being likely. 'I think you should get it!' Gabby points at me with her phone and laughs loudly.

'I feel like I should sing something from *Joseph and His Amazing Technicolour Dreamcoat*; God that's a long title.'

She points at me again with her glass, 'You could have just said "*Joseph*".'

'True.' I spin back to the mirror, singing the incorrect lyrics from one of the songs, '*fuchsia, and orange, and violet, and gold, and...*' I giggle and turn back to Gabby, 'You know what? It might be the booze talking, but I think I look rather good.'

'Definitely the booze talking.' She laughs, then takes another sip.

'I mean, it's anyone's guess as to where my hips are, but all I know is I feel great.'

She nods, 'Your waist looks tiny.'

I grin, 'I'm having the most lovely time.'

'Me too. I'm so glad we're here. Alright, next!' Gabby calls, quick to move on before I'm ready.

We both turn to the rack and there's nothing left on it, so move our attention to Janet, who reluctantly comes back with an audible sigh, before slapping a smile on her face. 'Any luck on this one, ladies?' she asks, knowing the answer already.

'It's a solid, maybe,' I find my mouth saying, then give a little hoot as I look at the £3,000 price tag. I suddenly don't feel grown up enough to be wearing this.

'Oh, you know,' Janet seems to have had a spark of inspiration hit her, 'there was a sample dress that came in a few days ago; it's still in the back, in its garment bag.' She points at me while pursing her lips, 'Yes. Yes, this is going to be the one.' She disappears with haste.

'But I've already found my one!' I say turning, and gesturing to Gabby; she raises her glass to me. Moving my gaze to the window, I enjoy a little tipsy sway on my podium; good thing they've only got light jazz playing, I might break out into a full dance with anything stronger. As I turn my attention to the window, I notice there are crowds of people, rushing from one hopeful bargain to the next; rather enjoyable to watch actually. An older couple is arguing next to a group of teenagers laughing; a stressed-out mum who looks riddled with regret for bringing her four kids shopping on Boxing Day; and, *huh*, a couple of men staring in the window at me. How rude. I adjust my glasses. *Oh, wait, I know him.* I burst out laughing and wave; I can't read Nick's expression from here, even with my glasses, he's a little blurry—I fear that's the booze, not my prescription. 'Nicks here,' I manage to say to Gabby.

She stands, looks over, and waves too. He's with the keyboard player and the drummer of Rise and Shine. They all wave back, then after exchanging a few words and hugs with each other, we watch as the band members continue on their shopping quest, and Nick heads towards the door, walking in with some apprehension.

'Hi,' Nick approaches us with a warm smile full of curious uncertainty. '*What-cha-doing*?' The smile carries into his voice.

'Wedding outfit shopping for me,' Gabby says, arms outstretched for Nick to take in the suit she's wearing.

'Very nice.' His head turns to me, 'And, you?' He raises a playful eyebrow.

'I'm finding a dress for your ball.'

'Are you now?' He takes in the gown I'm wearing with amusement. 'Well, I think this is the winner!' he says sarcastically and walks around to completely take it in. 'Wowzer, who knew there were that many colours.'

'Alright!' Janet-the-waif is back. 'Try this out.' She hands me a black garment bag, like a mystery present. 'I know it'll be creased as it hasn't been taken out to *breathe* yet, but that'll steam right out. Oh, hello,' she turns to Nick. 'How do you know the happy couple?'

'The happy couple?' Nick creases his brow slightly with confusion.

'Yes, Sophie and Gabby, here.' She looks at each of us, then Nick smiles wide, clearly clocking on to the little white lie we've told.

'I'm Gabby's younger brother.' He out-stretches a hand.

'Oh, welcome! Always nice to get a family perspective. Glass of champagne?'

Nick considers this, then shrugs, 'Yes, yes, why not! Thank you.'

'Great.' Her smile is back, perhaps thinking that her commission chances have increased with another person to share their opinion. 'I'll be right back to do you up,' she aims at me, then scurries off. Nick settles into the plush chair next to Gabby, taking off his coat. 'Well, come come, we must let the dress *breathe*!'

Feeling particularly silly, I scamper off to the changing room once more and playfully whip the curtain closed behind me. Hanging up the latest dress, still in its bag, I carefully make my way out of the *Joseph* one, remembering the price tag, and once I've wriggled out of it, I hang that up with exaggerated caution, on the hook behind me. Turning, I unzip the mystery sample dress bag, and smile, loving the fact that Nick is always up for goofing around. '*Ooh*, that's pretty,' I say to myself as I catch a glimpse of the indigo material which reminds me of a Cadbury's chocolate bar wrapper. Removing it completely from the bag, I see it's a strapless number, with a couple of sparkles here and there, like clusters of star constellations. Turning it around, I see it's got a lace-up back.

'Are you decent?' Janet calls from outside.

'Near enough,' I reply, and she makes her way in, then shuts the curtain behind her, while I'm still in my underwear; I'd imagine she's seen her fair share of brides-to-be in their mismatched bra and pants.

'OK, I'll lay it down for you,' she unclips the dress from the hanger, holds it up and then slowly lowers it to the ground, creating a hoop, 'now, step in.' I do as I'm told, then she carefully lifts it up and around me, adjusting it as she goes; I feel like Cinderella. 'Now, if you can just hold the dress at the front to keep it up,' I put my hands just above my boobs to keep it in place, then she gets to work on the back with expert speed. I feel her threading the satin ribbon through the loops, tightening it so it hugs my body. 'So, this dress really is a bargain if I say so myself. As it's a sample, it's already roughly 60% cheaper than any of the other dresses in here, then on top of that remember you've got the 70% off everything in the store today, so, I need to double-check with the till, but I think you're only looking at around the £200 mark; an absolutely steal if you ask me.'

'Gosh,' the word has escaped my mouth, as she expertly makes her way down my spine, and I feel the dress neatly drawing in, but not uncomfortably. My mind goes back to the price. I know that if I were buying a wedding dress for real, that would be a reasonable price, but honestly, I'm not sure I've ever bought a dress that cost more than about £80; I suddenly feel even worse for lying to her.

Janet carefully makes one more adjustment, I think tying the corseted satin ribbon into a bow. 'Alright, let's see, turn around for me.' Again, I do as I'm told, and a satisfied smile spreads across her face. 'You look stunning.'

I glance down and run my hands over my body, enjoying the material. 'Thanks.'

'Now, if you don't mind me saying, a dress like this often looks even better with hair up.'

'Oh, I don't have a hairband or anything.' I pat myself down as if one will suddenly appear.

She takes a clip from her waistband, that I didn't notice was there, and after walking around me, effortlessly swoops my hair up. 'I'll just do a simple chignon.'

'I have no idea what that is,' I confess while I feel her twisting my hair.

'Looks like a fancy updo, but in reality, takes seconds; it appears like you've spent ages on it.'

'I'll have to Google that.'

'Do. It's worth it. Alright,' she makes a few adjustments, then admires her work. 'Beautiful. You ready to show your bride-to-be?'

I giggle and nod. The assistant opens the curtain with purpose, holding it open for me. As I step out and walk towards Nick and Gabby, their faces are a picture, Nick's mouth drops open and Gabby's eyes widen.

'Holy!' Gabby is the first to speak, 'That dress is made for you.' I walk with pride over to the podium and stand on it, my back to the mirrors, so I'm facing them both. Nick stands, his eyes gracing over every inch of my body.

'What do you think?' I say with anticipation, nervous all of a sudden that he doesn't like it.

'You look...' he stutters and shakes his head ever so slightly, trying to find the words.

'Don't you like it?'

'No,' he says softly, shaking his head.

'No?' I feel my stomach plummet.

'No, I mean, *like*, isn't the word. Just look at yourself.'

I spin around, towards the mirrors, and standing on the podium, gazing back at me, is a young lady full of confidence and poise. I adjust my glasses, as she does the same. 'Wow.'

'Wow is the word.' Nick's standing at my side, and he reaches for my hand which I accept. 'God, you're beautiful.' Without thinking about where we are or what lie we've told, I step off the podium and into Nick's embrace. His lips are soft on mine, and for a moment, the world disappears. When we break apart, I catch eyes with Janet, whose mouth is hanging open.

'We're just such a close family,' I find my mouth saying, and I fumble for Nick's hand, and start swinging our arms.

'I'll give you all a moment, shall I?' she says, finding her voice, and starting to walk away.

'We'll take the dress,' Nick calls after her.

She stops, and grins, 'Perfect. I'll ring that up for you.' And with that, all judgement has left the building.

Chapter 28

Half an hour later, I'm bewildered to find I'm carrying a garment bag. After Nick paid for the dress, he kissed me on the cheek and left with the promise that he didn't need my help setting up the event tonight. We'll meet at the venue.

'I can't believe he paid for this,' I swing my new purchase from one shoulder to the other, as we weave our way through the car park, trying to remember where Scott parked the car.

'You know what? I can believe it.' She shrugs, clicking to open the boot of her ten-year-old Subaru Forester, nothing happens, so she has to use her key to unlock it. 'It's Nick. He's always been like that.'

I smile. Remembering countless times he would surprise me with a gift, or take me somewhere new and treat me, for no reason. He's a good man.

I gently place the gown down, feeling unbelievably unworthy of it and then step away.

I do deserve it. A small voice whispers from the back of my brain.

Gabby shuts the boot with gusto, then unlocks my door, before walking around to unlock hers. We both sit on the dog-haired backseats of the car, waiting for Scott to finish his shopping trip. 'Thank God we brought Scott with us, hey?'

'Definitely.' Gabby brushes a dog lead from the seat onto the floor. 'Hey, how's Aria? Not that I normally care about her well-being, but she did just have a baby and all...on Christmas Day. Poor thing, she'll never have a separate birthday and Christmas present either. Maybe she can have my idea of a fake birthday in July?'

'I like that, maybe I'll suggest it.' I smile, 'I mean, there's no way Aria will listen to me,' I'm not sure I care. 'Maybe I'll celebrate Holly's birthday six months before, regardless of what she says.'

'Sounds like you're already a great Aunt.'

'I'm not that old.'

'A great—as in super—not great, as in old.' She laughs. 'You're as young and spritely as I am.' Gabby yawns loudly; not sure that's encouraging.

'Anyway, both she and Holly are doing well; Chris messaged me this morning. *Huh*, feels weird to say that after going no contact for so long.' I find my eyebrows have knitted together.

'Any idea when they're coming home?'

'Not yet.' I swivel further round, to face my friend, and remove a dog toy from underneath my right thigh, 'and to be perfectly honest, it's kind of nice to know that Aria is out of harm's way—but being taken care of,' I add as an afterthought; I'm not a complete monster. 'I feel like there's less of them around to get anxious about.'

'Sure,' Gabby nods with all seriousness, 'your mum's really easy-going.' We both burst out laughing, then I sit up tall, composing myself.

'But you know, I'm proud of myself.'

'I like it,' Gabby nods, full of best friend approval.

'You've no idea why,' I laugh.

'Yeah, but you're never proud of yourself, so, I'm pleased to hear it.' Her eyes suddenly widen, and she starts clapping, '*Ooh*, are you proud of yourself because you've decided to stay, get married and have lots of babies? *Ooh, ooh,* double wedding! You've got the dress.'

'I have *a* dress, not *the* dress, and besides, you're the one who's engaged, not me.'

'Yes, yes, that's right; you're just the one who's had countless, wild, makeup sex with the man you ran away from.'

'Exactly,' I point at her then crease my brow. 'Did I really run away from him?'

We both ponder this for a minute. 'I don't think you ran away necessarily; you removed yourself from a toxic situation and he was the one consequence you lost because of it.'

'Christ.' I try to take that in, then remember I was going to say something before, 'What was I saying?'

'You're proud of yourself.'

'Oh, yes. I told my parents I'd see them tomorrow, and wasn't available today,' I say with a celebratory tone.

'Congratulations,' she says deadpan. 'You do realise that you don't *need* to tell them you're not available, right?'

'No, I don't know that. My brain does not realise that. My brain tells me that I need to be there all the fucking time, and if not, I have to justify why not.'

'Your brain makes me sad sometimes.'

'Me too.' I can feel my eyes wanting to well up; good God, day drinking is not the way to go.

'Well, I'm proud of you too. Always have been, always will. I didn't take part in our school musicals, without an ounce of talent, for just anyone, you know.'

'Shut up, you can sing!'

'No,' she corrects me sternly, '*I* can hold a tune; *you* can sing.'

It's then that Scott returns to the car. 'Sorry that took so long. Wow. Why does the car smell like a bar?'

'That would be us,' Gabby says, stretching her arms to the side.

'OK,' Scott nods, not needing to know why, but Gabby goes on to explain anyway.

'We went wedding dress shopping; apparently, that comes with bottomless champagne.'

'Oh really?' His eyes sparkle. 'Find anything?' Scott adjusts the seat and the mirror then starts the engine.

Gabby shakes her head, 'Nope. But Sophie got a dress for tonight. Nick bought it for her.'

'Nick? Nick's here? Does he need a lift?'

'No, no, he went home with the band; he's going to help them with their soundcheck before guests arrive.'

Gabby heaves a big sigh as we pull out and onto the road, 'I think I'm going to need a nap before tonight.'

I yawn, 'Me too.' I take out my phone to read the time but notice an email notification, from Freya. '*Huh.*'

'What is it?' Gabby snuggles down and leans her head so it's resting on the bottom of the window.

'It's from Freya. It's the first one since I left New York.'

'What's it say? Do you need to leave?'

'I don't think so. She just says: keep an eye on my emails, that she has some news and might message me at any time.'

Gabby brings her legs up to rest in the middle of the seat, between us, 'Didn't she give you the whole two weeks off?'

'Technically, yes. I'm not due to start until the 1st, but she tends to change her mind and demand me whenever and wherever.'

Gabby yawns, with her eyes completely shut now. 'Sounds like another unhealthy relationship to me.' Her voice is slow as she's clearly slipping closer to dreamland, 'But what do I know? I deal with dogs, not divas.'

'Sounds like you both deal with bitches.' Scott laughs at his own joke, while Gabby appears to be snoring.

I stare out the window and watch as the busy town morphs into county roads. I wonder what her news might be. Subconsciously I bite my lip, do I want to continue working for her? She never appreciates me or my work, or, at least she doesn't tell me that she does. Sure, I'm lucky to have flown on private jets, and who wouldn't want to say that they've not only met and had drinks with, but dined and had stimulating conversations with some of the top names in the industry? But is it worth it when I'm constantly treated like I'm unimportant and replaceable? Shouldn't I be worth more?

I am worth more. The small voice returns, and for the first time, I truly consider what that means.

I take a look at the email once more and type a quick reply before deciding to mentally put her down. Tonight, I'm going to do nothing but celebrate being with Nick, and my friends. Everything else can wait, right?

***

Every time Nick has hosted this event, he manages to hire ridiculously breathtaking buildings, and today's is no exception. Forty minutes out of town, Gabby, Scott and I pull up outside Langford Music Hall. The historic building was home to one of the most popular local dance halls of the 1950s and '60s, then after an electrical fire in the '90s, remained decrepit and abandoned for decades, housing nobody but squatters. But a few years ago, a rich kid came along, with a dream of recreating what it once was, with a wallet bigger than the dry rot problem. Today, as we exit our cab, and gaze up, the inviting red brick arches welcome us in, as beam lights theatrically dart from side to side, while shining upwards to give the building a vibe that's something akin to a Hollywood award show.

'Gosh, I feel very important,' Gabby giggles, wrapping her faux fur, knee-length coat around her.

'Shall we?' Scott offers us each an arm. I smile as we join the queue to the entrance. There's a light breeze tonight, but luckily, I took the advice from Janet-the-waif in the bridal store and decided to wear my hair up. Never one to have any idea what to do with my hair, Gabby took the initiative to ask Nick's mum, (a retired hairdresser), to take care of us both. She gave Gabby's always-been straight, shiny hair, some curling-tong treatment. As for mine, it has been lightly twirled, twisted, and pinned up; I feel uncharacteristically sophisticated.

As we draw nearer to the front door, I hear electro-swing music teasing us to come inside and have a dance. We walk up the stone steps to the mouth of the building, and standing on each side of the entrance, are two gents with silver trays. Instead of what I was anticipating (drinks), the entire tray is covered in masks; masquerade ball, of course. I select a lacy black one with a black ribbon to tie up at the back of my head. As I uncurl my arm from Scott's to tie it up, I'm grateful that I opted to wear my contacts for the first time in forever; my mum would be so proud.

'Feels kind of like we're going to a sex party, doesn't it?' Gabby remarks while modelling her own mask—a cream-coloured one that's soft and lacy like mine.

'How would you know what that feels like?' I can't help but ask.

Gabby shrugs, 'I watch movies. Not those kinds of movies,' she adds in response to my jaw-dropping. 'But you know, a series with a hint of erotica.' She raises her eyebrows.

'Not sure I'd know what to do at a sex party,' Scott contemplates while securing his mask.

'I'd say that's a good thing,' I shrug, 'but each to their own. Rock on and all that.'

We walk towards the main room, the music drawing us in. Looking around, the dance hall has two levels. The first, where we are, complete with a sprung, wooden dance floor and stage, and the higher level, with a low balcony railing, revealing small round tables, that I imagine were designed as the VIP section of the venue. Today, it plays host to all the guests who want to sit, chat with friends, and people-watch; I'm sure I'll frequent that section at some point this evening—ever the person to enjoy a good people-watch.

There's a DJ playing right now who looks like he's having the time of his life, playing random percussion instruments, as well as preparing the next track. DJs have always fascinated me. The ability that's needed to multi-task and mix the next song, is far beyond my skill set.

It's a fantastic turnout, and a wave of pride washes over me; I can't wait to give Nick a big hug. Looking around though, I can't seem to spot him. I guess he's busy backstage or something.

'Shall we head to the bar?' Scott asks.

'Let's have a dance first.' Gabby swings her arms around then grabs me and sends me into a twirl.

'If we're dancing, I need a drink in me first,' Scott laughs. 'What do you both want?'

'Bubbles, please,' we answer in unison. After my afternoon nap, I'm ready for more.

'We'll warm up the dance floor for you,' Gabby says, giving him a kiss on the cheek. 'He's a *good-un*, isn't he?'

'Maybe you should marry him,' I tease.

'You know, I just might do that.' She puts her arm around me, 'I was—very briefly, mind—engaged to a stunning woman, would you believe?'

I laugh. 'Fascinating. And what happened with that?' We place ourselves in the middle of the busy dance floor.

'Turns out she's in love with a man.' We both laugh and start bopping to the beat. 'But we decided to stay friends.'

'Well, all's well that ends well, then.'

'Exactly.' Gabby continues to grin at me. 'You know, I didn't think that I believed in soulmates.'

'Well, Scott is definitely yours.'

She nods, 'Yeah, but I'm not talking about him; I'm talking about you.'

'You think I'm your soulmate?' I smile affectionately at her.

'I do. I think in life we meet people who touch our hearts in ways that don't have to be romantic. Some people are meant to be in our lives and stay in our lives, forever. People who you have this connection with without trying, regardless of time, space, or life; they bring out the best in you and the world seems brighter.'

I nod back at her, 'That reminds me of something I saw on Instagram. An actor called André De Shields when winning a Tony Award said, "Surround yourself with people, whose eyes light up when they see you coming."'

'I love that. And speaking of...' Gabby points behind me. I turn and see Nick beaming towards me, dressed in a full tuxedo; it's all I can do to not rip it off right here on the dancefloor. When he reaches us, he kisses me on the cheek then stands back, his eyes sparkling, 'Wow.'

'Well, thank you, I do try,' Gabby says from behind me.

'You look lovely too, Gabs.' Nick gives her a quick hug, then turns back to me. 'Can I borrow you for a minute?'

'Sure.' I look to Gabby, asking her with my eyes if she's alright for me to leave her; she waves an arm at me.

'Go, I'm good. Always been more than content at a party for one.' She swings her arms around and enjoys a solo dance without the fear of judgement. 'Scott will be back in a minute, anyway. Go do what you need to.' She winks at me.

Nick leads me away from the dance floor and to the right of the stage with his hand on the small of my back. It's not until we're closer that I notice a door. Nick flashes a keycard and with a subtle click, the door unlocks, and we step through backstage. The moment the door shuts, Nick slides his arms around me and draws me in for a kiss.

In between breaths, he undresses me with his eyes, 'God, you're beautiful.'

I gently break away after a time. 'You haven't brought me backstage for a quickie, have you?'

He kisses me once more then his eyebrows raise playfully, 'Now there's a thought. But, sadly, no.' He grabs my hand, 'Come with me.'

Nick leads me around a dark corridor, and through to a greenroom. The Rise and Shine band are all sitting down, looking as though someone has died.

'Hey. What's up? Everyone OK?' I ask tentatively.

'It's Gina,' Jerry, the lead singer says.

345

'Has something happened to her?'

'Yes. She's pregnant,' the keyboard player replies.

'Well, that's good news, right?'

The bassist sighs, 'Of course. But it means we can't do our tour; or at least, we can't do the tour the way we planned. And, again, we're stuck for tonight. None of her deps are available.'

'Well, being pregnant doesn't stop her from performing; I remember seeing a local act, and one of her backing singers was at least eight months.'

'Yeah, the thing is, she's got extreme morning sickness,' the drummer adds. 'She's been throwing up so much in the last couple of months, she's dehydrated and needs bed rest and monitoring. That's not a match with a touring lifestyle, you know?'

'So,' Nick looks at me, 'since you did such an amazing job at the Christmas Light Switch On, I told the band I would come and get you, to ask if you'd sing Gina's part again.'

'Oh,' as much as I enjoyed it, I honestly thought that was a one-off memory to look back on and feel proud of myself.

'Please don't feel pressured,' Jerry, the lead, says. 'I know we did that to you last time, but if it helps, you were amazing.'

I exhale, breathe out the words my mum said to me after the last time, and take in the faces of the band around me. 'Well, sure. I can help.' The room explodes with cheering, whoops and high-fives.

'You're a lucky charm.' Jerry grabs me and pulls me in for a hug. I then take off my mask, put my phone on silent, and get to work.

Chapter 29

After messaging Gabby to tell her what's going on, I spend the next forty minutes rehearsing with the band. It feels nice to be a part of something; to belong, and I know I'm appreciated here.

Feeling prepared and more than capable, I allow myself to embrace the small spark of joy that's fully ignited within me; the glow of possibility. With not long to go before we're due on stage, I make my excuses to head to the ladies to freshen up and gather. As I push the door for the loos, it's at that moment, a small voice tells me to look at my phone. Taking it out of my small clutch, my heart plummets. You know that feeling of everything going so well, you, on some destructive level, want to shoot it all down, or find a problem? Well, mission accomplished.

As I stare at my screen, it glares back at me declaring twelve missed calls from my mum, and the voicemail notification. Exhaling, my hand hovers over the voicemail notification, then I catch myself in the mirror.

No. I am busy, and I don't need to drop everything.

Nodding at my reflection, I put my phone down on the shelf above the sinks, next to my clutch and do the necessary. Then while washing my hands, I see my phone light up. "Mum" flashes angrily at me and I wonder if I can just continue to ignore her; perhaps not the most mature response, but I know that Aria and Holly are OK—Chris messaged me again, saying they're going to be released tomorrow. And my dad messaged me about an hour ago, wishing me a fun evening, and saying that all is well with them, so I know deep down in my heart, she just wants my attention, and there's no problem; she is merely demanding my presence. The phone stops ringing and about 20 seconds later, another voice message pops up.

Something is wrong, Sophie.

I dry my hands then can't help myself, and begin to listen to my voice messages.

'SOPHIA! Where are you? We've been waiting around all day for you and you haven't bothered to show up....'

I did not arrange to meet them today, I try to reassure myself.

'...this is just typical of your behaviour, never thinking of others.' She hangs up, I delete the message and listen to the next one.

'How you go about and nonchalantly forget about us is quite frankly, disrespectful. You did say you were coming to see us today and...'

No, I didn't.

'...personally, I think about others, but unfortunately, you're just selfish.'

I delete that message too, waiting for the next message, while looking at my reflection.

Am I a selfish person?

'I thought you could have at least messaged today to see how I am. I guess you don't care about me, do you? Hmm.'

I delete that message then hang up. I'm about to go on stage, and I can't listen to potentially nine or ten more voice messages berating me for not being with them when I didn't plan to be.

I deserve to have my own, happy life, separate from them, don't I? It doesn't mean I don't want them in my life, but it shouldn't mean that I'm selfish if I have my own things going on, that don't involve them. Parallel, but not entwined lives.

Placing my phone firmly back in my bag, I exit the bathroom and head back to the band. 'Alright, we are ready; Soph, you good?' Nick says with a look of concern, the moment I step through the greenroom door; clearly, I'm not as balanced as I think I am.

I nod, 'Just had a few missed calls and voice messages, that's all.'

Nick nods, knowing exactly what I mean. He takes my hand and squeezes it.

'It's typical really,' I say quietly, just to him. 'I do something for me, feel good about it, and I'm selfish.' A hollow laugh escapes, 'It doesn't matter that I listened to a couple of her voice messages, she doesn't even have to say anything for me to feel awful.'

'Are we good?' Jerry comes over to me, and I slap on a smile.

'Oh, yeah. Let's do it!' I throw my clutch down on a nearby overused green sofa. Mum can wait. This is my time to shine, and I'm going to enjoy it.

Jerry puts his arm around my shoulders and leads me towards the middle of the room. The rest of the band gathers in a circle, all putting their arms around each other too. My heart lifts at the thought of being part of something.

'Nick, get the hell over here!' Jerry waves. 'You're one of us, man!' Nick grins and joins the circle of trust. 'Alright, we're going to go out there and kill it. We're sounding great, we've worked hard, and we've got this. Sophie, you really are our lucky charm; thank you so much for, once again, saving the fucking day!'

I laugh, 'You're very welcome.'

'So, let's go and just enjoy it.' He puts his hand in the middle of the circle. We each place a hand on top of the other and grin. 'Have fun, everyone,' Jerry calls and we move our hands down, then up and break, before all heading out of the door.

As I walk with the band from the greenroom to the stage, there's a mix of feelings dancing in my stomach: elation, deflation, pride, shame...quite the cocktail. I try to focus on the positive ones and leave the negative ones behind with each step.

As the band make their way onto the stage to get ready, I stand anxiously in the wings, staring straight ahead, all of a sudden doubting my ability as a performer.

'Soph?' I turn to Nick and he's looking at me with a mix of love and concern. 'Regardless of why she's ringing you, you deserve to have fun. You haven't done anything wrong, and you're not selfish.'

'I know,' my voice is a whisper.

'Soph, for years, I've watched this happen. You know that there's no emergency; you know nothing is actually wrong; she's trying to get in your head and make you feel bad for not making yourself available exactly when she wants you to be.'

I nod, numbly, then admit, 'Logically, I know that, but knowing isn't enough. Even being away for two years hasn't changed anything emotionally for me.'

'You are so much stronger than you were two years ago.'

Again, I nod. Apparently, I've lost my voice. Brilliant. Perfect just before heading on stage to sing.

'Do you want me to listen to the other voice messages to see if there's anything wrong?'

I shrug, then exhale, 'I thought these mind games would stop.'

'And what gave you that impression?'

'I've done work on myself and on some level, I assumed that she would have too. Stupid.'

'Not stupid, just, I don't know, maybe, hopeful.'

'*Ugh.*' I bury my head in my hands. 'This is ridiculous.' My neck suddenly feels itchy, and then I start massaging my head, a sign of a headache coming on. 'This is nonsense. I hate how much she's in my head; I'm missing the moment.' My voice, full of crazed outrage. 'I'm ruining my life because of her. No, it's because of me.' I feel my eyebrows have knitted together.

'What?'

I exhale again, and this time, my tone is softer, 'She might be the cause, but I have to be my own solution. I'm so bloody programmed that I automatically create a story in my head, based on what she's said or done in the past, and I'm reacting to that. She doesn't even have to do or say anything for me to punish myself; I have become the worst version of her in my own head.' I sigh, 'I am so tired of being my own worst enemy.' It's at the moment the music in the hall fills with Taylor Swift's, 'Anti-Hero.' I laugh out loud, 'Appropriate.' I realise my eyes have filled with tears. 'But there's this overwhelming feeling within me that says I've got to be prepared for being yelled at for not dropping everything.'

He tilts his head, 'Maybe you could practise *walking away* from being yelled at.'

'*Hmmph*, now there's a thought. You mean I don't have to just stand there and take it?' I say sarcastically.

Nick shakes his head, 'No you don't.'

'Well, that would be new.'

'They aren't going anywhere, and neither are these feelings. I guess the thing to practise is putting them down, putting yourself first, and coming back to the present. You deserve to enjoy every single second of your life. Don't let them steal any more of your precious time. Allow yourself to live in the moment.'

I lean in and kiss him gently on the lips. 'Thank you. You really are something, you know that?'

'No, *you* are really something.'

'OK. I'm choosing to put them down.' And with a smile and a deep breath, I march onto the stage.

***

The set is an hour long and I enjoy every single second of it; I honestly feel that I could do this for the rest of my life. Gabby and Scott were dancing in the front row the entire time, and the packed room was vibrating with positivity, you could feel it on every level.

As I gaze out at the room applauding, my heart feels full. I step forwards with the band, we put our arms around each other, and take a couple of bows.

'Are you sure you can't leave your job and come and travel with us?' Jerry says in my ear over the crowd's ongoing appreciation.

I smile wide, 'I don't know. Maybe I could quit and run away on tour with you guys.'

'Yes! Do it!'

'I'll think about it.'

He squeezes my shoulder as we go for another bow, then head off stage, just as the DJ takes over once more. Nick is standing in the wings, still clapping. 'That was nothing short of phenomenal.' He high-fives the guys, then brings me in for a hug.

'You're only as good as your sound man,' I hear Jerry say from behind me. 'So, Soph was saying she could quit her job and come sing with us on tour.'

'Did she?' Nick smiles.

'I said I'd think about it.'

'Hey, man, why don't you do the same?' Jerry raises an optimistic eyebrow.

Nick looks up in surprise, 'Really, me? And what instrument am I playing?'

'No. It's stressful having a new sound guy every night; new venue, new acoustics, different requirements, just ask any musician. We need you too.'

'Come run away with us!' the bassist says enthusiastically.

Nick looks at me with excited contemplation, 'Well, I'll think about it too.'

'Excellent. Meet you at the bar?'

'You bet,' Nick says and we let the band pass us. 'You were incredible, Soph.'

'Thank you.' I allow myself to bathe in the compliment rather than dismissing it completely.

'Can you imagine us doing this? Maybe this is our next step?' Nick's eyes optimistically search mine.

'Maybe. We could sell the flat, or Airbnb it, like Gabby and Scott do, and spend our lives making music together!' My excitement grows in my stomach as I allow myself to dream.

Nick looks at me with so much love, I'm not sure I can take it. 'Let's go celebrate.' He takes my hand and we walk from backstage to the main room.

It's heaving with people, all getting rid of any Christmas tension, throwing inhibitions to the wind on the packed dance floor.

'You created this,' I shout over the music.

He leans in and shakes his head, 'Let's head over there,' he points to the back of the room. 'It's behind the speakers; I'll be able to hear you.'

When we've moved behind the throng, he exhales, 'That's better. What did you say?'

'This,' I point around. 'All this joy; it's all down to you.'

He beams at me, 'Pretty cool, isn't it?' Then the colour drains from his face, and it's then I hear her voice,

'Oh, you are alive! Well, thank you for keeping me so well-informed.'

I feel like all the joy has been instantaneously ripped out of me, as I turn and face my mother.

Chapter 30

'Have you lost your mobile?' Mum glares at me, hands on her hips. I take in this hot-headed woman dressed immaculately in a black and red, floor length, mermaid number, complete with a black Colombina mask, reminding me of a pernicious Disney villain.

'It's backstage. Is everything OK?' I decide there's no time like the present, to get right to her point, whatever it might be, or however upsetting. I look around her, finding it implausible that she's come alone, 'Where's Dad?'

'He said your music was too offensive; he's gone to the car to get earplugs.'

Frowning, I attempt to ignore her clearly less than pleasing—though unsurprising—negative review of my performance. 'OK. So, what's up?'

'What's up?' she says with a tone somewhere between disgust and disbelief, 'You finally *bother* to come back to town at Christmas, and I assumed that after everything Aria and Christopher went through, you would be spending your time with the family.'

'Well, I am spending time with my family.' I grab Nick's hand and he gives it a supportive squeeze.

She takes a beat, then fires at Nick, 'You will never be a part of *my* family. Anyway,' she turns back to me, 'I was talking about your *actual* family; we haven't seen you since yesterday. This is a time that we should all be pulling together, and here you are, wasting your time with *him*.'

'Stop it,' the two words have flown angrily out of my mouth before my brain has time to censor them.

'Hello, darling. Wonderful set, I really enjoyed it,' Dad beams, walking over with a couple of drinks.

'So, you didn't need to get earplugs?'

'I'm sorry, what are you talking about, sweetheart?' Confusion reads all over Dad's face.

I glare at Mum, 'Yes, what earplugs?'

She flusters for a moment, then exhales, saying quickly, 'Well, I guess I misheard him; it is offensively loud in here,' she adds the last part of the sentence through her teeth while wearing a fake smile.

'Mum, what are you doing?'

'I'm talking to my daughter, who's forgotten we exist.'

'I was with you yesterday, and I said I'd see you tomorrow, even after everything.'

'And what is that supposed to mean?'

'Are we really doing this here?' Exasperation fills every part of my body.

'Doing what? I'm not doing anything, apart from pointing out to my ungrateful, privileged daughter, that she needs to think seriously about what's important to her. You're back now and you need to act like it.'

I can feel decades' worth of suppressed anger bubbling up inside me, threatening to erupt. I shut my eyes.

Breathe. Just breathe. You do not have to attend every argument you are invited to.

'The only reason I came to this ridiculous, waste of time event, is because you're here, and you refused to come and see *me*. He's probably not even raising money for charity, and is just going to pocket everything.'

'Aubrey,' my dad tries to steady her this time.

'Don't *Aubrey* me. Aria told us that he steals money.'

One lie from two years ago resurfaces.

'I do not steal money,' Nick's voice is calm but short.

'Well, that's your opinion.'

'It isn't an opinion, Mum, it's a fact.'

'Yes, a fact that he steals your money, and spends it on his lavish lifestyle. Aria told me. I know everything.'

Two lies.

'You know nothing,' I seethe at her. 'That is both ridiculous and insulting, and Aria is a jealous, psychotic liar.'

'She told me that we need to speak to you about *your* anger issues, I—'

'I think you need to think about what you're saying here, Aubrey,' I turn in surprise as my dad speaks up.

Mum turns to him angrily, 'I have every right to say whatever I like, wherever I like, whenever I like.' Her head now whips sharply to Nick. 'And just because you helped us get to the hospital yesterday, doesn't make you a hero.'

'And when exactly did I imply that I was a hero?' His voice is a lot calmer than mine.

'Oh, you could just see it all over your smug, arrogant, money-stealing, *abusive* face.'

'I am not abusive.'

'Aria said that you are.'

And there it is. *The third lie.*

The elephant in the room. The biggest lie that was told. The unthinkable story that was created in their heads. The thing that made me go crazy. The knife that my family pierced right through our hearts.

'She went to the mediums, they talk to the dead, you know. And my mother and Richard's mother are in agreement that you have been physically and mentally abusive to Sophia, for years.'

Hearing her say that with just as much unwavering certainty as she did two years ago, twists my insides. 'Can you hear yourself? You and Aria sound insane, Mum.'

'Nick's the one who created all of this tension that pulled our family apart.'

His mouth hangs open while outrage bursts out of me. 'That's not true!' I can't allow this to go on a moment longer; it's time to stop doubting my ability to distinguish what is real from what isn't.

'Well, what other possible explanation could there be for you leaving, then? *Huh*? Tell me?!'

'OK, you want to do this? We're doing this. I admit—'

'A-ha!' Mum points at me. 'There it is! It's all coming out now!'

'No,' I loosen my grip on Nick's hand and gesture my palms towards my mum, creating a physical barrier between us. 'Let me finish.' I compose myself with a deep breath. 'I admit that one of the reasons I left two years ago was because I couldn't take this tension between everyone anymore, but that was the tip of the iceberg. The ludicrous stories you and Aria created about my relationship with Nick spun me in dizzying circles, while I tried to justify and understand why you could possibly believe something so detrimental. Now, I've made peace with the fact that you have never accepted Nick, and probably never will, yet he was the first person to see me for who I am, to hold me up, to celebrate me and my talents.'

'That's a little ego-centric, Sophia; I'd hardly say you have something that stretches to the *plural* of talent.'

'Oh my God, why are you so infuriatingly insulting?'

'How *dare* you speak to me like that.'

'No,' I say strongly, 'how dare *you* speak to me, or Nick, like that. We are good people.'

'Are you saying that I'm not a good person?'

'Oh, Mum. You have no idea how much I want to believe that you are a good person deep down; why else have I put myself through all this? But there are so many layers it's impossible to wade through them all to find the true version. In public, you hide beneath the mask of a charming, charismatic woman, yet when we're alone, the facade slips, revealing a raging narcissist.' I stop myself momentarily from continuing; I didn't intend to ever say that to my mum, but, hey. Maybe it needed to be said.

'A what?' She stands tall despite her small frame.

OK, I'm doing this. Before I've thought about what I'm going to say, the words are falling fast, 'Narcissist, Mum. I've learnt that you are somewhere between a grandiose, and covert narcissist, depending on your mood, or if you're around Aria. You have a heightened sense of self, you live your dreams through me, then tell me I'm not good enough. You have gaslit me my entire life. You've used triangularisation against me. You use emotional manipulation all the time. I'm not allowed my own opinion or life, and when I try, love is withdrawn, and I am written off as selfish.'

'Well, you are selfish.' She nods her head.

'Completely missing all of my points! And this is why I vowed never to say any of this to you because there is no point having an argument with someone who is so stuck in their own existence, where no one else could possibly be right. You have your narrative, and everyone else is wrong. Full stop. No room for compromise.'

'Well, I'm so sorry I was such a terrible mother.'

Victoria Mae

I exhale, this is not the first time I've heard that.

'You think you had it bad? You should have been around my mother. You should feel lucky to have me as your mum. I have never done anything that was that bad to you.'

'Are you kidding? Apart from everything I've just said, and you've ignored? You're not even listening to me, Mum; this is the problem. You have never listened to me. I was never allowed to talk about my thoughts or feelings if they weren't positive. That's toxic positivity Mum; no one can be happy all the time. But fine, you know what? I've started, so I'm going to keep going. I am working on accepting an apology that I may never receive.'

'You think I owe you an apology?' She laughs, 'Alright, humour me; what could I have possibly done to warrant an apology?'

My anger starts to elevate, 'Oh, I don't know, to name a few, how about you and Aria, slowly picking away at, then ripping apart my *healthy* relationship with Nick, making me think that I didn't know how I felt, and then you both telling me that you were here to save me from him when I didn't need saving. Or saying that both my dead grandmothers hate Nick.'

'Well, that's what they said to the mediums.'

'And you took a stranger's word over ours?'

'Absolutely. Aria told me the truth: the mediums said there are bruises on your body that nobody can see.'

'The only bruises that are there are emotional ones, caused by you Mum. This is an example of what you've always done. You tell me that I don't know what's going on in my life, "because I'm too close to it".' I stop for a breath then psychotically continue, 'And what else? Oh, yes, you expected me to give my money to Chris, despite you refusing to support me financially when I was buying my home. And as if that wasn't enough, you celebrate Chris' failures and punish me for my achievements.'

'I do not.'

'He was taken to court, lost his job, moved back in with you and you act like they're triumphant acts, yet my successes aren't acknowledged. Every big life event, or everything that has meant anything to me, you have written off as unimportant. I work for one of the biggest pop stars in the world for God's sake, and you act like it's no big deal and you've never even heard of her. You have not supported me in any aspect of my life.'

'I have always supported you.'

'No. You support me when people are looking, Mum, or after I've made a success of myself; that is not support. It's trying to take credit for my accomplishments while making me feel like I don't deserve them in the first place.' I know I'm close to hysterical and I should probably stop there, but I can't seem to help myself; it's as if I've uncorked a bottle that's been waiting to pop for years. 'You have insulted me about my weight and my looks in front of people—complete strangers, whose opinions and feelings are always more important to you than mine. You have belittled my talents in front of others to build yourself up. You hate the man I love. You pinned Chris and I against each other our entire lives. Mum! You are awful to me, and yet, regardless of your behaviour, words and actions, you expect me to put you first.'

'Well, family should be put first.'

'Which is something that has been drilled into me my entire life, and is why I have put up with all of this absolute bollocks for so long. You hurt me, Mum, you continue to hurt me over and over again. I distanced myself to gain some perspective yet came back when you made me believe that something was wrong with Dad; but low and behold, nothing was wrong! It was just another control tactic with emotional manipulation on top. And me being here for the Christmas period, after two years, is still not good enough for you.' I exhale, not allowing myself to finish there. 'You haven't stopped to question *why* I haven't been here for two years.'

'Well, don't hold back how you really feel, Sophia!'

'And my God-damn name is *Sophie*, Mum. *Sophie*. Not Sophia. It has never been Sophia, and you know I hate it, yet you continue to say it.'

'You know why. Your father wrote it down wrong and—'

'Enough, Mum. This is just another example of your lack of respect for me. Do you have anything to say about what I've just said?'

She considers her words for a moment. 'Fine.' I pause, waiting with bated breath in the hope that something close to remorse or compassion is about to come out of her mouth, 'I think you are the most ungrateful person I've ever met. You had a roof over your head, and food on the table, and we supported you through your education.'

I feel my eyes prickling, 'Yes, you did do those things, and I'm grateful for them. But there was a distinct lack of emotional support that I needed as a child, and even as an adult, that I guess you were just incapable of giving.'

'You're talking absolute gibberish.'

'Exactly my point, Mum; you were, and still are, an emotionally immature parent.'

'And what is that supposed to mean?' I look to my dad, whose eyes are filled with tears, but he's remaining, as he always has done, completely silent.

'You never took accountability for yourself; if you'd done something to hurt me, I had to apologise to you. Your words and actions taught me that everything wrong in your life was my fault.'

'Well, you have no idea how much I sacrificed for you.'

'No, no, I do, actually. You used to remind me of that fact all throughout my childhood.' I take a deep breath before reeling off what she has always said, particularly in response to people complimenting me, 'Performing was your life. You were a lounge singer, and a backing vocalist, performing regularly in the West End and on Broadway. You even danced with The Radio City Rockettes for years. But then you decided to sacrifice your dreams, to have a family.' For once in her life, she's speechless, so I go on, 'And you even said that, after Jerry, the leader of Rise and Shine, was praising me, just this week, Mum.'

'I don't remember that.'

'You choose to not remember because you couldn't possibly paint yourself in a bad light. You couldn't possibly be the bad guy. You couldn't possibly give me a compliment, say you're proud of me, or that you love me, or even just take some—any—responsibility or accountability for your behaviour. It pains me to say that this family dynamic is toxic, and it hurts my soul.' My eyes are filled with tears now and a few escape down my cheeks.

'You need to compose yourself, Sophia. We don't cry in public.' Mum looks around her, smiling and waving to a few people, to pretend that everything is OK.

Swallowing my hurt, I lower my tone, and allow myself to continue, 'I want to spend my life surrounding myself with people whose eyes light up when they see me.' My parents are silent. Mum looks at me like I'm an offensive stranger. Dad's face is filled with remorse. I take a deep breath, 'As much as it pains me to say this, you aren't good for me.'

'You abandoned this family for no good reason, two years ago, Sophia, and now you come back and insult us like this? Talk about accountability, *you* are the one who took off without a care for your family and gave us all the silent treatment.'

'Do not mistake my not being here with not caring. I care more than anyone should and feel more than you will ever realise.'

She laughs, 'Fine. Enlighten me then!'

'That Christmas broke me.' My tears are flowing freely now as my sanity truly unravels. 'After you said those horrific—untrue—things about the mediums, Nick left your house, and I froze. Then you and Aria had decided *I'd* done something wrong, and neither of you talked to me, or looked me in the eye, for the remainder of Christmas day. I had to keep silently going off to the bathroom to sob. It was the straw that broke the camel's back, Mum.'

'So, because we didn't talk to you, you decided to give us the silent treatment? How very mature you are.'

'No. What I did wasn't an imitation of what you have done to me, my entire life: withdraw your love to punish me. This wasn't about punishment; it was about healing. It was about finding what way was up. I didn't know what was real, I wasn't allowed to feel my feelings, I had shame for having any kind of bad thoughts about your behaviour, because you are my mum, and you are supposed to love and support me more than anyone on this planet, and yet, for some reason, you don't. Why is that? Why am I so awfully disappointing to you? Why am I not worthy of your unconditional love and acceptance?'

My mum stares up into the air, tilting her head as if she's never even thought about these questions. She then takes the red wine that my dad is still holding, and I half expect her to throw it in my face. But instead, she takes a long sip, her eyes avoiding mine. She then hands the glass back to my dad to dutifully hold once more and takes a deep breath. 'I no longer feel welcome here. We're leaving, Richard.'

'No.' We all turn to the unexpected, strong voice of my dad.

'No?' Mum looks at her husband with shock. 'Sophia has insulted me, I'm upset, and we're leaving.'

He shakes his head, 'I'm sorry you're upset, Aubrey, but I'm staying, so I guess you're driving yourself home.'

'Richard, this is not the time to stand up and pretend you have some kind of backbone.'

'Actually, Aubrey, my love,' he says kindly, in spite of her words and tone, 'this is the exact time to do it.' He steps forward, closer towards her, 'We're on the cusp of losing our only daughter forever, and I for one, don't want that. Do you?' My dad puts both the drinks that he's holding, on a nearby table, then stands on my other side, facing Mum; he and Nick becoming my pillars of strength.

She shifts uncomfortably. 'We aren't going to lose her,' her tone implying the mere thought of me not succumbing is ridiculous.

'Yes, you are,' I manage to say with a wobble in my voice. 'This is it, Mum. I've hit my limit.'

'We both owe her and Nick, an apology.' Dad puts his arm around me, 'More than once, but we'll start there, shall we?' I smile with appreciation at my dad, as the tears continue to flow. He then turns back to his wife, 'So, what do you say, Aubrey?'

'Well...I...that's just...' she stutters then her voice fades away.

I look expectantly at her. After all these years of everything, is this the moment? Is she about to take accountability for something?

'This has become very upsetting for me. I came here to spend time with my daughter, compromising in fact, as you know how much I hate these kinds of events.' She stands tall. 'I will not be spoken to like this. Enjoy your evening. I'm sure you'll have a wonderful time without me.' As I watch my mum walk away, through the chuckle of happy people dancing, I scoff in disbelief, and if it's at all possible, my heart breaks even further.

Chapter 31

'Aren't you going to go after her?' I manage to say to my dad while wiping my tears.

'No.' His voice is calm. 'I think the person I need to make sure isn't walking out of my life right now is you, sweetheart.' I cry even harder and give my dad a hug; as strong as I think I've been, deep down, that's all I've wanted to hear from my dad—that I matter in his eyes. I hold tightly onto him as he continues in a soft voice, 'You have always had my unconditional love and acceptance; I'm sorry if you haven't felt that, or I haven't shown you, but I'm so proud of the woman you've become. I'm not sure what to say about your mother apart from maybe, give her some time.' He kisses the top of my head, 'I know that's a lot to ask, but I know she cares about you darling; she needs to just get over parts of herself that she hasn't been able to yet.' We break apart; he's wearing a half smile, 'However, I'm not sure where she thinks she's going, I've got the car keys, so she can't drive, and she asked me to hold her phone, so she can't call a cab.'

I laugh, 'She could ask someone else to call a cab for her.'

Dad nods, 'She could, but then she'd have no money to pay for it; I'm the one with the wallet.' He raises an eyebrow, 'I'm always the one with the wallet.' Then he smiles gently at me. 'I'll just let her cool off for a moment, then I'll go and find her,' he says casually. 'Let me buy you both a drink and then you can tell me all about your night.'

***

Nick and I spend about an hour laughing with my dad, sitting at one of the tables on the people-watching, upper floor. Nick kindly just went down to get my bag from backstage, leaving Dad and I to ourselves for a minute.

'So, tell me, darling, are you and Nick officially back together?'

I nod, while sipping my second prosecco, 'Yes, we are,' I grin.

'Does that mean you're moving back here?' he asks optimistically.

'I haven't worked out the logistics of my job, or the timings or anything, but, yes, that's the plan.'

'You don't always have to have a plan, or hold all the answers, just follow your heart my darling. And,' he smiles affectionately, 'I'm glad you're putting your happiness first. You were always a problem solver for everyone else, putting out fires you didn't start, or taking full responsibility for others' actions.'

'I didn't realise that I was doing that.'

He leans forward, 'I know it was Chris who threw Smudge out the window.' I smile at my dad and let him continue. 'You were always doing little things to make all of our lives easier or better. Like,' he thinks for a moment, 'doing the washing up before anyone even thought about it. I think it was your way of trying to control what was directly in front of you when you felt a lack of control around you.'

I raise an eyebrow, 'Deep. But sounds about right. Why am I like that?'

'I think you got it from me; you watched me try to create little wins in a long-term losing situation. Sorry,' Dad adds when he sees my face fall. 'I'm sure Mum means well. Somehow.' Dad buries his nose in his non-alcoholic mulled wine.

'I'm mad at myself for losing control and saying all those things.'

Dad shakes his head, 'I think it's a miracle you managed to keep all those things in for so long; God knows I have.' He makes a face and dunks his nose once more.

'You sure there's no alcohol in there?' I tease.

'I'm pretty sure,' he doubts himself, 'No, I don't think so. I think you're just inspiring me to open up.'

'Well, I'll toast to that.' We allow our glasses to clink, just as Nick returns, taking his place next to me, and passing my clutch.

Your phone's been buzzing constantly in your bag since I picked it up.'

'*Ugh*. Fine, I'll see what Mum's saying.'

'I have her mobile.' Dad taps his pocket.

'Oh.' I look at my phone and see all the notifications are from Freya. 'Oh, God.'

'What? Who is it?' Nick takes a swig from his beer bottle.

'It's my boss.' I start opening the messages and begin scan-reading them, my eyes widening with each one.

'What is it? Have you been sacked?' I can hear Nick's smile in his voice, then glance up to see his face matching his tone.

'No need to sound so pleased about it,' I say. 'She's flying into Gatwick.'

'What?'

'She says she needs to talk to me in person.'

'About what?'

'She doesn't say but says it's urgent and going to change my life.' I make a face. Freya's not usually someone to say they have something to tell me and then it be positive.

'Well, sounds like good news to me,' Dad chips in.

'She wants me to get her from the airport,' I say, practically downing my drink.

'When?'

I swallow, and place the glass back down, 'In an hour. I don't want to leave your party,' I lower my lip to Nick.

'Don't be silly, we'll both go.'

'We'll all go,' my dad gets to his feet. 'I've got the car.' He taps his breast pocket to indicate his keys. 'And I must say, I'm quite looking forward to meeting a superstar.'

I raise an eyebrow, 'You might regret that.'

***

As we whizz along the country roads at a surprising speed for a man who normally likes to go at least ten per cent under the legal speed limit, I start to feel bad about leaving my mum.

'I'm sure regardless of what Freya has to say, it will all work out,' Nick misinterprets my silence, and reaches forward from the backseat, to supportively squeeze my hand.

'God, I'm not even thinking about that; I'm feeling bad about leaving Mum. Even though, technically she left us,' I add as an afterthought, then my thoughts seem to fall out of my mouth without much consideration, 'I'm aware that she's a grown-ass woman who is perfectly capable of looking after herself. But still. I feel responsible; I always feel responsible.'

'You are not, nor have you ever been, responsible for your mother or what she does,' my dad says firmly, while briefly glancing sideways at me, his hands precisely at ten and two. 'And anyway, I found her sitting around the back of the building when you were in the bathroom,' Dad says casually.

'Why didn't you say?'

He shrugs, 'I didn't want to overload you.'

'Was she still mad?' I hate the crushing weight of shame upon my chest that so naturally attempts to suffocate me.

He sighs, 'She was…' he makes a face, 'cooling off and contemplating.'

'Great,' I say dryly, knowing that what's to follow is the wrath of expressing my true feelings.

'I arranged a cab to take her home, so put her to the back of your mind, darling. We're nearly there.'

As we pull into Gatwick Short Stay, it occurs to me that Freya isn't going to just be arriving via the normal *Arrivals*. 'Sorry, Dad, can you pull over for a sec? She won't be here.' Dad signals, and parks in a matter of seconds and I do a swift scan of my emails. Nothing new. Great. I then do a quick search of my previous emails and find instructions to get to the FBO, or Elite section, of the airport, from a previous trip we did.

After circling the airport, then re-entering in the right place, we slowly approach the gate for VIPs. My stomach fills with dread as I'm fully aware that we won't be able to go in unless Freya has registered the car, which she obviously hasn't done because that would normally be my job. My dad slows, and we park up in front of an inoffensive and remarkably dull gate.

'Well, I guess we'll just hang out here until she calls me?' I've been refreshing my email constantly, but nothing is coming through. 'Oh, crap.' I try to swallow my fear, and wave as a security guard approaches my side of the car; he gestures for me to open my window.

'Can I help you?' His voice is gruff and something tells me I'm not going to win.

'Yes, *hellooo*. I'm Freya's personal assistant and she asked me to bring a car.'

'Did she now?' He looks doubtfully at me, my gown, and checks out Dad and Nick too. 'Wouldn't a personal assistant be with her?' he says dryly.

'Well, yes, technically, normally, yes, but she's just come back from Bali.'

'Anyone could have read that in the news, Miss. Can I see your paperwork?'

'I have no paperwork; she just emailed me an hour ago.'

'Oh, she did, did she?'

'Yes, she did.' I attempt to say with authority, and without thinking, thrust my phone at him, 'See.'

He looks at it, unimpressed, 'That could be anyone.' And he hands it back to me.

'Look, I know this sounds fictitious, but all I know is that she'll be pissed if there isn't a car waiting right outside her private jet.'

'I can't let you in, I'm afraid, and you can't park here. Please move your vehicle, sir.' He leans close to my face, into the car, and glares threateningly at Dad.

Feeling deflation mixed with something akin to excitement, a little voice says this could probably help me move back to the UK quicker than expected, as I'll 100% be fired for leaving her stranded. I sigh.

And then it happens.

With a flick of my thumb, a refreshed email appears with an attachment. 'A-ha! A-ha! Here, look! Paperwork.' I shove my phone this time fully into his hands and he takes his time, before finally looking up.

'Thank you. Right this way, please.' He hands me my phone back, gets out of the way and the gates open for us to drive towards the private runway.

Chapter 32

As Dad drives slowly in, following another security guard in a high-viz jacket, I bend down to pick up the plastic bag at my feet, ready to jump out with it. 'Thank God there was that corner shop open.' Wondering if there was anything else I should have picked up, I scan through the items I chose. A medium (but relatively travel-sized-for-Freya) vodka bottle, headache tablets, water, some ready-salted crisps that I know she'll say she doesn't want or like, but will then demolish, several chocolate bars, and a stain remover pen.

'I think it's hilarious you're guessing she's spilt something on herself,' Nick laughs.

I twist my body to face him, 'It's not so much a guess, as experience; you don't know Freya.'

'Well, I'm about to,' he points, and I turn my head; her private jet is slowly taxiing. The guy in the high-viz jacket indicates for us to park on the right of him, and as we do so, I nervously unbuckle my seatbelt. 'Maybe you should both wait here, just in case.'

'Just in case what?' Nick asks amusingly.

'Just in case,' I say firmly. 'She could be drunk, violent, verbally abusive.'

'Then you'd need our help.' He looks at me as though I'm mad.

I smile at him, 'This isn't my first rodeo.'

'Well, we're right here if you need us,' my dad says, still with his hands at ten and two.

'You can relax though Dad,' I chuckle at his posture.

'I'm ready for a quick escape if you need one,' he nods, and as I smile at them both, a rush of love flows through me. I exit the car and wait.

I don't normally have several drinks in me before meeting Freya. I'm somewhere between nervous and nonchalant; she's never seen me anywhere close to tipsy.

I watch as the plane seems to yawn the airstairs in my direction; I wait patiently, with my plastic bag of possible Freya needs. An air hostess, who we haven't hired before, descends first, carrying the Louis Vuitton wheely suitcase I'd packed for Freya a little over a week ago, the matching handbag, sitting neatly on top.

The air hostess reaches me, places the luggage at my feet, raising an eyebrow, 'Sophie?' I nod, and she stands to the side, waiting to be officially dismissed by Freya. A moment later, there Freya is, standing at the mouth of the plane, posing, expecting photographers; I know she'll be disappointed that there aren't any.

Freya adjusts her sunglasses and looks like a bond villain as she carefully but expertly descends in her sky-high, knee-length, black leather boots. Her floor-length black coat, lined with fur, is open at the front, revealing a black, leather catsuit; not my idea of optimum comfiness for travel wear, but then again, I'm not an international superstar.

When she reaches the bottom, she uncharacteristically thanks the air hostess, who shimmies off back to the plane to get her things.

Freya stops right in front of me and pauses, before enveloping me in a hug. She has never hugged me. After a beat, I throw my arms around her and think this can't get any stranger. When she finally breaks free, she slides her Chanel sunglasses onto the top of her head, then holds onto my forearms.

'Hello, Sophie. How are you?'

'How am I?' I ask in disbelief; she has never asked this question before, or if she has, she's never waited for an answer. Her face is waiting patiently for me to reply and I'm confused by the sincerity of her tone. 'I'm…good, I think. How are you?'

'Never better.' She looks me up and down, 'You look stunning; I've never seen you dressed like that. Or, in a dress for that matter.'

'Oh,' I pat down my clothing, 'I—er, was at a charity ball when you messaged.' She nods, then we continue to stare at each other in silence. I look momentarily behind her, 'Did you travel alone?'

'I did.'

'You never travel alone.'

'Well, when I was away, I had some time to think, and I've come to the conclusion that I surround myself with too many people who don't care about me, and just want a free ride.'

'How profound,' I say this without overthinking how she'll react, but once more, we return to silence. I wait as I'm sure she has more to say, but for the first time, I think she's contemplating her words before speaking. I watch as her hair seems to gently and expertly flow, somehow in slow motion, behind her; it's as if she's brought her very own wind machine. Never being one strong enough to let a silence just be, I dive into the bag. 'I picked up a few items for you: snacks, drink, a stain stick just in case.' I offer it to her.

She takes the bag from me and begins to look through it. She then shakes her head, 'You're a really interesting character, you know that?'

I make a face, 'No.'

'You're the only one who anticipates me.' She picks up the stain remover pen, links the bag over her wrist, takes off the lid of the pen, and starts dabbing her coat.

'Well, thank you,' I say with uncertainty; I'm not sure she's ever complimented me before, or tended to her own stain for that matter. It's a bizarre thing to watch. 'Did you want to get in the car?' The worst of the snow may have gone, and it's definitely warmer this evening, but it's still December.

She replaces the cap, pops the pen back in the bag, then looks up at me. 'Yes. Thank you.'

My stomach twirls as I grab her suitcase, and we make our way, in silence, to the car. I'm not sure she's ever thanked me for doing my job before. As we approach my dad's Jaguar it occurs to me that she might not like the fact that my dad and partner are in the car; she normally likes to ride with drivers she already knows and doesn't like sharing a car with strangers. I'll have to ask Nick to move, I plan in my head, as she'll absolutely want to be in the back, not riding shotgun. '*Um*,' I begin nervously, 'Like I said, I was at a charity ball, so it's my dad who's driving, and my boyfriend is in the car too.

'You have a boyfriend?'

I smile, 'Yes. Yes, I do.' I pause and see Nick sitting in the passenger seat; he must have got out and back in without me noticing. He smiles and gives me a swift thumbs-up. I move to the back and open the back seat left door for her, directly behind Nick. She gets in without question or complaint. *How uncharacteristic.* Shutting the door, I run around to the back of the car, open the boot, hoist her heavy bags in, then after shutting the boot, run to the other side, afraid of what she'll say to them; thankfully they are all silent when I get in.

'So, Freya, this is my dad, Richard.'

Dad twists in his seat and extends his hand to hers, 'Absolutely charmed to meet you, Freya.'

'Charmed,' she imitates, practically sparkling at my dad's Englishness.

'I do hope you're comfortable back there.'

Freya strokes her hands over the plush stitched leather, nodding with approval, and I'm suddenly grateful that my dad has what is classed as a luxury saloon. 'It's similar to my usual rides; thank you, Richard.'

Where has this polite Freya come from? Maybe she did have a spiritual awakening in Bali. 'And this is my boyfriend, Nick.' I can't keep the smile off my face, after saying the word, "boyfriend."

'Oh, *Nick.* It's nice to put a name to a face.'

'What?' I say without thinking.

'That photo you have,' Freya says dismissively.

I shake my head, and think for a moment, 'You mean the framed photo that's lived in my bag for two years?'

'Yes, that's the one; where you're on his lap in an egg chair in a garden.'

I frown, 'You went through my things?' How have I never realised Freya is like my mum?

Freya shrugs, unapologetically, 'Of course. I'm a star. You need to make sure the person staying in your house isn't a psychopath.'

I want to point out the irony here of living with a psychopath, but maybe that would only be done with a few more drinks in me. 'Yes, the guy from the photo.'

'Pleasure to meet you, Freya.' Nick also extends his hand to hers and she looks deeply into his eyes.

'*Oof*, you're cute; shame you're taken.' She holds onto his hand and I can tell she's weighing up if that matters to her or not. Nick slowly extracts his hand and I swear I see her mildly shake her head, deciding against it.

'So, where would you like us to go, Miss Freya?' My dad asks kindly and again, Freya sparkles at my dad; I hope for not the same reason as Nick.

'Well, I didn't have Sophie with me to book a hotel; booking in my plane was enough of a hassle.' She turns to me with what I mistake for mild irritation, but it might be admiration, 'I don't know how you do that all the time.' She then turns back to my dad, 'So, whatever hotel in your town that you would recommend, would be fine.'

'Well,' I say after clearing my throat, 'the thing is, our town is pretty small.'

'A *small* hotel then, would be alright, I suppose.'

'No, I mean, each one is fully booked. You can stay here close to the airport; the Hilton has arranged for your usual suite to—'

'You know what?' She interrupts me. 'I think I should stay with you.' She sweeps her perfect hair back behind an ear in contemplation, 'Yes. I'd like to see your family home.'

I make a face, 'Oh, no, I'm not sure that's a good idea.' The idea of my mum and Freya under the same roof without me is enough to make my skin crawl.

Her eyes try to read me, 'You don't want to welcome me into your family home?'

'I think she means, you might be much more comfortable at mine; I mean, *ours.*' Nick smiles at me.

'You have a home here?'

'I do.'

She regards me, 'A real-estate portfolio; I'm impressed.'

'I'd hardly say that, but yes, of course, you're welcome at ours. That's where I'm staying, I'm not at my parents,' I say to both clarify and to avoid the horrifying thought of a Freya-Mum combo, with a possible side of Aria.

Freya nods, 'Yours it is then.'

'OK. Off we go.' My Dad taps the steering wheel gently, then starts the engine, and slowly makes his way to the exit.

'So, what inspired this visit?' I dare to ask.

Freya opens the plastic bag, selects a Crunchie bar, and points it at me, 'You never told me that you could sing.' She begins unwrapping the chocolate and takes a delicate bite.

I'm shocked by this sentence, 'Well, you never asked,' I say cautiously.

'*Hmm.* I guess I didn't.' She closes her eyes in delight. '*Um,* they didn't have anything like this at Greenway.'

'Greenway?' I question. 'I booked you into The Palm.'

Freya's eyes and mouth fly open, then she closes her lips once more, before opening them again, 'OK, so, I was going to share this with the whole team later, but I may as well tell you now.' She exhales, 'Greenway's an exclusive, private facility, in Antigua, for detoxing.'

'OK.' I remain silent to let her continue.

'It's the start of a long journey but they help fast-track you.' She exhales. 'I was in rehab,' she confirms. 'That's why I told the press I was in Bali; I wanted to throw them off. I changed the route after we'd taken off and made the pilot and air staff sign a non-disclosure agreement.' She gazes and waits for me to offer my opinion.

'You could have told me,' I say softly, 'I could have helped you. I didn't know you wanted to make that decision. You could have let me support you. Oh,' I reach forward, and take out the corner shop-bought booze, 'sorry about that.' I tuck it into the backseat pocket.

She regards me, 'You are without a doubt, the most decent human I've ever met.'

I smile at her. 'Well, I don't know about that, but thank you.'

'You don't need to thank me.' She takes another bite, then sighs, 'So, more on that later, but like I was saying, I didn't know you could sing.'

'How…*um*…do you know I can sing?'

'I do have access to the internet, you know.'

I shake my head in confusion, 'And what have you seen on the internet?' My mind flies to me having stage fright at the talent show as a ten-year-old.

She puts the chocolate back in the bag, whips out her phone from her coat pocket, and taps away before handing it to me, 'This.'

Taking the phone from her, the screen reveals the town Light Switch On, with us singing, 'Light in My Fire'. I smile, allowing myself to feel some pride; I actually sound quite good. 'How did you find this? It's just a little local event.'

'Can you not see the numbers below the video? It's gone viral.'

'It's gonc what now? Jcrry said it had 50 thousand vicws three days ago, that's not enough to go viral, is it?' I look back at the screen and see it's now had 8 *million* views, and burst out laughing. 'Have you seen this?' I turn the phone to Nick and he beams at me.

'The sound's good too,' Freya says, diving back into the bag and retrieving the crisps. 'You can tell even from my phone. Who did the sound?'

'Nick,' I say and he beams back at me.

Freya opens the crisps, then after eating a couple, she pauses to look at us both, 'Oh, you're not just a boyfriend; you're in love, aren't you?'

'Yes,' Nick says firmly. 'Always have been, always will be.'

'Well, I can't let that interfere with my plans.'

'Right,' I say with uncertainty. 'And what plans are these?'

Freya eats a few more crisps before placing them back in the bag, then with all the time in the world, takes another bite of the Crunchie and shuts her eyes, 'American chocolate is not the same as this,' her words just about audible with her mouth full.

I nod, then clear my throat, 'So, plans?'

She finishes the chocolate bar, discards the wrapper back in the plastic bag, dusts off her hands, then turns to face me, 'It's time to shake up the warm-up act. I liked the U.S. Tour guys, but for the European stretch, I've decided that they're out and you're in.'

I stare at her blankly, 'Excuse me?'

'You. And the band you sing with.'

'What?'

She looks at me with amusement, 'You and Rise and Shine are going to open for me,' her words are slow and clear.

It's all I can do to just stare numbly. I'm having an out-of-body experience.

'Did you hear what I said, Sophie?'

I nod, 'I…it's…what?' I laugh.

'Well, while she's thinking that over,' Freya turns her attention to Nick, 'I want an in-house Director of Sound. I used to have one but had to let him go. Every venue on the U.S. Tour was a different team; it was stressful, and I want to make the European stretch of the tour seamless. Are you available?'

'You've heard me do one Christmas Light Switch On.'

She narrows her eyes at him for a moment, 'Don't talk yourself out of a once-in-a-lifetime opportunity, boy. I'm not going to beg, but I make decisions quickly. I like what I heard, but if you suck, I'll fire you. How's that?'

Nick laughs, 'OK. When do you need me to start?'

'My tour starts on the 10th. Sophie and I were meant to start planning on the 1st, but as she's now an artist, she'll be rehearsing, and I've given her job to her assistant, Issac. We've got a full-crew meeting on the 3rd, rehearsals the rest of that week, and a final pre-show tweak meeting on the 8th.'

'I'll find a replacement for the studio tomorrow,' Nick says without hesitation. However, I'm still sitting there in shock. As Freya turns back to me, she laughs at my face.

'Am I going to regret this decision?'

I've no idea.

'I'll correct myself; I'm not going to regret this decision. I want your voice on my tour and I like the band. Can you handle this?'

I feel sick but I think it's with excitement and the possibilities of the unknown. 'Yes. Yes, I can.'

'Fantastic. We'll talk details tomorrow. So, you said you were at a charity event tonight?'

I whiplash at the conversation U-turn, '*Um*, yeah, a local dog shelter,' I say, still in a daze.

'Why didn't you say.' Her eyes sparkle, ever the mad dog-lover, and she waves a hand, 'I'll match whatever you've raised.'

'You'll what?' Nick says from the front.

'Match. Whatever. You've. Raised,' she says slowly, then grins. 'Always happy to support a dog shelter.'

'You've no idea what that'll mean.' Scott will be over the moon. Somehow, I find this more exciting than what Freya's just offered me. 'Hopefully, that'll mean it won't have to close.'

'Close?' Freya practically shouts. 'No, I'm sorry, I can't let that happen.' She thinks, then taps me on the arm, 'One of your last jobs as my PA will be to put me in touch with the management.'

I smile wider than I have in two years, 'Alright then.'

Author Note

Hello, Victoria Mae, here.

We have come to a fork in the road on our journey *Beneath the Mask*, as I've written two endings: *The Dark* and *The Light*.

Therefore, it is up to you, how you would like the story to end. You can read one over the other, or both, it's your path to tread.

From here, these are your options:

1. ***Beneath the Mask: The Light Side of Ambition***
   Skip to page 408, read Chapter 33-B and Epilogue B. Finish there and do not go back to read *The Dark*.
2. ***Beneath the Mask: The Dark Side of Ambition***
   Continue from here, (page 386), read Chapter 33-A and Epilogue A. Finish there and do not go on to *The Light*.
3. ***Both: Dark then Light***
   If you did want to read both, may I suggest reading in the order that it's written: *The Dark* first and its Epilogue, and *The Light* second, finishing with Epilogue B.

The ending is now in your hands, dear reader. You can choose your reality. You have always been strong and brave enough, but are you ready to face *The Dark Side of Ambition*?

Chapter 33 - A

The Dark Side of Ambition

If someone had told me a few years ago that Freya would be sitting in my old living room, I wouldn't have believed you. I'm sipping my Pukka Night Time Tea, while staring with disbelief at this person, who, after having conversations with us for the last couple of hours since Dad dropped us off, is seemingly, just a person. Far removed from the diva I've been working with for years, Freya has been asking Nick and I about our lives together, and listening to the answers. I sit cosily on the couch, hugging my tea, looking at the clock reading midnight. I've no idea how, but I'm not tired in the slightest.

'So, why did you break up?' Freya also sips on her tea and waits patiently for Nick's response.

'Sophie's family,' is his brief response.

Freya nods, 'Families are something else, man. I haven't spoken to my folks in, God, what is it now? Eight years?'

'*Eight* years?' I don't know why this shocks me. Freya has never wanted to talk about her family, so I knew they weren't close. I know that she's an only child, but apart from that, there isn't much written about them. They're never mentioned in the press, and I've never been asked to put them on guest lists or whatnot, but still. Perhaps if either of us were open enough, we could have bonded over this; maybe we now will.

'Yeah, they pushed me into fame then when I got it, it turns out all they really wanted was my money and all the perks that come from being,' she gestures to herself, 'this. We agreed on an amount of money I'd pay them each month, to stay out of my life. That's kept them quiet and happy for years. Turns out, they're not very nice people.'

I sigh and allow my mind to drift. No wonder Freya dove into drink; it's a self-medicating tool to numb thoughts and feelings, right?

'It was the only conclusion I could come to after trying to establish healthy boundaries and my family walking all over them. I decided that it was easier to set that payment up, and not have them in my life, or talking to the press.' She shrugs, 'Most people don't understand that having to distance yourself from your family isn't something you ever want to do, it's something that you feel you have to do, to protect yourself.'

'No, I get it, believe me; my—' My eyes dart to my phone as it starts pinging like it's possessed.

'Geez, someone wants to get hold of you; who is it?' Freya says, sipping her tea contently.

Without picking the phone up, I get a sinking feeling: there's only one person who messages me like this.

Aria.

'It's probably my sister-in-law-to-be.'

'The one who's just had a baby?' Freya asks with raised eyebrows, putting down her tea, and picking up a couch pillow to snuggle with. 'You think she'd have more important things to focus on.'

'Yeah. I'm guessing she's had a chat with my mum about tonight.'

'How do you know it's not your mum messaging to apologise?'

I give her a doubtful look. 'Because, if the past is anything to go by, she'll want to give me the silent treatment. Aria has no idea how to do that. 'She's quick to anger, and will tell you every thought she has about you; her words surround her like fog, she's hard to see.' The phone continues to flash and beep, causing my anxiety to rise with each unread notification.

'Pop it on silent,' Nick suggests, gently. 'No good can come of reading them right now—or at all,' he says after a beat. 'Maybe just delete them?'

I shake my head, 'No, I'm going to read them now. There's no point in putting off the inevitable; I'll just obsess and make up stories otherwise.' I grab the phone, exhale loudly, and start reading. As predicted, there's message after message from Aria. 'Aria's messaging me from her hospital bed,' I share with them while scrolling, 'Baby Holly's asleep, so's Chris, but she can't get a wink, due to her outrage at my behaviour,' I explain, deadpan to them both while feeling my heart sink. 'She says she was too polite to say so before, but now feels she has to. My behaviour has, in fact, over the last two years, caused tremendous trauma for them all, and now, I have crossed a line, and will never know just how much I've hurt my mum.' Tears start to fill my eyes.

'Wait a minute,' Freya says, 'all you did was call your mum out on *her* behaviour, and tell her, after years of being agreeable, how that's affected you, right?'

'Yup,' I nod sadly. 'I mean, perhaps I overdid it. I threw up thirty years' worth of hurt over her. I guess I was just desperate to hurtle towards a moment of change.'

'This was the same as my parents; they said I had upset *them*, by telling them that they hurt me, rather than apologising for hurting me in the first place or trying to make anything right.' She shakes her head, 'It's maddening.'

As I continue to scan the reams of abusive messages, her gut-slicing words begin to blur through my tears. I finally make it to the last message, 'She's telling me that everything is my fault; that I should never have come back, and that when I'm ready to apologise for my disgusting behaviour, to contact her again when I'm ready to be a proper aunt, sister and daughter.' I exhale. 'My God,' I look up at them both, 'Am I really that much of a monster?'

Nick rubs his forehead, then stands, coming over to kneel in front of me. 'The only monster is the one within you that allows you to believe that you are the person they describe you to be.' My tears fall fast now as Nick places my phone on the sofa next to me, and takes my hands in his, 'You have no idea how much I wish things were different for you, but I'm sorry to say that this is the reality. You can't spend the rest of your life trying to find logic where there isn't any, or waiting for them to change, and beating *yourself* up when they don't.'

'Yeah, I'm sorry to tell you, Soph,' Freya joins in, 'happy endings only exist in fairytales.'

'I disagree,' Nick's voice says softly, 'Your ending is up to *you*. It's a choice. You can't control the things outside of you, but I think it's about shifting your perspective, and it depends how *you* want to write your ending.'

'I want them to change. Why am I not worth changing for?' I say through my tears.

He shakes his head, 'Them being exactly who they are, has nothing to do with your worth.'

As my tears fall, I wish I could truly believe that on every level, but when you're repeatedly told everything is your fault, you start to believe it. 'I've held onto the hope that something will suddenly be different.' I swallow, 'I have to give up hope, don't I?' my voice trembles.

Nick gently wipes away my tears, then holds my hands once more, 'Perhaps it's not about giving up hope, but about practising accepting them for being exactly who, and where, they are, and then, if you're able, forgive them.'

I let out a shallow exhale, my breath, unsteady, while trying to ground myself and my racing thoughts.

'I haven't forgiven my parents,' Freya interjects, 'I can't imagine saying to them that I forgive them.'

Nick shakes his head again, 'Forgiveness has nothing to do with the other person. It's a decision that you make that you're no longer going to carry this pain with you; it has nothing to do with condoning anyone's behaviour or saying the words to them. Forgiveness is a release within you; it's putting yourself first.'

'I'm not sure I'm capable of that,' I admit.

My phone then pings once more, and looking down at the screen, I see it's not Aria this time. My heart plummets. I let go of Nick's hands, take my phone, and start reading. It's one line: *"I need to talk to you."* I numbly show it to Nick, who exhales.

'You don't have to respond to your mum right now.'

I then show it to Freya and sit, paralysed in my indecision. Freya's watching me with interest but doesn't say anything. Without overthinking, I type a reply, wipe my cheeks, and exhale.

'What did you say?' Nick asks.

'I said, "No, thank you".'

The phone begins to ring, and again, without overthinking, I press cancel. A moment later, it rings again, and my guilt picks it up, 'Yes, hello, Mum.'

'What do you mean, "No"?'

'I mean, no thank you; it's late, I think we should all get some sleep, and regroup.' Amazed at my strength, I allow pride to wash over me and then it's instantly wiped away as she laughs darkly.

'Oh, how lovely for you to be able to sleep; what a luxury!'

'Fine. What do you want to say?'

She falters, 'Well...I'm...I'm not doing this over the phone. Come to the house.'

'You want me to come to your house? Now?' I glance at the clock, 'At quarter past midnight?'

'Like I said, I'm not going to be able to sleep, so it may as well be now!'

I look to Nick and Freya, who can hear every word. They both give me supportive looks. Freya mouths, 'You don't have to.'

While Nick says quietly, 'It's your decision.'

I'm silent. I feel drained, and can't imagine that seeing her tonight is going to make me feel any better. But then again, putting off waiting to see her, is going to fill me with even more anxiety.

'Hello???' she huffs impatiently.

'Yes.' I sniff, 'Fine. I'm on my way.' She hangs up without a goodbye, and I look to them both. 'I want to end this.'

Nick places his hand on mine, 'There's not going to be an end to this, Sophie; it's a lifelong process, just like healing.'

I nod, 'Well, I'm going to see either way, aren't I?'

'I'll come with you,' Nick goes to stand and I stop him.

'Thank you, but I think I need to do this on my own,' his eyes are unsure, 'I'm alright. It'll be fine.' I stand up. 'Or it won't be. But either way, I have to go.'

***

I walk the ten minutes to my parent's house, still in my ballgown, but underneath I'm wearing boots, instead of heels. The icy wind hits my face and tries to whip my coat open. I'm sure my makeup is somewhat lost with my tears, and undoubtedly, she'll have something to say about my appearance. When I walk up the garden path to their front door and onto the porch, I have the feeling that this conversation is going to change the course of my life. I catch myself right there, just before knocking—what Freya has just offered me, is going to change the rest of my life, regardless of what is about to happen with my mum.

I deserve to be happy for myself.

Then why do I feel this unquestionable emptiness inside? With my hand still hovering, I close my eyes; I have to learn to be proud of myself, without the unconditional love or support from my family. I have to practise being proud of myself for myself, and that being enough.

Opening my eyes, and taking a deep, yet unsteady breath, I nod at the wreath on the door. Then gently knock, hug myself, and wait.

And wait.

I tap again, a little louder this time. *Is this a game?*

Still, no answer.

Now that I'm here, I'm not sure what to do. I step off the porch, and look up at the house once more, expecting to be able to tell if my parents are still awake, through the darkness. I imagine my dad is asleep, maybe Mum passed out on the couch? I turn and gaze up at the moon. It's full tonight, and beaming in all its glory. *What am I supposed to do?* I close my eyes, then whip them open again as I hear the door open behind me. I turn and lock eyes with my mum for a moment before she looks down. As I walk towards the house, she doesn't greet me, she opens the door a little further, then walks back in, with not so much as a word.

Stepping into my family home, I wipe my boots, then go to take them off, but my mum stops me. 'You can keep your shoes and coat on, this won't take long.'

I clear my throat, 'OK.' And shutting the door, I wait with anticipation.

'Took you long enough to get here,' Mum strides impatiently and dramatically in front of me, her eyes firmly on the floor, to avoid mine and express her disapproval. 'It's as if you think I have nothing better to do than to wait for you to bother to show up.'

'I was all of fifteen minutes.'

'Your dad said he picked up Freya from the airport,' she swiftly moves on; 'I would have liked to have met her, I'm a big fan.'

I exhale, *so she does know who I work for*, I think to myself, and fold my arms with mild annoyance.

'You know, we might look alike, but we are very different, Sophia.'

'OK.' Odd place to start, but why not?

Mum shakes her head, 'When I had you, I'd hoped to feel a connection with you, but I'm afraid to say that I feel more connected to Aria than I ever have to you.'

I nod. She didn't need to tell me that, it's obvious to anyone. Still hurts though.

'Although,' Mum looks up at me for the first time, 'you're not wearing your glasses this evening,' she says as if that's the first time she's noticed. 'That's why you looked so much better at the party, or at least you did; now you're red and puffy.'

'Wow. Alright. Well, this has been super fun, Mum,' my sarcasm is almost too much. 'Was there something I can help you with? If not, I think I'll call it a night.' I'm no longer strong enough to listen to her insult me. Still holding her eye contact, I reach for the door handle, with a mix of relief and sadness.

Mum shifts uncomfortably from foot to foot, then clears her throat. 'Yes. There was something I wanted to say. I would have said it earlier, but I hate to make a scene.'

'Alright, well, now we're alone. What did you want to say, Mum?'

She exhales, then bringing her hands up, almost in a prayer pose, she starts tapping the ends of her fingers, perhaps nervously, together. 'Yes. Well. Here we are.'

I wait patiently, as she doesn't begin immediately.

'Fine.' She turns, 'Firstly, I want to make sure that you know how you spoke to me is unacceptable.'

'Great,' I say, deadpan. Regardless of how she's spoken to *me* or has treated *me* countless times in my life, the *only* time that I say exactly what I'm feeling, it's deemed as "unacceptable". We're off to a fantastic start.

'Why you felt it was OK to talk to me like that, I don't know; I would never have dared speak to my mother that way.' I figure nothing that I say here will help me, so I remain silent. 'And, Nick is, just...' She searches for her words, 'the arrogant, pompous little child, I've always known him to be. He's changed you. He doesn't fit into our family. He took you away from us, and we lost our little girl.' She looks at me, waiting to be corrected or challenged, or for me to jump to his defence, but again, there's no point. And for the first time, I accept that it will fall on deaf ears. But most importantly, *I* know what he's truly like; she has no idea, and it's clear that she has no interest in ever knowing. 'And your father just left me there. You all just left me there.'

'Dad got you a cab. And besides, *you* walked off, Mum.'

'Well, how could I not after all those horrible lies you told about me.'

I look at this woman and almost feel sorry for her; she has no idea how she's behaved, and can't possibly comprehend that she might be in the wrong. My heart sinks a little.

'Why are you looking at me like that?'

I take a deep breath, 'You've asked me to come here. I'm here; what do you want to say?'

It's at this moment, that I think she's going to cry, but instead, her eyes fill with venom. 'What I wanted to say is that I will *never* forgive you for how you embarrassed me earlier. Insulting me, accusing me of things I haven't said or done. I have done *nothing* but love you with all my heart, and this is the thanks I get?'

I can't believe it. And yet, at the same time, I can. I feel my heart plummet into my toes.

'After all that I have done for you. My family came from nothing, and I made impossible choices and sacrifices you will never know about—'

'Then tell me! Share with me! Help me understand you. Apart from you saying your family came from nothing and you wanted to make Grandma proud, that's all you've told me. Have one open and honest conversation about your past, for once! Please,' I plead.

She shakes her head, 'Your grandmother would turn in her grave at how you spoke to me. I wouldn't have ever *dared* talk to her with the lack of respect that you have shown me today. You should be ashamed of yourself.'

My already broken soul feels like it's now shattering. How can I continue to be around this warped version of reality?

She takes a deep breath and continues, 'Tonight, the way you spoke to me, with your anger, it...' her voice drifts off and I feel she's stopping herself from telling me something.

'It what, Mum?' I say with tears now streaming down my face.

She stands tall, 'Stop crying. It made me ashamed to be your mother. I did not raise you like that.'

'You raised me to stay quiet, slap a smile on my face, and make me believe that everything is my fault!' I put my arms out to the side. 'This is the result of how you have treated me, and made me believe a twisted version of what is right and true.'

'How *dare* you say that you are the way you are because of me. *I* wanted to make *my* mother proud; all you're doing is making me feel immensely disappointed.'

'Well, I'm sorry that's how you feel.'

'You need to apologise to me properly, right now, or I will no longer consider you my daughter.'

I look at this woman. So much is undiscussed, so much hidden. I can't force her to have a breakthrough that she doesn't want to have. All she wants is for me to sweep everything under the carpet, apologise as if I'm the only one in the wrong, pretend that nothing has happened, and go on living a lie, because it feels easier.

I feel my lip wobble slightly and watch as my mum's barriers stand just as tall as they've ever been. We can't have a real conversation about anything. She isn't capable of letting me in and exploring her past traumas, that she must have; that door is firmly shut. She's not even capable of acknowledging that the door exists to begin with. How I wish that she would have a lightbulb moment in front of me, at the age of sixty-seven and help me understand. Heaving a large sigh, I allow myself to finally let go. 'Goodbye, Mum. I wish you a happy life.' I go to turn and she spins me back.

'The way I brought you and your brother up was the correct way;' she defends an argument I haven't started, 'it was the way I was shown. If I was tough on you, it's because hard work and success matters, how other people see you, matters, accolades matter, family matters! You swan off with Nick, Gabby, and Scott, and think your friends are better than family; blood is thicker than water, Sophia!'

'You know that quote is a misunderstanding.' I've no idea why I feel the need to correct my mother here, but the words have escaped my mouth before I've thought about them.

'Is that right?' her tone is sharp.

'Yeah, the beginning of the quote is something like, "The blood of the covenant is thicker than that of the womb", meaning the relationships we *make*, are stronger than those you *don't choose*, like family.' As soon as the words are out of my mouth, I regret them. 'Sorry.'

She looks at me, 'Finally; an apology.'

And with that, she disregards me, one last time, and closes the door on the conversation, and my heart.

She narrows her eyes at me, 'You think you have all the answers, but you have no idea what it's like to be a mother. You want the best for your child, and you spend your entire life trying to fight for that.'

'Life shouldn't be about fighting, Mum.'

Her eyebrows twitch this time, 'Nonsense.' She clears her throat again. She regards my face, and I almost let myself think she's going to apologise, but then she starts talking, 'Earlier tonight, you asked why you are disappointing to me, and not worthy of my love and acceptance.' I realise I'm holding my breath. She rubs her hands on her face and takes a deep breath. 'I *hate* who you have become,' her words are clear and measured.

Whatever I was expecting her to say, it wasn't that. I stare blankly at her. 'Pardon?'

She huffs, 'Everything I did was because I love you, yet, you have become a disrespectful, ungrateful, selfish human being, Sophia.'

I shut my eyes and exhale, 'That's not who I am,' I say with a small voice.

She huffs, 'Oh, really? Well, who are you then?'

Before I know what I'm going to say, I hear my voice, 'I am a kind, honest, and good person. I put others' needs ahead of my own, and I'm working on believing that I deserve whatever I want.' She stares at me blankly so I continue, 'And I want nothing more than to believe that everything you've done is a result of your love for me. But if you've loved me, I haven't felt it. What I have felt is rejection, heartbreak, guilt and shame.' I take a beat and then it hits me, 'I think you have projected onto me *your* lifetime of guilt and shame, whatever the origin, and I've carried it as my own.'

Beneath the Mask

'How *dare* you say that to me,' her tone is dark. 'I didn't think you could cause me any more pain, and that includes when you left us for no reason, for two years; this is worse.'

I exhale, 'Mum, do you realise that for two years, I have been mourning a family that is still here? You all made me think that all the good in my life and relationship wasn't real and that I didn't deserve happiness if it didn't include you. I had to step away from you all because I had lost all sense of self and rational thought. I was broken. You broke me!'

She swallows, and then a small voice replies, 'I did nothing of the sort. I am a good mother.'

I shake my head then sniff, 'A book I read recently said that a good mother gives her child roots and wings. What you did was try to glue me to the spot, and simultaneously try to rip off my wings, then punish me for wanting to fly.'

'I have no idea what you're talking about.'

'What I'm trying to say is, I may have moved to New York, but I didn't emotionally go anywhere, Mum. Regardless of what happened that Christmas, we are supposed to grow up and create our own lives, for God's sake. My entire life, you have constantly made me feel bad for daring to dream. You have made me believe that it is selfish to do anything for myself. That's not being a good mother, Mum.'

That comment hits her hard, and her eyes begin to well up. She presses her lips together, and takes a deep breath, 'You clearly don't want to be a part of this family anymore.'

'I want nothing more than to be a part of this God-damn family. I love you all so much; it hurts every part of my being that this is what our reality looks like. But I guess the people in this family aren't who I wish they were.'

'Excuse me?'

z

399

'A family is supposed to love and support you more than anything, not punish you for speaking your mind when you are in fucking pain!'

'How dare you swear at me!'

'I'm not swearing at you, I'm swearing near you!'

'You're always so sensitive. Stop crying right now, and keep your voice down. The neighbours will hear, and your father is asleep.'

I scoff. 'I have every right to be sensitive. I am distraught by this situation, Mum. For the first time, ever, in my life, I was honest. OK, I admit, the way I exploded thirty years of pain over you, may not have been the way to go, but apparently, I had reached my boiling point, and for that, I'm sorry. But I am not sorry for finally telling you how I feel.' I take a beat then have to ask, 'Do you honestly not have anything to say about what I said tonight?'

She looks at me squarely, 'I thought I already had; weren't you listening?'

I exhale, 'No. I heard you. Loud and clear.' Nodding, I notice, for the first time, how similar the line of freckles on her nose are to mine, 'Thank you for sharing how you feel,' I say sadly, knowing that there can never be anything deeper. She falters, confused by my comment. I look at her, trying to memorise every inch of her face, knowing that this is the last time that I will allow myself to see her. 'You know, I had an unbelievable, life-altering offer tonight, and I wish it was something that I could share with you, to make you proud of me.' Her eyes are full of anger, about to burst, 'But you'll never be happy for me, because you can't be happy for yourself, can you?'

'You've disrespected me this evening; how on earth am I supposed to be happy?'

I shake my head, ignoring her, and carrying on, 'You can't unconditionally love me, because you don't unconditionally love yourself.'

She narrows her eyes, 'You think you're so wise, when all you're doing is talking nonsense, quoting some stupid self-help book.'

I nod, my tears are flowing freely now. 'I love you, Mum, but it's time for me to go. I...I deserve better than this.' Sniffling, I turn, find the handle, and step out into the cold.

'*I* deserve better than this!' Mum calls after me and I turn.

'Yes. Yes, you do, Mum.' I stare into the eyes of the woman who's caused so much pain in my life. The mind games and emotional manipulation just aren't worth it anymore.

'You can no longer consider me your mother, Sophia!'

I nod sadly, and say softly to her, 'My name is Sophie.' And with that, I turn and walk away from the hope that things will ever be different.

I hear the door slam shut behind me as I walk back up their garden path. I turn into the road and take one last look at my family home. My eyes are stinging now and I give a little sniff, before turning and retracing my steps, back to my flat.

The little 5-year-old girl inside me, who desperately seeks to be loved, accepted, and understood, cries. The 35-year-old woman that I am, joins her. As I walk, I mentally hold my inner child.

It's going to be OK. We're going to be OK. I'm here for you, now, I find I'm saying to her, despite intensely feeling this gaping hole in my heart.

I guess that it's going to take the rest of my life to find ways to feel whole; I'm not going to get it from my mother.

It's time I gave that love to myself. I let tears roll down my cheeks, and from the slight shake of my body, I just let myself feel everything, not to punish myself anymore, but to let it try to move through me. I no longer want to stay in this dark hole, I deserve to step into my own light. I want the wounds of my past to finally become scars, always a part of me, but no longer raw, and unattended to. A part of my past, but no longer strangling the present, or dictating my future.

When I step over the threshold of my flat, I know that I'm safe and loved, but that doesn't stop the pain. The pain will stay with me the rest of my life, my hope is that it will no longer be all-consuming, and will get smaller over time, with acceptance of what is.

Stepping into the living room, Nick sits by himself; I'm guessing Freya has gone to bed. He gets to his feet, 'How did it go?'

I nod, 'I'm done.' I wipe my wet cheeks, 'I'm choosing myself.'

Nick's eyes fill with tears too, and without a word, he scoops me up.

'There's still so much hurt,' I sob in his arms.

'Of course there is.' He strokes my hair gently and holds me close, 'Nothing is going to instantaneously wipe out a lifetime of pain.'

When I'm able to find my voice through my tears, I stutter, 'I can't allow her words and actions to upset me anymore.' I exhale, 'I've got to protect my heart and who I let in it. I can't keep coming back to get hurt again and again, hoping for a different result. I want to see a light at the end of the tunnel. I just need to find it.'

'It's already inside of you; everything you need is already inside of you.'

'Kinky.' I laugh and he joins me. I then let out a long and low exhale, 'Thank you.'

'For what?'

I loosen my grip, so I'm looking up into his eyes. His arms remain around me. 'For everything. For standing by my side when you didn't have to, for taking their toxicity with poise, and for helping me believe that I'm worthy of anything.'

'You are worthy of *everything*. Like being the warm-up act for an international star, for example,' he gives me a small smile.

I burst out laughing, 'Oh my God, I'd momentarily forgotten that.'

'Can't imagine why, you haven't had anything else going on this evening.' He smiles gently at me. 'Did you tell her about it?'

I shake my head, 'I wanted to, but there's no point.' I swallow, 'They aren't capable of being happy for me, and I want to choose happiness; I'm so sick of being sad.' I shrug, 'I just want to be OK.'

'I want you to be more than just OK.' He kisses the top of my head. 'God, I love you, Sophie.'

I smile, 'I love you too.' In his arms, for a moment, I allow myself to believe I'm capable of anything. I just have to get out of my own way.

'I'm really proud of you, you know that?'

'I haven't done anything yet,' I laugh.

'Yes, you have. I don't think you give yourself enough credit for how far you've come.'

I nod, knowing exactly why, and determined to spend a lifetime reworking that blueprint in my head, 'I will though; it's just going to be a journey.' I smile up at the man I have always loved, 'But for now, this is exactly where I'm supposed to be.'

Epilogue A

31st July — closing night

There is nothing like the sound of a crowd. The stadium is packed to the brim, and my heart beats in time to the stamping, clapping, pulse of the audience, waiting with hungry anticipation for the show to begin. I'm wearing those boots that elongate my body and confidence, and smiling at the band, I glance up to the mixing desk. Nick mouths at me, 'You've got this.' I grin then look over to Jerry, who's awaiting my cue. I take my time.

No longer in the wings of my life, figuratively or literally, I gaze out at the crowd. On the front row next to Gabby and Scott is my dad; they're all waving and smiling.

O, our golden Labrador we rescued from the shelter (that's now back on its feet, thanks to Freya's generous donation), is backstage with Freya's chihuahuas, fitting in well with the wolf pack in the staff doggie creche.

I wave back at my chosen family then let my eyes trace from the stalls up to the balcony. Smiling faces greet me, and I allow joy and gratitude to flow through my body with positive adrenaline. This is my life. This is really my life. And I am deserving and worthy of all of it.

I'm still working on the fact that my mum remains exactly where I left her, as does Aria. Chris of course, has to stand by his wife's side, and I get that on some level; we occasionally message, but it's always in secret. He sent me a picture of their wedding day; I understood why we weren't invited. He updates me on baby Holly without Aria knowing, and I hope one day, my niece will know she can reach out to me. I'd love to get to know her, but right now, that's not an option. My mum and Aria are too strong, and I no longer want to enter the battlefield. My shield is down; I've walked away. I'm working on accepting that in their minds, there will always be a war that needs to be won.

Perhaps one day this will change but right now, I'm committed to surrounding myself with people whose eyes light up when they see me.

After signing a contract with Freya's record label, I can't wait to see what the next chapter brings.

I nod at Jerry, the introduction starts, the lights dance and the dry ice around us seems to sink dramatically to the floor. I take a deep breath and begin.

***

Beneath the Mask

Apologies You Probably Need To Hear But Never Will
by Whitney Hanson ©

I'm sorry that I wasn't there when you needed me.
I'm sorry for the pain I passed on to you because I didn't
know how to carry it kindly.
I'm sorry for leaving you when I should have stayed.
I'm sorry for trying to change you when I should have loved
you just this way.
I'm sorry that I convinced you that you didn't matter at all.
I'm sorry that I made you feel so awfully small.
I'm sorry that I didn't say what you deserved to hear: that
I'm proud of you; that I love you; please don't disappear; it
was never your fault.
I'm sorry that I let you believe that everything I did was a
reflection of you, instead of me.

***

This may be the end of *The Dark Side of Ambition* but
perhaps it's just the beginning of your journey.

Chapter 33-B

The Light Side of Ambition

If someone had told me a few years ago that Freya would be sitting in my old living room, I wouldn't have believed you. I'm sipping my Pukka Night Time Tea, while staring with disbelief at this person, who, after having conversations with us for the last couple of hours since Dad dropped us off, is seemingly, just a person. Far removed from the diva I've been working with for years, Freya has been asking Nick and I about our lives together, and listening to the answers. I sit cosily on the couch, hugging my tea, looking at the clock reading midnight. I've no idea how, but I'm not tired in the slightest.

'So, why did you break up?' Freya also sips on her tea and waits patiently for Nick's response.

'Sophie's family,' is his brief response.

Freya nods, 'Families are something else, man. I haven't spoken to my folks in, God, what is it now? Eight years?'

'*Eight* years?' I don't know why this shocks me. Freya has never wanted to talk about her family, so I knew they weren't close. I know that she's an only child, but apart from that, there isn't much written about them. They're never mentioned in the press, and I've never been asked to put them on guest lists or whatnot, but still. Perhaps if either of us were open enough, we could have bonded over this; maybe we now will.

'Yeah, they pushed me into fame then when I got it, it turns out all they really wanted was my money and all the perks that come from being,' she gestures to herself, 'this. We agreed on an amount of money I'd pay them each month, to stay out of my life. That's kept them quiet and happy for years. Turns out, they're not very nice people.'

I sigh and allow my mind to drift. No wonder Freya dove into drink; it's a self-medicating tool to numb thoughts and feelings, right?

'It was the only conclusion I could come to after trying to establish healthy boundaries and my family walking all over them. I think the final straw was when they said I had upset *them*, by telling them that they hurt me, rather than apologising for hurting me in the first place, or trying to make anything right.' She shakes her head, 'It's maddening. I decided that it was easier to set that payment up, and not have them in my life, or talking to the press.' She shrugs, 'Most people don't understand that having to distance yourself from your family isn't something you ever want to do, it's something that you feel you have to do, to protect yourself.'

'No, I get it, believe me; my—' My eyes dart to my phone. Picking it up, I see there's a message from Aria. I bite my lip, then open it, anticipating several more to appear, one after the other.

'Who is it?' Nick asks with anticipation.

'Aria.' I continue to read, 'She said she'd had a conversation with Chris, and she's apologising for how she's behaved.' Raising my eyebrows, I look up, 'I mean, it's in a very roundabout way where ultimately, she's blaming me, but even so, she's said the words: *I'm sorry.* Maybe that's progress?' I jump out of my seat at the sound of a knock at the door.

Fuck me, is she here now?

'You expecting someone? Do you think the press knows I'm here?' Freya's face is a mix of, "I'm not ready," and "Look, this is my best side".

'I don't think so.' I stand and walk over, looking through the peephole, my face drops.

Good God, help me.

I spin back around, to face the living room, my arms spread-eagled in front of the door.

'What's wrong? Who is it?' Nick asks.

'It's my mum,' I whisper.

'Sophia, I am perfectly aware that you're in there! I can hear voices,' Mum's voice cuts through the door and into my heart.

Freya looks with amusement, from me to Nick and back again. 'Fun. Do you want me to answer it?'

'Absolutely not.' The words have escaped my mouth before I can stop them. 'Sorry, I mean, no, it's fine, I'll get it.' I try to compose myself, then I lean towards Freya, 'You sure you want to be here for this?'

'Oh, yeah.' She smiles, settling back in her seat, and recrossing her legs. 'My mum sucks, and from the sounds of it, so does yours. Always makes me feel comforted when I see other people's pain.'

'How very supportive of you,' I reply dryly.

The tapping returns with increasing urgency. 'Sophia!?'

I take a deep breath and open the door. 'Hello,' I say with some strain.

'Took you long enough to answer,' Mum strides impatiently and dramatically through the doorway, her eyes firmly on the floor, to avoid mine and show me her disapproval of my actions. 'Really ridiculous of you to be whispering,' she mutters while taking off her coat. She then hands it to me, still without eye contact. 'It's as if you think I have nothing better to do than to stand on your doorstep, and—' Mum stops in her tracks after lifting her head, and spotting Freya. 'Well, hello!' Standing tall, Mum glides over, and stretches out a hand, 'Aubrey-Carter-Town-Council-and Sophia's-mother.' Her delivery is quick as if that's her full title. 'What an honour to meet you, Freya.'

I exhale, *so she does know who I work for*, I think to myself and shut the door with mild irritation.

'So, what's this?' Mum gestures to the room while taking a seat next to Freya. Mum sits on the edge of our couch, which she always told me was uncomfortable. 'A late-night secret gathering?'

I lean on the door, cross my arms, and decide that whatever is about to unfold is out of my control.

'Your husband gave me a lift here from my plane.'

Mum's eyebrows raise to compete with her hairline, 'He did, did he? He told me nothing of the sort.'

Dad won't hear the end of it whenever she decides to go home; she hates being left out of the loop, particularly on something she deems important. Freya, remains silent, just taking in my mum with her eyes.

'Is there something on my face?' my mum asks insecurely.

'No,' Freya shakes her head, 'You're just very similar to Sophie.'

Mum shakes her head, 'Oh, no, Sophia and I aren't anything alike; I'm more like my daughter-in-law-to-be.'

411

Freya's eyebrows raise, 'I meant, your eyes are the same shade as Sophie's, and you have a similar line of freckles across your nose.'

Mum seems to have lost some pep, but recovers well, 'Well, people would hardly know that, as she insists on wearing glasses; although,' Mum turns back to me, 'you're not this evening,' she adds, as if that's the first time she's noticed. 'That's why you look so much better.'

'Wow. OK. Well, this has been super fun, Mum,' my sarcasm is almost too much. 'Was there something I can help you with? If not, I think we'll call it a night, shall we? Because I'm no longer interested in listening to you insult me.' Still holding her eye contact, I reach for the door handle, with a mix of pride and fear.

Mum shifts uncomfortably in her seat, then clears her throat. 'Yes. There was something I came to say, but I didn't realise you had company.' She suddenly stands, 'Perhaps I'll just come back another time.'

'Why don't Freya and I go into the bedroom?'

'Sweet-talker,' Freya raises her cup to him.

'No. No,' Nick shuts that down by standing up and moving across the room. 'I meant, why don't I show you where you're staying, Freya, and then I'll go into *Sophie's and my* room. Alone. We'd be in separate bedrooms.'

'Good God, Nicholas, as if an international superstar would want to sleep with you.'

Nick frowns at Mum, 'On second thought,' he plants himself firmly back down in the nearest seat, 'please tell us why you've turned up, unannounced, and unwelcome at our home,' his open palm gestures to the entire room.

'How *dare* you say that I'm not welcome!'

'Alright. Enough,' I say, cutting everyone off. 'Why don't we just go for a walk, Mum?'

'Because it's freezing out there.'

'Fine. Come this way.' I lead Mum away from Nick and Freya.

'Nice to meet you!' I hear Freya say as Mum and I travel down the corridor towards the bedrooms.

'You too, Freya! I'm a big fan,' she calls, as I open the door to my bedroom, and wave her into it. After we've both stepped in, I shut the door, then walk over to the armchair in the corner, and sit down.

'Alright, now we're alone. What did you come here to say, Mum?'

She exhales, then brings her hands up, almost in a prayer pose. She starts tapping the ends of her fingers, nervously together. 'Yes. Well. Here we are.'

I wait patiently but she doesn't begin immediately. Instead, she takes several laps of the bedroom, tracing a finger along each surface, then inspects it for dust. There isn't any. Nick and I have always been neat, clean and tidy people. 'You could get a cleaner in here; I'm sure you could afford one, working for Freya.'

'Mum,' I exhale.

'Fine.' She turns, 'Firstly, I want to make sure that you know how you spoke to me is unacceptable.'

'Great,' I say, deadpan. Regardless of how she's spoken to *me* or has treated *me* countless times in my life, the *only* time that I say exactly what I'm feeling, it's deemed as "unacceptable". We're off to a fantastic start.

'Why you felt it was OK to talk to me in that manner, I don't know; I would never have *dared* speak to my mother like that.' I figure nothing that I say here will help me, so I

413

remain silent. 'And, Nick is, just…' She searches for a word and doesn't find one. She looks at me, waiting to be corrected or challenged, or for me to jump to his defence, but again, there's no point. And for the first time, I accept that it will fall on deaf ears. But most importantly, *I* know what he's truly like; she has no idea, and it's clear that she has no interest in ever knowing 'And your father just left me there. You all just left me there.'

'Dad got you a cab. And besides, you walked off, Mum.'

'Well, how could I not after all those horrible things you said about me.'

I look at this woman and almost feel sorry for her; she has no idea how she's behaved, and can't possibly comprehend that she might be in the wrong. My heart sinks a little, but somehow, I feel stronger than I've ever done. I don't need to say anything to her, and on some level, I don't care what she came here to say; I don't need to react to her, I'll wait to respond.

'Why are you looking at me like that?'

I take a deep breath, 'I said a lot of things earlier, now you've come to say something to me. I'm not going to do this for you. I'm here; what do you want to say?'

She takes her time, then begins in an unexpected place, continuing her pacing of my room, 'When I was a little girl, I had this favourite tree.'

'Right,' I tell my eyebrows to unknot.

'It was a cherry blossom, at the bottom of the hill on my grandparents' farm.' I watch as her mind clearly travels back in time; a mix of grief and nostalgia reads across her face. 'When we were growing up, we didn't have money.'

'I know, you told me,' I say softly.

'But I've never *really* told you about it, have I?' Her voice is unexpectedly vulnerable, so I don't answer; we've never had a *real* conversation in our lives, I'd convinced myself that we just weren't capable. I give her the room to continue. 'As you know, that's where we all lived; my parents couldn't afford their own house.' I find my eyebrows have twitched again; she's never admitted that or agreed to speak about it. 'So, since it was the family home and the family business, there wasn't a choice. I worked on the farm alongside my grandparents, parents, and sister; it was something you *had* to do. You couldn't have any dreams.'

'OK.' I take all that in. 'So, what does that have to do with a tree?'

'The tree was where I would go to hide.' She crosses her arms but still keeps to her pacing.

'You felt you had to hide as a child?'

Mum's reaction is hesitant, but she finally commits to a small nod. 'It's hard work working on a farm, and sometimes, I just wanted to be a little girl; apparently, I started helping even before I can remember. My sister found a book on meditation, and that seemed to work for her, but for me, I would go and sit under the tree.' Mum stops moving and closes her eyes. A smile, the size of which, I've never seen her wear, spreads across her face, 'I'd close my eyes, and suddenly, I'd be on a stage, twirling, lights shining, the unmistakable sound of applause filled with praise and approval would meet my ears.' Her face falls, as she opens her eyes once more, not quite looking at me, still lost in her past, 'When I shared this one time with my mother, she thought it was a ridiculous idea, and told me that it should remain a *dream*; after all, the family needs to stick together. We rely on each other to make ends meet. I had no choice but to work on that farm, doing back-breaking work, until I was in my early twenties.

'But no matter how old I got, I would still return to that tree, and allow myself to wonder what another life could look like. And then on my twenty-second birthday, my grandfather got me a train ticket to London. He told me there was an open audition for a cabaret dinner and dance, and I could stay with his old school friend, Gail.' My mum has never mentioned Gail, but I give her the room to continue, watching her face suddenly recoiling. 'The day I packed my bags, my mother was furious. She said I was abandoning the family, and that I would never amount to anything, chasing a ridiculous dream like that. She said that she had never been more disappointed in me, and told me never to come crawling back after I'd failed.'

A knot unties in my stomach; that's why she allowed me to have singing lessons, and take part in musicals at school, but not allow me to go any further, like I wanted to.

She stops pacing and looks at me. 'And tonight—' her voice fades, or she stops herself from continuing, I'm not sure. She takes a deep breath, 'Tonight, the way you spoke to me, I saw the exact same frustration, helplessness, and anger in your eyes, that I felt with my mother.'

'But I don't understand, Mum; you always told me that Grandma was a great person and that you wanted to make her proud.'

'Well, I did want to make her proud, and I think I might have, but then she got sick, and we couldn't ever talk about anything real, but I guess she…she was…a…complicated person.'

I try to take this in as my grandmother died when I was about two, so, my memories of her aren't really mine;

they're what I was told. Other than a vague recollection I have of the smell of her floral perfume and a fuzzy image of the large purple hat she used to wear.

'We could never agree.' Mum seems to be on a roll now, taking me away from my thoughts. 'I'm not sure we understood each other; and no matter what I did, I could never be good enough in her eyes, and she had no problem telling me so.'

I find my eyes have prickled with tears, as finally, I feel like I have something in common with the woman standing in front of me, but I remain silent.

'And, I guess without realising it, I've spent my life becoming her, to perhaps, win her approval?'

I feel my lip wobble slightly and watch as my mum has a lightbulb moment in front of me, at the age of sixty-seven. Somehow, it's even sadder. I finally know why she's behaved this way, but it doesn't make it any better emotionally.

'I thought the way I brought you and your brother up was the correct way; it was the only way I was shown, I guess. Hard work and success matters, how other people see you, matters, accolades matter, family matters. Blood is thicker than water.'

'You know that quote is a misunderstanding.' I've no idea why I feel the need to correct my mother here, but the words have escaped my mouth before I've thought about them.

'Is that right?' Her tone is soft, not sharp like it always has been when I've unintentionally corrected her.

'Yeah, the beginning of the quote is something like, "The blood of the covenant is thicker than that of the womb", meaning the relationships we *make*, are stronger than those you *don't choose*, like family.' As soon as the words are out of my mouth, I regret them. 'Sorry.'

'No, it's OK.'

She has never said anything I've said is OK.

'There's so much more information instantly available now, compared to when I was growing up. Or, when my mother was growing up, I suppose.' She walks over to my bed, and hesitantly, decides to perch on the edge. I watch as she pats down the mattress, and strokes it a little, I guess contemplating her next words. She takes a deep breath, 'When you become a mother, nothing else in your world seems to matter anymore. But what nobody tells you, is that you can lose yourself in it. You're so intent on keeping this little blob alive—'

'Thanks.'

'Creature then,' she uncharacteristically adapts her words to make them less offensive. 'It's terrifying. You want the best for your child, and you spend your entire life trying to fight for that.'

'Life shouldn't be about fighting, Mum.'

Her eyebrows twitch this time, 'Indeed.' She clears her throat again, 'Earlier tonight, you asked why you are disappointing to me, and not worthy of my love and acceptance.' I realise I'm holding my breath. She rubs her hands on her face and takes a deep breath. 'I *hate* that you are me,' she says quickly, now with her hands over her eyes.

Whatever I was expecting her to say, it wasn't that. I stare blankly at her. 'Pardon?'

She huffs while lowering her hands, 'You heard what I said.' She finally lifts her eyes so they meet mine. 'I *hate* that you have become the old version of me—the, life is for living, following your dreams—old me, and I hate that I have lost my youth and become *my* mother.' She bites her lip, then gives me a look so intense, it makes my soul ache. 'You mean everything to me, and I am sorry for making you believe that you are worthless and unloved. You are my heart.'

I swallow, 'Then, why? Why all of this tension, and fighting, and time lost, if I mean that much to you?' A few tears fall and I brush them away; Mum has never let me cry when I wanted to, but she doesn't tell me to stop crying, as she always has done.

'I'm not even sure when it started or why. But everything I did was because I love you.'

I shut my eyes and exhale, 'No, Mum. That cannot be true. If you've loved me, I haven't felt it. What I have felt is rejection, heartbreak, guilt and shame.' I take a beat and then it hits me, 'You have projected onto me *your* lifetime of guilt and shame. I want to say that I don't blame you, Mum, because I understand, I do, I really do. We had an honest and open conversation just now—something that you have never allowed us to have—but I am so hurt by your past words and actions. And, I meant what I said earlier, I'm not sure I have it in me to keep hurting myself over and over, just to have you in my life. Do you have any idea how hard it is to say that or to have to make that decision?' Mum holds my gaze but it's an emotion I don't recognise in her. Regret, maybe? I lean forward in my chair slightly, 'Mum, do you realise that I have been mourning a family that is still here? You all made me think that all the good in my life and relationship wasn't real and that I didn't deserve happiness if I did anything that didn't include you. I had to step away from you all because I had lost all sense of self and rational thought. I was broken. You broke me.'

She swallows, and then a small voice replies, 'I didn't mean to. I was trying to be a good mother.'

I shake my head and sniff, 'A book I read recently said that a good mother gives her child roots and wings. What you did was try to glue me to the spot, and simultaneously try to rip off my wings, then punish me for wanting to fly.'

'I was afraid of losing you.'

'I may have moved to New York, but I didn't emotionally go anywhere, Mum. Regardless of what happened that Christmas, we are supposed to grow up and create our own lives, for God's sake; you've just told me that you did. My entire life, you have constantly made me feel bad for daring to dream. You have made me believe that it is selfish to do anything for myself. That's not being a good mother, Mum.'

That comment hits her hard, and her eyes begin to well up. I'm not sure I've ever seen her cry for real. She presses her lips together, and takes a deep breath, 'You began to outshine me. I think I've always been jealous of you.'

'What?'

'Your talents—' she leans forward now, 'and yes, I said the *plural* of talent—far outgrew mine, even from the time you were a little girl.' I sit in shock and so she continues, 'You have more talent in your little finger, than I have in my whole body, and if I'd told you that, I thought I would lose you.' She shifts slightly on the bed, 'But I guess I lost you anyway.'

Exhaling, I don't know what to do with that. All these unnecessary mind games; do I want to open myself up to that again? Is she capable of change?

'I'm sorry that I let my pride and ego get in the way of our relationship.' She sighs then gets to her feet, walks over to my chair, and bends down on her knees, reaching for my hands. I let her take them. 'I am so sorry for everything. My words and actions, particularly those which make you believe such awful things about yourself. I am so proud of the woman you have become.'

What the actual fuck? My tears are flowing freely now, and so are my mum's.

'I love you and I'm so sorry.'

Sniffling, I try to find my voice, 'You have no idea how long I've waited for you to say that.'

'I'm sorry it's taken me so long *to* say it.'

I stare into the eyes of the woman who's caused so much pain in my life. Does this make up for a lifetime of mind games? I just don't know.

'I don't expect you to change how you feel about me right away, but maybe we can start again, somehow?'

'I think you need to go to therapy, Mum.'

'I couldn't think of anything worse,' she immediately shoots me down, and I raise an eyebrow. She bites her lip, 'OK, maybe that's something I could consider.'

I look at her and there's something that I have to know. I take a deep breath and go for it, 'Not that I want to push my luck here, but since we're airing some things out, there's something that I need to ask you.'

'OK, go ahead.'

'Why do you hate Nick?'

She almost lets go of my hands, but after a second's regroup, she goes back to her grasp. 'He changed you.'

'He helped me grow a backbone.'

'He doesn't fit into our family.'

'He doesn't drop everything he's doing, to the detriment of himself, whenever you demand.'

'He took you away from us.'

'He helped me believe that I was allowed to make my own decisions, and have my own opinions.'

She regards me, 'Fine.' She huffs a little, 'He's supported you, helped you, and grown up with you, and I felt that I lost my little girl.'

'People are supposed to grow and change in life, Mum.'

'Well, I wasn't allowed to.'

'So, neither was I?'

'Exactly.' She backs away slightly at the sound of her own voice. Dropping my hands, she stands, buries her head in her palms, and starts to sob.

I want to give her a hug but something makes me stay in the chair. She needs to feel whatever she needs to feel.

'Oh, my God, I'm a mess.'

Standing, I go into our en suite grab a couple of tissues, then hand them to her.

'Thank you.'

I take my seat once more and clasp my hands together.

'Why aren't you telling me to stop crying?' Mum wobbles.

'Because I'm not you. We need to feel our emotions so that they can move through us. If we don't, we keep everything bottled up inside, then they explode out of us, often at the worst times; that's not healthy.'

'Well, it's how I was raised.'

'It's how *I* was raised,' I challenge her. 'But we're doing this now, Mum. It's OK to feel whatever you're feeling right now.'

She wipes below her bloodshot eyes, and looks at me, 'You don't have to be this nice to me.'

'Well, I think that everyone deserves to be treated with grace and kindness.'

She blows her nose, then steps closer to me, approaching slowly, unsure, and insecure, 'You're a better person than I am.'

'Thank you.' I'm not used to getting any kind of compliment from her, so I shift in my seat, suddenly unsure of how to position my body.

'You've always been intelligent, but you've become a very wise woman, Soph–ie.'

My breath catches in my throat. 'You called me Sophie.'

'Well, it is your name, isn't it?' She gives a small smile, and I think that's as close to an apology for that, as I'll ever get.

'Yes, it is.'

***

Mum and I talk for another fifteen minutes or so, but when we go to leave the bedroom, she hugs me, really hugs me; perhaps for the first time. I allow myself to let down those walls I've built up, sink into her, and suddenly the little 5-year-old girl inside me, and the 35-year-old woman I am, smiles, and I start to feel whole. I let tears roll down my cheeks, and from the slight shake of her body, I can tell Mum is still crying too. I don't know how long we stay like this, but I allow everything she's just said to wash through me, attempting to cleanse me, and let go of whatever no longer serves me. Then there's a gentle tap on the door.

'Come in,' I manage to say. Neither Mum nor I move, and as the door slowly opens, Nick pops his head through the gap.

'I just wanted to make sure everything's OK.' He takes in our position, and his eyes widen in surprise.

423

I nod, 'We're OK.' I nod again, 'I'm alright.'

Nick's eyes fill with tears too, 'I'll leave you to it, then.' He smiles, going to close the door, but my mum stops him.

'No, no need, Nick.' Mum loosens her grip on me, holds my forearms for a moment, giving them a slight squeeze, and her face forms into a small, emotionally tired smile. 'It's getting late. I'll leave you to it. We'll continue this conversation.'

'How are you getting home? Shall I call you a cab, Aubrey?' Nick gets out his phone from his back pocket, and taps quickly, 'Amazingly for this town, there could be one here in ten minutes.' He looks up again to get the go-ahead.

Mum lets go of me, walks over to Nick, and uncharacteristically hugs him too, 'That would be lovely, thank you.' She releases the hug and looks him in the eyes, maybe for the first time, seeing him for who he really is, instead of the monster she'd created in her head. 'You are a good man, Nicholas.' She taps him on the arm, 'And, I'm sorry for how I've treated you.' She doesn't wait for a response, and walks past him, back towards the living room.

'What the hell was that?' Nick's frozen to the spot.

'I think I'd call it a breakthrough.'

'Really? Not a break*down*,' Nick's face is understandably doubtful.

'I don't think so. I'm not sure I fully believe it, and it certainly doesn't fix everything, but I think it's a step in the right direction.'

'Nothing is going to instantaneously wipe out a lifetime of pain,' he agrees. 'I think I can honestly say that I'm shocked.'

I shrug, 'Me too. Who knew she was capable of personal growth? She even said she'd consider therapy.'

He looks at me with doubt, 'Aubrey Carter, admitting how she feels, to a complete stranger? I'm not sure I can see that happening.'

'Me neither, but I think it was genuine.'

'*Huh*. Maybe she took your dad's words seriously and thought about losing you.'

'Maybe.' I shake my head, 'We'll have to see, I guess. I want to believe that she's capable of change, but at the same time, as mental as this might seem, I think I'm OK if she isn't. The fact that she said those things to me today, means a lot, but I think I'm at the point where I'm not going to allow what she says or does to upset me anymore. I'm going to practise protecting myself and deciding what I want to let in. I know where her hurt has come from now, not that that excuses anything, but it helps me understand. I've been doing the inner work, I've finally said to her what I felt I needed to, and now...' I glance around the room and exhale, 'I think I'm going to be OK.'

Nick looks at me with love, then scoops me up into his arms. We both exhale, holding onto each other. 'You're going to be more than OK.' He kisses the top of my head. 'God, I love you, Sophie.'

I hold him even tighter, 'I love you too.' Neither of us talks for a time, we just enjoy the feeling of our hearts beating in sync. In his arms, I believe I'm capable of anything, perhaps even letting go of a lifetime of hurt, and for the first time in a long time, I can sense a light at the end of a very dark tunnel that I've been stuck in, for far too long. I feel as though the wounds of my past are finally becoming scars. They will always be a part of me, but they are no longer raw, and unattended to; a part of my past, but no longer strangling the present, or dictating my future.

'So, on top of this breakthrough with your mum,' Nick says with his arms still wrapped around me. 'Can we just talk for a minute about the fact that you're about to perform as the warm-up act for an international superstar?'

I burst out laughing, 'Oh my God, I'd momentarily forgotten that.'

'I'm really proud of you, you know that?'

'I haven't done anything yet,' I laugh.

'Yes, you have. I don't think you give yourself enough credit for how far you've come.'

'How far *we've* come,' I correct him.

Nick loosens his body slightly, so he can kiss me on the lips. 'We should probably get back in there; who knows what your mum is saying to Freya right now.'

'To be honest, whatever it is, is none of my business.' I grin at the man I have always loved, 'This is exactly where I'm supposed to be.'

Epilogue B

31st July — closing night

There is nothing like the sound of a crowd. The stadium is packed to the brim, and my heart beats in time to the stamping, clapping, pulse of the audience, waiting with hungry anticipation for the show to begin. I'm wearing those boots that elongate my body and confidence, and smiling at the band, I glance up to the mixing desk. Nick mouths at me, 'You've got this.' I grin then look over to Jerry, who's awaiting my cue. I take my time.

No longer in the wings of my life, figuratively or literally, I gaze out at the crowd. On the front row next to Gabby and Scott, are my parents; they're all waving and smiling. My mum's holding up her phone, and I know it's Chris, Aria, and baby Holly, on Facetime.

O, our golden Labrador we rescued from the shelter (that's now back on its feet, thanks to Freya's generous donation), is backstage with Freya's chihuahuas, fitting in well with the wolf pack in the staff doggie creche.

It's not been an easy road with my family; habits are hard to break. But there's definitely forward movement on a healing journey of reconciliation. Chris and Aria's wedding was as elaborate as you can imagine, and I was very happy not to be asked to be a bridesmaid and to just sit with Nick, enjoying looking after baby Holly. It's never going to be the relationship I wish it was, but that's OK. I've reached acceptance, and my focus is me, Nick, O, and our lives.

I wave back at my family, then let my eyes trace from the stalls up to the balcony. Smiling faces greet me, and I allow joy and gratitude to flow through my body with positive adrenaline. This is my life. This is really my life.

After signing a contract with Freya's record label, I can't wait to see what the next chapter brings.

I nod at Jerry, the introduction starts, the lights dance and the dry ice around us seems to sink dramatically to the floor. I take a deep breath and begin.

The End

Appendix

Sophie and Gabby's Mental Health Tips and Resources

Recommended reading:
- Louise Hay, *You Can Heal Your Life*
- Karen McBride, *Will I Ever Be Good Enough*
- Fearne Cotton, *Happy*
- Mel Robbins, *The High 5 Habit*
- Dr Nicole LePera, *How To Do The Work*
- Dr. Joe Dispenza, *Breaking the Habit of Being Yourself*
- Brené Brown, *Daring Greatly*

Recommended watching:
- Rhonda Byrne, *The Secret*
- Louise Hay, *You Can Heal Your Life*
- Dr Wayne Dryer, *The Shift*

Recommended listening:
- Dr Wayne Dyer, *The Power of Intention*
- *Mel Robbins Podcast*
- *Mayim Bialik's Breakdown*
- *Happy Place Podcast*
- *Dr Ramani* YouTube Channel

Recommended mindfulness:

- 'The Five Minute Miracle', *Beyond Purpose* YouTube Video Channel
- *Boho Beautiful Meditation* YouTube Channel
- 'Yoga Nidra Nervous System Rest', *Ally Boothroyd* YouTube Channel
- 'Nick Ortner's Tapping Technique to Calm Anxiety & Stress', *Marie Forleo* YouTube Channel
- 'Affirmations for Recovery from Narcissistic Abuse and Gaslighting', *Rae du Soleil* YouTube Channel
- 'Say "Thank You." A Motivational Video On The Importance of Gratitude', *Fearless Soul* YouTube Channel
- 'Guided Meditation: Help for anger, anxiety, frustration', *MindfulPeace* YouTube Channel
- 'Positive Affirmations for Self-Love, Self-esteem, Confidence', *Lavendaire* YouTube Channel
- 'Chi Gong and Tai Chi (Qi Gong) Energy Healing Exercise', *The Art of Unity – Bill Farr* YouTube Channel
- *Yoga with Adrienne* YouTube Channel
- 'Paul Mckenna Official Sleep', *Paul McKenna* YouTube Channel
- *Jason Stephenson* YouTube Channel
- *Michael Sealey* YouTube Channel

Recommended social media:
- @Augustknoxcoaching
- @Carolinemiddelsdorf
- @the.holistic.psychologist
- @thefreedomalchemist
- @michael.galyon

Counselling suggestions:
- NHS Free six sessions of counselling
- Mind charity
- Samaritans
- BetterHelp Online Counselling

Affirmations:
- I am strong, I am brave, I am resilient.
- I am good, I am worthy, I am loved.
- Thank you for my healing.

The Serenity Prayer:
'Please grant me the serenity to accept the things I cannot change; the courage to change the things I can; and the wisdom to know the difference.'

Acknowledgements

Before my *thank-yous,* I'd like to take a mindful moment. Alongside a love story, Beneath the Mask was a passion project, and a book my soul needed to write. Mental health and wellbeing are very close to my heart and talking about uncomfortable subjects such as narcissism or gaslighting, especially within the Christmas period, is something that I wanted to shine a light on. There is no light without the dark.

It's my way of acknowledging that Christmas can be a tough and triggering time for many; it's not always mistletoe and merriment. I'm so proud of how it turned out.

For those wondering, it's not an autobiography or memoir. The characters are a creation of my imagination. (If you're reading this before the story, major spoiler ahead). It was important to me that Sophie's journey continued in both *The Dark* and *The Light* by moving on, either with or without the people who were at the root of her pain. My wish is that if this resonates with you at all (perhaps you too have been stuck in your own story) you can do the same. See the unhealthy relationships for what they are, and practise believing that your future can be whatever you choose it to be. You have a choice to step away. You are not the words that negative people in your life say you are. There is help available, and you can work towards healing yourself.

Alrighty, with all the heavy stuff said, a huge, *I don't know where I'd be without you* thank you, to James. Holy moly, we've done three books now! I am beyond grateful for the amount of time, love, and energy you have put into my books. From bouncing around plot points and holding me when my own writing made me sob, to bringing my front cover to life and helping me format the entire thing. Thank you for believing in my ability to make a difference in the world. I love you.

Thank you to my editors. A Celtic Manor cheers to Emma Webb. I'm so grateful not only for your eagle eye but for saying how important it is that I publish this book. Hip-hip-hooray, to Ann Jones, thank you for your patience: *'Next month...next month...next month.'* To Helen Foley, who insists I rescued her, but she continues to rescue me. My eyes will always light up when I see you.

Thank you to my tribe: Helen and Charlie Foley; Will and Khrish Preston; Rom and Ruth Arulanandam; Mina Chivite, Pere Sarrio; Suzie Bird; and Laura Groutides; my life is so much brighter with you in it.

Thank you, always, to the Hansens, Kerschtiens, Frasers, and Kissingers.

Thank you to Jill H, the cheerleader I didn't know I needed.

Thank you to my Rockies (technically not my Rockies anymore, but still), your support extends beyond anything I could have imagined. I hope you remember the reindeer moment and every other freezing cold light switch-on, lantern parade, and all the rest, with as much fondness as I do. I also hope you're enjoying your next adventure with Captain Karl at the helm.

Thank you to Whitney Hanson.

And last but not least, thank you to you, the gorgeous person holding another dream of mine in your hands. I hope it gives you hope to move forward, the encouragement to let go of what no longer serves you, and the sign you might need to march towards a life that fills you with joy. That is something we all deserve.

Suzie Anderson, who writes under the pen name **Victoria Mae**, was born in London and moved to the beautiful Welsh valleys for love. When she's not writing she's a musician and world traveller. She loves a glass of sauvignon blanc, the sound of the rain, and inspiring people to believe in themselves. Suzie is the author of three romantic comedy novels: Behind the Clouds, Between the Lines, and Beneath the Mask.

She loves hearing from her readers, and you can follow her on:

Facebook and Instagram: @victoriamaeauthor
Twitter: @VictoriaMAuthor

Praise for the Author

"From start to finish I was carrying this around like a second skin."

"Loved loved loved this book...I demolished it in one sitting...I felt like I had travelled the world by the end. Utterly brilliant."

"...it will brighten the winter evenings or be your chilled beachside read."

"...pour yourself an expresso martini and enjoy the ride."

"...felt like I was a guest at each and every wedding...a very talented author, leaves you wanting more. Keep writing."

"A ray of sunshine in book form!"

"If you enjoy travel and romance...this is the book for you!"

"...it's a travel guide and a romance novel all rolled into one!"

"Totally uplifting. Can't wait for the next book by this talented author."

"Should be a chick flick...can't wait to see it on the big screen, where it deserves to be."

Also available from Victoria Mae

Behind The Clouds

The lost love; the best friend; the blast from the past; the perfect man.

Teacher, baker, and romantic dreamer Melanie Butler is about to receive the icing on the cake of her life: her long-term boyfriend Evan is finally ready to propose...only thing is, it's to another woman.

Publicly humiliated and broken-hearted, Melanie's slightly unhinged sisters and eclectic group of friends help her find her feet as a newly found singleton—from a spot of mountain-range meditation to a surprise flight.

Grateful to have best friend Dave encouraging her to move on with her life, she starts dating the handsome and perfect fireman Julian. But when childhood nemesis Craig re-surfaces a little too close to home, his obnoxious words begin to reflect thoughts she's been trying to bury.

And when tragedy strikes, Melanie takes on a huge challenge, beginning to see not only what, but who is important in her life.

Can love defeat betrayals, and can you truly find happiness Behind the Clouds?

Also available from Victoria Mae

Between The Lines

Wedding columnist turned travel writer, Liv Bennett, has been left at the altar.

A year to the day later, in a bid to save the magazine she works for, Liv is asked to do the seemingly impossible: attend and write about a conveyor belt of weddings that will take her around the world.

Replacing the lead writer for the international best-selling bridal magazine, Blush is no mean feat, yet Liv packs up her feelings and embarks on this unexpected adventure with three strangers: hair and makeup specialist, Sarah; wedding stylist, Hugo; and the rude and impossible, photographer, Dom.

An around-the-world trip might be just the ticket for a broken heart. Across Europe, Asia, and North America, could this journey of a lifetime be the catalyst she needs to venture inwards, move on, or find some closure?

Before Liv can rewrite her own story, she's got to practise reading Between the Lines.

Printed in Great Britain
by Amazon

51763179R10253